"This book gives us what no contemporary TV program, movie, or magazine has even come close to—the tender, angry, funny emotional innards of the embattled daily life of working-class gay men. These could be the stories of the guys on the corner in my neighborhood—or yours!"
—Minnie Bruce Pratt,
author of *S/He*

"A very large percentage of gay literature produced in the United States is written by middle-class white men for middle-class white readers. There is a homogeneity to gay writing that reflects how, in our supposedly classless, multicultural society, issues of class and color are seldom worthy subject matter. If gays are 'The Other' in our predominantly heterosexist society, blue collar people and racial minorities (often one and the same) are 'The Others' within the gay community—a margin within the margin. The edgy, surprising stories in *Everything I Have Is Blue* are a tonic: they make an important contribution in terms of bringing to our attention characters and themes we seldom see explored in gay contemporary fiction."
—Jaime Manrique,
editor of *Besame Mucho: New Gay Latino Fiction*

"Finally! A gay story collection 100% free from scenes of Jeremy and Chad having tiffs by the Fire Island hot tub. Gay fiction needs books like Wendell Ricketts' *Everything I Have Is Blue*—and it needs them bad. Strapped to myths of upward mobility and disposable income, gay men are desperately short on books addressing working-class experiences. Thankfully this book steps up to the plate, serving up fiesty, sharp stories that stretch and challenge stagnant notions of class, masculinity, and gay identity."
—D. Travers Scott,
author of *One of These Things Is Not Like the Other*

EVERYTHING I HAVE IS BLUE

SHORT FICTION BY WORKING-CLASS MEN
ABOUT MORE-OR-LESS GAY LIFE

EVERYTHING I HAVE IS BLUE

SHORT FICTION BY WORKING-CLASS MEN
ABOUT MORE-OR-LESS GAY LIFE

EDITED BY
WENDELL RICKETTS

suspect thoughts press
www.suspectthoughtspress.com

Cover image and design by Shane Luitjens/Torquere Creative
Book design by Ian Philips and Greg Wharton/Suspect Thoughts Press

First Edition: June 2005
10 9 8 7 6 5 4 3 2 1

Library of Congress Cataloging-in-Publication Data

Everything I have is blue : short fiction by working class men about more-or-less gay life / edited by Wendell Ricketts.
    p. cm.
  ISBN 0-9746388-9-7 (pbk.)
  1. Gay men--Fiction. 2. Short stories, American. 3. Gay men's writings, American. 4. Working class writings, American. I. Ricketts, Wendell.
  PS648.H57E95 2005
  813'.01089206642--dc22

                                    2005003756

                          Suspect Thoughts Press
                       2215-R Market Street, #544
                       San Francisco, CA 94114-1612
                       www.suspectthoughtspress.com

Suspect Thoughts Press is a terrible infant hell-bent to burn the envelope by publishing dangerous books by contemporary authors and poets exploring provocative social, political, queer, spiritual, and sexual themes.

ACKNOWLEDGMENTS

The book you hold in your hand took six years to come into being. It was rejected by fifty-seven publishers.

Should I ever own a home—or maybe just live in an apartment where I don't care about getting the deposit back—I really do intend to paper the bathroom walls with the rejection slips I've collected over some twenty years as a writer. A wall of distinction—not to say honor—will have to be reserved for the rejections *Blue* received.

Ironically, many of them say the same thing: "This is a terrific (important, much-needed, exciting, valuable) project, but we could never do it." I was told that publishing short stories would be "professional suicide"; I was told that gay fiction was dead.

The best rejection for *Blue*, if I can say it that way, was the one from the publisher who admired the writing but "remain(ed) unconvinced of the validity of the category." (The category, that is, of working-class queer.) It might have been fun to introduce her to the gay publisher who told me, in his plummy British accent, that the writers in this book couldn't "really" be working class because, as far as I was able to follow his argument, they were writers.

Given all of that, is it any wonder that my first expression of gratitude is due to Greg Wharton, head honcho of Suspect Thoughts Press, for publishing this book?

He never knew (or perhaps didn't until he read this) that he was my last hope. Even someone who fancies himself inured to the humiliations and indignities of the writing life has a limit, and I'd about reached mine. The Italian novelist and playwright, Natalia Ginzburg, once wrote that disapproval is not what is dangerous to a writer. Rather, she wrote, "What really hurts a writer is a courteous, gloomy, opaque, and soporific indifference." She said it right.

Greg's enthusiasm for this book reanimated my own, and, were it not for him, *Blue* would literally never have existed. With great respect, I acknowledge Greg and his "partner in thought crime," the writer Ian Philips, who saw the potential in *Blue* and gave me heart when I sorely needed it.

I next record here a debt of thanks to my friend and teacher, Jim Colbert, from one of whose novels I cadged the title for this book, and whose gifts to me have never been less than substantial.

I am grateful in no small measure to John Crawford, John Gilgun, Rigo González, Beth Hadas, Jaime Manrique, Minnie Bruce Pratt, Susan Raffo, and D. Travers Scott, each of whom provided tangible support and encouragement at various stages of this project. The donor who gave *Blue* a cash grant at a critical juncture so that I could afford to do things like mail out copies of the manuscript and buy printer cartridges understood something profound about the nature of grace; though he asked not to be named, he will always be a hero to me.

I've never had any doubt that the effort to celebrate a fictionalized, literary dimension of "our" lives adds colors to the palate of American (queer) identity, confuses categories that deserve to be confused, and propagandizes where propaganda is well warranted. Though I spent years wandering queer literature in search of something like home, I now know that the writers in this collection are who I needed to find. I am proud of them for entering so willingly and so ably into a conversation that has barely started among queer men.

PUBLICATION CREDITS

Grateful acknowledgment is made to the following publications in which these stories originally appeared:

"My Blue Midnights" by Rane Arroyo first appeared in *Blithe House Quarterly*, 7(1), Winter Issue, "The Puerto Rican Issue," Aldo Alvarez, ed. (www.blithe.com).

"Food Chain" by Jim Grimsley is an excerpt from the novel *Boulevard* (Algonquin Books of Chapel Hill, 2002).

"Good Friday" by Alfredo Ronci first appeared in Italian as "Venerdì santo" in *Men on Men*, Daniele Scalise, ed. (Oscar Mondadori, 2002).

To Kenneth and to Paul, my original working-class heroes.

TABLE OF CONTENTS

FLOWERS, FLAMES

C. Bard Cole

Frankie's boy Raj is all like, what are you doing hangin' out with that fucker man, he don't care shit for you, what you bein' stupid for man dats ill. Frankie's all like, you my man okay and dats the truth but you don't know okay so don't be talking shit when you don't know.

Raj is, you know what they be sayin' 'bout chou now man and Frankie's you tell me okay—you tell me. Nobody says this shit to my face. That's the thing man, when bitch asses be talking behind your back nobody says shit to your face. If I need to know you tell me.

Raj is, don't fuck wit' me man.

Frankie's if you can't say it man, then fuck dat shit. People talk shit, that's their deal not mine. Frankie looks him in the eye. So whatchu have to say man?

They say you down wit' dat faggot, man.

His name David okay? I'm down with him, he's my man. You my man, okay?

You know what I'm sayin', Raj goes. They sayin' you gay together and shit.

Damn, says Frankie. They sayin' it, must be true.

Naw, Raj goes. I don't think so. I don't believe it man. I know you ain't a fag. I'm just sayin'.

Damn, says Frankie, waving his hand. You know it all man. You don't think so, must not be true. You say so, I guess I ain't.

David Florian's walking home from the F train, his laptop and portfolio slung over his shoulder. A menthol cigarette between his lips, he fumbles one-handed with a pack of matches. Looking up, he sees Frankie sitting on his stoop, kicked back, a bottle of iced tea resting between his big, immaculate white sneakers. David smiles, wonders how long he's been sitting there.

"Yo paps," Frankie says. "Where you been at today?"

"I was in the city," David says, sliding the padded shoulder strap down his arm. "I had a meeting. You been sitting here all day?"

Frankie shrugs. "I been lookin' in every now and then. You didn't say you were going to Manhattan."

David's a designer. He does illustration and graphics for a couple music labels, some independent, some corporate. Most of the time he works at home. Today he's wearing baggy khaki pants, a white button-down shirt, a gold-and-red striped tie, no baseball cap. He could dress sharper if he wanted but it's not worth it. The art directors he deals with wouldn't care if he came in wearing cutoff sweatpants and a T-shirt, his tattoos showing. They would actually expect that—it's what he looks like. The tie just gets him past the security guards and receptionists, stops people from showing him the messengers' entrance.

"They had some work I had to do in the office," he says, and then, remembering that Frankie dislikes his avoiding details, adds, "The color keys came in for a whole bunch of c.d. booklets and it's shit they had to send back to the printer ASAP."

Frankie nods seriously. David is sure Frankie doesn't know what color keys are, but if he cares enough he'll ask. Giving his portfolio an emphatic shake, David says, "Plus I got some sketches for the next job I'm doing."

"Warner?" Frankie asks with apparent casual indifference.

David nods. "This is my Rhino shit."

Frankie snorts. "Rhino?" he says. "You doin' the fuckin' Monkees?"

Rhino's a label that repackages old music into compilations, box sets, and collectors' editions. They do, actually, have all the old Monkees albums on their list. Frankie thumbed through the catalogue one day and made fun of its contents. David is working on a "breakdancing" themed boxed set, early eighties hip-hop. Graffiti-style text illustration is a specialty of his.

"I ain't doin' the Monkees," David says. Then, from the corner of his mouth, in a stage aside, he mutters, "Dumb ass kid trippin' this Monkees shit like he knows somethin'. His mother doin' the fuckin' Monkees."

This sends Frankie into ecstasies of boyish laughter.

He gathers himself together. "You say somethin' about my mother, yo?"

David's smile is slightly cockeyed. "Yeah. She Davy Jones's bitch. Don't be ashamed of your mamma, Davy Jones keep the food on your table."

David pushes past Frankie to unlock his front door.

"I know who keeps the food on my table," Frankie says, play-sulking. David doesn't turn around but he stands in the door frame, his back facing the street, until Frankie gathers up his backpack to follow him inside.

David has lived in this apartment for five years, pretty much since he graduated from college, working as a sales clerk at Pearl Paint in Manhattan and going out Thursday, Friday, Saturday nights to hip-hop clubs in the outer boroughs, tagging walls, subway posters, and sketch-books with a nice variety of fat art markers he'd stolen from work. He didn't find the job in a magazine art department—the job he'd promised his parents he could get easy—but he hadn't cared. He was happy to be on his own and thoughtless, happy not to have to move home to his childhood bedroom like some of his high school friends. He made friends with club promoters and kids running indie labels; he started up a little T-shirt company—nothing that made money, until it started to.

Frankie came with the building. He came with the stoop. He watched David move his possessions in five years ago, watched him run to the store for cigarettes and food three or four times a day. Maybe after the first year they finally started talking. The first thing David recalls Frankie saying to him was: "Yo kid, whassup? Donchoo never go to work or nothin'?"

David raised a supercilious eyebrow: "You're—asking me—if I ever go to work?"

"Damn...dat's cold," Frankie said, approving. "I am workin', kid." Frankie's uncle was supposed to be the super of a couple of buildings on the block, but whether that really was his uncle, or whether Frankie ever helped him out with anything, David couldn't say for sure.

David shook his head as he trotted off. "Workin' my nerves, maybe."

From that day on, whenever David was working in the front room of his apartment—he had his office set up there because it was too noisy and bright at night to use as his bedroom—Frankie might come by, reach up, and rattle the window grill. If the window were left open even a crack, David might find himself interrupted by an instant conversation. "Hey kid, whatchu cookin' in there? Damn, that smells good." It would be, for example, macaroni and cheese. Or Campbell's soup, simmering on the kitchen stovetop. Frankie had an extraordinary nose for food.

David had been reluctant to allow Frankie into his life. He did not credit Frankie with any strong appreciation of subtlety. He wondered what would happen if Frankie finally figured out that he was gay, for example, or, more practically, if it was a good idea to allow a neighborhood boy like this to see that he had six, seven thousand dollars of irreplaceable computer equipment in his street-level apartment—secondhand hardware it'd taken him years to put together and expensive software he'd pirated from various temp assignments. He had no idea what kind of shit Frankie was up to. One day you'd see him in some raggedy-ass shorts and T-shirt, drinking a forty of cheap Midnight Dragon, a few days later in a new hip-length leather coat and new jeans, new Walkman, mixing Guinness with St. Ides and bragging about his "mad loot."

"I don't wanna hear whatchu do for that loot, kid," David said.

"You wanna know, man?" Frankie said, winking slyly. "I'll tell ya."

What it was, was: Frankie had a girl friend who worked as a prostitute, a "role play therapist" at a West Side escort service. All the clients had secret desires they'd confess, eventually or right off the bat, and more than one wanted to be beaten up by a homeboy. "And she beeped me, said I got this faggot wants to be beaten up, and I go kick the shit out of this guy for like an hour and come back home with two hundred bucks in my pocket."

David had let Frankie into his home for this story. They were in his back room, the living room where he sleeps—futon folded into a couch—watching TV, smoking weed. The story made him uncomfortable. "I'm a fag, Frankie," he said finally.

"This one dude," Frankie continued indifferently. "He paid me two hundred bucks just to stand with my foot on his face."

"You really do all that shit?" David asked.

Frankie shrugged, looking down at his sneakers. "Don't tell me you wouldn't." After a moment he laughed, covering his mouth with his hand.

That was a long time ago. A couple years but a long time. David doesn't remember now that he was ever scared of Frankie. He remembers the fact, and they joke about it, but he doesn't remember the feeling.

"Hey bitch," Frankie says, flopping down on David's couch as David unloads his bags. "What's for dinner?"

"You the bitch," David says, grabbing a beer from the refrigerator. "You the one I keep around 'cuz you look pretty."

Frankie turns on the TV. *Roseanne* reruns. "Come on Flores, I'm hungry, man." He calls David "Flores," refuses to believe in "this 'Florian' shit,'" as he likes to say. This secretly delights David. He fears the opposite—that one day Frankie might regard him as a phony homeboy wanna-be. When he gets down to it, David's not really sure which is the truth. His life's always been about passing for something he isn't. Maybe he really is a Flores. Maybe it's just Frankie can see it.

"Serious man," Frankie says, "What's for dinner?"

David grunts, walking into the room. "Shit, man. I've been on my feet all day. I wanted to come home and take a bath."

"And not eat nothing?"

"Man, you are the all-time bitch," David says, taking his wallet from his back pocket. "I was gonna order Chinese or pizza or shit. Chinese. Broccoli with garlic sauce." He flips a twenty onto the coffee table.

"You taking a shower?" Frankie says, snatching the bill up. "I'll run down the street, get us some pork chops an' shit. You don't want Chinese food."

"Don't tell me what I don't want," David says, knowing full well he's going to be eating pork chops in the next hour.

"Do you," Frankie says, scrunching his brow. "Do you.... The thing I don't get about, you know, you being gay an' shit. Is you know a woman's body is...." He outlines the standard curvaceous form with his hands. "Is beautiful. And a guy's body is all flat here...." He smacks his chest. "And all knotty here...." He grabs a handful of haunch through his jeans. "And hairy an' shit. It's ugly, man."

David shakes his head, coughing instead of laughing. "I don't think so. I mean, you got your idea of what a woman looks like, how many women look like that?" He mimics the hourglass gesture. "What is that shit? I seen the girls you go with. Skinny like boys, they got muscles in their arms. In a bra and everything their tits are up here but take that off" — he indicates an area toward the bottom of his ribcage — "they don't stay up there like pretty little oranges."

"Oranges," Frankie laughs.

"Eggplants, whatever. Just don't bullshit me. Like you don't ever look at a guy and say, 'Damn, I wish I looked like that.'"

Frankie shrugged. "That's different."

"It's not different," David said. "That's what I like."

"Who?" Frankie says.

"Not who," David says. "What."

"No man. You said you look at a guy and say 'damn,'" Frankie says. "So who do you look at?"

David's not happy about finding himself right here. To explain this properly requires revealing more of himself than he'd like to do. The answer is: Any guy who can walk down a city street holding his head up, looking like he believes the glances coming his way show admiration or fear or respect, not contempt. That makes David say "damn." That's what David wants to be.

It took him years to understand, and to truly believe, that the men he saw and desired, men who advertised their manhood with their stance or walk, with telling gestures like overlong belts hitching up oversized jeans, the long leather strap folded over to dangle cock-like at the crotch, or one sweatpants leg pushed up over a tight knot of calf muscle — that these were, precisely, gestures, consciously made, and that David could imitate them if he wanted, that imitating men he desired and admired made him strong like them, and not merely an imitation, that imitating and admiring was what these desirable men themselves did with their stances and walks and telling gestures.

But David can't always believe this. Acknowledging the consciousness of his inspiration makes him feel like a phony. So he doesn't answer Frankie.

"Who do you look at, Frankie?" he asks instead.

Frankie doesn't hesitate. "You," he says. "I wish I had green eyes."

"My mom's Irish," David says.

"I always wanted to be one of them green-eyed Puerto Ricans."

"My dad's Cuban," David says.

"Whatever," Frankie says. "You look like somebody."

"Who do I look like?" David asks.

"No, man. You look like yourself. You look like somebody. That's what I thought when I first saw you. 'Who's this kid? He got something going on.'"

"Oh, you did not." David pushes away his plate—stray clumps of yellow rice and a stripped pork chop bone. "You're full of shit."

"Fuck off yo. I'm serious. I had to nose around after you. I had to know what the deal was."

David smirks. "So this is it," he says, gesturing loosely with his arm. "This is what the deal is." He thinks he's gesturing at a messy apartment, a pile of chaos signifying nothing. David doesn't recognize that he has made choices in his life.

"I don't know whas wrong wit' you, man," Frankie says.

Frankie understands more than David thinks.

They're watching TV, bellies full of pork chop and yellow rice, stretched out on the couch, David as close to Frankie as he dares place himself, close but far enough to seem like he doesn't mean to be close. Frankie understands more than David thinks. He puts his arm around David's neck. He's not going to kiss David. David is wondering. David is thinking, well, if I was less of a fag I wouldn't be afraid and we would kiss and make love and we'd never have to say that it meant anything in particular except we love each other. Frankie starts kneading the muscles of David's shoulder, saying, "Man, you gotta learn to relax." David wonders if Frankie means something metaphysical.

Frankie doesn't. He just means David's got to learn to relax. It doesn't bother him to touch David. It's not—well, first of all: his friendship with David is something unique in his life, almost a fantasy, in the sense that it changes nothing except the way he looks at the world. Second of all: he has a hard time thinking of David as a guy. David isn't what a guy is, as far as the rest of Frankie's life goes, so it isn't necessary to think of him as one. David with his small features, his olive skin just light enough to show freckles, just dark enough to set off his green eyes—his yellow eyes, Frankie thinks, yellow and blue. They look green but the two colors don't actually blend, they are blue shot through with gold. David's hair's cut in a fade, perfect, with no scars on his scalp. All the guys Frankie knows show scars beneath their buzz cuts.

It's not that he sees David as a girl. He's a fag and his features are soft but that's not enough to blur Frankie's basic understanding of gender. Frankie likes pussy and tits and sex with girls a lot more hard-assed than David. It's easy enough to say, but when you're in David's position you never quite accept things like this, especially when you're in this boy's arms and you're wondering if he's going to kiss you, ever. If he wants to.

Frankie knows that David thinks he is beautiful and Frankie likes this. There is no one else in the world that thinks Frankie is beautiful. His mom says he is handsome. His girlfriends say he is cute. The guy who paid him two hundred dollars to be punched said he was hot. But beautiful is different. Beautiful is wanting to look without touching because the fact that he exists provides a true and sufficient pleasure. They watch TV and Frankie's dark irises dart to the corner of his eyes, catching David in the act of this contemplation. "What are you lookin' at man," he says in feigned annoyance.

"I'm not looking at shit," David says, turning back toward the television screen.

"Well," Frankie says. "All right then."

Frankie's uncle Manny snaps, irritated, " ¡Oye, hazme caso! I don't need any more of your fucking suggestions!"

Frankie's supposed to be helping Manny with repairs to a newly vacated apartment. They're ripping up the bathroom and kitchen, putting in some new fixtures—this makes the place "remodeled," takes it out of rent stabilization. Carroll Garden's getting gentrified, a landlord can easily pull down twelve hundred dollars a month for a one bedroom on the open market. Manny's got basic super-slash-handyman repair skills; installing a stove or repairing drywall's kind of a challenge. Manny stands, rubbing his chin, legs apart, muttering at the new stove and the incomprehensible tangle of wires and tubing at its back. Frankie has just suggested, for the third or fourth time this morning, that he can find a "how-to" guide on the World Wide Web—if he can take ten to go over his friend's place.

But Manny's not muttering to elicit suggestions. He's just thinking. He can usually figure shit out. Frankie showed up an hour late this morning and that's already primed Manny to be pissed off. He doesn't want to hear any more bullshit about computers.

"Bendito, I'm just trying to help...," Frankie says. "I don't want to be all day at this."

Manny scrapes his hand on a metal edge of the back of the stove. "Coño fuckin'.... Jesus Christ, Frankie, will you shut up and do what I ask you? Go get my ratchet set outta the truck."

David never studied computers at school, Frankie knows. They've talked about it. He says his teachers were too old and they never thought computers would turn out to be important, and anyhow they're not too hard to learn just by playing on one. But Manny doesn't care, and Raj didn't seem too impressed either when Frankie told him if he got a laptop instead of a PlayStation he could download all the music he wanted and play it through his stereo speakers. ("What are you, on crack?" Raj had said. "I'm getting a PlayStation with my Christmas money. A computer is like five thousand dollars or some shit.") Frankie doesn't get it. Computers are the future, but nobody wants to educate themselves about it because nobody wants to see that Frankie knows shit that they don't know nothing about.

Chainsmoking Newports, David's staring numb-headed at a layout of a menu he's doing—a couple-hundred-dollar job for a restaurant on Smith Street that's opening in a few weeks: logo, menu, flyers, stationery. It just sort of fell in his lap and it's money but it's boring as fuck. He doesn't really give a shit how it turns out so it's hard to judge whether one font choice makes a difference over another, or whether tight letter spacing looks better than loose.

He's both relieved and annoyed when the doorbell starts buzzing frantically. It's almost ten in the evening so he knows it's Frankie. Walking to the door he's deciding whether it's better to look annoyed, to justify sending Frankie away so he can finish, or to look pleased and relieved, which he is. It's bad though. He does need to finish this job. He opens the door before deciding and Frankie's already in, hugging him violently, and he's got no choice but to smile and squeeze back. "Hey man," he says. "Whassup?"

"Fuckin' shit, man," Frankie says. "A lot of motherfuckin' bullshit's what's up. Damn."

Frankie's giving off disjointed vibes. "Are you stoned or something? Man, you are stoned."

"Whatever, man. I was just hanging out with my friend Angela. The whore—you know, I told you about her."

"Oh," David says, letting the door slam as he follows Frankie to the couch. "What were you—stepping on some old faggots again?"

Frankie shakes his head. "No man, we were just hanging out and shit. She wadn't working or nothin'. Hey you know," Frankie says, grabbing David around the waist and pulling him down on the couch in a kind of wrestling move. "Hey, I met this friend of hers, this kid Orlando. He's a fag, man. He's pretty good looking. Come out wit' me sometime, I'll hook you up."

"What," David says, forcing a laugh. "You're picking guys for me now?"

Frankie puts his weight on David's chest. "Fuck," he says. "You ain't gettin' it off me, you gotta get it somewhere, right?"

"That's cute," David says, pushing back. Frankie's roughhousing with too much strength, David can't force him off. He's obviously really stoned, David thinks. "You're a good matchmaker, I bet. This kid's a fag and I'm a fag, so we'll get together and fuck or something.

'Cuz we fags."

"Well man," Frankie says. "It's the start, right?"

David manages to wriggle free, sits upright. "I didn't know it bothered you, man," he says.

Frankie's legs are lying across David's lap so he folds his arms behind his head, acts like he meant to spread out that way. "What?" he says. "What bothers me?"

David grabs the remote, turns the TV on. "Nothing." David shrugs. "I mean, I thought you liked what we got going."

Frankie folds his eyebrows down, looking confused. He moves his hands to his chest. "What the fuck are you talking about man? Orlando's a cool kid, man. He's smart. He's funny as shit. You'd like him. He fucks guys."

David makes an unintelligible, sullen-sounding noise. He's sitting under Frankie real rigid, like he's afraid to feel comfortable like that.

"What do we got going, man," Frankie asks, serious.

David kind of sighs.

"Tell me, all right? It's cool, just tell me."

"I think you know what I feel," David says.

"I ain't your psychic friend," Frankie says.

He's looking at David, eyes wide, waiting.

"You fuckin' know," David says.

Frankie closes his eyes and feels the velour of the seat cushion at the back of his neck. He inhales the smell of David's apartment. "Tell me your words for it," he says.

David grabs for his cigarettes and lights one.

He checks Frankie's face to see if he believes in it.

"My life's kind of a mess right now," David says. "I don't wanna worry about dating somebody, all the bullshit and game playing. I just gotta—you know—have my life be solid. It's good to have someone around I can talk to. It's good to have someone I can touch."

"Uh-huh," Frankie says, uncertain. He almost understands but the words you choose for things matter and he wants to hear it.

"I mean, shit," David says. "You know I'm in love with you and you know I'm never going to pull anything on you you don't want. I don't want anything off you, you know that. I just like being with you."

David's right, Frankie felt this. But he didn't think that David would be able to say it. He'd thought maybe David didn't even know it for himself. It feels weird, and it hurts. "My uncle got real mad at me today," Frankie says, quiet. "It's such fuckin' bullshit to have to follow him around and carry his goddamn toolbox and shit all over the fuckin' place. I gotta find a better job than that."

"Frankie, you heard what I said, right?"

He shrugs. "So fuckin' what, you jack off at night thinkin' 'bout me or something. So fucking what? You don't need my okay."

David's not looking him in the face anymore. "But," he says. "But, do you ever think about it? What it would be like? I mean…. Come on, you told me to tell you what I was thinking."

Frankie ain't going to be what someone wants him to be, one more time: a disappointment. It's not my fault, he thinks—why don't they want something I can give? "You wanna know if I ever thought about us fucking?" he asks.

David nods.

"Yeah. I thought you'd probly like it and I probly wouldn't."

"All right."

"I mean, you want us to be boyfriends?" Frankie says. "Or you just want to suck my dick sometime?"

"I don't want to suck your dick," David says defensively.

"I'm not offering," Frankie says. "I just want to know."

"I'm sorry," says David. "I'm sorry I brought this up at all. I'm an asshole, okay. I'm fucked up. I don't want anything from you. It just makes me feel good when I'm around you and I don't know why. I don't want to have sex with you and I don't want to fuck some fag you just met. I'm sorry. We shouldn't be talking about this."

"Man, you just crazy, what's with you?"

David's folded his arms. He's staring straight ahead, wanting Frankie to disappear now. Or to shut up. Or something.

"'We shouldn't be talking about this'?" Frankie repeats.

It's been a while since David has hated himself this consciously. This isn't the first time he's made a relationship like this for himself. It's not the second or the third. Used to just be casual acquaintances, stupid crushes, always on straight boys. That he's made Frankie his friend, tied their lives together in various, sophisticated, tiny ways—he's appalled at himself. He didn't know he could be that devious.

He says, out loud, "I wish I could die or something and get it over with." And just hearing himself say that, seeing the look on Frankie's face, makes him wish it harder 'cuz he can see Frankie's upset.

"David, man," Frankie says in a whisper. "Why the fuck would you say that?"

David doesn't answer.

"Man, that makes me feel real fucked up. Don't say that, all right? I love you, okay? You're my brother. If you think you're a piece of shit, what does that make me?" With some effort Frankie works his hand into David's clenched fist. David doesn't relax. "Come on, man," Frankie says. "I don't know why you gotta be like this."

David shakes his head. "Okay," he says, putting his feet back on the floor. "All right." His hand relaxes, but it's just in Frankie's grip. He's not holding back. "Yeah. I want you to be my boyfriend. I want you to be my lover. This whole time, I think, that's what I've wanted. I'm friends with you because it turns me on to be near you."

"That's cool," Frankie says gently. "That doesn't bother me."

"It bothers me, all right?" David says. "That's the problem. It bothers me."

Frankie's stoop-sitting in front of his aunt's house when his friend Raj goes by. Raj says, Frankie, man, whassup?

Frankie thinks of a beer commercial, whassup? Frankie starts to say, jes chillin', but stops, and thinks about it, and laughs. Chillin'. What the fuck does that mean? So Frankie goes, I'm sittin' on the stoop in front of my aunts.

Raj is like, what're you, laughin' like a mutherfuckin' idiot.

Yeah, Frankie says, I'm a mutherfuckin' idiot. You wanna sip of this?

Raj laughs, takes the bagged forty. Frankie's in the doghouse, he says. What's up, kid?

Frankie just shakes his head, shrugs. Smiles.

Out on the street on a Friday night, Raj says. You ditched your man, huh?

Frankie's lip curls. Yeah, he says.

For real?

Yeah, Frankie says.

Raj is waiting for the punch line, or something. For real? he says again.

We decided, Frankie says wistfully, head held low. We decided we should see other people.

For five seconds Frankie can keep a straight face.

Man, Raj says.

Wha-a-a-ssup! Frankie says, like the beer commercial.

You are serious retarded, man, Raj says, laughing, sitting down.

MY BLUE MIDNIGHTS

Rane Arroyo

"The trees which grew along the broken arches
Waved dark in the blue midnight, and the stars
Shone through the rents of ruin...."
—Lord Byron, *Manfred*

1.

My ears are ringing so I can't help but think my family is already talking about me.

I don't think I'm that interesting once I get out of other people's beds.

The country of my own bed is only for invited tourists.

I stop at Little Jim's for a drink before I go to the family party for yet another cousin who is engaged.

It's only four o'clock in a Gemini afternoon but already the bar is crowded.

I see lots of businessmen eyeing unemployed (or unemployable, as my friend Linc insists) men in cowboy suits.

How has the gay world become so full of uniforms?

A younger man nonchalantly stares at me.

I look away and see one of the suits staring at him.

In the beginning was the triangle and it is still holy.

I walk over to the jukebox to see if there are any new Spanish songs and I find the same old one: "Feliz Navidad."

Jesus, why is there a Christmas song on this jukebox in the middle of June?

I swallow my warm Budweiser and hurry out of the bar before I have to reject a skinny man with an eye patch who is seeking rejection, and probably wouldn't believe that I'm late for a family party.

It's so strange but the inside of a gay bar is like being inside an imaginary country; rarely are there clocks or even clues to which city you might be in.

It's a no-man's land filled with men.

It's as if we're all amnesiacs without any other IDs other than what hangs between our legs.

I'm an exile who isn't an exile.

I think of my parents arriving in Chicago not knowing any words of English, their Puerto Rico becoming only Puerto Pobre.

I remember how they used to bundle us up in the winters as if we were going out to play in a new ice age.

My boots hit the sidewalks in a regular rhythm and I think of that song that Uncle Israel, used to sing, before he became Uncle Rachel: *There is a rose / that grows / in Spanish Harlem.*

He got the words almost right.

I arrive at the party, take a deep breath, and ring the doorbell.

The cousin who is pregnant and fifteen is being honored for trapping her man, an electrician who is even in a union.

She shrugs at me and cousin Tony embraces me and I'm pushed into the living room.

He is one of the family's heroes because he has been a rich banker's (I've never seen a poor banker) personal chauffeur for over ten years.

Tony's tragedy is that he hasn't had enough free time to make children, or at least "legal ones" as Mami whispered to me at another party for another pregnant cousin.

In our family, sometimes we had celebrations to celebrate the fact that nothing bad had happened in a long time.

Tony's wife, Rosa, kisses me on the cheek and sighs, "Ricky, you've finally got here. It's you and me against them. I've been doing my part."

It's a well-established, if undiscussed, fact in the family that I will have no children either.

Rosa finds this a more important link than I do, but it provides me an entry, or reentry, into the family.

Bells cut out of white tissue paper are taped everywhere so it feels like I'm inside a hot church.

My secret life is no secret anymore.

It's supposed to be my secret love.

Where is he?

Will I never sing: *eres tú / como el agua de mi...*?

Cousin Blanca walks into the living room, her body stuffed into a white Christian Dior yacht-dress, and rushes forward to embrace me.

"I told your mother this morning you would show up," she purrs. "Your parents told me that you wouldn't. That you had to go to the ballet or something that you—you know—you like to do."

"I like to do everything," I smile back. "That's how I get in trouble."

Rosa chokes and Blanca beams.

Sometimes I wish either of these women had been my mother.

"Where are Mami and Papi?" I ask.

"They'll be here. You know your mother. She's like a daughter of the tides. She only leaves the suburbs when there isn't any traffic. She wasn't that nervous when she was young. But who is young anymore? Not even you. I see gray hairs, hijo."

"That's because I am very good on some very bad nights." I feel drunk, strangely happy.

I like the sound of Spanish and English filling the room.

Some of the men are huddled, talking about the Cubs vs. the White Socks, that ancient argument where there are no clear-cut winners.

I join the women in the kitchen. They are never more than a few steps away from the liquor.

I grab a beer, look at it in case it's on the latest boycott list—it's not! Blanca hits my hand. "Put that back, you barbarian. I have a surprise for you."

She pushes me through the hallway into the dining room where a bar has been set up. "See something you like?"

I follow her gaze and see a handsome bartender. "Blanca, are you trying to get me in trouble?"

"Let's just say I'm trying to manage the trouble you're already in."

Jesus, I have a sudden taste for a cigarette even though I don't really smoke except when I'm drunk or nervous or sexed-out.

I rarely smoke.

I kiss Blanca. "Is this like a late graduation present?"

"It's up to you to make it a party. I know it's a fact the stud is suffering from a broken heart. So just keep it below the waist, you get me, huh? You'd be surprised what can crawl from down there to up here." She pounds her chest, winks dramatically, then walks away.

I savor the moment.

I feel as if I'm in *Brideshead Revisited*, but with a mambo soundtrack.

"Hola, hermano." I'm a fucking idiot, I think to myself.

Why am I calling such a stud my brother?

The bartender smiles back. "Are you my tip?"

I pull back. "What do you mean?"

"You're the Ricky that Blanca told me about."

I nod, "The little she knows to tell you."

He extends his hand, "I'm Pablo."

I hold his hand. "And I'm very happy that you are Pablo."

He breaks into a smile. "Ah, they warned me that you could be charming."

I smile back. "This is going to sound crazy, but I feel happy today. I mean, just being with my family—look at these criminals. I'm...here and you're...."

"Also...happy."

"Right," I wink back. "Happy."

"But you haven't asked me about my broken heart!"

"Tell me about your broken heart," I ask even as I offer my best *GQ* scowl.

Pablo gestures toward a drink. "You're too sober and I'm working."

"Can I ask just one thing?"

"As long as it's not the kind of question that is too inspirational."

"Was he Spanish or American."

"He was Spanish-American. A Latino. I only sleep with our kind. Who do you sleep with?"

The robot in me can't be stopped once again. "Usually myself."

Pablo puts his hand over mine. "Look, I've been hearing about you for nearly a month. And you are handsome. And you might even be sweet. I don't want to talk about me, okay? I want to talk about spending next summer in Madrid. Or some other adventure we might have. Stupid, right?"

I cock my head. "Are you a professional bartender?"

He shrugs. "I'm licensed. God, that makes me sound like James Bond, no? Did you see Rob Lowe, no wait, it was Tom Cruise in that terrible movie where he serves drinks in the Caribbean?"

"No, but I'll have to rent it now."

Rosa shows up. "Sorry to interrupt whatever this is but I need your help. The uncles are arguing about who will be godfather to our children."

Pablo points, "You two...?"

I shake my head, "No, it's a joke...."

Rosa yells, "We're two of a kind."

I'm dragged off into the living room.

I wave goodbye to Pablo and he waves back.

Forgive me this literary theft, but I'm surfing one of Virginia Woolf's waves and drunk on adrenaline: the waves, the waves.

Uncle Tony grabs me. "Am I or am I not your favorite uncle?"

I nod my head, "No."

Everyone laughs.

Uncle only pats me on my back. "America is still a land of choices, right?"

"Right," I laugh. "But you're always going to be my uncle. I have no choice!"

Uncle Tony playfully pushes me away and I watch the conversation slowly descend into a series of private concerns and confessions.

I can't help but think of Uncle Rachel and wonder what he is doing right now, at this very moment.

How many times have I tried to find him, but it seems he has legally changed his last name, too.

A transvestite in the family still has no place at the table during prayers, for our god is a jealous god and wants the spotlight all to himself.

Ask me about Spanish men I admire and I'll tell you of my Uncle Rachel, he who taught me how to dance to Aretha Franklin records, who said to me before he disappeared (los lost desperados in America):

Honey, I'm taking a slow boat to China and I may never see you again but think of me each time you open a fortune cookie.

Those were his last words.

Then he was gone.

I wonder if I'll disappear just like that someday.

I need a new drink, a new bartender.

Funny word — "bartender."

Tender bar.

Father Time, love me tender and I'll be so good to you.

I think of escaping my family, of making my way back to Little Jim's and being picked up.

I want to be seduced tonight and not be the seducer.

I avoid Pablo, feeling as unsexy as old bean burritos in a 7-Eleven microwave.

2.

I call Pablo and he meets me at the Chicago Diner, a trendy vegetarian restaurant blocks from the bars.

I'm a creature of habit, feeling safe only with the familiar, the explored, the tamed.

Christopher Columbus I am not.

I always have to know where the emergency exit is in the theater, the skyscraper, the airplane, and on first dates.

Little Jim's is two blocks from here and French Kissing is three.

Pablo shows up, looking a little older than he did at the party.

Perhaps that's because he is dressed more informally, in jeans and a tank top.

Or maybe I'm just sober.

We smile at each other, stumble through orders, and face each other without saying much of anything.

He breaks the silence. "So, your lovers — Americans?"

I smile back, but not so as to reveal much of anything. "You and I are Americans, too."

Pablo laughs and the tension breaks.

I like this man, although I don't know if I can love this man.

Why am I thinking about this over lentil soup, with a side of hand-shredded carrots?

He says, "When I was young I wanted to change the colors of my eyes. I wanted them to be sea blue."

I stare at his brown eyes, the eyes of a Marc Anthony before his encounter with destiny.

God, I have to stop reading personal ads.

I smile. "There are contacts for that now."

Pablo shrugs. "But I've changed. I came to realize that blue eyes wouldn't help me look like James Dean."

"I wanted to look like Sal Mineo, the smart one in *Rebel Without a Cause*."

Pablo pats my hand. "At least, you pick a dark hero."

"So what do you think?"

Pablo understands. He shakes his head. "It won't work. You, hijo, are too Americanized to live in my world. You know your family's party. Well, I belong there."

"I don't."

Pablo plays at twirling his pretend mustache. "And someday you'll succeed. And you'll get away from them, too."

"What do you mean?"

"Ricky, I watched you watch them. I'm not even sure if you know how far away you've placed everyone from you."

I must have been crazy, but I just put my right hand in his crotch and rubbed him.

"I'm right here, baby."

Pablo lifts the hand, kisses the open palm, and puts it gently in my own lap. "No matter how you try, you can't make the United States your real bed. You'll be Puertorriqueño again soon. I'm not talking about your body. I'm sure it knows how to sleep almost anywhere."

There is a pause and we're both laughing.

I feel so good.

I want to love this man.

"I want to love you, Pablo."

"I want to love you too, Ricky, but...."

I stop him from talking.

The dinner is excellent as usual.

I walk Pablo to Belmont Avenue and flag down a taxi for him, but before he enters it I kiss him slowly on the lips.

His hands wrap around my hips.

He pulls me to him.

We can't let go.

We don't let go.

I jump into the taxi and we go to his place near the Taco Bell in Andersonville.

We walk up the stairs past stoners in black T-shirts and underwear, munching on tacos.

I think how the neighborhood looks like a Mexican Disneyland.

Pablo's apartment is crazier than I thought it would be because he seemed so damn polite and not the free spirit he feels free to be at home.

There are cacti painted on the wall; orange chairs are all over the place.

They're like pumpkins that no one will carve with human faces.

There are different colored light bulbs in the lamps throughout his place.

Pablo has filled an aquarium with broken wine glasses.

"Souvenirs of parties?" I ask in an amused voice. "Or glass slippers that didn't fit?"

He gives me a look that makes him look like a brat, a mischievous little boy, a sideshow barker.

I thank Pablo for being my new brother, though I want and need him to be my lover.

I thank the men whose names I don't remember for giving me memories I'll never forget.

We mess up his place as our shadows rub against each other.

Making love with him is both silly and beautiful.

His brown skin covers me and it feels like I'm falling into the sun head first.

I wake up at midnight, my heart racing.

I look at the man next to me and Pablo looks uncannily like me; we're not twins, but we do look as if we come from the same planet.

I wake him up and insist we walk naked to his balcony.

"Los vecinos will call the cops, hombre," he half-protests.

"Fuck your neighbors," I growl.

"Dios, you're not going to be very faithful, are you, Ricky?"

He pulls me to him and soon I get him to look out at a city of lights.

Chicago, Chicago, Chicago.

We don't say anything.

We don't need to speak in Spanish or English about this moment as the weight of his body and mine are burdens we share.

Puerto Rico, my heart's devotion, let it sink back in the ocean.

I quote musicals at the worst times.

Hell, whatever scars I might have are only causes of celebration — that I've made it to the present, this now which is as naked as we are.

Pablo asks me where the North Star is, but what do I know of space, of cosmic forms?

I kiss him slowly and he rubs his face against me.

I don't care if we are ghosts among ruins.

Right now, we're dreaming without even having to close our eyes.

"What will happen to us in the morning?" I stutter.

"That's a million years away," he whispers.

"But in the morning?"

"We'll see."

I nod my head.

In daylight, one can trust one's eyes.

In the dark, the body knows the route to survival.

We have instincts that have developed within us after millions of years of living and dying on Earth.

I become cold and we go back to bed where our earlier forms have been etched out in the sheets.

Our desires are explicit.

3.

Over the next year, Pablo and I become friends and stop sleeping with each other.

I'm a little surprised one March night to see him waiting for me as I stagger home from Little Jim's.

I'm alone, broke, and tired of my clothes smelling like smoke.

I smell like a goddamn fireman; the bars are becoming more and more like the hearts of volcanoes.

The truth is that I spent most of the night hugging the jukebox.

I didn't really want sex.

I do right now.

Only, it's Pablo who is here and we are just amigos.

Pablo is as gone as I am, but I sense he is here for a safe place from some internal storm.

He loves my apartment because if you open up the balcony door you can smell Lake Michigan.

Not that you can see it!

My building is one of the last rental units in the lake shore area of New Chinatown.

Daily, I see yuppies shopping for $100,000 condos right in this building.

Soon I will have to move out, replaced by a young banker, a pretty actor, a successful photographer, or a dedicated accountant.

"Hola, El Cid," I smile. "Come inside. If you want to be cold, I'll put some ice in your wine."

He follows me inside, holds me, takes a deep breath.

"What are you doing?" I ask gently.

He holds me even harder. "I want to never forget how you smell like. The nose is one way that a poor man takes his revenge on a rich man's garden."

"Sit down. You're drunk."

"Ricky, you've been trying to pick someone up tonight? Why don't you take the bull by the horns instead. You know what I mean?"

Many glasses of wine later, we stop talking.

We grow sullen as we next finish off the rum.

Maybe this is what I miss most about not having a lover anymore: two bodies in one space not having to say anything to each other.

Pablo is still young, too young to be this unhappy. "So why are you here tonight?"

He becomes animated, as if a spell has been broken.

"You know about Chino. I mean, you know he's dead. You went to his funeral. They never caught the guys who did it, you know."

I move over by him. "I know, honey. Chino's probably in heaven looking down on us right now. Jerking off, I hope."

Pablo pushes me away. "Ricky, he tried awfully hard to go to hell."

We say nothing for the next ten minutes.

Chino stole Pablo from me even though Pablo was never mine.

My family asks about Pablo although they are afraid that if I find a companion then I will demand for them to treat us as a couple.

A couple of thugs.

A couple of what?

Pablo starts talking and I know it's going to be one of his monologues; I'm right but first, "Stop, let me piss and get bigger glasses for the vodka."

He follows me into the bathroom. "Why do you always know the right thing to say to me?"

"Pablo, a man needs his privacy sometimes."

"I've seen you at the Belmont Rocks doing God knows what. It was hard to tell from where I was but your butt...."

I zip up.

Glasses, vodka, ice, radio tuned to a classical station.

It's the *New World Symphony*; I'd laugh at the selection but Pablo might think I'm laughing at him.

He speaks slowly, deliberately. "It's my anniversary. Chino has forgotten all about me. The dead are putas, no. We went out just a couple of months. Then he got killed. And today is the fifth-month anniversary of our first date. Chino was something special. That's why he got stolen from me. You liked him, I know you did because you didn't make jokes around him. You listened to him. Not any more. Chino doesn't have a tongue. He doesn't have hands. He doesn't have those beautiful legs. He doesn't have a cock. He doesn't have a neck I wanted to bite tonight like I was Dracula or something."

He cries so hard that he is no longer saying words and I hold him.

Pablo's Chino was killed in a drive-by shooting.

He had been in the wrong place and in the wrong time.

Pablo's Chino.

Will I never belong to anyone?

I don't know what to say and end up making Pablo angry with these words, "Honey, you celebrate the sixth month, a year, twenty-five years. But the fifth month, well...."

"Ricky, we have five fingers on each hand. Five. You should know.

You jerk off enough. You should know that five is important. Five. Five."

He paces the room like a trapped animal.

I open the balcony door. "Take a deep breath."

Pablo almost says something, stops, and takes a long look into my tired face.

He then takes that deep breath.

"Lake Michigan!" I prompt. "There are some things you can't see even if they're there."

Pablo leans forward, throws his glass of vodka in my face.

Startled, I fall back. "What?"

"I want to lick it off."

He does and we end up kissing.

"Let's just sleep tonight, okay?"

Pablo nods.

"Sometimes, Ricky, I have sex with a guy just to sleep next to him. To breathe in the air he's just breathed out."

I push him toward the bedroom. "You're sick and you are the most perfect friend for me."

"I think I'm going to be sick in the morning."

"If you're human," I add.

He whispers in my ear, "I love you, Ricky Ricardo, Jr."

"I wish you did."

I put Pablo to bed and he floats away to some safe place in his head.

Why do I always feel like I'm being left behind?

Again.

My body is my true family.

My soul is the orphan that I've adopted.

My mother and father are sleeping in each other's arms and why can't I have the same refuge?

Is my Uncle Rachel going to make his cameo in a séance soon?

Again, I'm alone.

I am no loner and that is my tragedy.

I can't sleep.

I want to guard my friend against some invisible enemy tonight.

I sit on the couch, listening to my neighbors argue about alternative music not being alternative since it's so mainstream now.

Stupid shits.

I shake off my blue mood by thinking of someone I slept with (did he even have a name?) who stayed over on a night when these very neighbors were going for each other's throats.

My boyfriend (who hadn't been a boy in a long time) cooed, "They sound like jazz musicians without instruments."

He didn't know what a poet he was.

I remember him listening to the arguing couple some more, cocking his head like a dog that is left alone very often.

"Just listen to them go up and down the scale, baby."

I remember that much of him.

I still appreciate that much of him.

Is love possible?

I don't remember orgasm with him, just that moment listening to the neighbors.

Curious how the body is an amnesiac.

Are we all men of the mancha, our lances erect against windmills?

I'm glad to laugh at myself.

I turn on the television and fall asleep watching, of all things, *It's a Wonderful Life*.

It's not "La Vida Loca," is it?

Pablo talks in his sleep.

He talks in Spanish.

Angels gets wings on the television every time a bell rings.

Is it a wonderful life?

The blue midnight blows out my candles, one by one.

I end up in the dark, face down.

I spite the gods by dreaming about reality.

THERE ARE NO PRETTY GIRLS AT THE TABERNACLE
Marcel Devon

When Ma opens the door for me and Terry, it comes as no surprise that Pa is one of the first sights we see, enthroned in his usual place on the dingy brown sofa. His once-white T-shirt hikes up in rolls, exposing a pale, distended belly which one thick-fingered hand enthusiastically rubs. His other hand, complete with a half moon of black axle grease under each nail, loosely grips a can of Coors. A Saturday afternoon college football game bleats from the old TV.

Ma smiles warmly at me. "Who's this with you, son?" she asks.

"Terry, my roomie from the U." That's the University of Houston. My major—architectural engineering. I've just finished my first year.

Terry thrusts out his hand and Ma takes it limply. "My pleasure, Terry," she says with little interest. She turns to yell over her shoulder to Pa. "Dan! Scotty's brought his roommate from the university with him. Name's Terry." Ma motions for Terry and me to enter. As we do, we hear Pa's commentary.

"'Terry?' Thatta boy or a girl? Sounds like a girl's name. Thatchyur girlfriend, boy?"

No one bothers to answer him. Instead, Ma escorts us into the kitchen where Terry and I plop into uncomfortable wooden chairs. Ma pours out two glasses of warm orange juice. "I'll make you boys some sandwiches," she says, opening the bread box and moving several loaves to the cracked countertop "Did Scotty tell you he's going to be a pastor?" she asks Terry. Uh-oh, here we go.

Terry looks to me for confirmation. I roll my eyes. Ma needs to maintain her delusions, apparently unable to accept the fact that her son is godless.

"He took that class in…umm…Christian Science…," she begins.

"Philosophy of religion," I interrupt.

"…and right off I could tell a big difference in his spirit after that. The Lord reached him through that class. Terry, you want white or wheat?"

"Huh? Oh, wheat, please," Terry says. Ma already knows I like my bread wheat, my PB creamy, and my jelly strawberry.

"When Scotty came up to visit during Christmas break, we all saw a new boy. Creamy or crunchy?"

"Creamy," says Terry.

"He's thinking about joining that big church in Dallas," Ma continues. "What's it called? Strawberry, grape, or cherry?"

"Grape, please."

"Yes, Lord!" Mom raises her eyes to the ceiling, swaying a little. "My son!" She lets her words fade and sets two plates of sandwiches on the table.

"Ma, Terry needs a place to stay for the summer," I tell her, picking the crusts off my bread.

"You should eat your crusts, Scotty. Well, Terry can stay here. It's the best part of the bread. You shouldn't waste it, honey, eat it. Is he gonna...are you gonna be working, Terry?" she asks. Terry shrugs casually. "I mean, you'll have to buy your own stuff. See, Scott, Terry eats his crusts. Not rent, just pitch in with the groceries is all I ask." Terry nods between bites of sandwich.

Ma watches us eat in silence for a moment. Then: "Terry, you know how to work on cars?"

"Yes, ma'am."

"Then you can help out at the shop." Half of my parents' two-acre lot is a car shop.

I give mom a smile, my mouth full of PBJ, a small mountain of peeled crusts on my plate.

"Well, Terry," Ma says, picking up my empty glass for a refill, "we also have a great congregation nearby that you can go to. Our pastor— oh! Don't get me started." *No one was trying to,* I think to myself. "He's fire and brimstone, I tell ya! Sorta scares the young kids, but it's good for them to fear God."

As Ma goes deeper into her "Christian Mode," her sixth-grade education becomes ever more embarrassingly apparent. My head is bobbing on my neck like a hood ornament as I nod at things I struggle not to hear. At least this time I get the satisfaction of watching Terry's head wobbling in synch with mine.

"And he's a rowdy one, too!" Ma is saying. "Get t' jumpin' and hollerin' and speakin' in tongues! Lord's always there with the pastor. You can feel it in your heart. Ain't that right, Scotty?"

I don't answer.

"Lord all *mighty!*" she says. "I can feel the Spirit as we speak! You'll just love Pastor Rick. He went to U of H, too. Maybe you know him?" Here it comes. Terry feels it coming, too, as tangible as the taste of peanut butter against the roof of his mouth. "Are you saved, Terry?"

Squirming on the hook, Terry looks to me, pleading with his eyes for me to help him off. I like the show, but I also like Terry, so I do.

"To tell you the truth, Ma, Terry's going through some real hard times right now. His fiancée just ran off with someone else." I lean toward her over the table and whisper conspiratorially, "A Negro."

Ma gasps. Suddenly she's full of warmth and sympathy for Terry's plight. Terry, meanwhile, is displaying his very best trying-to-be-brave face, a product of the drama class where we met. My fable continues.

"You can imagine how much it's upset him," I say. "He was really in love with her. And, to make matters worse, Ma, she'd been fornicating with the Negro the whole time Terry thought she loved him!" With difficulty I manage not to smile in satisfaction. I knew, if I tried hard enough, I could fit "fornicate" into this speech.

"And Ma...." I lean even closer. "The Negro Terry's fiancée ran off with—it was another girl!"

I might as well have punched Ma in the solar plexus. She's choking and wheezing out her sounds of protest and outrage.

My mind wanders to Pastor Rick, whose favorite sins are for- nication and sodomy. I managed to cover them both. Ma, meanwhile, despises lesbians and is convinced that Tipper Gore, Janet Reno, and Hillary Clinton are in a kinky sex triangle. "That's why she doesn't care if Slick Willie sleeps with his interns," she has explained to me in the past, as confident as if she were declaring her discovery that the earth was round.

"So, Ma," I continue when she catches her breath, "I decided I should bring Terry home with me—to get him away from those dis- gusting girls." That statement is actually completely true, but not for reasons I'm about to tell Ma.

"Anybody want a cold soda?" Ma ventures. As she stands to go to the refrigerator, one of the dogs in the back yard begins to yelp. In a flash, Pa is up from his chair, his bouncing belly exposed under his beer- stained T-shirt. The floor shakes as Pa stomps to the rear door and straight-arms it, causing the door to fly back and crash against the side of the house. We listen as he kicks the shit out of one of the dogs, fuming and snarling, cursing the name of every god ever invented by the human mind. Ma covers her ears, squeezing her eyes shut against the blasphemy.

As quickly as it began, it's over. Pa returns from the back yard, stopping to retrieve another beer from the refrigerator, which stands open because Ma has frozen in the act of getting our sodas. "Scotty," he says, his brow furrowing, "where's your girlfriend?"

The three of us look at him stupidly. He snorts and trudges back to the sofa. The cushions hiss violently as his three hundred pounds displace the air inside.

Ma puts the three sodas on the table, one for each of us. "As disgusting as it is, Dan," she says, popping open her can of RC, the squelching sound a tiny echo of the sofa's more violent version, "you don't have to take our Lord's name in vain! Swear to your heart's content if you want, but I will not tolerate you blaspheming the Lord!"

Pa's only response is a belch. Ma covers her face with her hands. I see the edges of her ears turn red, as they do when she is about to cry.

"Ma," I ask, *what's* disgusting?"

"Those damn dogs!" she huffs, rising to pace the sticky linoleum. Her "inside" sandals slap against her heels with every step. "We got four boys, and one of 'em, the one we call Popper, can't tell the difference from a boy and a girl. I told Pa a long time ago to get a bitch, but Popper decided he can't wait on a bitch to come along so he's just gonna make himself one outta one of the other boys. It ain't natural. Like those Catholic priests going sebb-i-late."

"Celibate."

"Yes. Just ain't natural. It ain't in God's plan—that's why they molest those altar boys all the time. Same goes for the dogs, too. Pa says, 'Get 'em fixed,' and I say, 'We can't afford to, Dan,' and that's that."

"So Pa beats Popper?" I ask.

"You heard the other dog whimperin'. What's he supposed to do?"

"How much can it cost to neuter them? Just for Popper it can't be that much."

"Eighty bucks if we only get Popper done, but Pa says we have to do 'em all because it ain't fair if we only fix Popper."

"So why don't you just give Popper away?"

It must be half-time, because Pa has apparently been listening in on our conversation. "You know, we oughta get rid of that faggot mutt at that. Fact, Bernice has been bugging me forever to have one of these piece-of-shit dogs. I'll take 'im over to her house and she can deal with old fudge-packing Popper from now on." He digs a finger into his navel, wriggling it around before withdrawing it and wiping it on his shirt. "Shoulda done that a long fucking time ago. Dunno why I didn't."

In my mind I give the answer I would never say out loud. *Maybe it is because—although you can recite every college and NFL football player's jockstrap size; know how to dismantle any model vehicle and reassemble it, bolt by bolt, practically while blindfolded; can discourse on the differences between ale, lager, malt, stout, and bitters—you dropped out with Ma in junior high in order to become a mechanic in East Texas and have never been much of a one for taking action to solve your problems.*

Pa continues to watch the games, flipping through the channels whenever he is bored, while Terry, Ma, and I sip sodas at the kitchen table. Ma snaps out of "Christian Mode" and moves into "Gossip Mode," which I like better since it means Terry and I get to learn all our neighbors' dirty secrets.

First, Ma is absolutely certain that the teenaged girl across the street has had no less than three abortions. The girl's older brother had to leave town because he got two junior high girls pregnant, so that kind of behavior runs in the family. The neighbors to the right of our place are definitely swingers because another couple visits them for entire nights and all the lights go off as soon as they arrive. "With children in the house!" Ma exclaims. I suspect it must trouble her that they darken the house, making it impossible for her to watch.

The people on the corner smoke pot and continuously play loud "black devil music" (Ma is convinced that heavy metal is both African and Satanic in origin.) The family across from them is a bunch of crack dealers who have frequent orgies.

"I'm sure their kids participate," I offer. Terry cuts his green eyes at me, but Ma only nods distractedly. Her densely curled bouffant, shellacked into hardpan by repeated applications of hair spray, rides her skull like a blonde helmet.

Down the street lives a married woman who must be a prostitute because of her miniskirts, high heels, and makeup. Ma believes the alleged whore made a move on Pa, but he refuses to talk about it. Ma moves on to other topics.

It enrages her that schools are mandated by law to teach sex education yet don't teach how God created the world in six days. "It's a liberal conspiracy," she says. "I know it. Because they're also teaching kids that homosexuality is acceptable. Yes! It's okay to be an abomination unto the Lord, and anyone who disagrees is a bigot. And they're even brainwashing babies still in the cradle!" She's preaching now, and the tendons in her neck stand out like tent cords. "Teletubbies! Ever heard of them? Well, the purple one is queer. You can tell because of the way he just prances around. Plus he carries a purse! And, Scotty, this is a show watched by babies and toddlers!"

I keep bobbing my head, tuning out, as best I can, Ma's diatribes about the things she claims to hate yet is obsessed with, about the wickedness she spends hours observing throughout the dusty blinds. I recall how Ma was among the group of local women who were scandalized by the "oversized" bulge in the pants of a Sam Houston statue downtown. The same women who scaled the monument with ladders and ground down the offending swelling. But now she has moved on to abortion.

"Murder is murder," she's saying. "In those sexual education classes they teach ten-year-old kids that it's all right to kill the unborn. Get this—as a form of birth control! The world is overcrowded, they say, so it's not only okay to do it, it's necessary!"

I don't bother to remind her of her belligerent support for the state of Texas' frequent application of the death penalty. Or of how, each time an unlucky, unforgiven murderer is executed, she drives to Huntsville to be among the throngs of picnicking "Christian" families carrying posters that read, "Score One for the State."

"Ma," I interrupt, "Terry and I need to fix up our room. We'll be back down in a little while, okay?"

The relief on Terry's face is a bit too evident. I wonder if he's still as eager as he was to attend the Pentecostal Tabernacle with Ma each

Sunday for an entire summer. We excuse ourselves, thank Ma for the food and drinks, and walk past Pa, beached and immobile upon the sofa.

"Nice to meet you, sir," Terry says. A waste of breath. Pa does no more than grunt with impatience as we momentarily obstruct his view of spandex-clad college boys butting helmeted heads and tossing around an animal-hide bag.

We reach my old room, which, to Ma's credit, is spotless. Terry leaps onto the bed, test-driving the springs, grinning lecherously. I lock the door behind me.

"I'm sorry about all that, Terry," I tell him. "It's really embarrassing. Ma's a little lost in space, and Pa...."

"Did you have to tell her that crap about my girlfriend running off with some black girl?"

"Don't act like you didn't get a kick out of seeing the look on her face. Besides, she's got mucho sympathy for you now, Terry. You'll be her project for the summer. Sure you can handle the Tabernacle tomorrow?"

"Sure," he says without hesitation. "I'll just find some girl and give her the same sob story you told your mom."

"No, you won't," I answer back, perhaps a little too forcefully. "This summer, you're all mine. We agreed, remember? I'm not sharing you with any more girls."

Terry motions me to him where he sits on the edge of the bed. He wraps his arms around my hips, butting his head against my crotch. He gives me the same charming shrug he gave my mom when she asked him whether he had a job. I already know I'll have to keep an eye on him.

"What would your mom say if she caught us like this?" Terry asks as he unbuckles my belt.

"She won't."

"What if?" he insists, sliding my zipper down.

"Saw what Pa did to Popper, didn't you?"

"Well...when I go to the Tabernacle with your mom tomorrow, I'll make a good show of looking at all the pretty girls."

"No, 'cuz then Ma will just think you're a pervert."

"I am," Terry laughs, hooking his thumbs into the waistband of my jeans and my shorts and shucking the whole package down to my ankles.

"Anyway," I tell him, "there are no pretty girls at the Tabernacle."

SKINS

Rick Laurent Feely

"Let me also wear
Such deliberate disguises
Rat's coat, crowskin, crossed staves
In a field...."
—T.S. Eliot, *The Hollow Men*

I slap him across the face.

"But Rat," he says to me.

He's got a slippery voice that Crow. It's good for telling stories, or singing whiskey-slurred lullabies in those haunting hours between night and morning. When you finally nod off you can still hear it, subliminal and ceaseless, like the backbeat in a song. This time I'm not listening.

I look up, away, anywhere. The sky is the color of a grainy photograph left too long in the back pocket of your only pair of jeans. Jeans cured to ancient blue and frayed at the knees. One day you reach in, lookin' for a quarter, maybe a cigarette butt, and you come across this photo you been keeping, but you can't tell what it's a picture of anymore. That's what the sky looks like. A memory condemned to a smear of gray. Somehow the sunlight bleeds through, so I know it ain't yet night.

My gaze jumps from grainy sky to duct-taped boots to the tarpaper rooftop where he's sprawled, all jutting ribs and skinned elbows and black feather pants. His eyes are twice as black and just as shiny. So is what's left of his hair, a few clumps hanging ropy from the top, hanging like his wings would if he had any. I watch them flutter, a feeble, first-instinct response, like raising your arm before a machete. Makes me wanna hold him, promise it'll all be okay. It won't. He looks back up at me, underlip caught between his teeth. Crow.

Get up," I says. His eyes gloss over like spit-polished thrift store buttons. Like maybe he don't wanna see me, so he'll see through me instead. He's got an arrogant nose that Crow, sharper and straighter than a switchblade. A slag-like spurt of blood from one nostril. He licks it away.

"Rat. Please." I flinch at the word. My gaze scurries over the roof-top's cinderblock edge, reels at the dizzying drop that ends in a gutted alley twenty-one stories below us. There, squad cars howl red blue spirals and circle like wild dogs before a kill. I close my eyes. The pressure builds behind them, like a pipe before it busts. I wish I could believe.

Runnels of fresh sweat cut tracks beneath my leather, through last week's dirt and cheap cologne. "I'm sorry," I says.

And I am. Like it matters.

Let me tell you 'bout Crow. I was tanked on vodka and methedrine the night I found him on Crescent Boulevarde. He wasn't hustling then, just hanging out. All the boys wore jeans and maybe leather. He had on them black feather pants, and more Mardi Gras beads than a Bourbon Street lamppost. It must not a been Mardi Gras or I woulda been drunker. I thought he was a boy, but I weren't too sure. He's like that, Crow. He wears his skin in such a way as you can't tell, smudging the lines everyone else takes for granted. But I guess that's what I was drawn to. That sense of limitless possibility. Me, I stay close to the ground.

But the one thing I was sure of. He was beautiful and outta place, like somethin' sprouted from out a crack in the sidewalk. I felt my tail twitch, even though I didn't have one. I told myself it was just the drugs. Maybe even I believed it.

Thing is, most of the other queers I'd met that weren't on the boulevard were calling councils, begging the city for a few crumbs of civil rights. They wore their skins beneath their suits, if they still wore them at all. They came down to the strip sometimes, bearing gifts. The condoms found their way into greedy pockets. Sometimes we even remembered to use them. The instruction pamphlets, crumpled in junk-hungry fists, fell unread into the gutter. They always brought us more.

A couple of them invited me to council once, asked my name. I says my name's Rat. That's not a name, they says. Well that was it. They could keep their votes and rights and suits as far as I cared. I cussed 'em all as the worst kinda whores. They says, child you're the one we found on Crescent Boulevarde. I says I guess it takes one to know. Well I never went back to council after that, and I avoided them when I saw them in the street. Unless they were handing out condoms.

But this one wasn't getting into any cars and he wasn't a suit. More like a bright tangle of cheap beads and smeared lipstick and ragged black feathers, flinging gestures through the swears and spit and sully like he were fearless, or maybe just reckless. I saw through his beads, saw through to his wings, which trembled beneath my fingers later that night in my tunnel beneath the Atlantic building. Mouths running hot with rich, narcotic secrets. Skins rubbed raw by feather and fur.

"I love you," he says, afterwards.

I was digging through my crumpled jeans for a cigarette. My stomach dropped, like when that sixth-precinct rookie hit me in the ribs with his nightstick. But then I got this crazy idea that if I didn't say something, he'd maybe disappear. Don't ask me how. It ain't like he could fly.

Maybe it was just the skins we wore. But when I looked up from my cigarette and into his black-bulb eyes, I saw they weren't at all afraid. Of me, of anything. I thought, that is one reckless Crow. And suddenly I wanted to be reckless with him, wanted to shed the shit-skin of my only pair of jeans, festoon myself with Mardi Gras beads, part the spit-strewn sidewalks and lay him like a sacrament beneath the thrumming neon lights.

But I couldn't. Maybe it was the fear that started talking. Fear of the swears and spit and sully, fear of a nightstick in the ribs. Maybe it was that fear what told him flaunting his feathers would get him nothing but killed, that the going price of love was sixty bucks an hour. That he should ask for seventy and let them bargain him down. You ain't in bum-fucked Kansas anymore, Dorothy.

It's funny how the softest, most secret noises sound crazy loud down in the tunnels. His sobs echoed something eerie, like when an animal dies. It was so dark it was safe for me to reach out in silent apology. I held him soft and raw and shaking naked 'til he'd cried himself to sleep, skin sticky with tears and sweat and god knows, maybe blood. I mean, I wasn't sure whether or not he was a virgin. It was too late to ask.

"Y'ever have rat dreams?" he says.

This was weeks later. He'd been staying with me in the tunnel. It was a while 'til he stopped feeling claustrophobic. Or maybe he just stopped complaining.

Hiking down to the beach was his idea. My knuckle grip turned white when he stood up on the Ferris wheel, spread his wings. We fed each other cotton candy, took our pictures in the one-dollar booth. Then we climbed down the broken spine of boardwalk. Crow, he ain't so good at climbing, so he jumped, and I caught him, and we fell laughing in the sand. There wasn't a soul or skin around. Molt-stricken seagulls fought over scraps, and oil-slick tide pools sucked at empty plastic bags. The ocean hissed a fierce brown spray of sewer and salt.

"Rat dreams, huh?"

I picked a half-smoked cigarette from the sand. It was crusted with lipstick. I shoved it between my teeth, lit a match. Maybe I'd scavenge enough to fill my pockets. The sky was the color of the sea. The one bled into the other, erasing the horizon. I thought it was goddamn beautiful, like something you'd see on a flyer for the art museum. Only real.

Crow crouched down, plucked a feather from the sand, and I saw then that his fist was full of them. And I thought he had been scrounging for cigarette butts with me. I wrapped my arms around him 'til we stood chest to chest. Skin to skin. His hair was in two braids, like a schoolgirl, or a warrior. His thoughts soared above us, picking at things I couldn't see. I knew when we got back to the tunnel he would tell erratic stories by the flicker of a match while I fixed us up. Sad, wild stories of talking beasts and ancient forests and doomed love. They couldn't shake the acrid chemical reek of boiled meth and scorched tinfoil. There's not much that can.

The gulls wheeled. His eyes followed. They looked dull and dry, like he'd forgotten to polish them. Face pinched and eyes unpolished he looked more like a rat himself—not the kind you'd find in a tunnel, but some child's sleek, miserable pet.

"I mean like, do you ever dream that you're a rat?" he asked.

The gulls were calling and he called back, but his call was something awful, like a throat full of twigs.

"I don't have dreams," I says.

It wasn't like I turned him out or anything. I just didn't make enough for the both of us to cop. He didn't wanna be picking scabs all hellish night while I got straight. So it was his choice, as much as it ever is anyone's. I just made the connections, from skin to cash to meth to skin. A closed circuit, like this tattoo I saw once of a snake eating its tail. Ain't no end or beginning.

I don't remember when it was he got the lice. We'd been together less than half a year, but it's different out here. A day on the street is like a week anywhere else. A week is a month; a month is a year. A year is forever….

The lice eggs clumped in the crook between his braids, a live colony speckled white and itching mad. He crouched before me on a broken milk crate behind the 7-Eleven as I cut them free with my switchblade. I could count every button of his spine. The braids fell flapping to the blacktop, the lice scattered, the spine sagged. I tried to keep the blade's edge from touching his scalp, but we'd run out of needles sometime before sunrise and my hands jerked in withdrawal, laying open skin to blood. The blood sluiced tributaries down the shorn nape of his neck. My tongue caught the runnels, lapped him clean like I'd seen an alley cat do to all her kittens, but he only bled faster. Head wounds are like that.

We headed down to a new needle exchange at Thirteenth and Washington. It'd been a while since I'd seen Crow in the stark glare of daylight. The sharp spokes of his hipbones fought with gravity to keep his pants on. Most of the feathers had fallen off. Long fingernails scratched at the sores that clung to his lips. He'd tried to cover them with lipstick. It made him look both sultry and ridiculous, but I wasn't gonna tell him. He was still beautiful, in a relentless sort of way, like an autumn leaf before the wind rattles it free.

We straggled down Thirteenth Street, past flat glass stares and hidden slurs, his dirty fingers laced in mine. I didn't care who saw. The van where they gave you fresh works squatted on one corner, across from a Dunkin' Donuts and a twenty-one-story parking garage. Random street folks scuttled toward it, past skyscrapers and wind-blown bags and pinstripes driving silver bullet BMWs, too rich or too bored to follow common traffic laws. I thought of when I'd light a candle down in the tunnels, how some of the bugs were drawn toward it. Funny how only the ones with wings felt the pull, fluttered dangerously close. The smart ones scurried for cover, slid quick and deep into cracks to finish out their lives in subterranean obscurity. When you don't have to look at them, it's easier to pretend they ain't there.

He didn't wanna go with me to the van to get the needles. He's a shy one, that Crow. I dug a fistful of loose change outta my pocket. The window of the Dunkin' Donuts was tinted dark. It turned our reflections to faceless shadows, one all shoulders and stubble and scuffed leather, the other a skinny smudge of beads and tattered black.

"Here." I spilled nickels and pennies into the cup of his palm. "Go get a coffee or somethin'. I won't be long."

I crossed the avenue and got in line behind a woman old enough to be my grandmother, but she was wearing hot-pink jeans and plastic hair clips. Made her look like a wrinkled little girl with knowing eyes. The eyes were pus-yellow shot with red, like a sunset. I looked away. My knuckles tapped a nervous rhythm on the leg of my only pair of jeans.

The guy handing out the fresh needles smiled at me in recognition. I didn't know who the hell he was. A terrible ridiculousness struck me, that he coulda been someone I tricked with once, and my face went near bloodless at the thought. Then I remembered.

"It's Rat, isn't it?"

That was why I didn't recognize him. When people dress in suits, you never really see them. Today he slummed in pleated khakis and a green polo shirt. It looked as if it'd never seen a stain. The button pinned above his left pec caught my eye with white block letters. PLANT A TREE.

I chewed the inside of my lip, turned my eyes to cobble.

"I'm Matt," he says to me. Pretending not to notice my curled lip, slit eyes. I guess that's the polite thing to do when you're a suit. Expert hands shove condoms and vacuum-wrapped syringes into brown paper. Like a check-out clerk at some fantasy headshop where no one has to pay. I let out a bark of laughter. For some reason, he doesn't look at me like I'm insane.

"Listen, I'm sorry about what Gary said to you at council. He gets too big for himself sometimes, y'know? Thinks he's the king of Sodom."

It was his turn to laugh alone now. "There's a council tonight at six....
We'll be opening a gay-specific drop-in center soon. Y'know, somewhere to watch TV, eat hot food, take a shower. You should stop by
tonight to give us input. The Center for Civil Rights, first floor, second
door on the left. Bring your friend with if you want."

He handed me the brown paper bag. "I'll see ya later, Rat."

I walked to the corner, wondering whether this Matt guy was hot
for my tail or just retarded. Maybe it was neither, maybe he'd just got off
a bus from Idaho or bum-fucked Kansas, maybe some other ludicrous
place where people planted trees and voted and smiled too much at
drug-addicted strangers. I realized I never even said anything back to
him. What the hell was I supposed to say?

"Fucking faggot piece of shit!"

My head snapped up as if they'd called my name, but the fight was
already in action and the name was not for me. I heard the sickening
thwap of fists cracking connective tissue. The blond had on one of them
amber Cuervo T-shirts they give you at Shenanigan's for your twenty-
first birthday. The other wore a backward baseball cap and a gut-ugly
sneer. Maybe once he had been beautiful. They looked as big and dumb
and angry as cattle.

I dunno why I noticed the one standing in a widening pool of
spilled coffee last. Maybe because he was more like a shadow than an
opponent, bird-boned and shrinking backward until the wall of the
parking garage left him nowhere else to go. Maybe because he was
absorbing all the light as they reflected it—black clothes, black tufts of
hair, black eyes in a white face smeared lolly red with lipstick and blood.
Crow.

My first thought was that he had it coming to him, but that didn't
stop me from jerking forward into the street. Beetle-like cars honked and
swerved, whished rushing past like racing monsters and I stutter-
stepped back to the curb. Red light.

I watched powerless while drunken knuckles pummeled shots into
his stomach. It bent him over double so he couldn't see the next blow
coming from the side. Steel-toed shit-kickers met with a thunk against
the flower stem of his spine. Crow staggered, raised both arms over his
head like they would stop the blows, like they would fly him away, but
of course they didn't and the fuckers just went for his torso. I felt almost
responsible. I mean, I never thought to teach him how to fight.

There was the green light, arms piston pumping at sides, boots
carrying me quick over blacktop and boulevard. There was the last one
to hit him, knuckles busted and half out of breath, blond hair plastered
with sweat against his forehead. Then there was the terrifying thrill of
my adrenaline funneling into a fist, the satisfying crunch of cartilage
beneath my knuckles, the sluggish spurt of blood from a nose that had

been broken one too many times.

His breath popped like a busted condom. The one behind me hit me sharp in the kidneys, threw an arm across my throat. I slammed my heel into his shin, snapped my head back. Lips split warm like bruised fruit against my skull and the arm dropped.

But the blond had recovered. "Cocksucker," he spat, nose bleeding and bent at a crazy angle. His fist met with my jaw something terrific. I heard a crack, and blood burst on my tongue. I flailed, gulped air, tried to call for Crow, but something from behind hit me in the ribs first. I reeled gasping to my knees. My vision flickered like a broken neon light. I thought I heard sirens in the distance. Maybe my ears were ringing. Either way it was a bad sign. My hand went for the switchblade in my boot.

Someone yelped. The one in the baseball cap, cheek raked open. I swerved my gaze to Crow. His nails clumped with blood and shreds of skin. His eyes were polished, glinting bright with fear or madness. "You'll die of AIDS!" he shrieked. But I didn't get to see the guy's reaction. His friend kicked me in the head.

The world turned black around the edges, like a tunnel. I could see the blond guy's waist before me and beyond it the light at the end. No way I could let it end like this. No goddamn way. The blade trembled in my palm. They hadn't noticed. Blood dripped into my eyes, but it wasn't like I had to aim. I plunged it hilt-deep into his belly, through the fragile cotton layer. Through the skin. A dark stain blossomed on his Cuervo T-shirt and my knuckles drowned in blood.

I staggered to my feet. Still gripping the knife in his guts. Bile rose into my throat. My tongue pushed it back down, pushed up against loosened teeth, and an even deeper loosening, the loosening of that crucial stitch that sets a sweater to unravel.

I wrenched the blade and tore it free. The blood gushed slippery and dark down his jeans, down my arm. His hand went to the wound, pressing in his slick guts. Everything stopped. The stabbed guy's eyes went wild with sudden clarity. He cursed beneath his breath. They all looked at me in vague horror and awe, jaws slack and eyes gleaming, like I'd done something impossible and wrong. Even Crow. Especially Crow.

The sirens wailed louder closer faster. I shoved blood-slick knife back into boot and drug Crow to his feet. There was nothing to say. We ran into the shelter of the parking garage, pounding blood and breath and bones, hurtling over the candy-striped gate and into the elevator's hull.

He looked supreme. Forget the bruise and blood and lipstick. Forget the feathers and the scabs. His eyes glittered with a frightening peace. I couldn't meet them.

"Rat," he began.

"Just press a goddamn button!"

His blood-caked fingernail touched plastic square twenty-one. Magic number when boys become men in smoky downtown bars, friends and fathers nudging amber bottles past their teeth down their throats chug it down nice and easy 'til they throw up die pass out fall over get up go out and beat up a faggot. The orange numbers glowing as the elevator moved.

I want to ask Crow how old he is but I'm too scared of the answer. Up on the rooftop anything seems possible, he could be sixteen, fourteen, ten, or older than this city. Like some fairy tale he wove us into while I was sleeping. The sun bleeds stronger through the sky's grainy photo paper lens, melts it open like a cigarette's hot cherry. The wailing sirens die away below us, but the lights still pulse their red blue skywrite. There's nowhere to hide up here, nowhere to disappear to.

I look over. Standing two feet in from the edge I can't see much, but I'm afraid to get too close. Crow's not. Gray roof meets with gray sky under a drizzling of sunlight, flecking it all with tiny spots of gold. The gold's already there, in the cement; it's just that it needs the light to bring it out.

When I turn back to Crow, he's gone.

"I love you," he says to me.

My head swivels to his voice. He stands on the concrete ledge, the sun shooting fiery rays at his form, highlighting blood and bruise and beads. The wind ripples through what's left of his hair and torn T-shirt, sets what few feathers he's got left to dancing. The panic sends my heart thudding like a terrific shot of speed. Neurons fire at machine-gun speed from brain to battered body. I lurch forward, duct-taped boots crossing a tarpaper forever and the beat of the blood in my mouth in my veins like the beating of wings in the distance. Open eyes mouth fists guts heart and I'm split open gushing like a cracked glass bottle.

He spreads his arms. His face is turned up toward the sun. Still beautiful.

I lunge. He rocks back on his heels. The scuffed black leather of my arm stretches between us. My fingers, slick with straight-boy blood, clutch at ropes of plastic beads. For one brief still of a second the beads hold against the weight of his body in the sky, before the strain of gravity pops them open to rattle free in my fist.

I want to fling myself after him, tell him all the things I could never bring myself to say. Tell him how beautiful he is, how it takes guts to be beautiful, how I would do anything, fight for him, die for him. It doesn't happen. My heart is beating, my lungs are breathing, I am alive.

I step back, close my fingers tighter around the beads. I can't bring myself to watch. I'm afraid to get too close, afraid of falling. I haven't had my fix. Spastic shrieks echo up from the passersby twenty-one floors below me.

The sun will not stop shining. My eyes tear. Mouth ratchets open to birth some sob or scream. Nothing comes out but I can hear it anyway, silent and spiraling and endless.

Crow will only distract them for so long. I must get moving. I sneak slowly back into the building, scurry quick down through the floors, between the cars, between the cracks. They'll never find me.

I'm out on the street six blocks away when I reach into my pocket for a cigarette. That's when my fingers slide across it. Edges stained rusty brown and torn ragged in one corner. I can't make out the image at first, but then I remember—the beach, the booth, the buck, the blinding flash. It's a picture of him.

Six o'clock. The Center for Civil Rights. My reflection in the plate-glass window. Leather jacket. Beaded necklace. Broken teeth. I push the door open, follow the hallway, second room on the left. A milling of people, gray and tan and pinstripe blue, faces aghast and who can blame them. I spot the khakis and green polo shirt, stop. Matt. His eyes blink in startled recognition, face pale with however much he knows. I mean, he was less than a block away.

He starts across the room. I want to run but I can't move. My tongue curls dead and limp behind loose teeth. Matt says something soothing. A Styrofoam cup of coffee appears like magic in my hand. My hand starts shaking. He takes the cup away.

"I'm so glad you could make it." He's using that voice that people do when they're trying to get their cat to come back in, but I can tell he really wants to help me. It's not that I don't want him to. I'm just not sure he can.

I don't know where to sit. The table is a circle. Ain't no end or beginning. It reminds me what I done. He was so unreal to start with. I shoulda never tied his arm off. Shoulda never let him trick. The pain stretches open its claws. I pull out a chair next to Matt's.

"We usually begin by going around and introducing ourselves," Matt explains. Sitting this close, I can see the scars the track marks left in the crook of his elbow. The scars look old, faded. I wonder if any of the others here have noticed. Doubt it. I guess it takes one to know.

"I'll go first," he says. "I'm Matt, and I'm facilitating this evening."

My turn.

I feel the beads beneath the dried blood, beneath my leather, against my skin. I remind myself that under all their suits their skin's the same as mine.

"My name's Rat," I says.

RASPBERRY PIE

Wendell Ricketts

For D.H.G

Over lattes at Cafe Flore, I told Ehan that I'd gone to my first whipping over the weekend. He was eating a piece of raspberry pie, with filling splooging out the sides and spilling onto the plate. I pointed to the loose, crushed berries, oozing syrup. "The guy's ass looked about like that when they got done," I said. Ehan made a face like he'd tasted something foul, which was just the reaction I was hoping for.

It isn't that I like shocking people; I just like shocking Ehan. For the entire four years we were lovers, the thing I hated most about him was what a white-bread prince he was. Nice, nice, nice.

Right after we moved in together, Ehan came home one day with a bright red Macy's bag. Inside of it was omelet pan that hinged in the middle. "Look," he said. "Now we can make omelets without breaking them in half when you flip them over." He was referring to the fact that my omelets usually ended up looking more or less like scrambled eggs.

"Oh, that'll be good," I said.

A few weeks later I needed to take something bulky to work and Ehan got out the Macy's bag, which he had carefully folded and put into the cupboard with the broom and the lemon-scented bleach. "I'm not carrying that thing around," I said.

"Why not?" he wanted to know. "It's a great bag and it's got handles." He held it up by the thick strings that grew out of the stiff, red paper at the top, overlapping into an *M* like the golden arches.

"Because I don't want to look like someone who would shop at Macy's," I said. "I don't want to look like some fag who just popped over on his lunch hour to buy a sweater."

Offended, he put the bag back into the cupboard. "It's just a bag," he said. "Sometimes I don't understand where you're coming from."

The way Ehan is, if he came to your house, you'd hardly be able to suppress the urge to offer him tea. Something English. In a cup, with a saucer. I once heard someone describe Ehan as "patrician" and I couldn't get the word out of my mind. It bobbed around in there like an apple in some great iron washtub of language, bumping up against all the other words just like it: patriarchy, patrimony, patriotism. All the words that start out sounding like "father" and end up somewhere else entirely.

"Charming," my mother said, the first time she met him. Ehan complained later that she'd never asked him any questions about himself: but that's the kind of guy he is. The kind that prefers to be interviewed. Hardly polite to volunteer the Oberlin education, the Junior year aboard, the Fulbright. You have to be asked, so the information can leak out modestly.

But my mom's no fool: she doesn't "ooh" and "aah" any more sincerely than I do. I'm sure she took one look at that blood-in-the-face complexion and the parochial chin that I know won't hold up past forty, and she decided she didn't want to play. Though it isn't like she missed anything essential. Forced to improvise, Ehan found plenty of ways to work in all the important information he liked people to know about himself. Later, when we got back home, I said to Ehan, "Did I tell you that my mother dropped out of school when she was in eighth grade?"

Ehan blinked at me, owl-like. "Oh," he said. "Oh."

Ehan knows people who own lofts, which they call "spaces"; he goes to parties thrown by Herb Ritts. I go to garages painted black where people piss on each other and when someone screams it is because he is in actual pain. Stirring a third sugar into my coffee, I tell Ehan that the whipping was like theater.

"Why is this turning my stomach?" he said, pushing the pie aside.

Because you're a fucking coward. Because you can't stand the sight of blood. Because your castration fear is so immense that all I used to have to do to make you beg me to stop was to read you a squib out of the paper about some logger who chopped his foot off with an axe and later got it reattached. You would never have been able to discuss poor old John Wayne Bobbitt.

Because I loved you for years during which all you wanted was for me to throw you across the bed and fuck you until it hurt, and all I wanted was to do it; and rather than get what we wanted, we tortured each other, day after day, for years. If you do it the way we did, it's a relationship; if you get someone's consent first, you're a freak.

You'd lie beside me, jerking off, and talk about how you wanted me to fuck you in the shower, forcing you up against the wall and banging your head on the white tile with each thrust. You'd say you wanted me to gag you when I screwed you in our big, wide bed so the neighbors couldn't hear you screaming.

But fantasy isn't reality, is it? You liked to be screwed all right, but gently, sweetly, so it felt like love. You always had to be on your back, where you could see me. You didn't want to be treated like a dog, you said. And you never screamed, not once; instead, you'd groan politely when I finished you off with a greasy hand. After you left me, it took months until I could stop feeling embarrassed about the noise I made in bed.

I remember a day when we fought—one of the hundreds of extravagant, passionate, Talmudic arguments we had instead of good sex. All my words seemed to be tumbling off a cliff and into some deep, cold sea, as suicidal as lemmings. In my frustration, I punched you so hard that a cut opened up in the center of your chest, above your heart. I wasn't proud that I had hit you, but the blood thrilled the shit out of me. It was just your body, bleeding in perfect silence – a reaction that even you couldn't filter through all your bullshit and your reasons and your rational explanations.

I was transfixed, watching that dusky red stain spread out across the white field of your thin T-shirt. Here is my guilty secret: my dick had turned to stone, the way it did sometimes when I said things mean enough to make you cry. And I loved you so much I would have licked the blood up and wrapped myself around you later in utter, speechless gratitude.

This is what I wanted to say in answer to Ehan's question. What I said instead was nothing. Ehan was looking at me as though I were an object he couldn't quite identify. I had entered a room he couldn't get into, a place where the atoms of sex and love were so profoundly fissured that the danger of contamination must have seemed infinite. But it's in the Vedas, baby. Agni may have seven tongues and hair like flames, but he's also the guardian of humanity. If you want the healing, you've got to take the fire.

We stared at each other until I realized that, during all the years I had known Ehan, I had wanted him to understand only one thing: *I am not like you.*

On my way to meet Ehan at the Cafe that day, I had been angry. This is something else I realize: I am angry all the time. Even when I'm happy, I'm angry. I walked down the street hitting parking meters and pounding on the lids of trash cans, all puffed up with anger, swaggering with it, feeling invincible and doomed. My face falls easily into a frown, with no conscious effort on my part, and I was frowning. My shoulders felt huge and able to carry anything; my chest felt thick and strong enough to endure anything. I wanted to pick a fight.

When I am horny and want someone to want me, I am small and furtive, and I look at people out of the corner of my eye, and I am full of envy. When I am horny and angry, I don't want anyone, and I don't care if they want me. I stare people in the eye, and they always look away first. In fact, I glare at them, especially straight boys, and one day I know I'm going to find myself in a world of hurt. I take up space.

In this mood, the men I'm attracted to are bad-asses and punks; they look like Axl Rose or else like lads from the NLF. They're often skinny and have jail tats or a drug habit. But they strut. They are also angry and full of hate, mostly directed at themselves, and when we fuck those are the only things I want from them. I suck anger out of their armpits. I honor their suffering by rationing my tenderness with military discipline.

"I been tryin' to get my life together," says one black man to another on the bus, "but it's a struggle out there."

"Yeah," says the second man, "it's a hellified struggle."

I'd like to write about love. Believe me, I would. But rage is all I have to go on.

One of the few things Ehan and I did well together was go to movies. We always had a lot to say to each other afterwards. I think we used movies as a way to show off for one another—how smart we were, how much notice we could take of subtleties. Having such a convenient excuse to talk—without the fear of saying anything that might come close to the bone—what a relief! Most of the time, I liked the movies he liked. He rarely liked the movies I liked.

Once, and only once, I convinced Ehan to go with me to the kind of movie I usually had to see alone, one with gruesome murders and lots of blood: blood seeping from the trunk of a car where a headless corpse has been stashed; blood welling out of the disemboweled body in the upper bedroom, spreading languidly across the floorboards and pooling on the stairs.

I don't know what made Ehan agree to go, but he did. I think it was early enough in our relationship that he was still in his anthropological mood: still visiting me, the undiscovered country, to witness the manifestation of all the things he feared or hoped lay hidden within himself. Later, he'd turn missionary on me and make a project of rooting out those primitivisms, one by one.

In that respect, Ehan was playing out an age-old routine—what I sometimes teased him by calling the racial memory of his people—just like the real missionaries. At first, the naked breasts of native women fascinated them and turned them on, then their own desire became disgusting. In the end, they covered up their shame by covering up the breasts: Mother Hubbards as a symbol of the inability to tell the difference between what is out there and what is in here. The whole history of nineteenth-century Western civilization can be described as the refusal to look inward.

By the time we got to the movie, I felt like some sadistic teenage boy who had finally succeeded in dragging his girlfriend to *The Texas Chainsaw Massacre*—partly because he hoped she would bury her face in his chest whenever the movie got gory, and partly because he wanted to scare the shit out of her. They would leave the theater having had completely different experiences, the boy and his girlfriend—and she would say what Ehan always said to me when I suggested that we go to a film with rabid dogs or psychopathic killers or satanic ritual murders: "How can you stand to watch stuff like that?"

What Ehan didn't know—or perhaps what he did know but couldn't acknowledge about the person he loved—was that mayhem turned me on. It didn't necessarily make my dick hard; it wasn't what the Germans call *Schadenfreude*—joy in the suffering of others, which is the kind of thing they ought to know about. This sensation was entirely different. A kind of connection, a vibration full of savage intuition.

It was more like: I want to see these things because they look like how I feel inside. Cut up, howling, disintegrated, chaos, pain, raw flesh, pierced by knives. Eaten up. In that famous scene from *Alien*, when that creature—the one that looks like a turkey neck with teeth—chews its way out of John Hurt's chest, didn't everyone shiver with the same sense of recognition I did? At last, proof of what I had always suspected, that something else besides me was *in there*?

In the movie I convince Ehan to see, some psycho killer kidnaps this guy and chains him between the bumpers of two semis, his arms manacled to the front bumper of the truck parked behind, his legs fixed to the back bumper of the truck in front. The psycho has kidnapped the guy's girlfriend as well, and he has her handcuffed in the cab of the first truck. He gets in, starts the engine, and unlocks her handcuffs. He puts his foot on the clutch and then he hands her a gun.

"I'm going to count to ten," he says, "and then I'm going to take my foot off the clutch. Or you can shoot me before I get to ten. It's your choice."

Of course she doesn't shoot him, and of course he lets the truck roll forward, and of course the boyfriend gets ripped in half. I was disgusted with her: she couldn't save her boyfriend, but she could at least have had the satisfaction of shooting the asshole's balls off, or at least his kneecaps, before she blew his brains out. But she took no action at all.

I don't know how the movie ended because that's when Ehan got up and walked out, and I had to go after him. On the sidewalk, with the green and red neon of the marquee lights playing on our faces, Ehan screamed at me for long minutes. People stared. I tried to calm Ehan down, but he was on a tear like I'd never seen before. When he walked away, I tried to follow, but he told me to get the fuck away from him. Later, when I got home, Ehan was already there, and we picked up where we had left off. That was the fight when I hit Ehan on the chest and made him bleed.

Let's face it: in the movies, blood is Karo syrup and food coloring. It's always too thick and too red. But the attempt to represent a kind of impossible reality is mesmerizing. There's a scene in *Cat People*—the Nastassja Kinski version—where a leopard pulls some guy's arm through the bars of its cage and chews it off. Completely gratuitous violence. I rented the movie and watched that scene over and over, a frame at a time in slow motion, trying to figure out just when they had substituted the fake arm.

But the cut on Ehan's chest wasn't fake, and I've played that scene over and over in my head as well. And now I'm watching Ehan toy with the remains of the raspberry pie that he isn't going to eat, pushing the mangled pieces of crust and crushed berries around the plate with the edge of his fork, staining everything red. We need something to talk about; the silence is starting to menace the fragile peace we've stitched together in the years since the breakup. And I take a deep breath and I say, with comic exaggeration, "So-o-o, Ehan...seen any good movies lately?"

MEN WITHOUT BLISS

Rigoberto González

For Richard Yañez

At his "goodbye and good luck" party, Andrés looks around at the faces of his coworkers and tries to remember when he has had an intimate conversation with any of them. He can't recall a single exchange that warrants their theatrical display of last-minute friendship. In the corner, the silver helium balloon has begun to flatten, and Andrés knows that the blue-corn tortilla chips, a staple at every function, come from a garbage-can-sized bag in the storage room. He takes pleasure, however, in watching people parade up to him to say their goodbyes.

"You'll be missed," declares a tall, hefty redhead. Andrés had never been introduced to her until that afternoon. Her lipstick matches her blood-red nails. She retraces her steps to the center table for a second slice of chocolate cake. Andrés wants to watch her eat it but his view is blocked by another well-wisher.

"You'll be missed," he tells Andrés.

Andrés doesn't recognize the overweight white guy dressed in a white shirt and tie. "Why?" he asks him. The white guy titters uncertainly as he walks toward the punch bowl.

Thirty minutes after ushering everyone into the conference room, Mary Ann, the supervisor, announces that it's time to get back to work. The French, Spanish, German, and Italian tutors shuffle obediently out the door. Only a few of them walk up to Andrés to shake his hand or to give him a European kiss on both cheeks. The hefty redhead sways forward again and tilts her head to the left. Teary-eyed, she declares: "What's the Italian group going to do without you?" She's out the door before Andrés can tell her he tutored Spanish.

Only the ill-humored secretary—Program Associate according to the nameplate on her desk—stays behind to clean up. She mumbles under her breath as she wipes the conference tables and empties the uneaten chips into a trash bin.

Mary Ann returns with an envelope in her hand. "You'll need this," she says. "A letter of rec. Accrued sick days will be included in your final paycheck."

Andrés takes the envelope.

"I'm sure you'll do better in your next place of employment," Mary Ann says. She's shorter than Andrés, but in her high heels and with the tone of reprehension in her voice she seems taller.

"I'll certainly try," Andrés says.

"Professionalism cannot be compromised," Mary Ann adds as she shakes her head. "I'm sure you've learned your lesson here." Andrés taught individual and group tutoring sessions for a year at the language center, never once canceling an appointment or showing up late. And then they fired him.

"I don't think I've done anything wrong," Andrés mumbles. In the background, he sees the Program Associate roll her eyes. His teaching evaluations were generally noncommittal, but every other month one or another of his female students launched a harassment complaint. Not even Mary Ann, who was a stickler for policy and procedure, could clearly articulate what he was doing wrong.

"We've discussed this, Andrés," Mary Ann says. "With you we're risking a lawsuit that we can't afford." She'd said the same thing when she gave him his notice two weeks ago.

"But I've never done or said anything that was inappropriate."

"The complaints read the same: you make the women students feel uncomfortable when you look at them. That's enough for us to take action," she says.

None of the male students had complained, though it was true that he sometimes looked at them in a way someone might call funny. But they preferred to make their appointments with the female Spanish tutors, so he hardly saw them.

"Maybe that's their problem," Andrés says.

Mary Ann shakes her head in disbelief. "If you want to file an unlawful termination of employment form, you can speak with someone in human resources." She storms off to her office.

The Program Associate closes the cake box and wipes the knife with a paper towel. "I'd appreciate it if you emptied your desk out before four o'clock," she says. "I don't want to put in overtime setting up your cubicle for the new Spanish teacher. Do you want to take the rest of this cake home?"

Andrés walks out of the building with the cake box and the helium balloon. The bag over his shoulder holds a few blank pages of good, cream-colored paper he'll use for his résumé, three used Agatha Christie paperbacks, and a recycled manila folder to seal the damaged screen in his father's bedroom window. He's well aware that he's dragging the deflated balloon behind him like an empty dog collar, but he has no choice because the string is tightly bound to the cake box and he didn't want to ask the edgy Program Associate for the scissors. He throws everything into the back seat and drives off, taking one last look at the language center. He can't recall why he ended up teaching Spanish in the first place. His training that one semester at the community college was in psychology.

When he gets home he finds his father slumped on the couch. A janitor at the elementary school, he hasn't changed out of his dark blue work shirt. The name stitched above the left hand pocket reads "Rapael."

"They tried to spell Rafael the gringo way," his father explained when he first brought home the three regulation shirts he had been issued. "And then they left out the h. I really don't give a shit. They never call me by my name anyhow."

Andrés sets the cake box and newspaper on the table; the deflated balloon hangs over the edge like a silver placenta trailing its umbilical cord.

"Pop," he says to his father. "Do you want a piece of cake?"

"With my diabetes and high blood pressure?" his father answers. "I'll take two pieces. Is it my birthday or yours?"

"I lost my job," Andrés said. He rummages through the cupboards for a plate.

"Oh," his father says, disinterested. "What kind of cake is it?"

Andrés cuts a large piece for his father. "The store-bought kind," he says.

"I like those," his father says, twisting his pinky in his ear. "They don't skimp on the frosting."

As Andrés looks over the classifieds in the newspaper later that evening, his father watches television on the couch. He hasn't changed out of his work shirt. In fact he hasn't changed position all afternoon.

Andrés is fascinated by the exotic items in the "for sale" listings. "Do you want to buy a ferret, Pop?" Andrés calls out.

"A parrot? No, they stink," his father says.

"A ferret," Andrés says. "It's like a weasel."

"They stink," his father says. "How about another piece of that cake?"

After giving his father another helping of cake, Andrés circles potential jobs. Delivery Driver. Dental Assistant. Healthcare Provider. Housekeeper. Teaching Assistant. All of them minimum wage, but that doesn't matter. Healthcare doesn't ask for any previous experience, so he makes a note of the address.

"You know what this cake reminds me of?" his father says. He waves the fork in the air, dropping a few crumbs on his lap. "The day you were born."

"You had cake on the day I was born?" says Andrés.

"It's a birthday cake, ain't it," his father says, exasperated.

Andrés circles an ad for proofreader, though he isn't a good speller. But he figures he can run the documents through the computer's spellcheck.

"So what about the day I was born, Pop?" Andrés says.

"On the day you were born I went to see a movie," his father says. "Since you took your damn time popping out of your mother's oven." He laughs at his own joke and coughs a few times.

"Don't choke on your funny, Pop," Andrés says.

"Fuck you," his father says. He continues talking with cake in his mouth, spitting out crumbs. "Anyway, the hospital waiting room was making me sick, so I took a long walk and ended up at this movie theater. A few hours of distraction is what I needed so I bought a ticket. You were born halfway through the movie. I could feel it in the way my body relaxed. But I decided to stay and watch the other half. Your mother was pissed, God rest her soul."

Andrés suddenly looks up from the newspaper. He turns to look at his father.

"What movie did you see?" he asks.

"I don't remember," his father says.

"You don't remember the movie you were watching while I was being born?"

"That was like forty years ago," his father says.

"Thirty-eight," Andrés corrects him.

"Whatever, it's still a lifetime ago. Last millennium as a matter of fact."

"Don't you even remember what it was about?"

"Nope," his father says.

Andrés turns to the sheets of newspaper again.

That night Andrés tosses in bed. He can hear his father wheezing in his sleep in the next bedroom. He tries to guess what sort of movie his father had been watching and how it might have marked his own fate. Knowing his father, he'd probably walked into a porn theater, which is why he didn't want to say the name of the movie. Andrés tries not to think of his father sitting in a smelly dark room as the projector tosses out images of a naked woman taking it from behind, her breasts knocking against each other like water balloons.

Andrés overdresses for the visit to the group home even though he's only going in to drop off his résumé. On the porch, a cluster of old guys in faded clothes blow smoke into each other's faces. Cigarette butts are scattered on the porch, and Andrés pictures the shreds of paper left behind after a string of firecrackers explodes.

As he walks in, a musty odor invades his nose. His father's room smells the same.

"The title is residential counselor," the young female administrator says. She's wearing an ankle-length dress with a slit going down the side that exposes her calf when she crosses her legs. She looks closely over his résumé.

"Looks like you've got plenty of work experience," she says.

Andrés counts the piercings on her face: one nose stud, one eyebrow ring, two lip rings, six earrings on the left ear.

"We only have graveyard shift available at the moment," she says. "The hours are 11 p.m. to 9 a.m."

"I'm interested," Andrés says. "What are the duties required?"

"Primarily that you be awake and aware at all hours in case of an emergency. You'll need to get your first-aid and CPR certification. Secondly, you'll need to fetch anyone for meds if they haven't taken their bedtime pills."

Andrés pictures himself whistling from the front porch and the residents running up to him like trained dogs.

"And thirdly," she says. "Make them breakfast by 7 a.m., plus start handing out the morning meds to anyone who's awake. Usually only half of them are. You have to log it into the record book for each resident as you dispense meds. But it's super easy."

"How many residents?" Andrés asks.

"Twenty-five. Twenty of them are males. These are all developmentally disabled adults," she adds. "Pretty low maintenance. They do everything for themselves except they can't cook and they can't manage their own meds. They're very low-key. Nice people."

Andrés is suddenly aware that she's trying to sell him the position.

"So you'll let me know if I need to come in for an interview?" he asks.

"Oh, I thought this was it," she says, flustered. "I mean, you seem very capable and you're our strongest candidate. It's yours if you want it."

Andrés is suspicious but just as desperate as she is. So he accepts the position: full-time graveyard shift Sunday through Wednesday. Health and dental included. He'll start the next day. They give him thirty days to get his CPR certificate. He hopes no one needs CPR before then.

At home, Andrés opens up a can of minestrone soup for dinner. When his father arrives, he carries a bag of toilet paper, the partially dispensed rolls in varying thicknesses, and a stack of paper towels from a bathroom dispenser.

"Soup's on," Andrés says.

"What kind of soup is it?"

"Vegetable," Andrés says.

"Any more of that cake left?"

Later that evening Andrés stares at his father as he dozes on the couch.

At his feet, the untouched bowl of soup. On his lap, a small dish with crumbs. The fork dangles from his left hand.

"I found a new job," Andrés says.

"What?" his father responds in a sleepy tone.

"I found a new job. I'll be working nights, Sunday through Wednesday."

"That's good, son," his father says and falls asleep again.

In the morning Andrés fries eggs and sausages for breakfast. He also makes toast, oatmeal, and fresh juice, which pleases his father.

"Smells good," his father says.

"I'm practicing for my new job at the group home," Andrés says. "I'll be making breakfast for a dozen people every morning at work. Try the sausages."

"What kind of people are these, retards?"

"They're developmentally disabled adults,"

"Retards," his father says.

The young female administrator, Cassie was her name, said that most of the residents were paranoid schizophrenics. "But they're harmless," she was quick to add.

"You know, I think I remember a little more about that theater I went to the day you were born," his father says.

Andrés' ears perk up. "What do you remember?"

"A woman in a red hat," his father says.

"There was a woman in a red hat in the movie?"

"I didn't say anything about the movie," his father corrects him. "I said I remembered something about the theater."

"You met a woman with a red hat in the theater?"

"No, stupid, let me finish," his father snaps. He takes a long gulp of his orange juice and then continues. "There was a movie poster at the theater showing a woman in a red hat. That's why I bought a ticket in the first place. The poster looked interesting. You couldn't see the woman's face because the hat was tilted forward. You could catch a glimpse of her chin. And I think her fingers were resting on the brim of the hat like she was pulling it down to hide her face. Her nails were as red as the hat. That's it. Draw your own conclusions."

"And you're sure there was no woman in a red hat in the movie?"

"I don't remember," his father says. "The orange juice could use a little sugar."

Andrés tries to nap during the day, but ends up reading through the pages of *The Body in the Library* without much interest. He finishes the murder mystery before his father returns from work, but he can't remember who done it. He resolves to reread the ending at work since there will be nothing else to do in the predawn hours.

At 10 p.m. he drives to work early. His father is already wheezing away in his room.

Every light in the group home is on. The same cluster of residents smoke on the porch and a new cluster has gathered in the garden to smoke as well. They puff away without talking like a row of strangers at a bus stop.

"Are you the new guy?" one of the residents asks. He has a long beard and a pair of wide blue eyes that look as if they are being crushed open by his glasses.

"I sure am," Andrés says. "I'm Andy. Good to meet you."

The old guy shakes his hand.

"That's disgusting, man," another resident says. He has a large tattoo of a bird on his forearm. "He was picking his nose all afternoon." The other residents laugh.

Andrés walks into the hall and then into the small office where he was interviewed. The swing-shift person is surprised to see him. She's sitting on the chair with her feet up on the desk, a bag of yarn on her lap.

"Hello, there," she says, setting her knitting needles down. "Welcome. I'm Louise. You're Andy?"

"Yes," he says. "The graveyard shift."

"That's nice," she says. "The rest of us were taking turns with that shift. I told Cassie she better hire someone quick or she'd have a group full of disgruntled employees in her hands."

"Well, I'm here to relieve you," he says, attempting a smile.

"You sure are," Louise says. She stuffs her knitting in a plastic bag and rushes out of the office before Andrés can remind her that his shift doesn't start for another twenty minutes. He had been hoping to chat with her.

Andrés follows the instructions Cassie provided: he checks the record book—all of the residents have received their evening meds; he goes down to the storage room to bring up breakfast supplies—milk, coffee, eggs, sausage; he makes sure any lights not in use are off; he makes his rounds through the top floor, where residents watch television in their private rooms; he sweeps the dining area where a few residents watch television at no volume.

"It doesn't work," one of the residents says to him when he suggests turning up the sound. He leaves them staring into the screen.

He sits down at the desk with his book in his hand and by midnight he falls asleep. He's awakened numerous times during the night by the shuffling of bodies around the halls. Each time he thinks it is his father sneaking into the kitchen for a midnight snack.

One of the residents walks into the office. "Hey," he says. "You got any smokes, buddy?"

"I don't smoke," Andrés answers with a yawn.

"Then you're not going to be very popular around here," the resident warns. He's a large man in suspenders that stretch precariously across his belly. He's about to leave when he suddenly turns around and adds, "Well, I hope you last longer than the other guy."

"What happened to the other guy?" Andrés asks, curiously.

"Heart attack," the resident says. "I dialed 911 myself, but they didn't get here in time."

"Oh," Andrés says.

"I kept dialing the wrong number," he says, breaking into chuckles as he walks off.

Before dawn Andrés drags himself into the kitchen and gets the stove going to prepare breakfast. A few residents knock on the kitchen door demanding their morning meds, and Andrés maneuvers between the two tasks.

"What's your name?" he asks them as he runs his finger across the row of medikits.

"Brunswick," one of the residents answers, annoyed. "Haven't you learned my name yet?"

"I'm sorry, sir," Andrés says. "But this is my first day."

"It is?" Mr. Brunswick says in surprise. "Aren't you the guy who had the heart attack?"

Andrés finishes cooking and logs in Mr. Brunswick, Mr. Shepley, Ms. Calloway, Mr. Newman, and Mr. Harrison-Boyd. All of them have helpings of scrambled eggs and toast, spooning jam from a container the size of a coffee can. When it's clear no one else is coming down for breakfast, Andrés helps himself to a plate of eggs. They taste bland.

"Hey, buddy," the large man in suspenders says. Mr. Velasco, Andrés has learned.

"Ready for some breakfast?" Andrés says. "

"You got any smokes?" Mr. Velasco asks.

"Sorry, Mr. Velasco," Andrés says. "I don't smoke. Would you like some eggs?"

"Shove the eggs up your ass," Mr. Velasco says before storming off.

When the morning shift comes, Andrés hands over the keys to the office and walks sleepily to his car. Once in bed, he sleeps all day until his father gets home from work. The noise from the television wakes Andrés up.

"How was your new job?" his father asks. He has his hand stuffed inside a yellow box of breakfast cereal.

Andrés makes circles with his head, stretching out his neck. "I need to get used to staying awake all night," he says. "How was your day?"

"Nothing exciting. Except some kid brought a gun to school."

"Did he shoot anybody?"

"For show and tell," his father says. "Made one of the girls piss in her panties. They called me to clean it up. The kid didn't know any better. Say, do any of those retards take Lipitor?"

"They're not retards."

"Departmentally handicapped adults or whatever. They take Lipitor?"

"Some do," Andrés says. "Why? You want me to bring you some?"

"I'm running out," his father says.

"No problem," Andrés says.

He opens another can of soup and serves his father a bowl with crackers he brought home from the kitchen at work.

"Have you given any more thought to the woman in the red hat?" Andrés asks.

"Not as much as you apparently," says his father. He dips each cracker into the soup until it gets soggy before he pops it into his mouth. "I told you I don't remember anything else besides the red hat and the weird writing on the poster."

"What writing?" Andrés says.

"I thought I told you about that," his father says. "They had this weird-looking title above the red hat. Like those letters in the Chinese menus. But they were American letters made to look like Chinese letters."

"And?"

"And nothing. That's all I remember," his father says. "I thought that was the movie I was walking into but nope. The movie had no Chinese letters or woman in a red hat to speak of."

"Interesting," Andrés mumbles.

"I'm sure they're also taking Depakote," says his father.

"Say what?" Andrés says.

"Your people," his father says. "Check if they're also taking Depakote. Big pink pills."

"Oh," says Andrés. "Sure."

That night at work he has to track down Ms. Ryan to give her her meds. She won't open the door to her room.

"I've got keys, Ms. Ryan," Andrés says. "Either you open up or I do."

"Got to hell!" she screams. "I told them I wasn't taking any more meds. Been taking meds for thirty years and I'm losing my eyesight because of it."

"Is everything all right in there?" he asks.

"I'm not even decent so you better not open that door!"

He walks back into the office and marks the medication log: *R* for refusal.

"Hey, buddy," Mr. Velasco says. "You got any smokes?"

Andrés looks up at the old man in suspenders. "I just ran out," he says. "Mr. Shepley took my last one."

"That goddamn Shepley," Mr. Velasco says, and walks away.

Andrés checks the resident records, pulls out the medikits that have Lipitor in the small plastic compartments, and fishes out a few pills. Since the residents take up to half a dozen different pills, one less isn't noticeable. In the shelf marked refills, he finds entire bottles of Depakote. He stuffs the one labeled for Mr. Velasco into his coat and resolves to bring him some cigarettes the following week. For the rest of the night he simply presses his fists to his mouth as he leans on the desk with his elbows and thinks about the woman in the red hat.

"Say," one of the residents interrupts. He holds a large sheet of paper in his hands.

"What is it, sir," says Andrés. "Mr. — "

"Guilman," the man says. "Can I show you my drawing?"

"Sure," says Andrés. "What did you draw?"

Mr. Guilman turns the paper over. "A ship."

The drawing has been made exclusively with straight lines.

"Is that the *Titanic*?" Andrés asks.

Mr. Guilman chuckles. "Not quite. I have many more in my room if you care to see them."

"Why not?" Andrés says, and he follows Mr. Guilman into his room down the hall.

The room is small with an unmade bed on one side, a chair with an old suitcase on it. The wall opposite the bed displays a small gallery of drawings — ships, helicopters, cars — all of them drawn with ink and a straight edge. Andrés notices a picture of a space ship in the center of the drawings.

"That's interesting," Andrés says as he leans in closer to inspect it. "Is that like the *Star Trek Enterprise*?"

After a brief silence Mr. Guilman speaks up. "That's the mother ship," he says in a serious tone. "She's hovering up in space looking out for us."

"Well, thank you for sharing your drawings, Mr. Guilman," Andrés says as he slowly creeps out. "I need to get back to my office."

Mr. Guilman places one hand on Andrés' shoulder. "You understand, don't you?" he asks.

Andrés nods. "I do," he says.

The rest of the night goes by without incident.

The next afternoon, after waking up, Andrés goes into the bookstore at the mall. As usual, Helen J. waits behind the counter.

"Hi, Andrés," she says, waving him over. Andrés makes his way to her reluctantly.

She leans over to kiss him on the cheek and Andrés complies, slightly embarrassed. Helen J.'s hair feels coarse where it rubs against his skin; her own skin feels cold and slightly clammy.

"Haven't seen you in a while," she says. "Here to buy some more mysteries?"

"Not exactly," he says. "I came to buy a movie guide."

"Are you looking for video recommendations?" she asks excitedly. "I've seen some great ones lately."

"No, Helen J.," he says. "I'm looking for a book that will tell me about the movies that were out in the sixties."

"Oooh, the classics," Helen J. whispers in an attempt to sound impressed. "I love those old movies."

"Well, does such a book exist, Helen J.?"

Helen J. smirks as she walks around the counter and leads him to the reference section. She pulls a thick book from the shelf.

Andrés takes it from her hands and leafs through it.

"Is this what you're looking for?" Helen J. asks.

Andrés turns his back on her and begins to browse through the glossy reproductions of movie posters. There are so many. It will be a painstaking process, but he has the time, hours on end of time, at his new job.

"I'll take it," he says when he looks up finally, but Helen J. has returned to the counter to ring up another customer.

His father is already on the couch when Andrés walks into the house. The empty cake box sits on the floor beside him.

"Where were you?" his father says. "I had important news."

"About what, Pop?" Andrés says. He sets the bookstore bag on the table.

"About the woman in the red hat," his father says.

"Really?" Andrés says, holding back his excitement.

"She was using her left hand to pull down the brim of her hat," he announces.

"Oh," Andrés says, disappointed. "Why is that important?"

"You should know, stupid," his father says. "Left-handed people always notice other left-handed people. You're left-handed. So am I. So was your mother. One houseful of goddamn left-handers."

"My mother was left-handed?" Andrés says.

"Jesus Christ," his father says. "I can't believe you. You only knew her for about eighteen years."

Andrés remembers the day his mother died. His father wasn't home from work yet. His mother was in the bedroom and wouldn't come out. Andrés knocked and knocked but got no response, so he pushed the door open only to find her slumped over on the floor. The zipper on the back of her dress was wide open. He was shocked to see her freckled back and the pink strap of the bra. She'd had a stroke while changing clothes so she could be dressed nicely when she gave Andrés and his father their supper. Andrés zipped her up before his father came through the door.

While his father watches television for the rest of the evening, Andrés sketches a picture of the woman in the red hat with her left hand pulling down the brim.

Andrés decides to hold off on his search for the woman in the red hat until Sunday night. He uses the three days of rest to sleep and clean up the house, which is susceptible to ants. His father's couch floats like a small island surrounded by a reef of crumbs and spilled food, and Andrés circles it a number of times with the vacuum cleaner.

On Saturday afternoon he and his father take their usual outing to the bar at the end of town. When his mother was still alive, she wouldn't allow alcohol in the house, and his father had to drop in at the bar for a beer after work on Friday evenings. When Andrés came of age, his father invited him for a drink, and since Andrés' twenty-first birthday fell on a Saturday, his father changed his weekly outings to Saturdays. Andrés was surprised to learn that his father drank alone all those years and made no friends at the bar, except for Pirata, the one-eyed bartender. But Pirata had died ten years ago. His son, who took over tending bar, had invited them to the funeral, but Andrés' father didn't want to attend. The next time they came into the bar, Pirata's son didn't ask why they didn't go, but after that he never made any effort to be friendly with them. Not even after ten years.

"The usual," his father says to Pirata's son as they hop onto the barstools.

"Right," Pirata's son says, and brings them two bottles of Corona.

They chug their beers in silence while the jukebox plays the same tunes it played the Saturday before.

"What do you think of that new margarita-mixing machine?" Pirata's son asks.

Andrés' father glares at it. He takes out his glasses and places them on his face. After taking another swig of beer, he says, "What's the point?"

"Saves time, I guess," Andrés says helpfully.

His father looks around at the near-empty bar. "To do what?" he asks.

They chuckle into their beers. Pirata's son throws an annoyed look in their direction.

"Another round?" he asks.

"If you're not too busy," Andrés says, and they burst into laughter again.

On Sunday, nothing unusual happens at the group home, except that the television has been repaired and now the residents keep it on at full volume. Before she left, Louise warned him, "Good luck trying to get them to turn that down."

The dining room is cold. Andrés turns the television down and leaves. As soon as he's out the door, he hears the volume go up again. The pattern repeats itself twice before Andrés goes to the basement and shuts off the breaker to that part of the house.

"The lights went out," a voice comes to inform him at the office. Andrés flashes a flashlight on his face.

"I'm sorry about that, Mr. Shepley," he says. "We're on it. We'll get them back on as soon as we can."

He turns the flashlight on his video book and makes his way slowly down the columns of photographs as he searches in the semidarkness for the woman in the red hat.

By the time he turns the breaker back on, it's past two in the morning. A few residents are still smoking on the front porch. He looks through the medication record book. Five residents haven't taken their evening meds, so Andrés pulls out their medikits and drops the pills into the garbage can, logging in each evening's dose as if it's been taken.

The next morning he serves the same breakfast as always, eggs and sausage. He stuffs the automatic dishwasher with dirty dishes and then hands the keys over to the morning shift before heading home. As he drives into his neighborhood, he realizes that he's forgotten the video book in the office, but it will be safe there.

Andrés sleeps seven hours, waking at 5 p.m. When he walks out to the living room, his father greets him from the couch.

"I've got some more news for you," his father says.

"About?" Andrés yawns.

"About the woman in the red hat," his father says.

"Do tell," Andrés says. He opens the refrigerator to rummage for a soda. He finds two cans left in the door, both half-consumed and abandoned by his father. He takes one and sips the flat, cool liquid.

"She wasn't Chinese at all," his father says.

"How do you know?" Andrés says. "Her face was covered by the red hat, remember?"

"Yes, I know," his father says. "But her hand wasn't a Chinawoman's hand."

"What's a Chinawoman's hand?"

"You know," his father says. "Yellow."

"That's actually a misconception about Asian people. They aren't really yellow. Just like black people aren't really black."

"Well, what I meant was that I remember it was a Latina hand."

"You mean her hand was brown?"

"Oh, so brown people really are brown?" his father snaps.

Andrés takes another sip of soda. "Go on," he says.

"There's nothing more to it. I knew it was a Latina, so I thought maybe I was walking into one of those artsy foreign films."

"I think you're making it up," Andrés says.

"Why should I make it up? You're the one who wants to know what goddamn film I watched while you were being born. What the fuck does it matter anyway?"

Andrés pulls out a chair and sits down. He feels a slight tension at the temples.

"You know what, forget I said anything about any movie or any woman in a white fucking hat. I don't remember shit!"

Andrés says softly, "The woman's hat is red."

"Shut up with that," his father demands, turning up the volume on the television.

Andrés' headache worsens. He decides to lie down for a while longer. He still has a few hours before work. In bed he presses his fists to his eyes and somehow manages to fall asleep.

When he awakes his heart is pounding. The sound of the television carries into his room. He didn't set his alarm clock because he didn't think he would sleep this long, but it's close to nine o'clock.

On his way to the shower he calls to his father, "Turn that down, Pop." When he comes out again, one towel wrapped around his waist, another hanging over his shoulders, the television is just as loud. He's annoyed but decides to leave his father alone. He dresses, thinking he'll show up for work early again so he can make himself something to eat in the kitchen. The Sysco cheese is stocked in bulk, the odor pungent but appetizing.

As he makes his way down the hall he notices his father's left hand dangling over the arm of his chair. Andrés walks around him to turn the television off. He lifts his father's arm to drop it into his lap, the way his father usually falls asleep. His father's arm is cold.

Andrés bites his lip and his foot taps uncontrollably against the floor. Pressing his hands against his mouth, he releases a muffled wail. He squats, taking a few deep breaths, calming himself down. The need to cry surges and he grabs his face with both hands, piecing together an image of his father through the openings between his fingers.

And then suddenly the grief lifts, as if those few moments of panic were all he had to offer. He's uncertain what to do next. He looks around the room. Nothing seems different. Even his father's body on the couch is a familiar sight. It's as if he's sleeping.

After a few minutes on the floor he checks his watch. There are twenty-five people expecting him at the group home. Someone has to check to make sure they've taken their bedtime meds. In the morning, half of them will want their eggs and sausage. He turns off the living room lights and walks out to his car.

In his office, there is a woman in a red hat, waiting.

ADVANCEDELVISCOURSE
CAConrad

1.

Dear Elvis, I work in a gay and lesbian bookstore in Philadelphia. There's a six-and-a-half-foot lesbian who shops here. I told her she looks like a cross between you and Golda Meir; she said she was flattered by the comparison. She's invited me to play golf with her, she LIVES for golf! I think I'll go, just to see the old men react when she screams and bellows while swinging her club.

That's all for now.

P.S. Did you know there are no lesbian romance titles that begin with the letter *R*? Sometimes it makes me sad as a round dog caught in a tidal flush (as my Gramma used to say). But sometimes I'm elated for the possibilities of *R* in the realm of women who love women. If you were a woman, Elvis, you'd be a lesbian no doubt, and no doubt understand. Wish you had lived to do a duet with k.d. lang.

2.

On board the Lisa Marie jet for a tour of what Elvis called his Graceland In The Sky, I couldn't help but think of my uncle who wanted to be a pilot for United Airlines. He always dreamed of flying one of those big jets from Cleveland to Hawaii everyday, ever since he saw Elvis in *Blue Hawaii*. My uncle wound up driving a bus for Greyhound after failing pilot school. I used to imagine him driving a busload of passengers from Cleveland to San Diego, pulling over at the coast, gazing out over the Pacific, picturing Hawaii thousands of miles away, beaches full of airline pilots reclining with piña coladas and cheeseburgers. San Diego is about as close to Hawaii as a Greyhound Bus could every hope to get. My uncle died a sick, bitter man, having to drive from Cleveland to San Diego every week, the bus never lifting off the ground, no pretty stewardesses pacing up and down the aisles handing out peanuts and pillows. He would have loved the Lisa Marie jet. "Wow, this sure is classy," he'd have said, sitting down in the pilot's seat. "You know, those airline pilots all think they're such hot shit! I could've flown one of these things, no problem! Those fucking pilots are nothing more than glorified bus drivers if you ask me! I don't know who they think they're kidding?! Sons of bitches!"

3.

My friend Ken and I could never feel Elvis the same. We'd be driving down the road listening to "It's Now or Never." As soon as Elvis reached his peak in the song, Ken would turn the volume down a notch.

ME: Ken, you're doing it again.
KEN: What?
ME: Every time Elvis hits his peak, you dampen his flame.
KEN: I don't know, it just gets too loud.
ME: Ken, the volume is consistent throughout the song. You compensate with volume for the vibration Elvis puts in you.
KEN: What the fuck are you talking about?
ME: I'm trying to tell you you're afraid of the vibration of Elvis.
KEN: That's bullshit!
ME: No, it's not.
KEN: Yes, it is!
ME: No, it's not.
KEN: Yes, it is! Now shut the fuck up.
ME: All right. Have it your way.
KEN: Good! I will have it my way!
ME: There's no shame in being afraid of Elvis, though.
KEN: I'M NOT AFRAID OF ELVIS! If you don't shut your mouth I'm gonna pull over and kick the shit out of you.

4.

The truth of the matter is, if Elvis and Priscilla ever had a yard sale on the long lawns of Graceland, they would have sold everything in three minutes, customers screaming, crushing one another to buy the King's used socket wrenches and ashtrays. It used to take me hours to sell only half the things my mother wanted to get rid of. We had a set of Sonny & Cher napkin rings that always wound up back in the attic 'til the next summer's yard sale. For five years I put on my finest Capricorn salesmanship—"And over here, ma'am, we have a lovely set of Sonny & Cher napkin rings." None of our yard-sale customers ever had dinner events fancy enough to employ the likes of Sonny & Cher napkin rings. Of course, neither did we, that's why we wanted someone else to get stuck never using them. A set of Sonny & Cher napkin rings at Elvis' yard sale would have been swiped up by some shrieking, weeping yard-sale customer. If Elvis had dropped by my own yard sale and just touched my Sonny & Cher napkin rings, they would have been transformed into the Sonny & Cher Touched by Elvis Napkin Rings. Every one of my shrieking, weeping yard-sale customers (it was very uncommon for me ever to have shrieking, weeping yard-sale customers) would have wanted one of the eight Sonny & Cher Touched by Elvis Napkin Rings. No one would have had a complete set! Yeah, Elvis would have been a big help back then. But he had his own successful three-minute yard sale to worry about. Only a few other Americans could have had yard sales as successful as Elvis'—the president, for instance, as long as he was still in office. No one wants to buy used roller skates from an ex-president. I wonder if Jackie O was ever given a complimentary set of Sonny & Cher napkin rings. When she smiled for a photograph with them in her hands they would have become the Sonny & Cher Touched by Jackie O While Being Photographed Napkin Rings. Is it true there were also Elvis & Priscilla napkin rings? Did Sonny & Cher have a set?

> *"The President Lives in Washington, D.C.,*
> *but the King is from Memphis!"*
> (Graffito on the Graceland Wall)

5.

IF ELVIS IS NOT PARANOID, SOMEONE WILL HAVE TO DO IT FOR HIM

Elvis can't hide the fact that he has a penis. He's walking down the street and everyone knows he has a penis! It's outrageous! How dare they! But there's virtually nothing he can do about it. And they imagine other penises they've seen to visualize his penis. Which isn't fair either, but he's not whipping it out to say, "Hey, stop imagining things, this is mine!" He's sick of it. Sick sick sick sick of it! How dare they think about his penis! But there's nothing he can do about it. The best thing to do is not to mention it. When someone walks up to him and begins a conversation about the rainfall expected this afternoon, he just keeps talking about rain, never saying, "I know you know I have a penis!" It's ridiculous he should even have to say such a thing! But it's the way the world is! Better to ignore it. Yes, that's it, that's best.

6.

While I was walking to work today, another GODDAMNED fucking yuppie car nearly ran me down! I was FURIOUS! Then an old pickup truck stopped at a red light, Elvis on the radio rhyming tender and surrender, holding his darling in his arms underneath the bright moon.

Oooh, thank you, Elvis. I relaxed. Really, really relaxed. Sky overhead turning the jar lid of release. My sphincter opened its baby-bird mouth. Thank you, King.

7.

ELVIS AND THE ILLUSION OF HEMISPHERE

There are two windows on the wall. One for each of us. We fly through them and meet in the room. I come early, the sun catching me on its orange descent, reflecting off my back as I land on the floor, land in a rolling ball, a wreck as always. He never lands so clumsily. With him it's easy, gliding perfectly on the leather heels of his shoes. I come early so he doesn't see me crashing against the setting sun. I love him. I don't want him to see me sprawled and confused. My tender spots, my bruises, each of them a curiosity to him as we fold and unfold on the long sheets. What time is it? I'm waiting. Last time, he didn't come at all. He does that sometimes. Once, I waited half the night, making tiny pictures of him, a hundred pictures of him, smiling. They glued together nicely in the shape of an animal. Or a man, whatever you want it to be. He still hadn't come when I woke in the night and I found myself flying out the window, as confused as I had ever been about my feelings. Then I was sure of my feelings the next time I saw him. Why is that? He knows what time it is. He knows I know. If he were here I'd say I understand my feelings. Any minute now he will glide through the window, the scroll of white drapes blowing aside.

8.

I dreamed I was watching Johnny Carson interview Elvis on TV. Johnny told a joke and everyone laughed. Elvis told a joke and everyone laughed harder because everyone loves Elvis more.

> JOHNNY: So, Elvis, tell us what you think of Madonna.
> ELVIS: Oh, I think she's got some real good tunes — and she has a sweet pair of tits.
> JOHNNY: She sure is a beauty.
> ELVIS: Yeah, yeah, I wouldn't mind sticking my pencil in her knish.
> JOHNNY: Knish?! Are you, ah, Jewish?
> ELVIS: Yeah, well, you know, I thought I'd give it a try. I mean, hey, it can't hurt, right?
> JOHNNY: Well, sure, sure. Ah, MAZEL TOV to you, Elvis!
> ELVIS: Yeah, mazel tov, Johnny, mazel tov. (*Elvis says he has a surprise phone call to make. The TV audience gets real quiet while he dials. My phone rings.*)
> ME: (*Never taking my eyes off the TV.*) Hello?
> ELVIS: Hi, is this Conrad in Philadelphia?

ME: (*Silent. Can't believe it's true.... But I see him on TV.... Hear him and see him.... Talking to me.*)
ELVIS: Is this Conrad?
ME: Oh, uh, hello, Elvis. Yes, Elvis, it's me, it's Conrad, uh, hi.
ELVIS: (*Low and sexy.*) You've been a bad boy. Mmm. Haven't you?
ME: Oh! I mean no, no Elvis.
ELVIS: You're lying. Mmm. You want to suck my cock, don't you, hmm, don't you, boy? (*The audience oohs and aahs.*)
ME: Me, um, I, I, uh—
ELVIS: Yeah, oooh, yeah, you'd like that, wouldn't you? Hm? My big, fat cock in your mouth, hm? Yeah, yeah.
ME: (*I black out.*)
ELVIS: (*To Johnny.*) I don't know where he went.
JOHNNY: My goodness, Elvis. I think you put him into a coma! (*The audience laughs.*)

9.

An exhibition of the late works of Delacroix came to the Philadelphia Museum of Art. I wore headphones, listening to my Elvis CD, letting Elvis guide me through the nineteenth-century paintings. I wanted to spend time with the painting of Ovid in exile, but Elvis wanted lions, lions lions lions. He was singing "Don't Be Cruel," and I STOPPED in front of the painting entitled *Young Woman Attacked by a Tiger*. What is it, Elvis? What?

In the gift shop there are Delacroix T-shirts, Delacroix postcards, Delacroix jigsaw puzzles, Delacroix baseball caps, Delacroix note pads, Delacroix video tapes, Delacroix pencils and more! The yuppies roll their eyes at my Elvis T-shirt and whisper to one another while purchasing their Delacroix coffee mugs. They're fools, really. They think this gift shop is any different from Graceland with its Elvis wristwatches, Elvis cookie jars, and Elvis shot glasses. One man wearing a three-thousand-dollar Teton Brioni suit purchases a Delacroix baseball cap and a CD entitled *Music in the Time of Delacroix*. They're absurd Americans, just like me. We are the world's ridiculous, beautiful clowns!

They are going to launch a large vessel called a clipper at noon today. Another of these American inventions to make people go faster and faster. When they have managed to get travelers comfortably seated inside a cannon so that they can be shot off like bullets in any given direction, civilization will doubtless have taken a great step forward. We are making rapid strides toward that happy time when space will have been abolished; but they will never abolish boredom.
(Delacroix, 1854)

10.

ANIMATION FAMILY WITH ELVIS EVERYDAY

Every morning, Timmy pleads with Mama not to draw him a penis. "You're a BOY, Timmy, just shut up!" Just because he's a cartoon, doesn't mean he can't get what he wants. Elvis is never drawn until noon, gives us a chance to have some peace and quiet. First we draw the yard real pretty, lots of flowers. Mama draws flowers the prettiest. Elvis is drawn sitting on a picnic blanket with freshly drawn meatloaf sandwiches, mmm! Sure enough, Elvis will be singing us a song, telling jokes, and being particularly kind to Mama, when Timmy will stalk into the scene in a freshly drawn wig and evening gown to take Elvis's breath away. That Timmy ruins it every damn time! Elvis sings a love song to Timmy, stops halfway through, takes Timmy into his arms, and makes love to him right there on top of the meatloaf sandwiches EVERY DAMN TIME! We busy ourselves drawings walls around their lusty, moaning bodies. "Hurry!" Mamma yells. "Hurry, draw faster! I don't want to see THIS! That boy of mine takes Elvis away from us EVERY time! I swear, and I know I've threatened this a thousand times before, but tomorrow I will draw Timmy on horseback galloping away for the day!"

CREAM
John Gilgun

1.

"I know you stole the cream," Miss Kunert said.

"I didn't steal the cream," I answered.

"On the contrary, I have proof that you stole the cream."

"Give me the proof," I said.

"Why won't you admit that you stole the cream?"

"Because I didn't steal the cream."

"Were the other boys involved in stealing the cream?"

"I didn't steal the cream," I said.

"Perhaps one of the other boys stole the cream. If you tell me which of the other boys stole the cream, you can leave this room right now."

"If one of the other boys stole the cream, I don't know anything about it. How would I know?"

"You know because you're the one who stole the cream. None of the other boys stole the cream. I've already talked to the other boys. They all say they didn't steal the cream."

"Maybe they're lying."

"Maybe you're the one who's lying. Admit that you stole the cream."

"I didn't steal the cream," I said.

"You stole the cream," Miss Kunert said. "I know you stole the cream. Everybody knows you stole the cream. Why won't you admit you stole the cream?"

"Because I didn't steal the cream," I said.

It was March 1957. I was living as a chore boy at the Boston University Faculty Club on Bay State Road. Chore boy meant that I swept down the stairs, waxed and buffed the marble floor of the foyer, and washed windows. Those were my jobs. In exchange for my work, I got a free room on the top floor. The top floor had been the servants' quarters when this was a private home. There were six other chore boys living in rooms there—Paddy, a Korean War vet; Kim, a South Korean exchange student; Helmut, a chemistry major; Andrew, who was in the School of Theology; Adrian, a music major; and Pandit, an East Indian from Bombay.

I was two months from getting my BA degree in English.

I was poor. That's why they gave me the room in exchange for chores. In fact, at that moment, I had exactly six dollars to my name.

Helmut met me in the hall as I was about to enter my room. Miss

Kunert had finally let me go. She had not been able to break me down. My final words to her were, "I did not steal the cream."

Helmut had been smart to major in chemistry. He'd graduate in June and he already had a job with Monsanto. He didn't call them. They called him. "We want you," they told him.

You heard it everywhere: Better living through chemistry. Helmut had gotten the message.

I hadn't gotten the message. I had majored in English. I would be as poor after graduation as I was right now. Maybe even poorer. At least now I had a room. Once I graduated, the room would be given to some other needy student.

"What did Kunert say to you?" Helmut asked.

"She said I stole the cream."

"And what did you say?"

"I said I didn't steal the cream."

"But all the guys know you stole the cream."

"Did you tell her I stole the cream?" I asked.

"No. I didn't. But some of the other guys did. Anyway, I know you stole it. Everyone knows you stole it."

"Why did the other guys say I stole it?"

"You think they want to get kicked out of here a few months before graduation? Besides, you did steal it. You're as guilty as sin."

"I didn't steal it," I said.

Helmut laughed. "Bullshit," he said. Then he turned and went into his room, laughing his ass off.

2.

I was hungry. But I could go home to Malden, that grimy, blue-collar city where I'd been born. I could go home to my family. I could go on the MTA and that would cost me a dime which would leave me five dollars and ninety cents. If I jumped the turnstiles it wouldn't even cost me a dime. I could keep every one of the six one-dollar bills in my wallet. Jumping the turnstiles would be easy because it was Sunday. No one on the platform to see me, no one to turn me in. Once I got home, there'd be something to eat, Sunday dinner, mashed potatoes, pot roast, Birds Eye peas, Bond bread, a jelly doughnut from Cushman's Bakery for dessert.

I put on my parka and walked down the hall toward the elevator. Two of the doors to the other rooms were partially open. I could hear music coming from one of them. The other chore boys were in their rooms studying for midterm exams. I couldn't study. I was too hungry. I was going home. I needed food. I was weak from lack of food.

The guys had told Kunert I stole the cream. That's what Helmut said. But maybe they didn't. Maybe Helmut wasn't telling the truth. Maybe he just said that to get my goat.

It was cold outside, a bitter, blue-black cold, like a bruise. It was the kind of cold you only get in Boston. But what did I know? I'd never been anywhere else. I thought every place was like this. I was like a person born with some incurable disease. He lives all his life with pain. What does he know? He thinks everyone lives with the same pain. Nobody ever tells him they don't. They just lie and say, "Oh, yeah. We live with that pain, too. Everybody does." So he dies not knowing any different. Seven sorrowful mysteries. Life's a vale of tears. You can't escape the cross. Uh huh. Tell me about it.

3.

I walked through the Back Bay to Kenmore Square and entered the MTA station there. I didn't jump the turnstile. I got change and paid a dime. I was too beaten down to jump the turnstile. Jumping a turnstile takes optimism. I didn't have any optimism. I knew I'd get caught.

I didn't jump that turnstile, sir.
Six people saw you. We got the goods on y' now.
I didn't jump your goddamned turnstile!
Take him away, Officer Murphy. He's guilty as sin.

Because it was Sunday, it took a long time for the train to come. But finally it did come and I got on and sat down. The metal wheels started to sing under me: Hello, Central. Give me Doctor Jazz. Tell him I need everything he has. Hell-o, Cent-ral, gim-me Doc-tah Jazzzz-zz.

At Park Street a kid in a Loden coat got on, a rich kid carrying a green book bag, probably a Harvard kid, cute. You weren't supposed to think cute like that. He brushed past me as he went up the aisle. The edge of his Loden coat touched my left shoulder. Or was it his thigh? The edge of his ass? Brooks Brothers clothes. A blue-and-white-striped tie, a button-down shirt, chinos, and Bass weejuns. I wanted to wrap myself in that Loden coat with him still in it. I wanted to roll with him, hold him, stroke him, kiss him, rub against him naked, warm my hands between his creamy white thighs. I want to love him, wanted to know all about him, wanted to know what books he was carrying in that bag, wanted to sit up with him late at night in his Harvard dorm, a dorm where no one stole cream.

Hello, Central. Gimme Doctor Fag.
He's carryin' Physique Pictorial *in his bag.*
Are you now or have you ever been a fag?
No, Senator McCarthy. I ain't no fag.
Are you telling the truth?
Hey, Joe, would I lie to you? Nice workin'-class Irish-Catholic boy like me?

When I first moved into the room in the faculty club, I didn't know how good I had it. Needy boys like myself got one meal a day, the supper meal, courtesy of Boston University. Also, I had a job as a waiter in the faculty dining room so I got sixty cents an hour. I worked the lunch hour so I got lunch for free. The only meal I missed was breakfast and with that sixty cents an hour I could get eggs and bacon and toast with grape jelly any day at Hayes Bickford across the street from the Armory. Breakfast was only ninety-nine cents and you got fresh squeezed orange juice for the vitamin C to prevent colds.

Made in the shade with lemonade. Yeah. That's me.

Never get too comfortable with that shade or that lemonade. Someone always cuts down the tree and knocks the glass out of your hand. Miss Bunting, the nice lady who managed the Faculty Club when I moved in, got replaced by Miss Kunert.

Miss Kunert told us this was not a free ride. "You boys have lived high off the hog long enough." So the supper meal was eliminated.

Then I lost my job as a waiter. Cranky Frankie Boyle, the cook, took a dislike to me. Worse than that, he started pushing and slapping me every time I came into the kitchen to place an order. He'd come right around the steam table and slap me. Since he was the cook and they needed him, they let me go. They didn't need me. There were hundreds of needy students to replace me. They were standing in line all up and down Commonwealth Avenue.

I'd been assaulted by Cranky Frankie Boyle so I looked up Legal Aid in the phone book, called, and made an appointment. Legal Aid had offices in a building on Beacon Hill that went back to the Revolution. Paul Revere made silver dinner plates in that building. There was a plaque beside the white door with the fan glass. It said the Boston Tea Party had been planned there. The British were oppressing us with a tax on tea so we stood up for ourselves and fought back and after a while we won. Welcome to the Cradle of Liberty. Welcome to Boston.

"I've been assaulted and I lost my job and I didn't do anything to deserve it," I told the woman behind the desk.

"There's nothing we can do. Sorry."

"But he hit me three times. Isn't that illegal?"

"There's nothing we can do for you."

"But I thought there was something a person could do—I mean, legally—when someone assaults you."

"Sorry. Nothing."

I got out of the MTA car and transferred to an elevated train at North Station. This car took me on a loop fifty feet above the ground through Charlestown where I could see the Bunker Hill Monument as well as weary Irish women staring blankly out of tenement windows. Then the car rattled above Somerville, by the Whitman Sampler

Chocolate factory and Hood's Ice Cream plant where they made Hoodsies. My father had worked for Hood's for thirty years, delivering milk, before he got fired for being drunk on the job. Crossing the Mystic River by the Monsanto plant I could see a pile of sulfur, sulfur Helmut would process to make bombs. I got off at Everett Station and waited thirty minutes for the bus that would take me to Malden.

I didn't expect to see anything except pigeons at Everett Station on a Sunday afternoon. But there was a guy named Tommy Simpson I'd gone to Malden High with. He came up, stood beside me, started talking.

"Goin' home t' Malden?" he asked.

"Yeah. Sunday dinner."

"Me too. Sunday dinner with my fiancée and her folks. You remember Rita Quinn?"

"Sure I do," I lied. Of course I couldn't remember Rita Quinn. All I remembered were the guys.

"Her and me. Gettin' married in June. June, the month everybody gets married, ha. Yuh married yet?"

"Not yet."

"Well, you'll find the right girl. It takes time. It took me three years t' find Rita. Great girl. Works at Jordan Marsh now. She'll quit once we get married though. No wife o' mine's gonna work. Yeah. What are yuh doin' now? Workin'? Got a job?"

"College. Going to college. Yeah."

"Oh, yeah. Sure. Smart kid like you. I remember you in high school. Always in the library, readin' away. Sure, you'd be in college. Gettin' ahead in life. That's what counts, studyin', gettin' ahead in life through education. Yeah."

"Yeah," I said.

"See y' round," Tommy said. He walked away, crunching through some peanut shells the pigeons were pecking at. No peanuts. Just the shells. You peck at what God gives you, though. Take what's available. Any opportunity that comes along, grab it. Get ahead in life. Through education. Be sure you major in chemistry though. Otherwise, what do you get? Peanut shells.

After Miss Kunert cut out our evening meal, we went hungry. Kim the Korean bought a rice cooker and kept it in his room. He could eat. He lived on the rice. Rice was enough for him. Miss Kunert found out about it though and took the rice cooker away from him. She said it might start a fire. He shut himself in his room for three days and wouldn't come out. We thought he was sick and the other needy boys asked me to tell Miss Kunert he was sick. I did, but he wasn't sick. He was just doing religious devotions in there. Telling Miss Kunert that Kim was sick when he wasn't meant I got on her shit list. Her eye was on me from that moment on.

One night Paddy the Korean War vet saw me starving in the hall. "Shit, man. You don't know?"

"Know what?"

"C'mon. Come with me."

He took me down to a room under the kitchen. It was a dark place in the depths of the house. There was a refrigerator in one corner with a chain across the door and a padlock on the chain.

"Why drag me down here?" I asked.

"Wait. You'll see," Paddy said. He pulled up a chair, got up on it, reached up into a space over a cupboard, felt around, and said, "Ah, here it is."

"Here's what, Paddy?"

"Here's the key. Look, I'm friends with the woman who runs the dining service upstairs. We're like more than friends. Like she's a girlfriend. I'm goin' out with her. She feels sorry for us because we're starvin'. So she had a copy of the key made and she leaves it up here for me. Why starve if you don't have to?"

"What are you doing?"

"I'm unlocking the friggin' refrigerator. I'm takin' food out. I'm eatin'. What do you think I'm doin'?"

"But that's food to be served tomorrow upstairs in the dining room. What's Cranky Frankie going to do when he comes down here tomorrow and he sees that someone got in there and ate the food he was going to cook for the faculty?"

"He's gonna order some more. Here. Have a piece of shrimp."

"No," I said. "Thanks, no. You're gonna get caught. Your ass is gonna be grass."

"What caught ? I've been eatin' like this for a week, I haven't been caught."

"No, Paddy. It's gonna hit the fan. I don't want no part of this."

"So go hungry," Paddy said.

"I will," I said. And I left.

You read novels about rich WASP kids, they're in some fancy prep school, someone steals something or breaks the honor code or cheats on an exam, it's a big deal, an ethical issue, and they get an opportunity to anguish over it, learn from it, come to some conclusions, grow up, become responsible adults. After all, they're going to run the world, right? With the needy kids living as chore boys at the Boston University Faculty Club, stealing food had nothing to do with any of that shit. It was hunger, pure and simple. Miss Kunert was a new version of the Potato Famine and we were starving. I didn't steal slices of roast beef and cold macaroni and cheese but everyone else did. They'd had their supper meal taken away from them. So they stole food. What would you

84

do? They weren't getting food any more. So they raided the refrigerator. Like Oliver Twist.

More, Miss Kunert. More!

More? Did you hear what he said? He wants more!

Please, Ma'am.

The Faculty Club was built on a vast Charles River dump. Its foundations rested on trash and garbage thrown there in the nineteenth century, trash and garbage through which the starving Irish scrounged for food and firewood. A foot under that chained and padlocked refrigerator, ghostly Irish women were still eating garbage. In my nightmares, I heard them keening.

Please, Miss Kunert. For the love o' God, more!

No. Go back to Ireland where you came from!

4.

In Malden, the streets were empty. Everyone was in church, brooding about their sins. Or they were home eating mashed potatoes with butter and salt. Or they were drunk on their ass in some alley somewhere. I entered the flat where we lived. I opened the back door, a door with frosted glass, and stepped into a hall that opened into the kitchen. My seventeen-year-old sister Reenie met me there.

"What are you doin' home?" she asked.

"Reenie, you ask me that question every time I come home."

"Yuh sure. Because every time you come home I wonder why you're home. So I ask. So why are you home?"

"I'm hungry. I need to eat."

"We got food. You come to the right place. What's the matter, no food in Boston?"

"No," I said. "Not a crumb. Even the rats are starving."

My mother was out working as a waitress, feeding rich people at the Hancock Inn in Peabody. But my father was here and my thirteen-year-old brother Jimmie. They were sitting at the kitchen table now with plates of food in front of them. My mouth began to water.

"So sit down," my sister said. "Make y'self at home."

They say that if you're starving and you see food, your eyes get bigger. They tested it on people. They put plates of food in front of starving people and their eyes got bigger. They proved it with the scientific method. It's science. Which makes it true. I looked at the plates of food and I'm sure my eyes got bigger.

My brother was wearing a black leather jacket. He was hunched over his mashed potatoes and pot roast and Birds Eye peas. I thought he was in a real hurry to eat and get back on the streets with his gang because he hadn't even taken off his jacket. I kept looking at the studs on the jacket as I ate. I also got the smell of the cheap leather.

My father said, "It's not right to wear a leather jacket at the dinner table."

My brother laughed. "What? If I take it off, all I got under it is my T-shirt."

"Well, take it off," my father said.

"No. It's cold in here. No."

"Take it off or I'll take it off for you."

"You and whose ole lady?"

Reenie said, "Pretend it's a tuxedo. He dressed for dinner. He's like Cary Grant. Ha."

We continued eating. Then all of a sudden my brother said, "Hey! Who cut the cheese?"

My father's face clamped together like the head on a wrench and he said, "Don't talk about things like that at the dinner table!"

"But you farted!"

"But we don't talk about things like that when we're eatin'."

"But how can we eat when you fart?"

"Keep quiet about it. A man farts, he can't help it. But it's wrong to talk about it."

"It was a big smelly beer fart."

"It don't care what kind of fart it was. Eat, don't talk. No talkin' at the dinner table."

"Should be no fartin', too."

"You keep it up, you're gonna get it, Bozo."

"My name's not Bozo. My name's Jimmie. You named me Jimmie. Can't you remember what you named me?"

"I shoulda named you Bozo because you're a bozo."

Reenie said, with a whine in her voice, "Please. Please quit. My stomach's upset enough already and I have to meet Mike on the corner in twenty minutes." Mike was her boyfriend.

We put our heads down and shoveled in food in silence. Then Reenie said to me, "What are you learnin' now in college? Tell me about it. I want to hear. We'll get something at this table besides what we're getting."

"I'm learning about different religions," I said.

"I don't want to hear about that," my father said. "No talkin' while we're eating. Eat and shut up or get out."

"Go ahead," Reenie said. "I want to hear."

"I'm sitting in on this class called Comparative Religion. I'm sitting in because it's not a required course for graduation but I'm interested in it."

"Can you do that?" Reenie asked.

"Yes, they don't care. I just sit in the back and listen. Last week it was about Buddhism. I guess I got interested because this Korean kid, this Kim, he has a room next to mine and he's a Buddhist."

"You're a Catholic, that's enough. That's good enough. What more d' you need? I don't want to hear. No talkin' at the table," my father said.

"Buddhism, shit. What next?" my brother said.

"Go ahead," Reenie said. "I wanna know."

"Well, one guy in the class said, 'What does rice taste like to the bowl that holds it?' Then he explained that taste is only an arbitrary conception of what he called our taste organ, the human tongue. Taste has no substantiality outside of our awareness of it. Taste isn't real."

"What the hell's that supposed to mean?" my brother said.

"It means nothing's real until your mind makes it real," I said.

"No talking," my father said.

I continued. "Suppose you're suffering. You're in pain. That's all in your mind. It's a conception. You can deal with pain if you realize it's just a conception. You can overcome it. What if you're hungry? Say you're starving. You can overcome the pain if you have Buddhist mind control."

"That's interesting," Reenie said, encouraging me. I could feel this menacing thing coming out of my brother and my father but she was encouraging me. She set me up. I took her bait and went on.

"Yeah, it is interesting. To me anyhow. Look, it's like, I can feel this table or this chair I'm sitting on but it's only an arbitrary conception of my dualistic touch-organ, my body and its touch-mind. The feeling of this plate, the smell of this food, the butter on the mashed potatoes has no substantiality outside of my mind. This whole kitchen, all of us sitting here, everything, it's just a conception in my mind. It's not real until my mind makes it real. The kitchen sink, the range, the boiler, the linoleum, none of it's real until I make it real in my mind."

"I think it's shit," my brother said.

I knew he'd say exactly that before the words came out of his mouth. It was as though I could see the words forming themselves in his mind. I shrugged. I'd anticipated it.

"Don't say shit at the dinner table," my father said.

I anticipated that, too.

"Shit," my brother said. "It's shit." Then he picked up his plate, turned it over, and dumped his food on the table.

I hadn't anticipated that. But everything that happened after that was predictable.

"Don't waste food!" my father said. "It's a sin, wastin' food!"

Then he stood up, leaned across the table, and slapped my brother across the face. My brother stood up. His chair crashed against the sink. He started crying.

Reenie said, "Quit! Quit now."

My father grabbed a handful of the mashed potatoes lying on the table and threw it toward my brother's face. It went all over his black leather jacket. My brother ran crying out of the kitchen. The door with the frosted glass opened and shut and he was gone.

My sister said something and my father slapped her. She started to scream and ran crying out of the kitchen. The front door at the end of the hall slammed, and she was out of the house, running to the corner to be with her boyfriend Mike.

I sat there looking at my father's face. It told me he was insane. That twisted-up face—it was the face of an insane person. But I'd known that for years. My father's insane. So what else is new?

"Are you satisfied?" I said weakly.

He didn't answer. He walked away, leaving me alone in the kitchen. He went into the parlor, picked up the Sunday paper, sat down, and started to read it. I could hear him talking to himself. He talked to himself for hours sometimes. My father the nut case.

But with my brother and sister out of the house, things were quiet. The front door had locked automatically when my sister ran out, slamming it shut behind her. I locked the back door, the one with the frosted glass. Reenie would be with her boyfriend for the rest of the day and Jimmie would be with his gang on the corner. So we'd have some peace in here. No one could get in. My father'd be off in his own nutzy world, sitting in the parlor talking to himself.

Peace, it's wonderful.

It didn't work out that way. Peace lasted as long as peace usually lasts—that is, about twenty minutes.

But before it ended, I cleaned up, in a calm, blissed-out trance. I was in a trance because I'd eaten. But also because putting things in order always puts me into a kind of trance. I found a plastic container in the pantry and put all the leftovers into it. I would cover the plastic container and bring it back to Boston. I'd hide it in my room. Then I'd have something to eat through Tuesday. I thought about the Buddhist insubstantiality of the container, of the pot roast, the peas. But I drew the line at the insubstantiality of the mashed potatoes. For an Irishman, mashed potatoes can never be insubstantial. An Irishman may come to doubt the existence of God and his angels but the nonexistence of the potato—never. Irishmen make piss-poor Buddhists and it's all the fault of that substantial potato. They can never get over the substantial hump of that ever-lovin' potato.

I was also thinking of my anima because a friend had given me Jung's *Modern Man in Search of a Soul* and I'd read it and knew I had a feminine side, my anima, as well as a masculine side, my animus.

It was my anima that enjoyed washing the dishes, stacking them in the plastic rack, wiping food off the kitchen table, wringing out the dishrag under the faucet. They'd always said I had too much of a feminine side. I was a sissy, a pantywaist. But Jung said that was all right. I shouldn't deny my feminine side. I should just try to balance it off with my masculine side so that I could attain harmony, unity, and wholeness. Okay, I'm all for that. But where did I put that masculine side? I knew it was around here somewhere. Can't find it, though.

I was also thinking of insanity because my father was insane and so that interested me. I'd said to Kim the Korean, "My father's insane. What does the Buddha tell us about insanity?" And Kim had told me, "Buddha says insanity isn't caused by anything. Insanity means the true mind hasn't been revealed yet. The false mind covers it."

"How do I get my father to his true mind?" I asked Kim. But he said he was busy, had to study for an exam, didn't want to give me the answer to that. I figured there was an answer because the Buddha had an answer for everything, but it was complicated and Kim didn't have time to talk to me about it right then.

So I was into these deep thoughts.

A violent pounding at the back door shook me out of these thoughts.

It's my brother, I thought.

I heard my father yell, "Son of a bitch!" Son of a bitch. My screwball father was up. He was out of the parlor. He was reeling down the hall toward the door. My brother knew enough to stay away. If he was foolish enough to come back and bang on that back door, I wasn't going to intervene. He'd brought it on himself. I heard my father turn the key in the lock. Son of a bitch. I heard the door open. I heard my father say, "Son...son of a bitch!" Then I heard a voice that was not my brother's voice scream, "You fucker! You ever touch her again, I'll kill you, you fucker! I'll kill you!"

I looked into the hall and my sister's boyfriend Mike exploded like a bomb through the open door, threw himself at my father, pinned him against the wall and started pounding him, pounding him, pounding him. When he had pounded him long enough, he dropped him on the floor. Standing over him, he said, "Fucker, you deserve to die."

That Mike, man! He was a big bruiser. No one fucked with him. No one. He had a big mop of red hair that kept flopping over his face as he pounded the bejeezus out of my old man.

My father looked up and said, "Don't say 'fucker' in my house." He was bleeding from the mouth. "Nobody says 'fucker' in this house. Watch your language in this house."

"Fucker," Red said, and he nudged my father's fallen body with his foot. Then he stepped over him and walked up the hall toward the front door.

My father got up and followed him, saying, "Let's talk this over.

Can we talk this over? I wanna talk this over."

Mike opened the front door and stepped outside. My father knew that the door had an automatic lock. Once it was shut, Mike couldn't get back inside.

"Let's talk about this," my father said, approaching him.

"I don't want to talk to you," Mike said.

"C'mon. Let's talk." My father's hand was on the door.

"No. I'm not talkin' to you," Mike said.

With his hand on the door ready to slam it shut, my father raised his foot and kicked Mike in the balls. See, he figured he could get that door shut and lock Mike outside. He was wrong about that. Mike was fast. The shock of being kicked in the balls registered, and he threw himself at my father, pushed him backward into the parlor, got him down and began to beat his head against the floor, screaming, "You kicked me there, you kicked me there, you kicked me there!" Bang! My father's head hit the floor. Bang bang! It hit the floor twice more. "You dared to kick me there, you fuckin' dared!"

My sister ran in through the open door, crying. "Stop, stop, for God's sake stop. Please stop. Oh stop. Oh, God, just stop."

5.

The house was quiet again. My sister and Mike had left. The front door was closed, locked. I had closed and locked the back door. My father was sitting on a kitchen chair holding toilet paper to his bleeding mouth. Through his bleeding mouth, he managed to say. "That mick thinks he's ever gettin' back in this house, he's got another think comin'."

"Is that all you have to say?" I asked.

"God damned harp. They're all alike."

"You kicked him in the nuts and that's all you got to say? That's all it means to you?"

"Not back in my house, he's not."

At that point the bottom dropped out of my world and I fell through. I started to cry. So I stood there crying. There was no response from my father. So I turned and walked into the ratty bedroom with the bunk bed in it. I threw myself down on the lower bunk and cried. I cried for an hour. I'd swim up through the crying to hear the house making noises around me—the furnace turning over down cellar, the outside walls cracking in the cold. Then I'd go down into my crying again, like lowering myself off a fishing pier into Boston Harbor. I cried until I forgot who I was and where I was. I cried 'til I hit bottom and couldn't go any deeper. I scrambled around on the bottom among the rocks on my hands and knees and then I cried some more.

6.

My mother came in from her waitressing job at nine o'clock. We sat facing each other across the kitchen table. She was tired. It showed in her face. She worked too hard and it wore her out. She had a can of Narragansett beer in front of her from which she sipped as we talked. She still had her pink waitress uniform on.

"He said you cried," she said.

"Yeah," I said.

"Well, you always cried too much. As a baby, you cried all the time. All the paregoric we poured in you to shut you up, it never shut you up. I never seen a baby cry like that in all my life. The neighbors complained. I told them I couldn't do anything about the noise. You wouldn't stop."

"I didn't want to come into the world. It was a big shock to me. I didn't like it. So I cried."

"Well, you're here," my mother answered. "Get used to it."

"I don't think life is worth living," I said.

"Well, Bishop Sheen says it is. Besides, what else you got?"

"I got pain."

"We all got that. What do you think life's all about anyhow?"

"I don't know. Pursuit of happiness? I read that somewhere. I forget where."

"You got a lot to learn," she said.

"I stole some cream," I said.

"You stole some what?"

"Some cream. At school. I stole some cream."

"Your old man delivers milk for thirty years for Hood's and you steal cream? You want cream, you come home and get cream. Jesus, stealin' cream! Have you gone crazy?"

"I don't know why I did it. But I found myself in the basement of that place I'm livin' in and there's a chain around the refrigerator and there's a padlock on it and I found I could open the door and get a bottle of cream out and I drank some of it. The chain is loose so you don't even need to unlock the padlock, though I know where they hide the key. You can reach in and get what's in there and get it out if it's small enough. A pint bottle of cream. But I didn't need that cream."

"You needed something," she said.

"What did I need?"

She shook her head. She wasn't about to tell me what she thought I needed. Maybe a kick in the ass. Maybe something else. She wasn't saying.

"The other guys have been robbing that refrigerator blind for weeks and no one said a word. I steal a tiny bit of cream and all hell breaks loose. I didn't even drink the whole bottle. And it was only a pint."

"Well, you got caught and they didn't. That's the difference."

"They ratted on me. But I lied. I said I didn't do it. Because if I said I did it, then they'd kick me out and I wouldn't graduate and everybody's sacrifices would have been in vain. But Kunert knows I did it. She couldn't break me down, though. I got it fixed in my mind that I wouldn't say anything except 'I didn't steal the cream, I didn't steal the cream, I didn't steal the cream' and it worked. Anyway, I broke two of the commandments. I stole and I lied."

"Well, that means you got your whole life to break the other eight," she said.

"Yeah. My whole life. Life. Who needs it?"

"Well, yes. You can kill yourself. But then you die and go up to heaven and they show you all the great things you might have done if you'd stayed alive. How do you think that's gonna make you feel? You watch all the things you didn't do on God's television up there and you never got a chance to do them because you threw your life away when you were twenty. You might accomplish a lot of things. So do them. Don't sit up in heaven telling yourself, 'I didn't do this, I didn't do that.' Give yourself a chance. You're still a kid. Don't throw your life away. You want a beer?"

"Sure."

She opened the fridge, took out a beer, applied the church key to it, popped it, and handed it to me. I took a sip. A couple of these and no more pain.

"Thanks," I said.

"You got the best years of your life ahead of you. Bein' dead is bein' dead. There's nothing to it. You just lie there in the ground. Being alive is like.... Being alive is better. Believe me. There's nothing worse than bein' dead. Anyway, you'll get there some day anyhow like everybody does. Why rush it?"

"I'll keep that in mind," I told her.

"Yeah, do that," she said. "Finish your beer now. Jeez."

SUE & hELLBOUND oO tHE sTRIP

Ryan Kamstra

"O mother dear, we're not the fortunate ones."
—NY's beloved poetess, C. Lauper

The rose under his Harley T-shirt. His heart-shaped fist. His narrow
pushy lip. The tight body. The almost virginity there.

You can barely see for the alcohol. It's been several days of this now.
You've caught yourself giggling.

He says his name is Sue. He says he got his foreman to cough up a
fifty-dollar advance and it's Friday. He's out to party. You're out to
party. He's got a fifty-yard stare when he's out to party.

He has a girlfriend who is a boy who lives her life as a girl. From his
wallet, he shows a picture. She is angular, pouty, and sweet. He has a
bona fide girlfriend, biological and all that, back home in small-town
Northern Quebec. He shows you a picture. She is round, homely, and
sweet. He's flirting with you.

How great is it to be a boy? Leggy, irresponsible, broke, high, infi-
del, tough.

Sue is hilarious. He moves his hands really fast when he talks.
Squints hard whenever the train comes into the hi res of the next station.
Teenage toughs, unspoiled and predatory, size up minky girls spread
pell-mell on chalk-blue seats.

If life is sometimes like a series of losses, your body feels more like
a series of crashes.

You lost it first to rock and roll. With banger girls, hair out to here.
Half-dykes who were never innocents, never unknowing. Malleable like
videogames, you would do anything on a dare or from bullying—
parents away, booze, oil, got tossed around for a while, spread. Sex for
welfare kids—like chewing gum, it's impersonal and you spit it out
later. Sue's own hair is blonde, almost white. Lips touched with a gob of
saliva.

The world he has no use for.

You can't hold a job. He resorts to boredom with a selective
attention span.

Looking to party?

You are. You are without cash but jonesing. You follow him off at
the next stop. You decide to regret it in the morning.

C'mon give me cash and we'll go party.

You do. He has a sweet face, tortured only by habitual amphetamine use and a mission. He is playing three, maybe four people to-night. Just playing them is its own high. Like all addicts, he is superhuman and impossible to keep sight of.

He keeps getting his face in your face.

O, he tells you, first we drop off at the ex's. We'll party there. He's such a sweetie.

You come over the glare of the stairwell and into a quiet twilight station. He is walking fast, tunnel vision, an incorporeal beat keeping time. You two parting the crowd, a maniac pair. You follow him, churn-ing turnstile, into gaytown. Pass purses, handbags. Professionals wear-ing protective masks.

You have to ask.

I have to ask. Are you picking me up, or...

The word carries a lurking enchantment.

...hustling?

He scowls at this. He'd prefer to insulate you from the facts. The cost of it all, his extra-relationship sex life, his current girlfriend's wild possessiveness, his debts. Questions like yours belie seduction.

He is not entirely living here. Who would want to?

Through glass doors, the village secretes trim boys in neon joggers, patios of wealthy men dining on pastas with curious hybrid sauces, waiters who could be models and models who could be actors, a thin woman strumming a Patti Smith tune on a nylon-string guitar. Buildings are low and white with rectangular windows. Security condos watch over, imperious and weightless.

He waves vaguely.

Dude, my ex lives in that one. Give me a sec, I gotta score something for someone. I'll score for us too.

So you let him. He vanishes up a closed system of alleyways. There is a ninety-nine-point-nine-percent chance you'll never see him again.

They are around your age, and pass you, giving you one stern, demeaning look over. You can almost hear them. *O, honey, please, not T-shirt and jeans*....

Faggots, you mutter.

A middle finger is raised from behind a head. You see his one, raise him one.

Aggravation and this city. Everyone in everybody's face.

Everything Sue says, there's a layer of accusation to it, a shell enclosing something too furious to contain. Like you. You don't always sleep well.

He emerges from the alley, bright eyes, saying, You look really hot in that shirt.

You smile tolerantly.

Fuck off, you tell him.

It's a red T-shirt that reads: Florida.

Sue shakes his head, turning the corner archly.

He'd tell you anything. He's out for a good time.

Okay man, let's just steal in that peelers bar, and then we'll go to the ex's.

He is making for the outskirts of gaytown where cafes diminish and the sex trade picks up. Where women, biological or not, lean into the stream, just obvious enough for the buyer, not enough for the cops.

Ya hot, you ask grimly, motioning to go.

What man?

Fuck, all right, I'm gonna go have a beer somewhere.

Stop worrying man, look, look, look.

He clasps a little foil stone between two fingers.

What's that, crack?

Stop worrying man, I promise we'll party.

Show it to me.

Not here. We'll go to the peelers bar. We got to get a can or something to smoke it with.

Show me it.

Why are you worrying all the time?

Because if it's crack. Show it.

As you dodge up alleys, he is still too squeamish to take it out of his pocket again. Or even to pull a can from one of the various blue bins. You begin to suspect he's been picked up by the cops a few too many times. You take a can from a colored assortment worthy of a supermart while he skulks to an ambiguous distance.

Fingernails the foil, shows a peep to you.

It's hash.

You resume your sweep toward the peelers bar. He's going on about his crazy girlfriend now. How she's threatening to go through with full surgery. How he's told her, if she goes through with full surgery, he'll leave her. You know, then she'll be just another chick.

You're bi, aren't you? he asks.

You say, How old are you?

So am I, he says.

Hmm, you think.

In the brown lobby of the peelers bar, there's trouble. It seems they caught Sue earlier smoking rock in the bathroom. Imagine. You pay for beer for the two of you while he argues to a balding mustached managerial type with dreads.

He argues that the waitress who said that has it in for him. The managerial type agrees she has it in for him, and for good reason. The managerial type looks you over twice and deems Sue more respectable if in your company. You have that effect sometimes, when you're drunk.

You sweep to the back, to the lap dance area. There are only empty chairs there now, empty and oversexed.

He is puncturing the can, making a pipe. He talks, half a con, half a cool pink lady giving an interview to *Famous* magazine. His eyes look right through you. You try to place the expression. It's like how ever since the first man hit you, you've had that same smile.

No offense, you smirk, but you are a bit of a hustler, no?

Why look for absolutes, gawd. Stop worrying. Sit down, relax. Watch the chicks. I'll be with you in but a moment.

He is wiry as an adolescent, definitely older. Not that he looks older. There is a certain youthful cunning that comes with age without place.

You watch the peelers, professionally bored at humping poles.

Several minutes pass, and he has the little lump of hash lit in the homemade pipe, passing it to you. You drag enough to get spinny. He takes more, his eye the whole time on any sign of management. And on the back door.

You both take a table, still out of view. Feeling silly and high, kiss while the girl dances. Unsung, her legs wrap around the brass pole.

Kissing him, if you were both violent like the swans, perhaps this caress would hold some great promise for you. Holding his face, remembering him this way, living. Shaking, if boys shook.

A peeler and a businessman now join you.

Labor is her ass touching the cool root of that man's lap, and him barely able to open his eyes. The night begins to feel like that. Like this one trope locked inside. It's not fair. It's not fair, the ones who get over it the quickest. Wed in suburbs, with crisscross gardens, dying their gray every month and slowly going blind.

You begin to wish queer were still a disease.

He says he has to go to the washroom. To whack off. That you and the girls are getting him hot. You offer to go with him. He fidgets, says he prefers to jerk off alone. But that he gives fantastic head.

You're going to a party. He'll give you fantastic head there.

You briefly wish you could marry like that. On a cul-de-sac, at the edge of light.

He takes too long. He's doing something in there, lines. When he returns, he's in a hurry, shaky-eyed, and one of the management is following him out. A wiry dude, in fatigues, with a close-shaved scalp.

Fags, the militia dude calls.

Tall walls of monitors throb hiphop from certain windows.

The lobby of the condominium tower is like walking onto the bridge of the *Enterprise*. The security guard eyes you from the perch of his desk. He's positioned like he's playing checkers against himself in glass columns.

You ride with Sue up a slow-moving elevator of women in jackets.

As you come through the door, a very, very tall man with bluish-brown skin, wrapped in a sheet, orders, You sit down there.

It is a single chair by a mirror. You do.

And you, go in there.

Sue does. A door closes. The very, very tall man remains on the other side. A soundless interrogation ensues.

I am sorry about this, says the man, his high cheekbones chiseled as if by a team of precise alien divinity.

I'm Iggy Pop, you say, extending a hand.

He sighs, wipes his hand on the sheet.

Sorry, jerking off before you came.

He then extends his hand draped Halloween-like in the sheet. You take it, fondly. You shake.

Patrick, he says.

Is that your ex then? you ask.

Iggy, listen, Stew is a good guy, but with him it's all about getting to the next high. Why I had to dump him.

Stew? you ask.

So nothing personal, but I will not have him showing up at all hours of the night, unannounced.

You feign innocence. He told me there was a party here.

Rolling of eyes. He only visits when he needs drugs.

Patrick shouts into the next room. Isn't that right, Stew?

You're upset now. You say, Nice to meet you Patrick. I'm only sorry it was under these circumstances.

You open the door to the main space. And say, Stew, I'm leaving.

Wait, he says, getting up.

He, too, had been seated on a single chair. A balding dude with a close crop-cut and glasses like TV screens sits opposite him in silky pajamas on the edge of a fine bed. He gives you a goofy smile.

Iggy, says Patrick, this is Iggy.

Nice to meet you, you say.

Sue lurches toward you,

Hold on, jeez. Man, I got us stuff to smoke.

For a moment you want to stay in the room with the plants, the cheesy velvet prints of divas, the arabesques, the huge TV.

See you, you say.

Fuck it, why is everyone so down my throat tonight.

You touch Patrick's shoulder once before turning out the door.

Thanks, you smile, slow.

He nods.

You pause one full beat.

You can feel Sue's body racing after you as you turn down the hall.

EVERYTHING I HAVE IS BLUE

What do you want me do with your drugs!
Fuck it. Keep them. Have a good time.
He throws up his arms. You don't have to tell him. He will.

FOOD CHAIN
Jim Grimsley

In the morning he made himself bathe and dress again, down to thirty-five dollars and forty cents, his stomach in knots, but when he looked in the mirror he still thought he looked all right, his black hair neatly combed, his smooth skin between the color of sand and brown hen's eggs, his nice lips, and in the T-shirt his shoulders had a good shape, you could tell he wasn't all skin and bones. Looking in the mirror he thought better of himself, and the panic about money subsided. This could be the day he found a job, after all. He walked to the Circle K, and the manager, Curtis, was there, in the middle of a rush, and could only pause to talk to Newell for a moment. Newell figured that meant bad news, and Curtis kept rushing from table to table anyway, so that Newell had to stand and wait. Curtis pushed by with a tray full of plates and glasses and said, "The dishwasher didn't quit, but wait a minute," and turned the corner, with Newell's heart sinking, there was no job, the dishwasher stayed, and here was suddenly Curtis again in his face. "But the busboy left. Do you want to be a busboy?"

He grinned, he could hardly believe what he was hearing. "Sure."

"Well, I can't stop to talk to you right now. Come back this afternoon about three o'clock. Can you start Tuesday?"

"Sure. That's fine."

"Good. Come back and talk to me this afternoon."

Curtis rushed away and Newell went on standing there dumbfounded. After a while he realized he had to leave, the place was too busy for him to go on standing there, so he drifted to the door, walked outside, realized he could relax now, the anxious feeling could dissolve. He would come back this afternoon, he would talk to Curtis, he would go to work as a busboy. He figured that was the job Curtis had been doing while he was talking to Newell, clearing the tables and carrying the dishes to the dishwasher and setting the tables again. For doing this he would earn money, and it was only the third of June, he had plenty of time to earn the rent. He felt himself relaxing over and over again. He could stay.

At three o'clock he stepped through the door to the restaurant again. The tables in the various rooms that he could see were mostly empty now, a few pairs of men or women sipping coffee or glasses of water. Curtis was sitting at the desk crammed against the corner near what had once been a door leading to the back gallery of someone's house. He had Newell sit down and fill out some papers, explained the tax forms to Newell and showed him how to do those. He told Newell the job paid four dollars fifty cents an hour plus tips. The waiters he worked with would each tip him at the end of their shifts. How much would depend on how busy the restaurant was, but if Newell felt like he was being cheated, he could say so. Had he ever worked in a restaurant before? Well, that didn't matter. What mattered in the Circle K was that Newell could keep the tables clean, keep the water glasses filled, and look cute while he was doing it so people would keep coming back to the restaurant to see him. Curtis said that with a perfectly straight face, and when Newell giggled, Curtis merely smiled, though in a rather tired way. "You don't think I'm kidding, do you? I wouldn't hire you if you weren't cute, sweetheart. Not to work out front."

He would work breakfast and lunch shifts Tuesday through Sunday, with Monday off. He was due at work by 6:30 a.m. every day except Sunday, when the restaurant opened later, and he would get off work by two in the afternoon. Absorbing every detail as if his life depended on it, Newell studied the rooms, the neatly placed wooden tables, the framed prints on the wall, drawings of men with no shirts and tight pants, big crotches, big eyes with long lashes, in pairs or groups, eyeing one another greedily.

"When is payday?" Newell asked.

"End of shift on Tuesday. For the week before. But you'll get your tips every day."

Walking home, Newell could hardly believe it, that it was done, that he had a job, that he started in three days, that he would have to get up very early every morning, even earlier than for the IGA; he would have to buy a cheap alarm clock, he couldn't rely on his watch. But he could buy an alarm clock out of the thirty-five dollars he had left, a sum that appeared more substantial now that it only had to last a few days. He could buy something to eat besides soup, and starting on Tuesday, he could eat two meals a day for free at the restaurant.

He called his grandmother, Flora, the next day, to tell her he had found a job. He caught her at home with a headache on Sunday morning, puffing her cigarette audibly, sipping coffee and trying to clear her throat. "Honey, I am so glad you called me."

"Yes ma'am. Well, it's good news, don't you think?"

"Well, I hope you don't have to work in food service for very long," she intimated. "Jesse has been in food service his whole life and look where that's got him."

"Yes ma'am." Newell understood from this that Jesse, Flora's boyfriend, was sitting at the kitchen table too, scratching his nose or the inside of his ear, looking completely vacant as he usually looked in the morning.

"You being careful in that French Quarter?"

"Yes ma'am. But I don't think it's dangerous."

"You'd be surprised."

"Really. I been walking around since I got here, even at night, and I never feel like anybody is following me, or anything."

"Well," she took a puff on the cigarette, "you walk around with that kind of careless attitude and somebody will drag you off in an alley one of these days, you watch. And nobody will know what happened to you."

"Yes ma'am."

"I know what I'm talking about. There's things that happen in New Orleans that you'd rather not even imagine." Her words took on a curious authority over the long-distance line. Jesse must have coughed, with the cigarette smoke swirling around him in that trailer kitchen, because Flora snapped, "Go in the living room if you can't stand my smoke, you tattooed son of a bitch."

"Are you going to church, Grandma?"

"No. I didn't get my dress out of the cleaners this week." They had made this joke before, they both laughed and felt better, and he imagined Jesse sulking in front of the TV with his toes buried in the shag carpet. "It's a lot of Catholics in New Orleans," Flora noted.

"I know. There's a great big church they go to. In a square right here in the French Quarter."

"I know exactly the one you're talking about," she agreed, and after a moment said her phone bill would be sky high with the two of them gabbing about nothing. They said goodbye and there he stood across from the Verti Mart on Sunday morning. Wondering why he had asked about Mama, after such a long time. Wondering what had put her on his mind.

On Tuesday he woke up when the clock said 5:30 a.m. He had hardly ever waked up so early before, and he stumbled to the bathtub and ran hot water. He lay in the tub waking and sleeping, waking and sleeping, 'til finally he washed and rinsed himself as best he could. Got dressed in jeans and a shirt, like the other guys he had seen in the restaurant.

He headed for the Circle K with plenty of time. Some people were already seated in the dining room, and a thin waiter in a tight T-shirt slouched over them, writing down their order. Curtis was at his desk, looking half asleep, yawning as Curtis walked in.

"Oh, hi, it's you," Curtis said, and yawned again. He showed Newell the kitchen setup, introduced him to Felix the breakfast cook, and Alan the morning waiter. Umberto the prep guy was out back washing out the garbage can with a hose, visible through the open screen door.

Newell picked up dishes and brought people water. When they were gone, he cleaned off tables. He was the only busboy for the breakfast shift, until Tyrone came in at eight. The job seemed easy until the tables were full, and then he was walking back and forth from the kitchen through all the dining rooms and back again, one thousand times at least. Curtis helped him at first, then sat back and only pitched in to clean a table when there were too many for Newell to handle.

Whenever Newell looked that way, he found Curtis watching him, though pretty soon he was too busy to notice what Curtis was doing. Alan tapped Newell on the shoulder and said, "Those people have been asking for water for fifteen minutes. You need to move your behind." Or came up to him and said, "If you can't clean these tables any faster than this, I'm not going to tip you. I could do it myself this quick." Or, while passing to the kitchen, said, "Come back here and help me take out these plates to that party of eight. That woman at that table has an attitude about me." A woman was in fact scowling at them both, and Newell set her plate in front of her. She asked for something and he took the message back to Alan, and Alan said, "Well, here, take it to her," and what it was, Tabasco, turned out to be a bottle of hot sauce that she sprayed over her eggs. So that half the morning he spent running around doing what Alan told him to do and the rest trying to keep from listening while Alan harangued him because his own work wasn't getting done.

Help came and things settled down, and sooner than he could have guessed, the rush was done and Curtis clapped him on the back as he came through the kitchen door. "You got through it."

"It was all right," Newell said.

"Except you're so slow and clumsy," Alan added from the side.

"Shut up, Alan," Curtis said.

"I will not shut up. He's slow and he's clumsy with the plates."

"He didn't break anything."

Alan whirled away with his order pad. Curtis watched him go and said, "You did okay. But you need to wear a tighter T-shirt."

"A what?"

Curtis laughed nervously. "Your jeans are all right but your T-shirt's not tight enough. You need to wear a tight one. We have to keep the queens happy."

In the lull between breakfast and lunch, he ate his own eggs and bacon, served without a word by Felix, who watched Newell eat the first couple of bites, then grunted and lumbered back to the kitchen. Alan ate his breakfast, too, but sat at a different table than Newell, refusing to look at him or speak to him. But by then there were other waiters, Frank and Stuart, and they were friendlier than Alan, and cuter.

Lunch shift shocked him with its intensity, so many dishes on the tables, so many empty water glasses, everything to be done at once, and people crammed into the restaurant, leaving only the narrowest space through which Newell could slide. He moved as fast as he could, did everything he could see to do, and hoped for the best. His whole mind focused itself on the need to note the level of water in a glass across a room despite cigarette smoke swirling in the air and bodies moving this way and that across his field of vision; he concentrated on the balance required to haul a heavy tray of dishes over the heads of the customers, who were often staring at him as he moved, trying to make eye contact. He was assigned to Alan's and Stuart's sections and kept them clean as best he could, kept the customers flowing through, kept the water glasses full and picked up the used napkins from the floor, but even so, Alan found plenty to criticize, that he was setting the tables the wrong way, that he took forever to fill a simple pitcher of water. That he was bumping into the customers as he walked, that he was so slow he couldn't help to carry out the food.

At the end of the shift, Stuart tipped him eight dollars and some change and Alan refused to tip him at all, at first, until Curtis and Stuart took him aside and talked to him for a while, after which he gave Newell four dollars even and said, "You're lucky I give you that much, as slow as you are. I think you're in the wrong line of work, honey."

"Don't pay any attention to her," Stuart said, indicating Alan. "Her stars are all in the wrong place this month."

"Fuck off, Stuart."

Stuart smiled and glided away. Newell imitated the glide, though not the smile, and said, "I'll see you tomorrow, Alan."

So his first day was over, and all he had to think about for tomorrow was finding a tight T-shirt to wear. He tried on the ones he had brought from Pastel, all six of them, including the one that had Bruce Springsteen's picture on the front; that one was tight, and one other green one from high school was also a bit tight.

He put the twelve dollars and some change from his tips with the rest of his money, which grew to nearly fifty dollars again. The fact pleased him, and he thought, *I can start saving for the rent right now.*

But at work the next day, with Newell in the Springsteen T-shirt, relations with Alan were even worse. Every dish Newell touched was the wrong one, every time he carried out the water glass he went to the wrong side of the restaurant first, or when Alan asked him for a simple glass of orange juice he needed ten minutes to find it. By the lunch shift, Newell was wondering what bothered Alan so much about him.

"He really liked Travis, the last guy," Stuart told him when they were eating breakfast together, Stuart lowering his voice to float just over his eggs and potatoes. "But Curtis fired Travis for coming in late all the night and then not showing up one day, and Alan has been pouting ever since."

"That doesn't have anything to do with me."

"Honey, to a princess like Alan, that does not matter one little bit."

"It's because you're cuter than he is," Frank said, sitting with the two of them with a cup of coffee. The restaurant had gotten quiet around ten thirty, just before lunch would start. "And younger."

Alan, sitting alone at the window, legs crossed like a girl, smoked a slow drawling cigarette, his elbows sharp and dark against the window. Hair combed straight back, long sharp nose, thin lips, narrow eyes, soft chin. His parts had a look of hanging together only loosely, an uncertain whole. *He's not cute*, Newell realized and then, at the same moment, *but I am. I am cute.*

Curtis had that day off, but came back for the next, when Newell wore the tight green T-shirt from high school and the tight faded jeans with a slight flare at the bottom. Curtis said the T-shirt was better, was more like what he had in mind, and all morning he found reasons to talk to Newell, helping him with tables during the breakfast rush. Newell had to concentrate on his work and hardly thought about Curtis or what he might be up to, but as the morning wore on, he noted that Stuart was angry about something. He began to harangue Newell pretty much as Alan continued to do—get the water faster, there's too much ice in the pitcher, this orange juice is sour, didn't you check it?

For breakfast, Felix prepared Newell a nice omelet, a change from the usual eggs. Frank handed Newell the plate, noting, "Well, I guess Felix is in love with you too."

"What do you mean?"

"He never fixes omelets, you have to beg him."

For Frank, Felix had made the usual breakfast, scrambled eggs and bacon, potatoes on the side.

"Who else is in love with me?"

Frank laughed. "Are you kidding?"

"No."

"Well, darling, Curtis is following you around like a puppy. It's got Stuart all upset. Haven't you even noticed? You cold bitch."

From there on through lunch he did notice that Curtis was more or less following him around the restaurant, and Stuart was watching the whole thing, slamming dishes around and getting in a fight with Umberto the prep cook about the bad salad. Alan was meanwhile sitting calmly by the window, puffing the usual cigarette, off his feet for a moment, as he called it, but glaring at Newell whenever he passed.

You cold bitch. He liked the ring of the words, though he had simply been oblivious and not really cold. But he liked that he had appeared so to Frank.

The work was what absorbed him, the novelty of it, which he knew would wear away; but for the moment it was what he needed. Alan and Stuart tipped him, if poorly, and his stock of cash grew, if slowly.

Payday was coming. Saturdays and Sundays, the restaurant was busy from the time it opened till the time Newell got off, and the customers were all in a jolly mood, ordering big tall glasses of tomato juice and vodka. The dining rooms became so crowded that every trip he made through the mazes of chairs and tables became a performance, and he became easy at making eye contact with the customers for the most fleeting of moments, but enough to fulfill the apparent requirement; he twisted and shimmied through the chairs with his pitcher, his tray, his cloths for cleaning, and he forgot whether Curtis was watching him or not, he forgot whether anybody liked him, he did what he was supposed to do and remembered that he was getting paid money for it, and with the money he could pay his rent, and with that accomplished he could stay here, in the city.

Monday he slept late, luxuriating in the bed 'til long after sunrise, then getting up and taking enough money to buy breakfast, not at the Circle K, god forbid, but at the White Biscuit, where he got a table to himself. He liked the thought that he could afford to buy his own breakfast out of money he had brought home last night, money he had meant to spend in the bar. The waiter kept watching him a moment longer than necessary for all the transactions, and Newell thought it was nice to get the attention but pretended not to notice.

In the afternoon he went to the adult bookstore. He waited 'til the heat of the day, when his room was becoming too close for comfort, and he walked across the Quarter to the building with the fine galleries. Today the carriageway was open and a car was pulling out, a long white car with tinted windows. The car glided past Newell slowly, and he waited for it to turn onto the street before he went inside.

He stepped into the fluorescent light, walked down the long dark passage to the lit counter where the same bored Louis was slumped over the cash register with his chin in his hands. The pattern of his acne had changed, but the T-shirt was the same. Newell stepped toward the room where the men's magazines lined the walls and at the same moment, from a curtain at the back, the old guy Mac appeared. Today Newell noticed a big mole on his cheek and his saggy, wrinkled facial skin, his rounded, soft belly with his pants pulled up high, the white short-sleeved shirt with the pens and pack of cigarettes in the pocket, the T-shirt visible beneath, and the belt buckle in the shape of a leaping dolphin. He had come out of the curtained doorway near Newell and stood there watching the magazines briefly as if taking an inventory. He said, matter-of-factly, "We got some good new stuff in here this week. Good thing you came back."

Newell nodded.

"Let me know if you need any help finding what you want," the man said politely. "But take your time and look all you want." He started to shuffle off but then paused, leaned forward, and snagged a magazine to hand to Newell. "This one," he said. "You like this guy, don't you?"

He shuffled over to the cash register and lit into Louis about sticking his gum on the edge of the stool; Newell heard the words but he was already lost looking at the cover of the magazine, where he saw Rod the Rock, shirtless and tied to a wall or a post with his hands raised over his head and a look on his face of pain or fear, and though the picture might be posed the pain or fear seemed real, and Newell gripped the magazine tight.

This one cost even more than the other, fifteen dollars, and Newell had only that much in his pocket. His heart sank at the thought, because he had not meant to spend so much money when he came here. But his heart was pounding and his grip tightened on the magazine. He glanced at the cover again, at the black-and-white photo of the big man's body, of his face with that unearthly expression, and at the title, *Bonds of Love*. From the cash register, Mac watched, belly sagging onto the counter, magazines fanned out in front of him, the greasy-faced boy hanging behind his shoulder. Mac's hair was neatly combed and oiled straight back over his skull and Newell could smell the hair oil all the way across the room. Mac watched Newell without any self-consciousness while taking a cigarette out of a packet in his shirt pocket, raising it to his lips, and lighting it. Finally Newell stepped up to the cash register and pulled out his money.

"I thought you might like that one." Mac rang up the sale while Newell stared at the other magazines, afraid to answer. Mac shoved the magazine into a bag and folded the top over, fastening it with a strip of tape. He handed the package to Newell. "Come back to see us."

"Yes sir," Newell said, and wondered why he had said it, "sir."

But Mac simply watched him as if the "yes sir" had not surprised him at all, and said, "I could use some smart people around here, anyway. I got nothing but dumb asses working for me. Like Louis here. You're a dumb ass, ain't you, Louis?"

Louis had been squeezing a pimple near his temple, an angry purple rise, but stopped when he heard his name, blinked, and said, "I ain't so dumb, Mr. Mac. It's just too many magazines to keep up with."

"Yeah you dumb shit, you're a dumb ass, all right." He winked at Newell, who blushed and turned away, and at the doorway paused when Mac said, "Good night, son. We get the new magazines on Thursdays, come on back and take a look."

He took the magazine home and spread it out on the bed. The cover promised something harsh, and inside was a picture of Rod trussed up in chains, hanging in a sling, a kerchief through his mouth. Rod Hardigan in the magazine had been captured by a gigantic hairy blond man, stripped and tied up, and page after page he was forced to do things, endure tortures, pains. Some of the pictures shocked Newell, Rod being penetrated by various objects, and he only glanced at them but even so he could vividly remember these glimpses, the blond man shoving a long dark stick inside Rod from behind, and pinching Rod's nipples with metal clamps, other pictures that Newell had turned quickly past. What amazed Newell was the look on the face of Rod, the almost starvation, almost ecstasy, almost oblivion in his eyes, as if they had become windows on a hollow space. As if inside Rod the Rock were an emptiness waiting for this, nothing else.

He stayed in the room that night, washed his Springsteen T-shirt by hand, spread it out carefully to dry. The magazine lay facedown on the bedside table. A banner across the top read, "The bondage that is love," with a picture of Rod with his hands tied behind his back, face down on a bench looking backward at the camera, his fleshy ass exposed, his feet padlocked together, altogether helpless. *Bonds of Love*. He lay the magazine in the bottom of the wardrobe on top of the copy of *Brute Hombre*, and he went to bed,

He overslept by a few minutes the next day, and arrived at work a few minutes late, only to find the place in an uproar. Alan had caught Umberto looking in Curtis' desk drawers without permission, presumably for the cash bag from last night, as if it would still be there. Everybody was shrieking at everybody and the dozen or so customers sat struck with a mild astonishment. Newell went back to the office to the time clock and stuck his card into the punch slot. Alan said, "Well, Umberto, if you're so innocent, what were you doing in there?"

"I was looking for a book of matches."

"We have matches right at the register."

"I wasn't at the register."

"Well, ten steps would have taken you right there. You were not looking for any matches."

"Everybody knows Curtis takes the deposit to the bank at night."

"Sometimes he doesn't."

Umberto waved his hand at Alan and headed back to the kitchen, and Alan followed him there to argue with him some more. Alan came out in a few minutes and spotted Newell with an empty tray, heading to the tables where the customers were paying their bills and fleeing. "And don't think I didn't notice you were late."

"I forgot to turn on the alarm," Newell said.

"Convenient to be so forgetful. When the rest of us have to do double work."

"It was only a few minutes, Alan," he said, but this time he looked Alan in the eye. Alan wavered and looked away. Newell cleared the empty tables, his stomach already in a knot, and the week was only an hour old.

At the end of the shift Curtis handed Newell a pay envelope and gave him a receipt to sign. Inside was a check for one hundred and fourteen dollars and thirteen cents. "I can cash it for you if you sign it over to me," Curtis said, and Newell waited, and Curtis looked at him, and then turned the check over and said, "Sign it across here. Sign your name."

So he rushed home and put all his money together, and had over a hundred ninety five dollars, nearly enough to pay the rent in just one week. Now he felt better about buying *Bonds of Love* for fifteen dollars. Especially since he'd been afraid to look at the magazine once he saw what was in it. He sat on the edge of the bed with the folded money in his hand. The room, small as it was, could belong to him now.

On Bourbon Street he bought a tight, white T-shirt with the words "Vieux Carre" printed across it, and the outline of an ornate gallery, intricate ironwork, in shiny blue appliqué. He bought a small and figured he couldn't get any tighter than that, so he paid seven dollars for the T-shirt and felt pleased that he would have something new to wear tomorrow.

The next day, in the T-shirt, he felt as though he were putting on a show in the restaurant, slipping between the tables, with men watching him from all sides, and some of them flirting, trying to talk to him. Later, Curtis called Newell to his office and said, "You're really getting into this, babycake."

"I like it all right," Newell said, but he felt suddenly uncomfortable, knowing Stuart was somewhere in the dining rooms, watching all this.

"How long have you lived in town?"

"I just got here a couple of weeks ago."

"That's too sweet," Curtis said, and his tone offended Newell, something about it he could not place, but Newell showed nothing except that he was listening. "Anyway, you seem like you're settling in all right."

Stuart appeared suddenly in the doorway, across from Newell, close enough to touch, and smiled in a brittle way. "You two look so comfortable together."

Curtis turned to face the wall, lifting a pencil. "Stuart, did you want to talk about something?"

"No, Curtis, I just wanted to find out how much you two have to talk about, you know?"

They were staring at each other now. Curtis had started to blush again, and Stuart was about to start an argument. Newell figured it was a good time to leave, and so he did, with Alan waiting for him at the server's station, complaining that there was not even a pitcher's worth of ice in the bin, Newell needed to bring in some ice, where had he been anyway, the little nitwit?

He went to Lafitte's after work, still wearing the T-shirt, taking a seat in the upstairs bar. The cool beer soothed his nerves, three in the afternoon and him drinking, you'd think he was Flora or Jesse. He had quarters from his tips and played the jukebox, a song he had started to like, Dire Straits, "Sultans of Swing," and some other songs that went with it, a nice set. Sitting on the barstool, he could only sway a bit to the music, but he felt himself content. He stayed in the bar long enough to spend three dollars on beer, an achievement, with prices as cheap as they were, but when he walked out of the bar he felt better about the world, more like he could face going back to that job tomorrow.

The next day, Thursday, Alan was off work so at least there was only Stuart to worry about, and he appeared to have made up with Curtis, because they were both acting very warm and friendly toward one another. Stuart hung out in the doorway talking to Curtis and looking back at Newell to see if he was getting the message. Newell ignored the drama, bussed his tables, and did his other duties, ate his eggs when Felix cooked them and tried to stay out of the way.

Stuart and Frank tipped out and left the restaurant, Stuart lingering for a while to hover over Curtis, while Newell was still eating his lunch. He felt the comfort of his day's tip money in his pocket. Stuart kissed Curtis goodbye on the lips and left the restaurant. Curtis hardly waited for Stuart to get out of sight before he sat down with Newell himself. He was watching Newell. Something hangdog in his air. "You doing all right, Newell?"

"Sure."

"Things are working out pretty good for you, here."

"Yeah. I like it."

"Stuart likes you."

Newell gave him a look.

"No, I mean it. He's fine about you. Look." He pulled his chair closer to Newell. "You could probably be a waiter, don't you think? Those guys pull down the real tips."

Newell felt something pressing on his midsection, a strange pressure that he had never felt before, a bit hard to breathe while Curtis was sitting so close, talking so low. "I'm fine with being a busboy."

"But you'd like to make the real money."

He let that go. Curtis was still watching him. After a while, Newell wiped his mouth with the napkin and laid it across his plate. "I like to make money, that's a fact."

"Well, then," Curtis said, but he was looking down at his plate. "I'll have to see what I can do about it."

"See you tomorrow."

"Why don't you sit for a while? Talk to me."

"I have something I have to do," Newell said.

"You sure?" Curtis asked, and there was something suddenly cool in his aspect.

"Yes. I have a friend coming over to my house."

Curtis nodded.

"See you."

Curtis nodded again, staring down at the table.

Umberto had been watching the whole time, and partway through the scene brought Felix to the kitchen door to witness too.

Newell walked out of the restaurant with a sinking feeling, already dreading the next morning. Curtis was off the next day but Stuart was working and it was clear that Stuart had heard something. He was cold and unfriendly to Newell all day, and that coupled with Alan's continual harangues made the day nearly impossible. The next day was Saturday, and Curtis was working even though it was usually his day off. He treated Newell very coldly all day. But there was so much business in the restaurant, nobody had time to say very much to anybody. At the end of the day Alan left with the restaurant still full, Curtis interviewing people in the office, the rumor going around that Curtis was hiring another waiter.

When Curtis went out of his way to say goodbye to Newell in the coldest tones possible, in front of Stuart, Newell left the restaurant fearing the worst. In fact, it was as bad as he expected, because the next morning, a Sunday, a new busboy was on duty when Newell came to work, and Curtis called Newell to the office and fired him very first thing. Almost a week's pay for the days he had worked since the last payday, plus an extra fifty for getting fired, as best Newell could understand it.

"What did I do?" Newell asked.

Curtis shrugged, looked down at his desk.

"You were too disruptive," Alan said, passing the door. "Nobody could get along with you."

"Was this because I wouldn't go out with you?" Newell asked.

Curtis never answered at all, going back to his books, and Newell asked, "Well, what am I supposed to do now?"

"Leave, honey," Alan said. "It's just that simple."

In a daze, he headed back to his room. He went upstairs immediately and counted out two hundred fifty dollars from what he had, leaving him about forty dollars. This was the rent; he put it aside. The forty dollars would have to keep him alive till he got another job. He had a couple of cans of soup and some crackers left from when he had been employed; at least Curtis could have fired him after breakfast. Could you really be fired because you didn't care when your boss flirted with you? Newell ate a can of soup slowly to make it last longer, counted his money again while he did, discouraged that the folded bills and precise stacks of coins added up to such a tiny sum. The hot soup calmed his belly and he felt less anxious and tried to lie across the bed, but when he did, with the afternoon sun slanting across his belly through the slats of the blinds, when he drifted toward sleep he felt his belly rumbling as if hungry again and turned over on his side and counted his money again in his head, worried that it would not be enough. He had meant to stay in the house, but with thoughts like these churning in his head, he sprang up from the bed and splashed water on his face, folded the money into his pocket, and went out walking along the boulevard. But whenever he saw a sign for help wanted, he surged first toward the door of the business and then away from it. Sunday, it wouldn't do any good to ask, most places the managers didn't even work on Sundays. His heart pounded and he talked himself out of each opportunity, and walked away, and finally drifted toward the bars again.

He went into a bar and got one of the cocktails that worked so well to dull his thinking before. He moved from bar to bar. Late in the evening, in the Bourbon Pub among a lot of men dressed like cowboys in flannel shirts, cowboy boots, and belts with ornate silver buckles, Newell felt a wave of nausea pass through him and sank to the barstool and hung his head down. There was a drink in his hand, somewhere distant, and he concentrated on that, because he knew if he did not keep the thought of it in his head he would drop the glass, and that would be unpardonable, to drop the drink glass, with the whole bar watching. The bar was spinning and the music was making him dizzy, but he thought he was okay sitting there, he thought the nausea was going away and he was acting pretty normal, he thought he blended in pretty well, until someone leaned into his face and asked, "Honey, are you all right?"

In the morning, Newell woke to a pounding head like nothing he had ever imagined and a feeling that his stomach was slowly wringing itself inside out. As soon as he dared sit up, the flashes of agony in his head and the topsy-turvy state of his stomach sent him reeling to the bathroom, where he hung against the toilet and heaved bitter-tasting, yellow bile into the toilet bowl. After a while he rinsed his mouth and brushed his teeth and rinsed his mouth again, and he wanted to take a bath but his head throbbed with sharp bursts of pain. He had broken out in a sweat and hung on the sink looking at himself in the mirror, his hair matted in clumps of curls, his eyes ringed with shade, skin so pale it was almost blue. He drank a cup of water and waited to see whether his stomach would accept it, ran a tub of water and slid into it, sweating into the hot water with his head throbbing.

He found his clothes from the night before and went through all the pockets. Laying out the money, counting all the bills and change, he found he had nineteen dollars left. He had expected to find he had spent all forty dollars or something like that, he remembered drinks in the disco and in the Bourbon Pub, but now to find out he only had nineteen dollars! His heart sank at the thought, and he searched all the pockets again, and came up with another dime and a nickel, and added them to his careful piles. Sitting there dumbfounded, he stared at the money as if willing it to grow.

He slept through the rest of Monday, got up for a while, too depressed to do much more than eat chicken noodle soup and go back to bed.

In the morning, he woke up and bathed, his head still tender but no longer throbbing. He went to breakfast because he was starving from the day before and ate a big omelette and a lot of potatoes and toast, and he felt better after that, though the meal cost five dollars with the tip. He bought a *Times-Picayune* and read the want ads in his room. He sat on the front gallery with all his money in an envelope in his hand, and he listened to the sounds of the city in the hot afternoon and felt its strangeness and indifference, and this scrap of money in his hand was all that protected him.

He slept for a while that afternoon, real sleep, with the effects of all that alcohol finally gone, and when he woke he went for a walk and ended up, he never knew quite how, at the adult bookstore on St. Ann. This time of day the cool, high-ceilinged room was mostly empty, but Louis was nowhere to be seen. Mac himself slouched behind the cash register, a cigarillo in his fingertips, brown and thin, trailing a signature of smoke up toward the drop lights. He had something on his mind and merely nodded at Newell when he passed, which made Newell shy, so he strayed along the shelves of magazines and scanned them. Standing in front of the magazines that had women and men on them, the women shoving their breasts toward the camera, bending over to show the creases and pinknesses of their inner parts, sometimes sprawled on a bed with a man hovering over them, a man with a pale, flat, white ass and a limber cock in his hand, and the woman staring up at him and pretending to have some expression on her face that somebody told her to try to have, and all the while the invisible camera hovered there, and their relationship was with the camera, and with Newell, and with anyone who wanted to watch. Newell thought this effect must come from the fact that the regular magazines were not made as well as the magazines that had only men in them, because the magazines with only men seemed very real and exciting to him, while these big-breasted women and sag-assed men were flat and lifeless.

"You like that stuff too?" Mac surprised him, walking over from the cash register, scarcely lifting the cigarillo from his lips.

Newell blinked and watched him.

"You like this stuff too?"

Newell shook his head. "Not much."

"I didn't think so."

They blinked at each other in mild surprise. They were suddenly watching as if they might know each other, in a friendly way, nothing too personal, and Newell became less nervous. He moved away from the racks of magazines with their endless sets of breasts and big gaping nipples, and Mac gestured to him and said, "Come look at these."

He lifted a stack of magazines to the counter. These had not yet been wrapped in their plastic covers, and Newell lifted each one and smelled it and opened it. Every kind of magazine offered itself, magazines with thin pale boys, smooth bulbous asses, a little fat at the lower back; with tall lanky men in cowboy hats, sometimes with cowboy clothes on, maybe a vest or chaps or just boots; with men who were dressed like sailors in a cheap motel room, or what looked like a cheap motel room, though it might have been someone's cheap apartment or even a room in a mobile home in Pastel, Alabama, and the sailor men taking off their clothes, and one was thickly muscled and one was thin and hairy, and they both had moles on their butt cheeks; but occasionally one of the magazines contained someone beautiful and he felt his tongue go thick, and these he laid aside in a pile, as if by instinct, since Mac had only asked that he come and look. He spent some time sorting the stack into the magazines that he liked and the ones that he didn't care much about. Now and then Mac would chuckle and say, "You like that one," or, "There ain't much to that one, right?" Pointing with the little cigar.

A couple of other customers came in but Newell and Mac went on talking, even when Mac was taking the money, making change, answering the phone. Newell helped put the magazines into the plastic covers, and to tape them shut, and write up the price tags. He had heard Mac mention this sort of task to Louis, and knew he was up to something but wasn't altogether sure what it was until he had a thought, and asked, "Where's the guy that works here?"

"Louis? That fucked up motherfucker? He don't work here no more."

"No?"

"His ass is gone back to Mississippi where he the fuck belongs."

"That's too bad," Newell said.

Mac fixed a look on him and chewed on the end of a match. "You want his job?"

"You bet I do."

"You want to start right now?"

A weight lifted off Newell and he took a deep breath and took a look around the store. The fluorescent lights were humming in the sweetest way. "Yes, sir."

"You ever cashier before?"

So Mac began to teach him how to work the cash register, and pretty soon Newell stood on the other side of the counter, and he relaxed, and he was able to breathe for the first time since Curtis fired him the day before, maybe even since he stepped off the bus that first morning on Tulane Avenue. He learned the operation of the cash register without trouble and soon he was making change or ringing up sales himself with Mac supervising, arms folded; Newell's first sale was a magazine called *Suck City* with women and men on the cover, and for the rest of the day Mac sipped root beer and sat on the stool while Newell operated the cash register, made change, and checked in magazines from below the counter, ticking them off on a handwritten invoice sheet that he could barely read, then bagging them and pricing them and, with Mac's advice, moving them to the shelves.

That night, in bed, satisfied, having eaten two whole cans of chicken noodle soup, he stared at the shadowed stains on the ceiling and was aware of the ridiculous smile on his face, here on a day that had begun so badly and that was ending so well. Visions of naked breasts and stiff nipples rose before his eyes, and something in that parade of body parts pleased him, as if he had found something for which he was destined. He would continue to have money now. He would be able to call Flora and tell her he had a job at a bookstore, and she would think that was nice, and she would not worry about him so much, and he would leave out the part about the exact type of bookstore, and everything would be fine. She would stop being afraid he was about to go bad.

GOOD FRIDAY

Alfredo Ronci

Translated by Wendell Ricketts[1]

*"Human beings live their lives in constant search for the idealized or
remembered father."*
—Anna Maria Ortese, *Alonso e i Visionari*

Nasty weather. Not enough to cause any undue concern, but for my
sister, nasty weather meant Good Friday. For years I had tried to
understand if the weather was bad because it was Good Friday or if it
was Good Friday because the weather was bad. The simplest calendar—
or just a little common sense—would have made clear that the latter
hypothesis could be jettisoned. But the first one did allow a consideration of the unique character of geography.

Did that mean, for instance, that the weather was bad all over
Europe? And in those countries where Catholicism had taken hold? In
that case, excluding Asia, Russia, the Balkan Peninsula, and the major
part of Africa, Good Friday ought to be a very nasty day indeed. Still, I
wondered what the weather could be like for the sixteen percent of
Catholics on the Island of Tonga or in the Federated States of
Micronesia.

By the age of fifteen I had already understood that meteorology was
capable of expressing ugliness in a thousand different ways. March and
April would surely bring rain to Italy, snow or frigid temperatures to
Northern Europe, a dense and threatening overcast to Central America,
drought to the Christian part of Africa. All of that remained true, my
quasi-religious and semiscientific doubts notwithstanding.

That day the weather was nasty, but it wasn't Good Friday.

Nicola had been looking for me. Somehow I'd managed to avoid
him. I didn't even know why I did it, but I had no doubt that our little
role-play was just as beneficial for him as it was for me.

His excessive worrying and his habit of making so much of my
absences aggravated me no end. He said I tried to avoid the respon-

[1] Kind thanks go to Emanuela Canali of Oscar Mondadori, the publishers of the *Men on Men*
series (Daniele Scalise, ed.) in which "Venerdì santo" first appeared, and to Alfredo Ronci for
permission to include this story in this collection. I am indebted to Fabrizio Rossi and, in
particular, to Alessandro Amenta for their insights and many helpful suggestions regarding
the translation.

sibilities of couplehood. The phrase—the way he said it—embarrassed me, not because I didn't share the idea of a union as complete as the one he imagined, but because it made me think too much of *family*, of an institutionalization of our emotions that cut me like a knife.

And yet he'd used every lover's trick in the book to try to win me over, including telling me how the former Secretary of the Italian Communist Party, Luigi Longo, had been the source of his awareness of his sexuality.

In August 1968, when Nicola was ten, he discovered he was homosexual just as the Warsaw Pact troops were running rampant through the streets of Prague.

"Could you tell me what in hell that has to do with anything?" I'd asked him.

"It has to do with it because my father was anxiously awaiting the Italian Communist Party's official statement on the matter."

"And so?"

"And then it came, but only because Armando Cossutta tracked Longo down with a phone call to the Soviet embassy. Longo happened to be visiting Moscow at that very moment."

"I still don't understand."

"My dad was an old-style Communist. And he was worried."

"Worried about what?"

"That the Italian Communist Party would lose credibility in the eyes of Italians. But what happened instead was that, in the middle of the election campaign, the Party leadership expressed '*the solidarity of Italian Communists with the brave struggle of Czechoslovakian Communists for the defense and the empowerment of socialism in their country and for the full development of socialist democracy.*'"

He recited the communiqué with his eyes closed, making all the necessary pauses and reserving the most dramatic emphasis for the final reference to socialist democracy.

"And you?"

"I took advantage of the fact that my father was so happy and locked myself in the bathroom with a soccer card that had a picture of Pierino Prati on it."

"And that's when you realized who you were."

"Yeah, but that wasn't the only thing...."

When he kissed me for the first time he told me how he'd stolen 230,000 lire from the Radical Party.

"I was in charge of a table for a referendum they were holding, collecting signatures and contributions."

"You stole from the donation box?"

"No. I stole right out of the hands of the people who were paying their dues."

"And no one ever caught on?"

"There was a notary there to verify people's signatures, but he winked at me when I put the last of the money in my pocket. Then when we closed up the table he came over and invited me to have a drink with him."

I never understood why Nicola told me all of this, how his sex drive had gotten mixed up with political debates about abolishing hunting and fishing, the art of petting with arguments over whether or not to remove a branch of the police force from under the control of the defense ministry.

Perhaps he wasn't confident that he could offer with his body what he could provide with his words. And yet that white, gymnastic figure fascinated me, putting me in mind of milk and of sports. He taught me that allowing oneself to become obsessed with some cliché of physical perfection was a true obscenity.

His smooth stride pleased me, slightly unbalanced as it was toward the right, with a head that, rather than act as a counterweight, accentuated his posture: he described an arc in space, the outline of a bird cage for hunchbacked parakeets.

I was much less pleased by the fact that he had placed so much hope in me—expectations beyond all dignity. It meant recreating my father, bringing back to life a newly youthful parent with whom we could play out—painfully—another thirty years.

"You exhaust me," I told him one day when he was far away: New York. "It's like carrying you around on my shoulders all day long."

When he came home again he was a rag. He'd lost so much weight and was so thin that at first I thought he'd deliberately misunderstood my meaning.

"I don't want you thin. You didn't understand a damn thing I said. I love you, if that's the issue, even when you're gone—with my mind and body. But most of the time you go around here like some worn-out elephant."

"I'm what? I do what?"

I loved torturing him with words—he who was so enamored of his own verbal inventiveness, a slave to the desire to impress with his clever storytelling. He was a disingenuous virtuoso, even when it meant parting with reality.

"You know what I mean. Why don't you try making like the birds in autumn."

At that point, I was the one talking bullshit—like when I confessed that I had been raped by my uncle when I was thirteen. It was believable enough. I didn't know anyone who wasn't hiding, behind a calm and patient smile, or perhaps behind a kind of feverish agitation, some childhood violence.

And now I was the calm and thoughtful one. He was upset and emotional.

He hold me that he wished he'd been there.

"What do you mean 'been there'?"

"Sometimes it's hard to imagine your past without me. Even if I wasn't there, I like thinking about maybe having shared some of your life with you."

I still consider such an idea alarming, but at the moment I took it for a declaration of true love, tied up in a bow, a passionate and lucid (imagine such a thing!) testimonial.

But I didn't spare him one small jab.

"It was a lucky thing you weren't there. By now you ought to know me well enough to know what I'm like when you're not around." And I cut my eyes at him, making them hard and a little violent.

Lately I'd been thinking about having him knocked off. That's why I'd started seeing Vittorio. Vittorio was a plumber of Pasolinian ugliness, one of those young guys with so many muscles you can barely count them, and just making the effort takes your breath away. But they have devious eyes, like whipped dogs, and teeth like a piano keyboard, one black and the other the color of vanilla ice cream.

The evening before, we'd seen each other at his place. His nearly theatrical passivity had always irritated me, his desire to render himself the slave of every situation. He handed his body over to me like a gift, with the same ease with which a child extracts his favorite toy from the grasp of a playmate—in other words, with an almost embarrassing determination. Fucking him meant putting a cock into a mechanical and adjustable opening.

I fucked him halfheartedly—as for the other half, I truly didn't understand it.

"I want to see you," I told him when I called him later. I was using my most persuasive voice.

"Like last night?"

I knew what he meant. I felt my saliva starting to go down wrong. "I need to talk to you. It's important."

"Did someone find out about us?"

"What the hell are you talking about?"

"What then?"

"It's something else. I'm too embarrassed to talk about it over the phone."

"Does it have something to do with me?"

"I'll tell you when we see each other. What time?"

"Right now then. Do you want to come over here?"

I said yes, but I didn't like the idea of going to his house. He acted like he owned the place: he showed you in with an air of total indifference, neither asking nor expecting the slightest consideration in return for your presence.

I couldn't have gotten away with anything like that at my own house. There, I always had the feeling that my presence was rather supplemental—adequate, but by no means inevitable.

When I arrived, Vittorio was scratching his ass. It was a gesture that he performed in a kind of convulsive frenzy, and the intensity of the movement was anything but playful. There was no genius in the act and no elegance. How could I be surprised, then, that I saw him only as flesh? Good flesh, but flesh still meant for the butcher and tasting of death.

"I love you," he said suddenly.

I wasn't expecting that, just as I hadn't expected him to have gotten cleaned up after a hard day at work. He was wrong about that, too. He didn't understand that the dust and the dirt and the bad breath were products of nature and that they kept me just fascinated enough to hold my desire to escape at bay. The plastic mannequin in front of me left me feeling slightly nauseous.

"What are you saying?"

"It's true. I realized it a little while ago."

I didn't tell him that such sudden declarations of intimacy were not what I would have chosen. I much preferred the long, slow road. Nor did I ask him who else he had been in love with, whether the men before me had felt the same horror in the face of such a sudden and ill-timed effusion of love.

"It was a stupid thing to say, huh?"

"No. I'm just surprised."

In fact, I was deeply bitter. All I had been seeking was a body to distract me from the strange life that seemed to be taking shape around me.

"How surprised are you?"

How the hell do you respond to something like that? What was I supposed to say? Was I supposed to tell him in grams or meters exactly how disorienting his declaration was?

I shrugged my shoulders and said nothing. The ball was back in his court.

"I'm sorry. I thought hearing something like that would make you happy."

"Happy, sure...."

"So?"

"I belong to another man."

"Just one?"

That stopped me. The astonishing intelligence of Vittorio's response surely deserved a medal, but I just as surely didn't take the time to tell him so. He started scratching his ass again, but so forcefully that his body tipped forward. He almost fell on top of me.

"What are you doing?"

"Sorry. I needed that."

"You needed what?"

"I don't know. It's a habit. Like the way I need oxygen when I make love. You never caught on, right?"

I hadn't caught on, but I had suspected something. On those few occasions when we'd had sex, he'd allowed himself to be fucked only from behind, and there wasn't any way to convince him otherwise.

"I use an inhaler with therapeutic oxygen in it."

"What?"

"I need it. What did you think? When we're doing it, I get short of breath."

"But not when you're surrounded by all that shit where you work!"

"So now you're criticizing what I do?"

It was the first time he had ever stood up to me, though he still managed to do it with elegance.

"Have you seen a doctor?"

"No."

"Where do you get the oxygen from?"

"My father uses it. He's got a serious respiratory problem."

"So it runs in your family."

"My father is a war invalid."

"Oh, sorry. So does scratching your ass mean something?"

"Oh, well, that...."

He came closer and he kissed me. One way or another for taking the words out of my mouth.

"So what was it you had to tell me that was so important?" he said.

"Is it about me?"

"No, me."

"You know I'd do anything for you."

"You'd better wait until you hear what it is."

"What is it? You want me to knock someone off?"

"Touché!"

"What?!"

"You guessed it, blockhead. How much would you want to kill someone?"

He let himself be fucked in the usual way. But this time, I stayed on guard. I was more fascinated by his asthmatic sucking noises than by the muscular body that flashed and twisted beneath me like a fish.

He kept a green-colored inhaler by his side. When he had trouble breathing, he practically engulfed the small plastic tube that protruded from it. The hiss that followed was wet and metallic at the same time.

Then he would swallow, nearly exhausted by the effort.

"I've never killed anyone," he said later, stretching himself across the bed.

"It's the first time I've ever asked anyone."

"I'll bet. Are you sure you haven't lost your mind?"

"You've never once wanted someone dead?"

"No."

"Not even when they screwed with you?"

"You don't kill people for something as small as that."

Ten-cent philosophy, I thought to myself, but in that moment, I admired him. I appreciated his sense of calm in the face of my dogmatism, of my efforts to demonstrate my lack of decency.

He watched me, and at the same time he used one finger to smooth out the hair on my chest. He rolled a curl around his finger, then he unrolled it again.

"When I was seven I almost killed a boy at school with a stone," he said, sniffling.

"It wasn't premeditated."

"But I came close...what are you doing?"

I had climbed over him, leaning across to reach his side of the bed.

"I'm taking this with me." And I grabbed the inhaler.

"And why's that?"

"You don't need it."

That was a mistake, because I actually believed him: he couldn't have sex without the inhaler, and as long as I held onto it he couldn't have sex with anyone else.

"I just want to know what it tastes like."

"Careful. It's pretty disgusting."

"You're supposed to squirt it up your nose, right?"

"Give it a try!"

In reality, it had no taste at all. It was like licking a pane of glass that had been left outside in the winter dampness. Like swallowing snow.

"I thought it would be worse. And anyway, I don't understand you. I'd bet my right arm this isn't doing you any good."

"That's what you say."

He tried to grab the inhaler out of my hand. I aimed a fist at his balls.

"So are you going to tell me how much you want?"

He didn't make a sound. He covered his sex with his two cupped hands and gave me a sideways look. He wasn't even remotely handsome, but I thought again of Pasolini and of the expressiveness of the faces in his movies. Vittorio was marked by an appealing ugliness, a joke of his features that was both bitter and sweet. He was a kind of alloy, a compound of rusted iron and warm winter cotton.

"Want for what?"

"I told you: Would you ever kill someone?"

"You're asking too much. Besides, I already have a job."

With Vittorio, people were always tempted to take on the role of father or big brother. He was one of those guys. He had a square head and his gaze tended to veer off suddenly, only to land on some insignificant detail. And a cocky smile: his lips were drawn in roughly, a kind of reddish mark that formed the outline of a mouth, a slash across his cheeks that gave his face the appearance of an insect's. Short as he was, he always seemed an abbreviated version of other men. When the sun was out, Vittorio stood beside them like a second shadow.

When I went to visit him at the construction site, I found him conferring quietly with his supervisor, a fat giant of a man: Vittorio half the size of the other. But Vittorio's stature was relative—the monumental dimensions of the other man were an optical illusion of blubber—whereas Vittorio's physical vitality resulted from a specific combination of details. His proportions were augmented by the slightly off-kilter perfection of the way his body moved through space. Alcoholics aren't the only ones who know that good wine comes in small bottles.

"I need to talk to you."

He ignored me for a while, then he turned, his eyes fastened on the ground.

"I've got things to do. Can't you see that?"

"I see something else."

"And what's that?"

"A man who's scared for no good reason."

The giant suddenly burst out laughing, also for no apparent reason. He yanked his belt upward, mashing his balls against the spherical overhang of his immense belly.

"I'm not frightened."

Vittorio was a useless man. I realized that. But I rode over his uselessness like an armored tank.

"I still need to talk to you."

Vittorio took me into a tool shed where the only light came from a window covered with a sheet of yellowing plastic.

He posed a little, his hands in his pockets and his legs slightly spread.

"So?"

"I need to explain. Really...I'm not nuts. Up to now we've been kidding around, but I'm serious."

"But you can't make me kill someone...come on...that's crazy."

He'd said it. He'd taken the words out of my mouth. Instead of skirting the issue, he'd stepped right into the middle of it.

"What if I were to tell you the whole story?"

"Because then I'd think you had a good reason?"

"I know...it's not easy."

"It's not easy to think about. Imagine actually doing it."

He moved closer. I took him in my arms and started chewing one of his earlobes. He smelled like plaster and dried sweat. He had no idea that his own smell was better than any promise and that it cut the distance between us like a knife cuts through butter.

"They'll see us."

"You worry too much about other people."

"And you're a monster."

He said it with a smile on his lips. I licked his sweat. It tasted like bitter chestnuts.

Nicola came back from yet another trip to New York on the morning of Good Friday. The sky was covered with an embroidery of white-chocolate Easter eggs.

He called me the minute he got into the house.

"I've lost three kilos."

He was clever that way, always knowing how to ingratiate himself, a master juggler of the feelings of others.

"What do you expect me to say?"

"I don't know. Whatever you feel like...."

He snickered, the sound of a flushing toilet punctuating our silences.

"How'd it go? Did you have a good time?"

I didn't know what else to say: I expected him to drown me in fears. His fears. I expected him to confess that the world had suddenly become dangerous and unlivable. That his life was hanging by the merest thread. I even hoped he'd tell me that he'd die without me.

"New York was about the same...but then once I got back here...."

"What about here?"

I quickly counted the beats of my heart and then, like some cold-blooded mathematician, I multiplied. Twenty-five beats every fifteen seconds. Which meant a hundred per minute.

I was just getting started.

"Something very strange happened...."

"Strange? Tell me what."

"I don't know, maybe it's just...one of my neuroses, but I feel like someone is following me."

"Where?"

"Wherever I go...I even thought I saw him outside the house."

One twenty-five. A bicyclist who had to face the start of a climb at this point would have collapsed. Because of his outstanding physical condition, the great cyclist Eddy Merckx had a resting heart rate of forty beats per minute, which rose only as high as seventy as he made his way to the top of Coppi Hill, the steepest climb in the Tour d'Italia.

One thirty-two. Which, divided by four is thirty-three, like the age of Christ.

"Don't talk nonsense. Who'd be following you?"

"I told you...maybe it's just exhaustion. All this traveling. But it seems so real."

"Why don't you come over and we can talk about it?"

There was a reaction, but I struggled to make sense of it. At first it seemed like a sob, one of those involuntary reflexes that come over you when you don't want to talk, but the words are determined to force their way out. And then a muffled cry, like a call for help. When Nicola finally spoke, I realized my mistake.

"I love you."

What I'd heard had been the guttural, drawn-out sound of a smile forming. Hardly a moan of pain! And with that he took complete possession of my body, something that gave him no trouble even over the telephone.

"I might be making too much of things. Maybe I'm one of those guys who wishes he could make his intentions clear, but who's afraid to show his real feelings...."

"Right. One of those guys who isn't satisfied until he's made you furious."

"Why?"

"Because you always need certainty."

"You never give me any, and yet I'm still here."

Now it was my turn to react, and I did my best to make sure he wouldn't understand me. But it wasn't important. What difference did any of it make: a scream, a shout, a sob, a yawn, a belch, a moan, an entreaty, a plea, a prayer? I waited for him at home, prepared to hoist him back into place on my shoulders, no matter how much weight he'd lost.

Vittorio showed up instead.

I had set the table as if for some grand occasion—that is, for one of those grand occasions that most people would consider a picnic: a drop or two of wine, just enough to give one's face a little color, stomachs full of vegetables, because everyone knows that the consumption of meat is ill advised when dining al fresco.

He was wearing a pair of jeans faded down the front where the hands go to play but not to pray, and a white, short-sleeved T-shirt with black embroidery at the collar.

"I was just passing by."

And yet he'd found time to make a detour to my door, which he now closed behind him.

He smelled fresh from the shower—though he hadn't quite reached the point of being ready to be stamped "deluxe" and put on the shelf for public consumption. Still, he was no longer covered with mortar. In short, for the first time he'd found a way to present himself to me that was something of a compromise.

When he moved, his prominent pectorals stretched the material of his T-shirt as if they'd been filled with air and left to float above his abdominals. The effect was irresistible. Beneath his shirt the imagination roamed freely: the hardness and the firmness of him, the slight softening along his sides, the shape of his bellybutton, the way the hair grew across his chest.

I was well acquainted with Vittorio's body, but seeing it in front of me meant discovering it all over again, reconfiguring, with the evidence of my eyes, the image I'd held in my mind. And he knew it. He knew that behind the way I looked at him, even when I looked at him in anger, applause was always hiding.

"Don't tell me you were expecting me."

He glanced at the table.

"Actually...."

"I see. Another man."

I was stunned. I'd have preferred it if he had at least said a name, if he'd proposed a suspect or two. But he stood there, a stolid presence—making clear that there was no point in asking him to come back in and try the scene over—his slightly crooked mouth and his stained teeth threatening to arrange themselves into a smirk.

"I invited my mother, stupid. Today's Good Friday. It's important to her."

"Your mother?"

"You know how mothers are. Since I lost my dad, she feels lonely. And she wants to spend the holidays with me."

"She didn't invite you to her house? I mean, usually...."

"For Easter. Good Friday is my turn."

No one is born a liar. The successful lie is achieved in sweat and with a pounding heart. I don't believe anyone ever really manages to feel comfortable telling lies, even those who do it habitually. Sooner or later you have to give it up, or the symptoms will kill you.

"You can't stay. She doesn't know about you."

"I'd have bet on that."

"What do you expect me to do? Tell her all about your oxygen fixation? The way you open right up for me like I was the master of the universe?"

"Tell her how you want to kill someone."

"I never talk about my bloodiest fantasies."

I hoped he would understand, that he'd read between the lines, but he was curiously resolute, nearly immovable. I was having a hard time recognizing him. At any other moment, his body would have betrayed him, reducing him to a puddle at my feet. But now he towered over me, making me consider the possibility that other mountains lay behind this one.

"You're expecting Nicola, aren't you?"

"And if I were?"

"You wouldn't deserve me."

"Look, I tried everything I could to make you understand how things stood between you and me, I even tried to scare you. And believe me, that was no small effort."

"And I just took it...."

He tried to smile, tried to find some way to distract himself, because the standoff we'd come to weighed on him, all but unbearable.

"I'd even imagined I was building this body for you," he said, "even when you weren't here, because I thought you'd like it."

The usual story, the old call-and-response between lovers, bouncing back and forth like a ping-pong ball.

"I know you followed him."

He came nearer and put his mouth next to mine. His breath was barely tolerable, so who knows why I tried to chew his lip.

"I followed who?"

"Come on, don't act like you don't know what I'm talking about."

"I told you. You can ask me anything, but not that...."

"But somebody followed him."

"It wasn't me. I have other things to do."

He was far above me now, in a way I'd never imagined, light years from the patina of a man (that was all I'd noticed!) he had always been. And that was why I didn't believe him.

"I hope you didn't make him suffer...."

He laughed.

"Are you nuts? As soon as he gets here, you ask him. I'm going now."

As he made his way to the door, he held his hand out to me.

"Take it for once," he said, "without asking anything in return."

HEAVEN

Royston Tester

A month before I was due to leave for Blanchland House, I started to fool around again. Nicking stuff. Don't ask me why.

It kept me going while I waited for the court-imposed sentence to begin.

Worked on me like a coke rush. Easy pickings all round. On Sunday nights.

My stepfather Graham was in the pub—the Jolly Fitter across from St. John the Baptist. And Ma—Vera—was at home wailing along to "Songs of Praise" on the BBC. Once her piety was over for the Day of Rest—holy communion at eight thirty of a Sunday morning, family service at eleven—she could resume what she'd been doing with Graham every Friday and Saturday night since we'd arrived in Longbridge, spitting distance from Birmingham's sprawling Austin Motor Company: at the bar until closing, "never more than a rum and orange."

To make herself feel holier, she'd enrolled me in the church choir.

St. John the Baptist was a stripped-down place—heavily polished lily-white pine work and bleached walls. The building smelled of honey and the elbow grease Mrs. Fidgeon and Mrs. Hawkesford worked off on its maintenance and "floral improvements." To my nose it was tooty-fruity.

There, every Sunday morning, I churned out hymns and Ma would appraise the congregation. She never missed a trick: attended coffee mornings, socials, jumble sales, scout and cub bazaars, the works. Girl Guide and Brownie bingo nights. Christian Fellowship of England club. You couldn't fault her for trying to blend in. But Ma had all the regulars down pat. According to her, no one passed the rinse cycle.

With their dowdy slip-ons and cheap velvet hats, the women of St. John's were, according to her, "gormless to a bunion—sooner they climb into their litter boxes the better." Men didn't count at all—"most of 'em are women, anyway," she'd say.

And yet Ma spent more time with the *harridans*—those, grim God-fearing ladies—than with anyone in her life, even Graham. She detested the parishioners—men, women alike—no matter how kindly they behaved.

But I don't believe Ma ever troubled to ask herself why. What was so wrong? Did we look so different? Was it our accents from a canalside, country area only thirty miles away near Bloxwich? Were we gypsies selling clothes-pegs? Or had someone, once too often, put her down?

Found her girlish, deferential, social ways too stagy? Who knows why newcomers didn't fit in. Ma sold football pools for *our* living. Graham was on the dole. *They* were all bricklayers', plumbers', and carpenters' wives. And Austin car people. *Skilled.*

Ma wanted out, that's my guess, but didn't know where else was better. So Vera and Graham went on being the cheeriest outcasts in all Longbridge, doors closed all around. She ingratiated herself, never inviting a parish soul into our home. Nor they us into one of theirs. Ever. Except Nelly Barton next door—and she was heathen.

But church was like living in our council house in Edenhurst Grove, too. Infiltrators, each one of us. Fear hovering beneath every confident gesture. Upbeat pass-bys on the stairs and in the cramped hallway. Thin cheeriness. Masks. None of us daring to speak honestly about our lives, what we really felt. Questions we yearned to ask. No wonder my philosophy had blossomed at wanking and leveling war veterans for the life savings hidden in their squirrel teapots (hence the magistrate's sentence). What the hell did it take to turn my family circus off? Find some tenderness in our eyes? An honest word?

Wrongness loomed large over Edenhurst Grove, like David and Goliath entwined. One face ignoring the other. Not surprisingly, I was ready to explode.

I'd been at St. John's since 1970. Two years chanting and prattling my adolescence away. But after the business with the magistrate, Ma discreetly asked the vicar if I could join the senior choristers for weddings and funerals, held on Saturdays, as well as for the two Sunday services and Evensong at six thirty. A weekend of blistering Protestant devotion, not to mention the choir practices of a Monday and Wednesday night. Shrouded in her guilt over my criminal lapse, I was heading for a bishopric. A spiritual high for the damnation that was surely to follow at Blanchland House.

The Reverend Langston Garnett from Bradford via Bloxwich—"a meddling wog and the oddest you'll ever meet," as Ma liked to put it behind his back—had not hesitated. Or so she said. They always needed a good alto. Moreover, he'd offered to counsel her "delinquent Enoch" if I had *need*. Reverend Garnett would pray for my soul. And, of course, the circumstances would be safe with him. Not a word to anyone about reform school or Borstal. "This is Longbridge, Mrs. Jones," he had said— meaning a cut above any place you've known to date and compassionate about its fallen (although he didn't say that bit). He would expect me for three Sunday services. No monies paid. And would enroll me in the Catechism Group for Young Britons. It would help me on that yellow brick road to enlightenment, if not to Damascus.

And there went Tuesday and Thursday nights! Up in more chants and responses. Nothing like a script and routine to purify the damned,

I thought. The whole enterprise stank of abuse. You should have seen the other devotees around the table: blubberbods, spinsters, a cub mistress for scouts-in-waiting, and an alcoholic factory worker who saw existence in terms of gear-cutting. Some hippy freak from Northfield Lending Library. I was drowning in righteousness.

The real knives came out over the matter of Sunday at six thirty, however: Evensong at St. John's.

Nobody in the choir—except the old-timers—enjoyed this hour-long excruciation of canticles and psalms. With a congregation of five or six widowed pensioners and the occasional refugee from the Jolly Fitter, this was the low point of St. John's week, illuminated solely by candles that trembled from many a draught in the hold—and from the merciless gaze of a certain Mr. Ketland, the new and exemplary church warden, who seemed especially devoted to the pearl-faced boy choristers.

Even Reverend Garnett appeared downcast by it all—or was this *faith?*—especially as he declined to allow heating until December ("the numbers don't warrant"). And Mr. Swithin, organist and choirmaster, who used the nocturnal occasion to rehearse his frenzied Bach before and after the actual service, scratching his buttock between the thunderous seizures of music. Melancholy Mr. Swithin, he lived for religious abandonment. And for conducting his sopranos. Pick, swerve, pluck. They broke his heart—which explained the twitch on him; and on all of us at his practices.

Evensong was purgatory. I was opting out.

On the third Sunday in September, I left the house at six o'clock as usual to walk up Longbridge Lane to Calvary. I stopped by Windeatt's for some Polo mints and then, bowels stirring with mischievousness, I ducked behind some trees on a patch of wasteland across from St. John's.

Waiting and watching in the darkness. Drizzle. Until Evensong resurrected itself for yet another spine-tingling week. If God only knew what people put themselves through in His name.

Someone should write a letter.

From between the branches, I could see the maneuvers commence: Mr. Ketland—alongside a table of prayer books at the rear of the church—his head bowed but one eye kept on his favorites among the teenaged angels; the skeleton choir, led by Reverend Garnett, making its way through a congregation that had survived to see another day. After five minutes or so I hurried across Longbridge Lane to the church's side entrance, past the choir vestiary on the right and into the men's washroom.

And there they were. The Apostles. Three of them, all flush for the reaping.

It took seconds. There was always some spare change, cigarettes and, the previous Sunday, a wallet with fifty quid. Overcoats in a welcoming row.

As I was clearing out the third set of pockets, I heard the distant squeak of a St. John's door.

I rushed to a urinal, unzipped, and desperately tried to splash onto the fragrant porcelain.

The washroom door eased open. In walked Mr. Ketland, a dusty-faced, straitened Welshman — anywhere between thirty and sixty — with a brusque manner and polished shoes. Recently promoted from assembly-line Austin worker to foreman, he was therefore newly converted to Tory politics as well as to spiritual rigor. And neckties. A factory menopause like no other. He stood and observed me as a hysterectomy might the immaculate conception. No go there.

"Evening, Mr. Ketland," I said. "Damp night."

He nodded and put his hands in his pockets as though seeking guidance. How do you supervise a parish lavatory, O Lord?

I smiled and looked away. Had he noticed my three absences from Evensong? Had Ma been informed? Reverend Garnett? I'd never considered that my last week's harvest might have led to *complaints* and *investigations.*

My ears felt hot.

"Arrived late for choir," I told him, shaking my dick of nonexistent pee. "Better get off home."

Mr. Ketland was looking stern. I was in for it. On top of the Blanchland fuss. It'd be jail next: Wormwood Scrubs — skinned alive. Maybe I should invite Foreman Ketland to the Catechism Group?

Desperate measures, Enoch.

So instead of slipping the cock back into its jeans, I let it flop out, turning around slowly so that he could see my uncut length. He stared at it, his chest rising and falling beneath the phony regimental tie.

I spat into my fingers and began massaging the head like I was soaping in the shower. With finger and thumb I pulled the foreskin back and forth: see it stretch and have a nice day. Happy teatime marshmallow rising from the flames, Mr. Ketland?

I offered him a lick.

Cheeks stained red, he murmured something foreman-like but walked toward me, breathing rapidly.

Hit me or fuck me, I thought patting the shaft of my dick left and right.

As he approached, I reached deftly for his groin and there, beneath his neatly pressed twill trousers, lay the stiffness of redemption.

Slipping his cock out from beneath layers of flannel, I began jacking him.

"You're bad news, Enoch Jones," he said hoarsely, pulling me against his Norfolk jacket. He smelled of Old Spice.

"Aren't I," I replied, adjusting my grip.

He knelt down heavily and sucked for a minute or two as I rested my hand on his Brylcreemed head.

Eventually he struggled back to his feet. "Sooner you're in reform school, the better for us all."

"First line of a hymn, Mr. Ketland?"

He started kissing me on the lips. I felt sick to my socks but liked the taste of skin. Even his. How did he know about Blanchland House?

"Minute you and that Vera Jones walked in here...," he began, throat straining, "...trouble."

I yanked the Austin prick harder and harder.

He buried his face in my shoulder.

"Oh Jesus," he moaned, thrusting for eternity and God himself. Almost there.

"Jesus, yeah," I whispered encouragingly, steadying myself against a urinal.

"The lot of you," he gasped, beginning a lengthy choking sound as he reached for my ass, "not from around here...."

"That's it, man."

"Trash," he managed to say, trembling from tip to toe.

And he came—or rather, sputtered—over my anorak sleeve.

"You were right then, Mr. Ketland," I said, squirting jism onto the tiled floor. Something simultaneous to remember me by.

"Caravan runts," he said, still gripping my elbow.

"Yeah," I agreed, fastening my jeans. "Not your sort at all."

"Next time, you'll be reported," he added, zipping up and checking himself in the mirror.

"For bringing you off, like?" I replied, hurrying toward the line of coats.

"You know what for," he said, turning off a tap. With wet hands, straightening his tie.

"Thanks, Mr. Ketland."

"Hop it before I change my mind, lad."

Before you could say "Jack Robinson," I was out on Turves Green, taking the back route home by the Carisbrooke flats so I wouldn't bump into Ma on Longbridge Lane. She of a Sunday night. Imbued with holy spirit, serenading the pub for a wee dram more.

Loose change and cigarettes in my pocket. "God, I love Evensong!" I yelled out loud. Benediction felt sticky in my Y fronts as I started to catch on. Ma, Graham, and me, we really weren't from around here. And it showed. Trailer trash. Caravan runts: love 'em, fuck 'em, or hate 'em; it's all the same.

Christ, I'm dim.

It's truly eye-opening what you learn when you're in communion with everything you're not supposed to see. Maybe my family was not so out-of-the-ordinary, keeping everything that mattered under wraps. We'd fit right in if the locals let us. Still, it isn't pretty when grown-ups — well, mothers and fathers and church wardens, so far — will do anything to keep you in the shadows, fingers and thumbs in front of your face.

But I had Mr. Ketland to thank for letting me see beneath a pair of Longbridge trousers. The way you discover things about yourself — Nancy-boy? Trash? Bog whore? — is when you're not expecting to. Even the worst sounding places — and people — can turn you right around.

If I'd had a breakthrough that rainy Sunday night, it was downright confusing. Nothing seemed to mesh except for one small thing: the taste of someone's lips, the solid heft of him in my hand. And the way it could end with you back on the street and no harm done, wanting to yell to the sleeping houses from something like happiness.

The Word made flesh.

No St. Paul, me, but finally, at one of St. John's blessed services — albeit in the wrong room — I'd had a fearful glimpse of heaven.

At seventeen, more than most would wish to see.

I was growing more optimistic about reform school.

HOOTERS, TOOTERS, AND THE BIG DOG

Timothy Anderson

I spent last night with a fugitive
Tonight with a saint
Tomorrow with a drag queen
Who isn't as bent

Don't know where I'm going
Don't know who I've been
Don't know if I'm doing good
But I'd do it all again

The eyes just weren't cooperating. It was morning, and although I'd gotten three hours of sleep the night before, they refused to stay open in the spring morning sun. Running westbound on I-40 between Amarillo and nowhere, I was just east of New Mexico. The last of the Texas plains were a memory, and the rough country of New Mexico loomed ahead. I hightailed it into the San Jon rest area and grabbed an hour of shuteye. The fertilizer wasn't in a hurry and neither was I. Dallas was home recovering from surgery for an old rodeo injury, so it was just me and my big red truck, Little Red Ride 'Em Good.

I awoke an hour or so later. Groggy but ready to roll. The truck eased out of the parking lot slow and easy. Not much weight but enough to make each gear work. Eighteen gears and a dozen poses as we smoothly profiled our way out of the large vehicle parking area, past RV coaches and lost tourists and other sleeping drivers. On the road again.

The CB was active. I merged onto the freeway and heard some lady driver in the background. She was going by the handle "In Between," and, although she sounded like Bodacious, I was relieved to hear she wasn't. Unless Bodacious had changed her handle. The last time I'd met up with Bodacious and her chicken truck on I-40, she'd goaded me into racing her from just outside Barstow, California almost all the way to Kingman, Arizona. She taunted me, and I'd gotten my ego involved. Chicken haulers, as a breed, aren't known for lollygaggin', and I was proud of myself for beating her fair and square, but my partner, Dallas, was plenty skeptical when I tried to explain how a thirty-two-year-old grown man had gotten involved in a pissing contest with a nutcase of an outlaw hauler. The thought of restarting a race with Bodacious and her chicken truck was intriguing, but it would be hell on the fuel mileage. I was looking forward to a 6.5 average. If Bodacious was around, that number would plummet like an express elevator.

Hitting the top gear, I set the cruise control and sat back. In the background, Brad Pitt was reading Cormac McCarthy's *All the Pretty Horses*. The speakers echoed with each inflection, and the sun got hotter, and the story fell headlong into starkness and strife. Pitt was the perfect reader for the story. In his quiet voice, descriptions rolled off the tongue. Words became the tales of New Mexico meeting Mexico and cultures clashing and youth slungshot out of the passivity of protection and into reality.

In Between was gaining on me. She was in a green W-900 KW coming up fast in the hammer lane—definitely not Bodacious. Momentarily distracted by a hill, she seemed to pause. Behind her a Blue Classic Freightliner pulling a freight wagon was hot on her tail. From the CB I gathered his handle was "Big Dog." In Between and Big Dog were making miles. Running hard.

She wasn't pulling a chicken wagon but had a load of beef. Kansas style. Fresh from the packing plant and late before she started, In Between rolled into the sun. Chrome sparkled and clean paint caught the light. Behind her, Big Dog was the definition of likewise.

Caught up on the hill behind me, In Between groaned when I pulled out in front of her to get around a slow JB Hunt truck. Then I knocked off a couple of U.S. Express trucks and a Werner. The Who's Who of those not making miles with their governed, castrated, wanna be "large cars." Been there, done that. Crawled up those hills in what seemed to be a cruel version of reverse. I waved at the drivers and they waved back.

"Look at that, Big Dog," whined In Between. "A freight hauler just pulled in front of us. We are gonna have to slow waaaayyyy down." She was referring to me.

"No way. Damn freight haulers," commented Big Dog. Neither he nor In Between could see around my back doors to take in the fact that this company trailer was not pulled by a company driver in the standard issue, gutless company truck. I stroked it over the hill and left the two of them scrambling and struggling behind me.

"You see that, Big Dog?" In Between asked.

"Yep. That truck has either got a load of sailboat fuel on or it ain't no company truck," he said.

"We'll get 'em," she said.

I pulled out Brad Pitt and *All the Pretty Horses*, shut down the radio, and started concentrating on the 525 horses I was running. It was decision time. Be good, get passed, and get the going over from In Between and Big Dog, or make a hard run for it. The way they were pulling I could easily lose them in just a few hills, and it would be

Albuquerque before they even thought of catching me again. Fuel mileage would go to shit but I could hear the rest of my cassette without any further interruptions. True, the CB could be shut off, but that was asking for rude surprises if I lost a tire or the road got shut down ahead and I missed the news.

Up ahead, a Winnebago passed an Airstream and made the decision for me. Two sets of grandparents proudly displaying "We're Spending our Children's Inheritance" bumper stickers clogged up the works as traffic bottlenecked and everything slowed to ten miles under the posted limit. Big Dog and In Between cussed. I was boxed in and found myself staring into In Between's cab as she came up next to me. She had a rider. A pretty young lady. In Between was older but not bad herself. Almost a Reba McEntire look-a-like. She had some miles on her, and a person could tell that innocent wasn't exactly in her vocabulary.

"Big Dog, you should see the pretty truck I am passing. That ain't no ordinary freight hauler. It's a large car. Driver's kinda cute. Hey there, what's your handle there, sweetie?"

"I can't tell you," I told her.

"Sure you can. I'm harmless," she said.

"Nope. Can't. And I already know you are anything but harmless," I told her.

"How's it that you know so much?" she asked.

"Just do. I can tell. My handle, it would trouble you. So I can't."

"Yes, you can. It must be a good one. Talk real quiet so just I can hear it and I won't never tell no one. Swear." She was looking at me then looking at the road then back at me. Her rider was trying her best not to get involved. Yet every once in a while she'd look over too.

"Nope. Can't." I kept on keeping on. Traffic was rolling again in the hammer lane, and she could have rolled ahead of me, but she stayed steady next to me instead. I was boxed in. All I could see on my horizon was an aluminum monstrosity with Airstream plastered all over it.

Big Dog was getting impatient. "In Between, what are you doing up there?"

"Looking," she said.

"At what?" he asked.

"This purty little thing running next to me in the High Mountain truck. I got to get me one of him. I ain't budging until he talks. He's hiding something and I can smell it. He won't tell me his handle but I'll get it out a' him. I'm good." She talked in that famous Kentucky Fried Chicken Hauler voice. Low, scratchy, and sexy. She had the looks to match the voice. Her rider, on closer view, was much younger and a different definition of pretty. She didn't look old enough to be In Between's co-driver. She glanced over at me and rolled her eyes.

"C'mon, In Between. Let's get it going. We're making a mess back here. Hell, even JB caught back up." Big Dog was getting impatient.

"Nope. Not 'til he talks. I want to get a handle on his handle." She looked over at me. Red tangles of teased hair dangled across her forehead, just this side of mall hair. A cigarette hung suspended between long, painted nails. Every once in awhile, she flicked it out the open window. She was grinning at me, and her rider was trying to pretend that she was anywhere but in that truck.

"Listen, In Between. You and I, we got to get one thing straight. I ain't telling you my handle. I can't. I won't. No matter what. You JUST ain't getting it. It's JUST the way things are supposed to be. And I know it's JUST killing you and it's JUST killing me that it's killing you but we both JUST gonna have to deal with it or JUST roll over and die. Because that is what's gonna have to happen before I tell you my handle. Now I'm sure y'all got much more important things to be fretting about and my handle sure ain't one of 'em." The last thing she needed to know was that I was known as Northern Exposure on the highway. I gave her my best "catch me if you can" grin. Luckily for my ass, that Airstream finally pulled off at the bottom of a good hill, and I powered down into it.

Pulling away from Big Dog and In Between, I left them struggling in the hammer lane to get over that whoop-dee-do of a hill. Behind them, both lanes were a mass of traffic.

"In Between?" I asked.

"Yes?" she came back.

"You look mighty foolish sitting there holding up all that traffic. I just want you to know that it was a pleasure running with you." It was arrogant of me to say such a thing. I knew it just added fuel to her fire. I suppose it even made me a Male Chauvinist Pig, but damn, if it didn't feel good just to walk over that hill and put a half mile on her and Big Dog in no more than a few.

"Big Dog?" In Between asked.

"What?" he responded. He almost sounded irritated.

"We got to catch that High Mountain truck. I'm gonna get that handle." She sounded determined.

"Oh for Chrissakes, In Between, just leave it be. You ain't ever gonna catch that boy. You just gotta put it out of your mind. Forget about it." Big Dog was frustrated.

"Can't," she responded.

Big Dog groaned.

I stayed out of traffic bottlenecks and made good time. Big Dog and In Between got smaller and smaller in my mirrors. Soon enough it seemed they were on to other topics. Forgotten, I listened in amazement at the goings-on behind me.

"I am a full Irish redhead," In Between was saying. "It's all real.

Ain't no dye on this head. I got me red on my head and a snatch to match."

Big Dog was intrigued. "Let me see," he begged.

Apparently she stuck her head out of the window as he passed her.

"Look, In Between, I already seen your head. I want to see the other," he pleaded.

"Uh uh," she said.

"Please...," he begged.

"Nope, I can't. But if you slow down I'll show you something else." I instantly recognized that tone in her voice. I hadn't known her for even an hour but I knew. It meant mayhem. Trouble. I turned my CB up.

Things were quiet for a minute.

"Damn, In Between...that is a fine set of hooters you got. Mighty fine." Big Dog was impressed.

"Why, thank you, Big Dog. I'm rather fond of them myself." She sounded tickled.

I wondered what the hell was going on back there. So did every other driver within earshot. Both eastbound and westbound.

"Where's the hooters?" driver after driver asked. Mile markers were exchanged. Locations given. The suspect's vehicle was identified. Chaos reigned.

Big Dog wanted to see the hooters of In Between's rider next. She wasn't cooperating. I watched in my mirrors as the blue Freightliner came around on the passenger side of the green KW. Big Dog was pleading with her. "Please show me your hooters, darling...I'll make it worth your while, I promise."

I wondered what Big Dog had to offer that would be worth her exposing her breasts to a leering, middle-aged driver. In Between answered my question.

"Damn, Big Dog.... You are one BIG DOG. You better put that away before someone gets in an accident!" In Between exclaimed.

"No. I'm gonna leave it out until that purty rider of yours plays, too," he said.

They went on rolling down the highway, and I heard Big Dog tell everyone listening that In Between had entirely removed both her blouse and her bra and was now driving down the road completely topless. Big Dog continued to expose himself and continued to plead with In Between's uncooperative passenger.

Then it happened. Without warning, I saw the two trucks, running side by side behind me, do a strange dance. The radio went silent. The commotion only lasted a few seconds. But when it was over there were several pregnant seconds of silence while everyone regrouped. Big Dog was now trailing In Between by several truck lengths. In the meantime, she seemed to have regained possession of her lane.

"Sorry 'bout that, Big Dog," In Between finally exclaimed breathlessly.

"You better be. What the hell happened?" Big Dog responded. They both sounded like they'd seen a ghost.

"I dropped my cigarette. Burned my hooter. I missed it and the damn thing fell into my lap. Burned my tooter, too." She was stunned.

"No shit?" asked The Big Dog. "You okay?"

"No shit," she responded. "And, yeah I'm okay. It burns a bit...but my hooters'll be okay. Don't know 'bout the other."

"Well, I almost lost Little Big Dog in the steering wheel trying to stay out of your way. You don't know what a scare like that does to a man." He was still shaken.

"You don't know what a cigarette out a control does to a woman either." Her voice wasn't quite the same as it had been before.

"Damn, In Between...you gotta be more careful," he commanded.

"Okay, okay. I will. Still ain't putting my hooters away though," she replied.

"And we wouldn't want you to," another driver responded.

Chaos returned to the radio as drivers tried to figure out where Big Dog and In Between were. The terrain was flatter now. As we flew by the junipers and cedars on the plateau west of Santa Rosa, the radio was a constant hum of speculation about the whereabouts of the runaway hooters.

Company drivers cussed their predicament, frustrated at governed company tractors that wouldn't allow them to tag along or get a long enough glimpse as the two truckers flew by. Still other drivers did manage to catch up and joined the procession led by a proudly topless redhead.

Another couple somewhere ahead of us seemed bent on adding more topless hooters to the mix. A woman named "Go Figure" announced that her husband was convinced she had a finer set. He wanted Go Figure to compare her set with In Between's. They weren't sure where we were. In Between asked them for a mile marker and to identify their truck, which Go Figure's husband proudly did.

They were in a red Freightliner. I realized, as they announced it, that I was in the process of passing the very same truck. I looked over into the cab and the husband smiled at me. I also saw his wife, Go Figure, who hadn't realized that another driver was passing them and suddenly scrambled for something to cover herself. She belted her husband for not warning her and then grabbed the CB mike.

"Did you see 'em, High Mountain?" Go Figure asked.

"Yeah, I saw 'em," I answered.

"What did you think?" she asked. "Who has the better hooters?"

"Well ma'am, I can't rightly tell you. I ain't seen In Between's

Hooters. I have only seen yours. They're nice though. You ain't got nothin' to be ashamed of."

I could appreciate the artistic merits of mammary-gland form. It was all academic. A pursuit of the highest standards of excellence. I shared my vision of Go Figure's hooters with everyone who was listening, and I felt no misrepresentation. In fact, my credentials as judge were unquestionable. I pondered my grandfather's well known love for all things hooter and used his finely tuned skills and criteria (which he had often shared with me) to make my call. She had a fine set.

In fact, right up until just before Grandpa died, he had continued to refine his judgment in this area. In Spokane there is a quaint little franchised club where he used to hang out with his buddies.

For "lunch."

Known as Déjà Vu, the home of ninety-nine beautiful girls and three ugly ones, it was also the home of the Texas Couch Dance. It wasn't until late one evening several years ago, when Dallas's and my pickup truck broke down outside this establishment, that we found ourselves inside the place my grandfather had so frequently and fondly spoken of to my grandmother as having the "finest food in town."

We sat down at the bar and waited for the menu. A beautiful woman approached and asked what she could do for us. Although it was obviously a strip joint, we were still under the impression that they had a full menu. Imagine the surprise on our faces when we learned they didn't serve any food. Never had. Never would. They only served beverages. Suddenly my grandfather's curious development of diabetes was explained. It wasn't grandma's cooking but all those years of going without a midday meal so he could have "lunch" with the boys at Déjà Vu. Imagine day after twelve-hour day of hard work without a bite to eat.

He got caught several years later. Ill with terminal cancer, he sat across from a hospice worker who explained to him the progression of his disease. My grandmother and I sat with them in the living room, taking it all in as he asked many questions of the pretty young woman. After a long silence, Grandpa finally asked the hospice woman if he could continue to have lunch with my uncles at the Déjà Vu. The stunned and blushing hospice worker looked at my grandfather in amazement. Frail with cancer and worn from the treatments, he still wanted to go to the Déjà Vu. She finally laughed and told him, "Orin, you know they don't serve food there."

My grandmother shot me an alarmed look, and I quickly interjected, "Oh, yes they do serve food. I've been there." Grandma was looking at me now, puzzled.

"Damn right," Grandpa interjected. The hospice worker gave us one of those condescending smiles that women sometimes give men who are in cahoots together. It said, *Well, aren't you two just a fine work in progress.* Thankfully, she didn't pursue it any further. And my grandmother, horrified that the subject had been brought up to begin with, was content to let the matter drop. I think she knew all along what my grandfather and my uncles were up to. Montana women are just plain smart that way.

Still, my grandfather would have approved of the compliments I'd directed toward Go Figure.

Go Figure responded enthusiastically, "Why thank you, High...."

Go Figure was cut off by In Between's booming voice. "High Mountain? Is that you? I'm gonna catch you so you can see mine. Why won't you run with me?"

I responded, "Because I know you are trouble, In Between."

"How do you know that?" she asked.

"What color is your hair?" I asked.

"Red. Naturally red." She said.

"See, that's how I know you are trouble and that if I run with you, you will get me into trouble. I have a lot of experience with redheads. They only lead to trouble. I've been down this road before." I was determined to stay out of this one. I didn't want to see In Between's hooters. I didn't want to get Big Dog pissed at me for moving in on whatever he thought he had going with In Between. And I didn't want to be forced to judge who had the nicest set. The irony of the situation was not lost on me. I knew there were far better judges than me in the very near vicinity.

"I will never get you into trouble. I am very good. I never get anyone in trouble. You should trust me." She wasn't giving up.

"I can't. Besides, I saw what you did back there when you dropped your cigarette." After I spoke there was silence. In Between's green KW was now running next to Go Figure's red Freightliner. I wondered if Big Dog was just beside himself that there wasn't a third lane. I knew right where he'd be if he could. In the middle.

Over the next few miles there was a lively roundtable discussion over who had the best set. The old timers were voting for In Between because she had "Class and the Sass to Match." The other drivers were inclined to vote for Go Figure because she was from the "Show Me" state and had promised never to drop a cigarette anywhere that might "alter the mood." I wondered what her husband was thinking about the competition. I considered that things might be getting just a little bit out of control. Looking in my mirrors I figured there were at least twenty trucks bunched up behind me in the hooter procession.

Unfortunately, In Between tired of the competition and once again focused her sizable attention on me. "High Mountain?" she asked.

Oh no, I thought. *What now?* I'd stayed close enough to keep tabs on their goings-on but far enough ahead to be out of harm's way if In Between dropped another cigarette. Big Dog was silent.

"Yes," I responded.

"I have to go pot-tay," In Between announced, using the Arkansas French pronunciation for piss.

"OOOOhhhkkaaaayyy," I answered.

"Why don't you stop with us at Clines Corners? I can use the ladies room and I'll buy ya' a cup a' coffee. Then we can keep running together. Where you heading?" she asked.

"California."

"Me, too," she said.

I groaned to myself. "I can't stop, In Between. I gotta keep going." It was a lie but it was necessary. I could imagine the convention that would descend on Clines Corners when she stopped. I already knew who the keynote speaker would be.

"You are no fun," she responded. "You won't tell me your handle. You won't look at my hooters. And you won't run with me. I think you are hurtin' my feelings. You don't want to piss off a redhead, now, do you?"

I felt the jaws of strife descending on me. "No, ma'am. I certainly would never want to piss you off. You are way too pretty to be walking around pissed off or with a frown on your face. Just look at all those nice drivers who are willing to escort you across the 40. Now why would you want to hang out with an inexperienced hand like me when you can be surrounded by people who know how to do right by a fine woman like you? I just can't fill those shoes. But I appreciate the offer and hell, if I told you my handle, it would just upset you no end so I am gonna keep it to myself, 'cause I can't do that to a lady such as yourself."

I hated myself. I had no pride. Big Dog confirmed it. "That was smoother than Slick Willy, In Between. You gonna let him get away with shinin' you on like that?"

"Yeah, it was smooth, wasn't it? I liked it, though. He knows how to talk. He claims to be sweet and innocent, but that boy knows something. He ain't worried about me getting him into trouble. Nope, that boy is worried about him getting me into trouble. I know it. And as soon as I go pot-tay I am gonna catch him. That's some trouble I gotta find out about."

We said our goodbyes and I started wondering where I was going to hide out for twelve hours while she got ahead of me. I finally settled on the Ranch in Albuquerque. Behind me, I watched as the whole pack of trucks exited off the freeway. Clines Corners would never be the same.

In my mirrors, I also noticed one lone truck that hadn't exited with the other hounds. A red, long-nosed "Pete" pulling a bull wagon. A truck I hadn't passed. I wondered how long it had been back there, sneaking up on our back door. Listening.

The truck was immaculate, with a big chrome Texas bumper and painted in the kind of red that glows in all-type weather. I watched the truck quickly catch me and was surprised when it moved out into the hammer lane and then slowed as it came up next to me. The truck was piloted by a cowboy with a big, dark, bushy mustache and a straw Stetson cowboy hat. He wasn't wearing a shirt and I could see that he hadn't been eating a lot of chicken-fried steak. He studied me for a minute, then extended a muscular arm across the passenger seat. He threw me a big smile and gave me a thumbs-up. And then he was off.

I took out after him toward the looming Sangre de Cristo mountains. He was running hard and after a minute he came over the radio in a low voice that was quiet and calm. "High Mountain, you know she won't rest until she finds you."

"Yeah, I 'spose you're right," I answered, sullen.

We rode in silence though Moriarty. Then he spoke again. "So how about it. You fixin' to tell me your handle or am I gonna be chasin ya, too?"

I thought for a minute. Considered my options.

"Well?" he said. "I only ask once...then...." He got quiet, like he was also considering options.

I told him to take it to another channel. Here was a hand I'd have no problem sharing my name with.

BLEEDING TOY BOYS

Dean Durber

1.

The room was starting to look hazy. I noticed again the gray stains spread over walls whitewashed for the first and last time years back, long before my arrival. I wondered how many students had sat on this fraying chair, slept on this tiny bed, its mattress weary and sagging toward the floor.

This place was never built for the likes of me.

I stumped out a cigarette that I had smoked right down to the tip. My lungs breathed freely for a while as I twisted another cigarette in my fingers, staring down at it. I was enjoying relief after nearly a year of addiction to the inhalation of intoxicating, infuriating fumes.

"I'm going to quit one day," I told myself. "I am."

I lit up and started to choke.

A pile of books balanced on my desk, closed now and resting beside an overflow of ash. Books I will never open again.

I stared out of the window and listened one last time to the shouts of summer rising up from the scorched patch of grass down below. I puffed out a circle of smoke and watched it climb to the ceiling.

I raised my feet and pressed the soles of my dirty shoes hard against the wall. I held them there while I watched him. He jogged across the lawn, into the trees and into the distance. I noticed how he wore a small white towel wrapped tightly around his neck.

I pulled my feet away and smiled desperately at the imprinted memories they had left. I knew I should feel guilty about what I'd done.

2.

"Where ya goin'?" my mother asks me, a half-smoked cigarette hanging from her lips.

I feign a cough as I wave the fumes away. I turn to offer an exaggerated stare at the boxes that I have packed so neatly into my car.

"University," I spit.

Her still face dangles somewhere between puzzled and pleasure. I'm not sure. I notice only the depths of her wrinkles and the yellow of her crooked teeth.

"What, today?"

"Yes, today. Like now. I've packed my car. Didn't you even see me packing?"

The shared grayness of the houses around me makes this place seem so desolate. The streets are filled with the sounds of unwanted children running around in tattered clothes. They scream endlessly. Drunken old men stagger home to Sunday lunches covered in cold, solidified gravy.

"I thought you knew," I said.

"Maybe. Yes, maybe I did."

"I'm sure I told you."

She lets the cigarette fall to the ground and leaves it to burn. I use the sole of my new shoes to crush its embers. I lean down to pick up the extinguished butt and hold it tidily in my hand.

"I guess you just forgot then."

I think I catch a tear in her eye, but I try not to let her see me looking. She moves to hug me. She squeezes me too tightly. I can hardly breathe.

"Mum, I...."

"No, you go now, son. You go to your university and you make us proud."

She pulls out a crumpled green note from her pocket and pushes it into the palm of my hand.

"I don't need this," I insist, thrusting it back toward her. "I'll find a job. I'll be fine."

She squeezes my palm closed.

"I know you will, son. You'll be fine now. I know that."

She turns away and wobbles back toward the house, a graying box squashed in the middle of squalor. I never want to come back here.

"And don't you ever come back here!" she shouts back.

"What?"

She doesn't turn.

"Don't you ever be coming back to this shitty life!"

She closes the gate. And suddenly I am filled with rage.

3.

His voice is what first grabbed my attention. That's what attracted me to him, I suppose. If attraction is the word. I don't know for sure, but I know that I listen intently to the way he speaks as if every word were important, e-v-e-r-y w-o-r-d meant something. There are no apostrophes in his life. No missing syllables.

"Joseph," he says to the girl beside him. "But most people call me Joe."

She smiles.

I can see the huge streams of dirty smoke rising from large chimneys way in the distance in a world outside of these windows. I hate their presence, their reminders.

"I'm from down south," I hear him say.

His voice is so soft, so clean.

"From just outside of London."

The girl smiles again. The anger won't leave me.

"In a place called Tunbridge. Tunbridge Wells, to be exact. It's just outside of Tunbridge."

I sit through that lecture not caring what is said or if it will ever end. My notepad is filled only with rough scribbles of faceless mutated bodies and a sprawl of random dot-to-dot patterns that I piece together to form nothing. I know that I need to be paying more attention, but I can't. I can smell smoke. It's everywhere. It's in my clothes, clinging to my skin, on my breath. It will never leave me.

The sudden clatter of desks wakes me and I jump up. I hang at the end of the row of chairs where I have been sitting, fumbling with bits of paper in my hands, waiting. The girl beside him gets up to leave.

"Nice to meet you," the boy shouts out.

I step forward, forcing myself between them, following slowly behind her, feeling the slight breeze of his breath on the back of my neck as he moves closer. I step through the swinging door and push it backward, purposefully, harsh and hard. I hear the thud. The silence that follows. That moment stretches for an eternity of my joy. I can feel the ache of my smile.

"Fucking Jesus! Fucking Jesus Hell Christ!"

The corridor stills. People turn in slow motion while I grip the edge of the door with the very tips of my fingers and peel it back just enough to see his fallen body sprawled, his books scattered, his hands clinging to the side of his head where already a lump of flesh starts to thump and grow. His eyes are streaming with shameful tears. I squat down.

"I am so sorry," I say.

I reach out to touch his hurt.

"Are you all right?"

A hand flicks out and knocks my caring touch clear away. It takes all of my strength, all of my patience to resist forming my hand into a fist and smashing it down into his face. I know how badly I want to hurt him. I am not ashamed of that.

"Jesus fucking Christ!" he screams again.

People pass us by. They exit through other doors.

"It was totally my fault," I repeat. "I am so sorry."

Again my hand starts to move. This time it manages to come to rest on the top of his head where I stroke him.

"Maybe I should get you to a hospital."

He looks up, stares at me. His nose is dripping blood.

"I'm a total idiot. I just let the door go. I didn't even know you were there. I was miles away. I'm sorry."

Still he stares. Still my hand runs over his hair.
"I'll take you to the hospital." I stroke.
"I'll be fine," he whispers.
"But I feel so bad. Really. I feel so bad."
"It wasn't your fault. I'll be fine."
His eyes don't move.
I cup my hand beneath his elbow and help him to his feet. I can feel the flesh of his arm as I pinch it between my fingers.
"Can I at least buy you a drink? To say sorry."
He rubs fingers over the swelling, over the uncertain flesh of his elbow. He stares at me again, begins to smile.
"Yes. A drink would be fine."
I like watching him in the bar as he dabs himself clean, his blood soaking through onto my handkerchief.

4.

She tells me she's fine, things are fine, work is fine. I know she lies.
"How's the weather with you there?"
"Cold," I say. "Too cold."
"You keepin' warm then?"
"Yeah, yes, I'm keeping warm."
"I should try 'n' send ya some money, 'elp with ya bills a bit." She coughs, and then the sound of sucking as she inhales.
"I'm fine, really. It's warm. Not too cold at all."
"And your friends?"
"Yes, they're all fine."
"I bet you got some lovely friends there. It's good that you have some good friends. You'll need them."
I don't answer.
"Better than the likes of round here that's for sure."
She laughs, but I know she means it.
"They're not so bad," I lie.
"No, not too bad. But you can do better than the likes of us, son. I'm proud of ya, ya knows that don't ya?"
"So you keep saying."
"Well I am. And I don't care 'ow many times I say it. Ain't nothing wrong with bein' proud o' me own son, now is there? Not many folks round here got any son of theirs goin' to bloody university 'av' they now?"
"Guess not."
"Too bloody right not. So I am proud of ya. I'm glad I got the chance to see ya makin' someat of yoursel'."
She coughs again.

"I could have 'ad them brains you know!"

She laughs. We are silent. I hear the click of a lighter.

"And you're talkin' right posh now and all."

"Am I?"

"So when ya comin' home to see us then?"

I leave the question to hang.

"Been well on three months by now."

"I know. But I have to study all the time. And then there's work. I can't really get time off work. I'd lose the job."

"Ai, I know luv. Happen if I had a bit more money...."

"You work hard enough. I'm fine."

"Thank Christ you'll never 'ave to do the kind o' work we does."

She coughs again and again, this time louder and harsher. It goes on forever.

"How are your hands?" I ask. "You still rubbing cream in every night?"

"Sometimes."

"You've got to do it every night to keep them soft."

"Listen to you there."

I feel my face blush. We both know that no matter how much we rub them, no matter how much cream we force into the cracks of her skin, those hands will never heal.

"You're a good 'un, you know that."

Silence.

"Well you take care, son. You be good. And don't you worry about us now."

I hear the phone go click. Her voice is gone.

"You're a good 'un," I repeat into the silence.

And I cry.

5.

I didn't make it home for Christmas that year. Drove straight past my town and continued further south, heading to London, to Tunbridge, Tunbridge Wells to be exact. Here the doors of the houses open out onto scrubbed cobbled streets. There's a touch of frost in the air. It might snow. It should do.

"I understand, son," she sobs quietly, sniffling like it's only a cold. "You have your own life now. Don't wanna be spendin' all ya time here now."

I pull up outside Joe's house and grab my bag off the back seat. He is already standing at the open door, his face flushed red. I can't tell if he is cold or shamed, maybe neither. He smiles too much.

"Mom, this is Dan."

He looks at me, smiling.

"This is my best friend from university."

I reach out to shake her hand, feel its softness. I notice how her skin is so clean, so healthy, alive.

"You'd be bored comin' down 'ere anyways," she insists.

The coughing has grown worse.

"And besides, things aren't too happy round 'ere right now."

She wheezes. I know she's finding it harder to talk.

"It's very nice to meet you, Dan."

Soft, gentle hands.

"Joe has been telling us all so much about you."

Behind her, waiting on the kitchen table, I notice a large lump of bread freshly baked. I can smell it. I see the unpacked butter. And a single silver knife, very sharp. Everything seems so tidy in here.

"Please make yourself at home," his mum says. His mom. "We are very happy to have you."

I imagine what it would be like to have my tiny infant mouth sucking on the nipple of this lady with silvery graying hair. I watch her slender body as she bends to pour juice into a small glass with not a drop spilled. She passes it to me, but all I can see are gleaming white teeth.

"So where are you from?" she asks me.

I give the name of some town that isn't mine but close enough.

"Oh yes. We have been there. A lovely part of the country."

"Yes, lovely."

"I thought you must have been from around that part of the country. I can hear it in your accent."

I stare at the knife.

"Come on, Dan. I'll show you to my room," Joe says.

"He can sleep in the spare room if he wants," his mother interrupts. "He might not want to sleep on the floor."

She looks at me, waits for an answer, but Joe pulls at my arm and drags me out of the room. He whispers to me as we climb up the tiny, crooked stairs.

"The spare room is tiny. It's too cold. I thought you could sleep in my room."

"Look, Joe...."

"It's so good to see you."

He goes to kiss me, lands on my cheek.

"Maybe I should just sleep in the spare room."

"Why?"

"Just because."

"But it's really small. The bed's tiny. We could just get you a mattress and put in on the floor in my...."

"It'll be fine!"

My hand stretches out. I push him away, but during the night he comes back and rests his head sleepily on my chest.

"I'm so glad you're here," he tells me.

He starts to kiss at my naked flesh while I think of what it would feel like to slide that silver bread knife across the perfect smoothness of his cheek. How the blood would trickle down the curve of his neck.

"Do you ever think about cutting yourself?" I ask.

6.

I know I should have called to wish her Happy Christmas or Happy New Year at least, but time just ticked on by. We had turkey for lunch. Fresh potatoes with steamed vegetables. Christmas pudding and cream. I didn't want to make her cry.

"Hey, why don't we go out for a drink?" Joe says.

Too many. I tried to walk upright on the way back to the house, but then I pretend that I need his support so that I can drill my knuckles into the top of his head. I stumble forward and fall, pulling him down. I punch him hard on his nose, spraying blood onto the cobbled pavements of Tunbridge Wells. My heart races so fast. My hand grabs at his flesh through a torn T-shirt as I roll him on to the road and force him to dodge cars whose horns blast out. I feel my fist penetrate into the fleshy softness of his stomach. Joe pukes. I like how this feels.

My mother would have had chicken for lunch. Chicken and sausages wrapped in bacon. She would have sat at home listening to the sounds of screaming kids and drunken old men outside her window, and the sky would have stayed dark and gray. The cold of the house would have hurt. She would have closed her eyes and slept.

We stumbled home together, his body all sore and bleeding. Crusts of blood have already started to form to cover his wounds. I think I am sleeping when I suddenly hear his voice whisper beside me.

"I'm sorry."

I lie silent.

"I'm so sorry," he cries.

I open my eyes and turn him over onto his back, his face staring up at the empty ceiling. I have never noticed before the darkness of hair on his legs, the smoothness of his chest. I try not to look.

I sit on top of him, my legs stretched across his naked pelvis. My fingers pinch the razor blade that I use to slice gently across his chest. Blood trickles into tiny wrinkles in the skin of my fingers, under nails, seeping into my pores. I watch his face, his silence. I lower my face toward his wounds and touch his bleeding flesh with the tip of my tongue. For a moment I think I might puke. The taste of him slips down the back of my throat as I come.

My face stares down now into his open, pleading eyes. I lower my lips and kiss him where kisses between us should not go.

"Thank you," he cries, his eyes widened in shock.

7.

I throw my bag onto the back seat of my car and start the engine. It takes a while for the heat to show a hole through the mist on the windscreen. I sit shivering.

Through the cleared side window I can see him as he stands in the doorway, his mother stroking his hair. He kisses her and opens the door to sit beside me.

"Please take care of him, Dan. To think that this sort of attack could happen here." She touches his cheek.

"I know. Awful, isn't it?"

My hand rests caringly on his shoulder. "I'll look after him. Don't you worry. And thanks for a great Christmas."

When we are out of sight of his home, he dares to place his hand on my thigh. It stays there.

8.

"Hey, mom. It's me."

"Hello, son," she sighs.

"I just called to let you know I'm leaving university. I'm coming home."

"You make me so proud, you know that."

I speak through my tears. "I.... No.... You make me proud."

"Don't you be silly now."

"No, I'm serious. You do."

There's a silence while I wonder if she understands me.

"You don't know how much I love you," I cry. "It's like sometimes, when I'm here, I feel I'm in a completely different place and the people I meet are like, well, they're not like us. They.... Mum?"

I hear the phone click.

9.

I look down at the crumpled sheets and can still make out the stain. My cock throbs with pain.

It is dark outside. Streetlights flicker through the open window.

"Come on," I say as I take his hand and pull him to his feet.

His face is red, sore, hurting. His body is bruised.

"I think we should get you into the shower."

He nods his head and cries then, heavy sobs of passion while I think about hating him and all the reasons why. In that moment I love him, and I know all the reasons why.

"You and me, we don't belong together, you know that, don't you, Joe?"

He cries and cries.

"We're from different worlds. Different times. We want different things. We don't even speak the same language, for Christ's sake."

"But I love you."

I raise my fist, watch it hover above his head. My finger falls on his lips.

"I know you do, Joe."

I stand him in the shower and watch as warm water pours over his naked body. His hand moves backward and forward, gently rubbing between the cheeks of his arse as he stares out at me, his face smothered in dried tears.

"Does it hurt?" I ask.

"Not much. It's okay."

I want to hold him.

"I know what you're thinking," I add.

He waits.

"But you're wrong."

I glide the back of my hand over his shoulder and along the breadth of his arm.

"I don't want to be like you. I don't want to be the things you are. The way you talk. The house. Your mother. I thought I wanted all of that. But I don't. I want...."

I stop to kiss him gently, on the lips. His eyes widen with sadness and fear. But when he cries, I pull him tightly toward me. My lips rest on the softness of his cheek.

"I'm sorry," I whisper.

Through his tears he is silent. He tries to speak but can only splutter phlegm from the back of his throat. I can smell her now. I can feel her.

"It's okay," I whisper. "It's okay now."

10.

I haven't seen Joe for days. I have kept my door locked, holding my breath when I hear him knocking and knocking. After the knocking stops, I hold my breath for a while longer, counting the seconds. Seventy-two. Seventy-three. I find it hard to dare to breathe.

As I watch his body disappear into the trees, I feel lonely. Sitting in this room, my life packed into boxes. This space echoes with his presence. I smoke another cigarette.

Right then, smoking is such a joy, and I decide I will never quit. These burning embers remind me of her. It's her smell on my fingers, in my clothes, in the disease of my blackening lungs.

Uncontrollable tears suddenly begin to pour down the side of my face. My body spasms into a tiny ball. My legs crush up tightly against my aching chest. I cannot breathe. And I don't want to. I hold my breath and hope to turn blue. Ninety-two, ninety-three. I dare to breathe.

I place the last of the boxes in the boot and sit staring out the window. Joe's face appears in the mirror. I see a car driving down the road and I wonder what it would be like to have its metal body smash against our fragile ones and tear our flesh apart. To feel our heads crushed beneath the weight of its wheels as our bones crumble together into dust.

HOW TO GET FROM THIS TO THIS
Keith Banner

1.

My brother Lucas leaves a message on my answering machine.

"I am out here in my car on my cellphone, Danny, and I swear to God you better not be in there hiding. They've towed your car. Are you drinking? Call me. We love you."

One time I caught him and his high school boyfriend out in the tree house he and I had built. They were hot and heavy, and I climbed up to smoke a joint out there. He looked so happy and helpless on top of his sleeping bag. His face was extremely alive.

I just had to say something.

"They can hear you guys in the house," I said.

Lucas got up real quick, terrified, and the boy who had been so joyfully sucking him off jumped up like he'd just been electrocuted.

"I mean, quiet it down." I laughed under my breath, trying to seem cool.

Lucas, sixteen and full of venom because he was caught, goes, "Get out!"

From then on it was like he was superior to me because I had caught him. And even though I said not one thing to anyone, still he had that superior attitude, like at any moment I would go stool pigeon on him and he would have to defend cocksucking at a family reunion. Which he kind of had to do eventually anyway when he brought his college butt buddy home with him and was real serious about how much he loved him and nothing would change that, not his parents or God or anybody.

2.

A few months back, Jill said, in the ironed jeans and fresh crisp blouse she wears to work: "Do you think you are the only one who sees how fucked up and shitty everything is?"

"Watch the language," I said.

I lit up a joint. I am thirty-three years old and she's twenty-four and we met in a community-college English class when I was still trying to get my degree in whatever. At that time, I think it was computer graphics.

She said, "Give me a toke," standing by the bed. She took it in and walked backward a little, bumping into the treadmill Lucas had given me for Christmas. She's got short blonde hair, and she goes to a tanning

153

booth but not to get extra-crispy, just to look healthy. She is so beautiful I want her to leave most of the time.

I got up and went into the bathroom. This was when I was not drinking, when I maybe had a chance at management at Applebee's Neighborhood Bar and Grill. I was helping to open a brand spanking new Applebee's out by the overpass. I was that good at that shit.

I came out of the bathroom, smiling.

Jill noticed the look in my eyes and said, "Oh shit," kind of laughing.

When I kissed her, I could tell she liked it. It is so goddamn mysterious how she could give herself up to me knowing stuff like she did, how weak I was, but right then I was strong, I guess. When I pushed her onto the mattress on the floor, she yelled and laughed, and we did it even though she had just gotten ready for work.

3.

I finish the bottle around 6 p.m. I go outside. It's August, and the hot wind smells from the shit-filled river by the water-treatment plant. The apartment complex parking lot is filled with just-bought used cars, and the big dumpster sits next to the chain-link fence like some fat, pissed-off robot waiting to eat what's left.

I start walking at the side of the road in my 1982 Rush tee and jeans and no-sock Converses. Cars pass by. No one seems to see me. I trudge through some ditch slime, past a big diamond-shaped church, past the half-built Wal-Mart, past a neighborhood of brand-new cardboard houses, under a huge water tower, and then into the little town, drowsy and abandoned, sidewalks and a bridge. It gets dark but being fucked-up makes the dark seem like I'm a little kid wandering through a carnival in my pajamas.

At Mutt's Sports Bar, I order myself a Jack and Coke. I say to the bartender, "I wish you guys took coupons," taking some money out of my pocket.

He doesn't even laugh, just gets the drink. It's not that crowded, and the four-man country-rock band plays "Sweet Home Alabama" followed by "Cuts Like a Knife." I gulp and wonder what time is it, and then the bartender goes, "It's for you."

I take the receiver from him.

"I am out in the parking lot right now," Lucas says.

"Mutt's parking lot?"

"Yes."

"Jesus, Lucas," I laugh. It feels like bubbles in my bloodstream, real slow, kind of like an old, worn-out game of Pac-Man going on inside my veins.

"I am going to come in there and kick your ass," Lucas says.

We both laugh.

"How's Craig?" That's his boyfriend.

"Fine…. Come on, Dan. Jesus. You can't keep doing this. They towed your car. What the hell are you going to do without a car? Aren't you supposed to be working?"

I am shocked at how Lucas never gets it.

I give the receiver back to the bartender, and he goes, "There's a pay phone outside."

"I'm done with phone calls."

"If he calls you again, I'm telling him to call you on the pay phone."

"Fine."

I realize this must happen a lot, my brother calling me here. I always come to this place, like my journey is on a tape loop, but every time I come here I don't remember it.

Right then, the Wayne Man makes his nightly appearance. He is tall and gangly and retarded, wearing a T-shirt and work pants and flip-flops. His three-wheel bicycle is out there on the sidewalk.

The bartender goes, "Wayne, hon, we're closing."

"I know. I know. I just wanted to come in and say hi."

Wayne's got greasy hair. Wayne's overweight, and his voice is low-pitched and dull and prissy. He has acne bad. When he talks, he kind of spits a little all over the place. The people left here back away from him instinctively, like a really sick animal just got in through a window

I am almost out of it, about to sink properly into the sinkhole. Wayne comes over.

"Hey, Danny," he says.

"Hey, Wayne."

"How's it going, bud?" Wayne says. He sits down next to me on a stool, smelling pretty ripe. Everything is now so blurry it feels like I am inside a car that is going through a car wash really slow.

"You seen *Spider-Man* yet?"

"Not yet."

"It's great." His eyes are afire due to *Spider-Man*. I notice people are leaving now. I feel frozen next to Wayne.

"It's really great," he says.

Lucas comes in. He is in shorts and a T-shirt and sockless canvas shoes. His hair is combed back perfect like Michael Douglas. I'm proud of my brother with his slicked-back hair and his great job and his condo, and next his boyfriend and he will probably adopt some kid from China. One time Lucas got beat up at school, and I remember how my mom wanted to help him clean up his face, and he scowled at her, and he said, "This is mine." He was pointing at the bruises and the blood on his face.

Lucas comes over and whispers, "I'm taking you to my place."

I laugh. I am not ashamed to be handled by him, like a bad-boy movie star being escorted out by his manager. It's kind of touching. I smile up at Lucas. I want to take back everything about myself and give it over to him in a little wrapped-up box with a letter that says, "Lucas, I love you." But it ain't that easy.

"I'm staying," I say.

Wayne says, "He's staying."

Wayne and me, two buds. But Lucas is stubborn. He has glassy eyes from trying to hide his disgust, and I see it from the point of view of the ceiling fan: me and Wayne. Me the skinny pale thin-lipped nobody with no job about to be evicted, his car towed, in his 1982 Rush tee, sidled up to a bar next to some flannel-shirted moron with major zits. Not a pretty picture.

All of a sudden I get real mad.

"I'm fucking staying!" I scream. I swing my arms at Lucas, trying to hit him.

Lucas backs up. There's not a sound in the whole place then. The band has stopped playing. They are quietly packing up their gear. Lucas glares at me. I swing at him again like I am trying to kill his face, that look he's giving me, and I love the faggot but then again I can't take much more. I want the freedom of everybody hating me, the only true right a real full-blooded alkie has in this country: the right to get rid of everybody.

Lucas says, "Fuck you."

"Fuck you," Wayne says to Lucas. He's got my back.

"Get out of here!" I yell. My voice is like a cartoon-dog voice all of a sudden, mumbled and barked. I like the feel of this sudden exposure, this embarrassment. It fills me up with heat and sparks, and even as the regret starts to kind of flood in around me, even the regret makes me happy that I've done what I've done: something final and real. Something that maybe will change my life.

Lucas has some tears in his eyes.

"This is it, my man," he says, trying to sound all masculine. "Everybody is tired of you."

I feel so sorry for the guy, even though I'd like to hit him all over again. I pity him in a way. I try to get back on the stool, turning my back on Lucas, but then I fall to the floor. Wayne tries to help me up, and I get a big whiff of his piss stains and sweat.

The bartender comes out from behind the bar.

"Get up," he says. "Get up and get the fuck out of here."

I stand up. I think Lucas is still there, behind me. When I turn around and he's not there, I tell myself, *See? See how much that fucker loves you?*

4.

It is me and Wayne against the world. It is Wayne helping me into the big wire basket on the back of his three-wheel bicycle. It is an orange August moon and the back of Wayne's head as he pedals the bicycle up a hill and talks and talks and talks, and me wanting to puke, but holding the puke back.

Wayne knows where I live. He parks his bike in front. Chains it up.

"Can I see your comic book collection?" he says, sweat rolling off his nose.

I don't say anything.

I get out of the big basket and stand. The world is a bent piece of cardboard. I feel so dead I might as well start going up to people and screaming boo. We walk up to my studio apartment, which I did not lock. We go in, and Wayne makes himself right at home. He knows the routine. I see my apartment the way it truly is, a mouse-bit bag of bread, Old Crow bottles, old textbooks I never sold back to the bookstore. The magical couch with no cushions. Now what the fuck did I do with the cushions?

Wayne lies down on my mattress, after grabbing six or seven of my comic books which I keep in a few big cardboard boxes beside the bathroom. I have collected comic books since I was nine years old. I have a goddamn fortune in those boxes. *Justice League of America* #12. *Black Lightning* #6. *Green Lantern* #21.

Wayne takes off his shirt. Lies back, reading a comic, and I flop down beside him.

"I wish I had this one," he whispers in awe.

I look over at the comic book in his hands. Wayne's fingernails are painted black. On the yellowed page is a beautiful rendering of a woman turning into a laser-beam butterfly. On the page next to it is an ad for a miracle workout herbal supplement with a picture of a geek next to a picture of a bodybuilder, and under the picture are the words: *HOW TO GET FROM THIS TO THIS.*

"That is beautiful," I whisper.

Wayne kisses me.

"I love you," he says.

"Thank you."

Wayne kisses me again, and I can taste myself through him. He awkwardly pushes aside the comic books, yanking off his work pants. Naked, he looks like a big white barrel-chested amoeba. I smile up at him, drunk and stupefied. *There is a reason I am on this earth*, I'm thinking, the boy going down on me, even though I'm not even hard and he sucks and he sucks, as hungry as hungry can get. I want all the sadness of the whole universe to be wiped out by this somehow. Then I see Jill in my head, laser-beam butterfly, tanning booths, and Frappuccinos. I remember the message she left me on my machine about six days ago: "Danny, don't do it anymore. Jesus fucking Christ."

I fall into the sleep I always sleep, Wayne doing whatever else he wants to me. It's kind of like being attacked by an invisible dog. Loneliness needs a socket. Wayne is the dude you see and run away from: the mental case you shield your children's eyes from, the reason neighbors sign petitions. But tonight he's in my dreams with me. The Wayne Man and me on a gondola in Venice, right?

5.

Jill and I drove to Ruby Tuesday's in the mall that day. I had a Diet Coke and a hamburger. She ate a third of her Caesar salad with grilled chicken.

"You look healthy," she said.

"I feel good."

She smiled. The reason she loved me, I thought, was because of all the other times I looked like a goddamn zombie, but here I was today in my plaid shirt and khakis, clean and sober, only smoking pot, still spilling out my sadsack bullshit, but working and making plans and thinking about the future at the same time. I mean, soon enough, there I'd be at Applebee's, inside its empty half-decorated shell, teaching new hires how to make nachos. You know: believing in myself. At this juncture, there were definite reasons for making a regular paycheck, like taking Jill out to eat and/or buying her perfume at Lazarus and/or thinking about buying a used Honda Civic I'd seen in a dealer's lot, shiny and blue.

Jill and I went out into the mall-proper after I paid. There was that cold-cinnamon-android odor of mall. I loved her very deeply because it was so easy to do right then.

"Walk me to work," she whispered.

We held hands up the escalator at Tri-County Mall. Past all the stores lit up so clean and still, walking past other couples, past families, past a screaming baby. It was like I was delivering her to her savior at the entrance to the Gap, and standing beside those huge photos of half-smiling guys and gals in crisp, casual clothes I felt like we might be a version of them: models without names, worth photographing, leading the good life.

We kissed goodbye. I swear to God I really wanted to tell her something good about the world, but she walked into the store and I walked out to the parking lot and my fucking piece-of-shit car would not start.

At that moment, there was an avalanche on my home planet. It was time to get it back: *Green Lantern* and Old Crow, closed curtains, and the smell of an empty can of Pringles. People probably think you just fall into that stuff, like tripping. But you have to make plans. I wanted a whole fucking bottle poured directly into my brain—not really through my mouth, but through a *Matrix*-like portal. I was living in a world where you could go from air-conditioned cinnamon smell and shiny new clothes to the cough and coma of a dead car in three seconds.

I called Lucas up, and he came and gave me a jump. He was nervous around me because he knew what shit like this could do to me. He was being real helpful. My Ford Taurus came back to life in no time.

"That was easy," Lucas said. He unhooked the jumper cables like it was a little dance. "Nothing to it."

"Thanks," I said, but I hated him so much my teeth felt like they were rotting from it.

"How's Jill?" he asked, outside the driver's side window. I kept revving the engine.

"Fine."

"Great."

He was smiling out there. I just pulled out without saying goodbye, like it was his fault he had come here and saved me.

6.

It's about 10 a.m. when I wake up. Wayne's snoring and naked. My head is so heavy I have to let it slide back to the mattress. I lie there, trying not to breathe, listening to Wayne.

Eventually he gets up, yawns. He stands up and slides his dirty underwear on.

"You got any hot chocolate?" he says.

"No," I say.

Then there is a knock on the door. A pounding. I pull Wayne back down onto the mattress and put my hand over his mouth. We stay like that while the pounding continues. I hear Jill. She says something that I am not going to write down.

7.

Wayne is loading up what he can. He looks almost cross-eyed. He carries down a plastic grocery sack full of *Green Lantern*s. He puts the bagful very carefully into the basket on his bike.

"You're sure about this?" he asks me as he picks out more upstairs in my apartment.

I go over to my closet. "What size you wear?"

"Extra large."

"I think I have a few extra-large T-shirts maybe. Maybe this jacket?"

He comes over and I put it on him like a butler. He struts in it for a second, excited about getting more stuff.

"Yeah, it fits," he says, almost proud. He can't zip the thing, but that's okay, he takes it. This motherfucker is a survivor. I go in the kitchen and empty out my cabinets. He takes a box of mac-and-cheese and some cans of pork-n-beans. He takes an old model of a *Star Wars* TIE fighter I made long ago that was decorating my windowsill. He loads himself up. I help him carry some of it down, until his bike basket is overloaded to the point stuff is falling out.

Out there in the parking lot, I feel superior to Wayne, as if everything I've given him is a big joke, like he doesn't know I would throw it in the dumpster anyway, but still it's like a gift. I don't even get choked up or morbid or anything.

We shake hands and the sun kind of gets in my eyes as it glitters through some tree limbs. I watch him get on his bike.

"Thanks, Dan," he says, deep pitch in his voice.

He starts pedaling away. His wheels crunch over the rock and pavement. It's a soft, sweet sound, like someone eating cereal.

I go back up to my apartment. I can feel all the stuff I gave him missing, like phantom pains. I catalog it all in my head. Then I sit down on the mattress. Eventually I will fade into what I've given the Wayne Man. I will be what is in Wayne's apartment. I won't even be here, just there.

It's pretty simple.

I always seem to know what I have to do next.

8.

I mean, I had that place perfect, that Applebee's I was helping to open by the overpass. I wasn't a manager or anything, just someone who really cared, a hard worker that the managers always wanted working for them. Older than most of the other kitchen guys, but being older made them kind of respect me. I would hang out with managers, in fact, bum a cigarette, shoot the shit, help them with their inventories anytime they asked.

Hard worker, I stayed after off the clock (district managers frown upon overtime), arranging the kitchen area, Windexing all the windows. I unloaded trucks and had that place stocked to the max, a clean, organized library of canned and paper goods.

When I took that money opening night, right out of the cash register, right then and there, I was thinking, "It's over." I was kind of happy. I was glad there was an end to all my hard work. I think I took the money so I could buy Jill a dress. Or maybe it was for a new alternator.

It was opening night, like I said, people lined up to get in, business booming, and one of the bartenders left the cash drawer open behind the bar, and when the bartender was in the back getting glasses, I took what I could. Just grabbed the bills, shoved them into my pockets, and ran out the back door, past the manager who thought I looked weird, I'm sure, past fellow Applebee's employees, out into the night.

I didn't have that much really, just a few hundred dollars, I guess, but I ran into the field behind the place, turning around to see all the parked cars, the grill smoke coming out of the top vent.

It was a chilly April night. I thought about what I had done and my whole life. I was always on the verge of being a good guy, I had the smile and the look down, I had the feelings, I had the whole thing ready to be activated, but then something stopped me. My human-being card was always being spit out of the ATM.

I left. I abandoned the restaurant I had helped to open, kind of like a man would abandon his wife and newborn kid. I went to the liquor store and I bought myself what I wanted: three bottles. I went back to my place and I crashed, and I drank a whole bottle in an hour. I puked and I drank some more.

Hey—this is the secret nobody ever tells you: there is so much happiness when you finally give in. There is a kind of happiness no one knows about, until they get to the very bottom. It's a magical little pond you slip into headfirst, drowning quickly, but taking your time too. It gets real quiet, and then there's not even quiet. It's just like that. And you're grateful. You really are.

SOMETHING TO BE

Jan-Mitchell Sherrill

Like all inveterate pessimists, Jed was ready for the emergency phone call when it came. There was no searching for car keys, no retracing his steps to the location of his wallet: he was down the stairs and out the door—from call to car—in five minutes.

When he arrived at his destination, Jed found that the police station was nothing at all as he had expected it to be. For one thing, there were no brightly colored prostitutes strung together by handcuffs in raucous little groups around a high magistrate's bench. The paint was not peeling off the walls. The linoleum floors were not buckling. He walked across the subdued beige carpeting directly to a woman sitting at a modern, blond-wood desk.

She looked up at him with a blatant, defiant kind of eagerness. "Can I help you?" she said.

"Are you a police officer?"

"No, I'm the receptionist. Did you want to see an officer? Did you need to report a crime?"

"No. I'm here to post bond for someone."

"Name?"

"Mine or his?"

"The person arrested."

"Reynolds. Barnabas Reynolds."

"Reynolds, Reynolds...." She looked through a ledger sheet. "They bring them in too fast to alphabetize. Was he arrested tonight?"

"Yes. He called me about forty-five minutes ago."

"Here it is. They brought him in from Wyman Park about three thirty this morning. You're not posting bond. He's already pled guilty. You going to pay his fine?"

"What was he charged with?"

The woman closed the ledger sheet, punched one of the twinkling buttons on her phone, and stuck a pencil into an electric pencil sharpener. "They brought him in from Wyman Park?" She smiled at the needle-sharp point of her pencil. "What do you think?"

For a second, he thought about strangling her.

The woman sniffed. "One hundred dollars. Make the check out to the City of Baltimore." She continued to smile as Jed wrote out the check and went on smirking until, accidentally on purpose, Jed overturned her small cup of thumbtacks, paper clips, and rubber bands. He apologized over and over as she retrieved them from across the surface of her desk.

The elevator opened onto a wide room, paneled in white with chilling, soundproofing squares. Other people were seated on plastic orange-and-blue chairs against the wall. At the opposite end of the room was a doorway through which people were occasionally brought as Jed waited, drawing one or another of the seated figures up to meet them at the room's center. A policeman stood next to the door, collecting the receipts of bond or fine from those waiting. Jed went to him and handed over his pink receipt. As the policeman went through the door into the back, Jed stood with his hands in his coat pockets. He wasn't sure how to wait; there was no smoking.

Barney came into the room mumbling something to the officer and feeling through his pockets. Jed moved a few steps in his direction. The left lapel of Barney's jacket was torn almost completely off. There were holes in both pant legs at the knees, and the front of his white shirt was streaked with blood in such even, definite columns that Barney seemed to be festooned with red ribbons.

"Where are your glasses?" Jed whispered. "You know you're practically blind without them."

Barney squinted into the light above Jed's head. His swollen face was mottled with cuts and discolorations. Over one eyebrow, a square gauze pad had been taped, though it now hung raggedly down into Barney's eye.

"That's what I was trying to find out."

Another policeman came out and handed a pair of glasses to the officer who'd escorted Barney, who handed them to Barney. One lens was missing. Barney put them on gently.

"Is it all paid?"

"Yes," Jed said. "Can we go?" he asked Barney's escort, who hadn't left their side.

The officer told Jed to pick Barney's personal property up at the desk. He would need to sign for it and then they could go. That final task completed, they took the elevator down and walked out the front doors to the street.

Under the street lamps Jed stopped and, his hand on Barney's chin, tilted his friend's head into the light so that he could see how badly he'd been hurt.

"I've never seen anything like this outside of a *Rocky* movie."

"Pretty gruesome, huh?"

"You're going to lose that front tooth. Come on, we're going to the emergency room."

"No. Jed, please. Let's just go back to my house. There was a nurse in there. He saw me when they brought me in. Nothing is broken; I just need to go to bed."

"Fine. Then let's get in the car." Jed shivered. "I'm sure this place is swarming with rats." Jed helped Barney—his shoulder under Barney's arm—get into the car very slowly. They were not used to physical contact between them, so their movements seemed choreographed and formal, like a dance rehearsed by strangers. Once inside, they sat for a few moments, waiting for the car to warm up.

"Are you going to tell me who did this to you?"

"I didn't catch his name."

"They don't have names, do they? Nameless Hampden boys. Though I thought they at least had their first names stitched above their shirt pockets. All the janitors I know do." Jed sounded angry.

"How many janitors do you know?" Barney asked. Jed pretended not to have heard.

"How much of it did the police do? They shove you around when they arrested you?"

"They put me on the rack back at the station house. Can't you see how much longer my arms are? I'll need to get all new coats."

"I don't find this even a little bit funny."

"I'm thrilled to be alive. In case I don't look it, somebody nearly beat me to death. No lectures."

"I'm not lecturing you. I just don't understand how you can be so blasé."

Barney leaned his head back against the seat. "I'm usually pretty good when I do the park. I like it because everything operates completely on instinct. You watch for how somebody walks, whether they look at you directly when your paths cross, and you take your good sweet time. You watch for the Hampden boys—blue-collar, blue plate specials."

"Are you on crack? What the fuck is the matter with you? Those 'blue-collar' specials are third- and fourth-generation hustlers; getting blow jobs from old lawyers in heat is a cottage industry with them."

Barney ignored Jed and continued. "Only tonight, I had been out a long time, and I was getting cold. There was a kid I've seen almost every time I've been to the park, and I assumed he was a hustler. You can usually tell the Hampden guys; they're too disdainful, too macho. They have grease on their hands."

Jed snorted, "You asshole; it's Valvoline; they use it like makeup; like stage blood."

"But I was cold, so we went behind the Union Soldier Monument."

"And?"

"And he beat the hell out of me."

"What did he want, your wallet?"

"It was confusing. He took my money, but that seemed like an afterthought. I don't really know what he wanted. He was beautiful. That I am certain of."

"He's some sort of berserko, a basher. I've warned you about this."

"Well, dear, you warn me about everything." Jed started to argue, but Barney cut him off. "No, he wasn't a basher, I don't think. I couldn't help but feel that he didn't really want to hurt me. He hit me with such, I don't know, *resignation*. He sort of did it without being there. Just *resigned* to it."

"Ah, poor guy. Resignation? Shit! It's called precision, methodical precision, and all psychotic murderers have it in common. I wish you'd had a gun to blow his fucking guts out."

"I couldn't kill anyone that beautiful. Once, a guy I met in the park—he was in his twenties—told me that his father, when he was young, used to work Wyman Park."

"Hustler and Son, a Baltimore blue chip company."

"You're a snob, Jed. You really are." Barney was barely audible.

"I'm not a snob. But I hate anyone who hates me. Shit! You think you're Richard Gere in *Pretty Woman*, don't you? Discovering the truth about the lower class? Fuck you, Barney. Start carrying a gun."

"Please calm down, Jed. Stop shouting, at least. I'll carry a gun; I'll shoot all white-trash boys on sight, okay?"

"*You* couldn't. *I* could."

Then Barney was quiet, and the sound of his even breathing told Jed that he'd drifted off. Jed put the car into gear and drove them back to Barney's house. He took the long way, by the park. He slowed as he circled. The walkways were deserted. Only the really serious ones—Jed had seen them, the ones who made you shiver when you looked at them, when they looked at you—they might still be there, waiting. The committed ones. The auto mechanics who pretended to hustle; the high school boys in the acid-washed, Kmart jeans, who were silent first and last, without even an audible intake of breath when they came all over your cashmere coat. The collarless, beer-drinking men who wanted you but hated you. Over by the Union Soldier Monument, a cop car was parked. Only beyond that, inside that dark center where the trees were tightly clustered, only there might anything have been moving.

At the house, Jed woke Barney and got him out of the car. They made the stairs with some difficulty. Barney seemed dazed from medication, and his ribs ached where he had been kicked.

"You mean the bastard kicked you, too?"

"When I was down, dear." Barney tried to laugh but had to pause in their climb to catch his breath. "Isn't that sordid? You know, I think I'm going to throw up."

"Really?"

"Really." Jed left Barney on the stairs and ran up to the apartment for water and paper towels. Finally, after a delay to clean up the mess, he led Barney into his own bedroom and sat him on the edge of his bed. He turned on the table lamp and helped Barney out of his ruined clothes.

"The only thing I still don't get is how you got arrested; I mean, they could take one look at you and see that you weren't the heavy in this piece."

"Jed." Barney was wincing, pulling his arm from his shirtsleeve. "Nobody walks through Wyman Park at that hour for anything other than a particular kind of pleasure. They know that. Besides, the park officially closes at midnight."

"But you're a lawyer. Didn't you threaten to sue them for false arrest?"

"You don't think I told them I was an attorney, do you? For Christ's sake. The most I said to anyone was when I said I wanted to call you to come and get me. I told them nothing. They don't want to hear any bullshit, anyway. I wanted to go home. I didn't want anything to do with them. The whole business is entirely my risk. I don't need law-and-order either for me or against me."

"What a groundbreaker you are!"

"Shut up and get me some aspirin, please. Be my nurse, not my judge." Jed brought the aspirin and Barney rolled under his blanket. "And stop looking at me that way. What do you want me to do, sing a chorus of 'What I Did for Love' or something?"

"'Working Class Hero' might be better."

"Well," said Barney, and he began to sing, falteringly, the refrain from the John Lennon song. Look, this just isn't that big a deal. I'll be fine."

Jed crossed to the windows, looked down on the street, and lit a cigarette.

"*That*," said Barney, "is more hazardous to my health than cruising Wyman Park." Jed turned back to him and laughed. He jabbed the cigarette out in a used coffee cup. Barney waited a second, then asked, without looking up at Jed, "Are you going home?"

Jed folded his arms tightly against his chest and stared down at Barney. "No, I'll stay here with you tonight. You might get sick again, need something. Will I hurt you if I kick in my sleep?"

"I'll probably be the one to have the nightmares." He paused. "You're terrified by this, aren't you? It's you; this scares *you*."

"What terrifies me is how stupid you are. Christ, if you're not worried about getting all your teeth knocked out, aren't you a little concerned about disease? I'm sure that kid's been everywhere. A sponge for microbes."

"Do you expect me to kiss through a surgical mask? Interesting once, maybe, but...."

"You are stupid. Well, you're getting tested tomorrow."

"I've been tested. What am I supposed to do, get tested after every intrigue?"

"*Intrigue*? Listen to you. Wake up, Barney! *Wake fucking up!*" He was going to shake Barney by the shoulders, but stopped himself. Barney noticed and involuntarily flinched, and then to cover up, he put his hand up to touch the bandage on his forehead.

"I know, I know. What I can't stop thinking about is how sad that kid seemed. He was just so resigned to hurting me."

"Yes, you've told me. I'm not crying for any goddamned gay-basher."

"Well, you're a notoriously hard woman." Barney closed his eyes and let his breath escape in anticipation of deep sleep. Jed sat down beside him on the bed; Barney stirred and moved to give him room. In the oblique light, the shadows made the bandage over Barney's eye seem huge; the cuts and crazy-angled scrapes looked sharper and deeper. Sleep would bring Barney some relief from the pain, and he could probably stay in bed until late afternoon. Jed would call Barney's office, and tomorrow — or, actually, later today — he would force him into going to the doctor.

Jed lay stiffly in the bed. His feet touched the brass rail at the bottom. He pushed so hard that his right foot began to cramp. He extended his leg out from under the blanket to watch his toes separate involuntarily.

It hadn't been that long since some psycho had gunned down all those men outside a bar on Christopher Street. And there'd been that pipe bomb at The Hippo right here in Baltimore. How awful to be killed like that, on the verge of love, kissing, or down on your knees in the gentle abbreviation of love that so looks like prayer. Barney was right: it made him afraid even to turn out the light.

Barney was sleeping soundly now. Jed raised himself on his elbows and leaned over him, turned his cheek to one side above Barney's mouth to feel the regularity of his breathing against his own skin. He looked terrible. The bruises were already deep purple beneath both eyes, violet along the edges of his cheekbones, as though big, determined morning glories had bloomed on Barney's face. Jed bent closer and kissed them as secretly, tenderly as he could.

Over in Hampden, who put the hustler to sleep? What does he dream? Some sixteen-year-old girl, a shag haircut and a homemade tattoo, winds her skinny arms around him. Barney's money, in neatly folded twenties in his jeans back pocket, the pants dropped by their bed. Does he dream of Barney? Jed eased himself back onto his pillow, reached to turn out the light, and pulled the blanket around him. Barney's breath caught sharply. Half in sleep, he extended an arm across

Jed's chest.

"Don't be afraid," Barney whispered. "A working class hero is something to be...."

Jed didn't move. The bedroom windows had become gray oblongs, the only things visible in the cautious sunrise.

MY SPECIAL FRIEND
Christopher Lord

By the time Harley and I leave to visit my parents for Christmas I'm barely speaking to him.

A few weeks ago I was promoted to night manager at Shari's Restaurant and I've been having trouble making the switch from days to nights. These days our—formerly my—little apartment has been feeling pretty close.

Because we were going home for Christmas I decided we wouldn't get a tree even though Harley wanted one. Just when I think we're agreed he goes and buys a Noble fir, some strings of lights, and puts everything up while I'm at work. I'm still cleaning up his mess when he comes in the door.

"Why didn't you pick up this shit?" I ask.

"I ran out of time, Rudy," he says, slipping out of his coverall and letting it fall to the floor.

I'm on my knees, the fir needles in the carpet pricking my fingers. "You should've thought of that before you started."

He walks over to me, puts his business near my face.

"You wanna play?" he asks, a little shy, a little teasing.

"Play with your own self," I say. "I'm busy."

An hour later, after eating dinner in silence, we're on our way, the first time I've ever brought a man home to meet my parents.

We're off the interstate now and familiar signs tell the miles to Foster, Sweet Home, other rural Oregon towns. Side roads beckon as they trail away in the fog and darkness.

I see the house—it's a little box with a low-pitched roof, the porch a pouty lip drooling out rickety stairs. Chimney smoke trails into the fog and spreads in veins. Already I can feel the heat inside, the cramped rooms, the low ceilings.

I pull the car into the gravel driveway. "We're here."

It's the first time I've spoken to Harley in more than an hour. My voice is husky, probably sexy, too.

"It looks nice," he says.

The house looks the way it did when I was growing up, only smaller, a few cedar shakes loose and paint peeling in the light of the full moon. Not quite in the country, not quite in town, my parents' house sits on a quarter acre at the end of the paved road that crumbles into gravel the next house down. It's the first house past the trailer court where OotieMae lived until the second hip replacement, the reason for the telephone call from Mom that has led Harley and me here. Mom—or more probably OotieMae—has persuaded Pop to put up Christmas lights. They are stapled in place. Clown colors of orange, yellow, red, blue wink at us as we get out. The curtains are closed; the triangular glow of the tree shows through.

Harley stumbles on the porch. I reach out and grab him so he doesn't fall.

"Thanks," he says, brushing his knee.

As I'm holding Harley's arm the front door opens. Mom and Pop are standing in the doorway, Pop squinting into the darkness. I let go of Harley and we finish climbing the steps. My parents are on the porch now. Pop's arms come around my sides. He smells like dry firewood.

"Good to see you, son," he says.

Mom gives me a closer hug; the dough of her body is warm, a hint of bath talc.

Pop is shaking Harley's hand. "You must be Rudy's special friend," he says.

"Harley, Mr. Sampson." Harley uses his deepest, most polite voice.

"Call me John."

"And I'm Wilma," Mom says, clasping Harley's large flat hand in her own small hands. "So nice to meet you."

Pop steers us into the house. My glasses steam up.

The pellet stove is decorated with garlands. A Douglas fir—a real one from the woods—holds strings of white lights and Hallmark ornaments.

"Take off your coats, men," Pop says. "Set a spell."

The stove's hellish warmth radiates to every corner of the living room. The furniture is familiar—the long couch with the orange-and-brown crocheted afghan on the back, the twin green Barcaloungers. The new big-screen television competes with the tree in trying to illuminate the room. Somebody's hit the "mute" button. Bing Crosby and Rosemary Clooney move ghost-like across the screen.

Harley and Pop sit across from one another, big crooked smiles on their faces, but they're not talking.

"Is that who I think it is?" The voice is a rasp, a growl, a wheeze.

"OotieMae?" I ask.

"Bet your ass, kiddo."

From the kitchen comes OotieMae Winsocket, my father's stepmother. She's been old since forever—she's about eighty now. She's a dynamo not quite five feet tall, once somewhat broad, now thinner, racked with lung disease and every other ailment known to man. She's wearing a white velour caftan decorated with a giant sequined Santa face. She's got a hand on one of her bony hips, which project out from the caftan like antler buds. Her elbow propels her upper body forward as she takes one step, then another, in jerky motion. Her other hand

SHORT FICTION BY WORKING-CLASS MEN

holds a wooden cane, gnarled and polished, almost black. A cigarette
hangs from her lip and produces a wreath of smoke that envelops most
of her face.

"Give Ootie a hug," she says, sidling up to me, her voice somewhere between Tallulah Bankhead's and Andy Devine's.

Even though I'm only five six, I tower over her, and my face gets
buried in her engine-red hair, scratchy, smoky, and flying in all
directions. She tries to put her arms around me, pokes me in the side
with the handle of her cane.

"It's about time you came back," she says.

I pull away. "You're right, Ootie—it's been too long."

She looks at me, swivels on one foot, gives Harley the once-over.
"Who's this tall drink of water?"

Harley's just over six feet. Some of our friends call us Mutt and Jeff.

"This is Harley," I say.

"Come here," she says to him.

"Harley is Rudy's special friend," Mom says. Her hands are clasped
in front of her flower-print dress.

"Well that's just ducky," Ootie says.

Harley bends down, lets Ootie hug him. She pulls back, puffs on her
cigarette. Her fingernails are two-inch talons polished in alternating
green and red.

Mom and Pop sit in their recliners. Ootie has a special chair of her
own, a cracked vinyl rocker that's piled with throw pillows that she can
arrange around her achy bones.

Harley and I sit together on the couch, several feet apart.

"So," Pop says, "any bad weather on the way down?"

"The weather's the same in Portland as it is here," I say. "It's less
than a two-hour drive."

"Then why don't you visit more often?" Ootie asks. Ash falls from
her cigarette onto a metal tea tray sitting next to her chair.

"Let's hear about the big promotion," Pop says.

I can't tell what it is: the heat, the strangeness of being here with
Harley, Ootie's eyes ranging over us both, or embarrassment at Pop's
pride when he emphasizes "big." Whichever, I feel my face flush.

"Do you like it?" Mom asks.

"It's better than serving—well, not always, since I could get good
tips most days, especially the breakfast crowds. I miss days. But I like
the managing. I'm getting to use my education."

After waiting a few years to start college I finally finished night
school a year ago, got an associate's degree in business from Western
Community College. My parents came to Portland for the graduation,
took me out to dinner.

"You're the boss," Ootie says.

171

"I guess."

Harley's spatula hands are on his knees, large fingernails, flat and square. I notice that he's scraped away the grease.

"Are you hungry?" Mom asks. "There's tuna casserole in the refrigerator."

"We ate before we came."

"What about you, Harley?" Pop says.

He looks at me, shuffles his hands. "No, thanks," he says.

"You work for Midas?" Mom asks.

"Yes, ma'am," he says.

Mom's hair picks up the light of the television, shimmers with the colors. "Wilma, please," she says.

"Wilma—yes. I do brakes. Discs, pads, fluid—you name it." Harley pushes himself back in the couch.

"We go to Midas here in town," Pop says.

"They're a good employer. I've been there two years."

"Steady job," Pop says.

Mom's face, Pop's, Ootie's inscrutable pucker—I'm looking for signs that they're wondering about the two of us in the bedroom, whether the difference in height is a handicap. I shiver in the heat.

"Well, Munchkin," Ootie says, after she finishes a cough, "I'm sure as hell glad you're here."

"We got a turkey—first one in several years," Pop says.

"I haven't cooked a big Christmas dinner since you moved out," Mom adds.

"You're making me hungry," Ootie says.

Harley and I go outside to get our luggage; when we come back in we start up the stairs.

Mom stops us. "Ootie's staying in your old room." I put down my bag. "Since the hip replacement. We had her in the family room until she could climb the stairs. But she didn't like sleeping there."

Harley and I go upstairs to the guest bedroom. I turn on the light. Twin beds pushed against opposing walls, tight neat bedcovers. A framed poster from Aunt Tilda's trip to Germany twenty years ago. Mom's waterfall Lane cedar chest, topped with a yellowed crocheted runner, hugs the wall opposite the beds. The room is chilly, with an empty smell, but it's clear that it has been cleaned, straightened, made ready for me and my "special friend."

I open the top drawer of the dresser and I put in my underwear, socks, extra shirts. Harley does the same. Our clothes touch; we don't.

We go downstairs. Harley looks like a man too big for his skin. I can't tell what he's taking in. I told him about OotieMae—but I didn't expect to see her so frail, even after what Mom said on the phone.

Pop's standing at the foot of the stairs; as we come down he puts his hand first on my shoulder, then on Harley's—he rubs Harley's pretty hard.

"You fellas have everything you need up there?" he asks.

"I put extra towels in the bathroom," Mom says; she's talking to me, but looking at Pop. She almost sings the words. "All I had were the ones with seashells."

"I left the bedroom door open to warm the room a little," I say.

"I'll check the vent," Pop says. "I'm about ready for bed anyway. I still have to work tomorrow—half a day, at least—and six o'clock comes pretty early. But you boys can sleep like slugs."

My dad's a plumber; he plans on working just one more year until he's sixty-two. He's put on weight; either that or the plaid pattern of the Pendleton shirt makes him look broader than when I last saw him.

"Night, Pop."

"Night, Rudy," he replies. "Harley, glad to meet you finally."

He gives Harley a good look, shakes his hand again, then climbs the stairs one at a time and disappears into the dark.

Mom is at the bottom of the stairs, takes Harley's hand, too, then stretches up on her toes, kisses me on the cheek. "Good night," she says. The rustling of her dress fades as she climbs.

"You get your butts over here by me," OotieMae says, a bony arm flailing out from her caftan like a twig in a storm. Her fingernails wink the reflected light of the television.

"Nice nails," I say, as Harley and I sit down in the recliners.

"You like them? Delpha at The Hairport does them for me."

"How long does it take?" Harley asks.

"How would I know? I'm never there!" She slaps a hand on her brittle knee. "I love that joke—Dolly Parton says that all the time about her hair."

"It's a good one, Ootie," I tell her.

"I glue 'em on, honey," she says to Harley, fanning the nails at him.

I go to the kitchen. The fridge is filled with cellophane-wrapped bowls, casseroles, fresh vegetables. The turkey's thawing on a towel. So much food for only five people—four, really, since I suspect OotieMae doesn't eat more than a child. A part of her stomach is missing.

Mom's always had a clean kitchen, little appliances lined up and covered with plastic or fabric. The room hasn't changed—the thick, white-framed glass cupboard doors with the old-fashioned pulls, the Formica countertop clean but discolored. Mom's duck collection—ceramic, wooden, glass, clay, and other odd materials—lines the counter.

"What are you rooting around for in there?" OotieMae calls out.

I get a couple of Barq's and a Bud for Ootie.

"You're something in shoes?" she's asking Harley when I get back.

"Brake shoes," he says. "I repair brakes at Midas."

"Oh, yeah. You said that before. The muffler people." She sucks at her beer bottle, smiles, and shows both sets of dentures. She leans back in her chair, gives us a long look. "You've been away too long, Rudy."

"I get so busy."

"You're never too busy for family," she says.

"What with moving and all—" I start to explain.

"And you, Harley—" she says, "well, you're the real megillah." She drums her Christmas nails against the head of her cane.

"Thank you," Harley says politely.

"You're going shopping tomorrow?"

"Yes," I say. "I still have to get a few things. So busy, you know...."

"Nothing like waiting until Christmas Eve to buy presents," Harley says.

"I want you to buy something special for John," Ootie says. "He and your mother have been extra good, letting me come here after the surgery and all."

"Sure," I say. "What?"

"A new fishing rod. It's on sale at the G.I. Joe. I'll give you the money." She reaches into some fold in her caftan and pulls out a wrinkled newspaper ad. She holds it between two fingernails, one red, one green. "This one." She hands me the crinkled paper.

"We can get this tomorrow, no problem," I say. I put the ad in my wallet.

She finishes her beer. "I better be getting up to bed," she says. She closes her fingers around the head of her cane.

Harley rises, starts to help her, but she whips out a bony arm and shushes him away until she's standing as tall as she can. Her hair is wild, maroon flames.

"*Now* you can give me a hand," she says to Harley, her voice breathy. "I still hitch up on the stairs."

I turn off the lights, the television, and make sure the door is locked. When I finish they're still making the climb, Ootie putting both feet on each tread before starting up the next one. Harley towers over her. He's cradling her small craggy elbow with the palm of his hand. Ootie is talking to him in a low voice. I can't hear and I stay back so I won't crowd her.

Harley walks Ootie to the door of my old room. She pats his hand, says good night to me, and shuts the door behind her. She starts to cough almost at once; more than a minute passes before she stops.

I go into our room while Harley leaves to brush his teeth. I leave when he returns and when I come back he's undressed and in bed already, the covers pulled up to his waist. I see his broad hairy chest. I want to be naked next to him, want not to be mad at him.

"I like your parents," he says.

"My friends always have," I say.

"And OotieMae—she's a real trip."

I turn out the light, undress in the dark, and climb into the cold bed, the sheets crisp against my skin. The room is black, a hint of bitterness and Harley's cinnamon aroma.

"What's a megillah?" he asks, his deep voice poking a hole in the dark. "Some kind of monkey?"

It's Christmas Eve and I'm pissy.

I wake up, hard as a rock, and see that Harley's already gone.

I think about Harley again when I'm in the shower, him snaking out of that coverall last night, and the soap and water feel good, sexy. I think about relieving the pressure but that's too weird and anyway, I'm still mad at him.

When I come down, Harley's at the table with OotieMae, almost lost behind a shroud of cigarette smoke. Mom's frying bacon—some things about home stay golden.

"Hey, sleepyhead," Ootie says.

"Morning," Harley says.

I respond with a yawn, give Mom a kiss on the cheek, and steal some of the bacon that's on the plate under paper towels.

"We've been having a little visit, Harley and me," Ootie says.

Harley looks up from his plate; he's been stoking himself with scrambled eggs. He smiles.

"Ootie did most of the talking," Harley says, as if the scowl on my face told him what I was thinking. "About when you were little."

"A little shit is what he was," she says.

Her hands are even smaller today; she's removed the press-on nails and her fingers look like crinkle-cut French fries.

"He was a good kid most of the time when I came for a visit," Ootie says, "except when he'd come around when I was standing in the bathroom in my undies and bra and slap me on the butt saying 'bosom bottom bosom bottom' until I'd shoo him out and slam the door."

"Bosom bottom?" Harley works his mouth around the words like they were foreign.

"Maybe I picked it up in church," I say. "I never could sing 'Rock my soul in the bosom of Abraham' without thinking of OotieMae."

"And my big ass," she adds.

"And the smell of Avon Skin-So-Soft."

"I still use it," she says, "and Christmas is coming."

Mom nods at me from near the stove, her smile small and thoughtful.

Ootie's taking Harley in with great big gulps of her eyes, checking him out as he shovels in the food. He doesn't talk with his mouth full or anything like that, but he looks like a big child as I watch her watch him, a big child with huge muscled forearms and wide shoulders. I'm getting hard again, and I'm still mad at him, but I'm beginning to forget why.

Ootie drags on her cigarette. I forgot how those Kools smell, rotten minty dirt in the air.

"Say, Harley," Ootie says, "I need some things downtown, some special things to make Christmas perfect. Could you get them for me?" She stubs out the cigarette, pushes herself up from the table with her spindly arms. "You come in the other room with me," she says. "Where they can't hear." Harley rises to help her and they disappear into the living room. "Rock my soul...," she sings, then cackles.

Mom loads the dishwasher, turns it on, and sits at Ootie's place with a cup of coffee. She pushes the beanbag ashtray away, wipes her hands on her apron. Her eyes are warm brown pools, the skin around them wrinkled at the edges. The pupils are dark too.

"Ootie thinks quantity is as important as quality when it comes to presents," she says.

"I'll keep that in mind."

"Harley's a nice man." Mom sips her coffee. "Your father and I—"

"I should have shopped earlier," I say, "but this job change really has me jumpy—I've got my days and nights all tumbled up."

She waits. I see her thinking. "Are you happy?"

"I like the new responsibilities—I feel too young sometimes to supervise the older servers."

"Are you happy at home?" The voice is patient.

We've never had this talk before. I've told them the minimum things they needed to know.

"We get along fine," I say.

"Harley's been there—what is it—five months?" Her hands cradle her coffee cup.

"Almost six."

"He's got a good job."

"He wants to go to night school for an associate's degree, maybe do bookkeeping or something. He doesn't want to be a grease monkey forever."

"There's nothing wrong with manual labor," she says.

"He wants to learn stuff, too."

"You're careful, aren't you?"

"Mom—"

"I read horrible things."

"Other people, Mom. Not us." I put my hand on hers, warm from her coffee cup. "Yes. We're careful."

I see her face change, a twitch at the corner of her eye. She looks away, then back at me.

"We haven't bought Harley anything," she says. "We didn't know what to do for him until we saw him."

"You don't have to get him anything."

Ootie and Harley come back into the kitchen. "He's big *and* he's smart," is all Ootie says before she starts to laugh, then gives way to a long, painful cough.

Even in the car I'm getting horny. I want Harley to mention the tree, say he's sorry, and then we can go back to the way it was, sex nearly every day, the yeasty smells of sweat and semen.

"What did you and Ootie talk about?" I ask.

"Just some errands she wants me to run. Nothing special." Harley's voice pushes the warmed air.

We split up at the mall and agree to meet in a few hours.

I've made a mental list and I need to follow it. Something personal for Mom. For Pop, Ootie's fishing rod and something from me. My usual gifts for Ootie. For Harley—well, I haven't made up my mind, yet. I could use a little more charity in my heart, move the feeling for him up from where it seems to be stuck.

There's Harley a hundred yards ahead, going into the music shop. From the back—that's how I saw him the night we met at the Cinco de Mayo party. I'd had a boyfriend for six weeks but he dumped me and I was in a lousy mood. I was planning on drinking a lot of margaritas and going home early when I saw Harley's broad, flat back. He turned and I saw his face and instantly I got interested. But he was too handsome until I saw the chipped tooth when he smiled.

That's when I knew I wanted him. I remember staring at Harley's hands, grease under his nails, and I started imagining those flat big fingers on my back, my stomach, the other places. I liked everything about him and didn't mind at all that he didn't have any college or a career job.

I was jittery that night but the more we talked the more I noticed that he was calm, at home in his skin, had some deep center that was at peace. And that took the edge off me as well.

I could tell he was interested. Since I lived alone my place was the obvious choice. I started cleaning up the bedroom but he was right there kissing me, taking off my clothes, being both gentle and demanding at the same time until we fell on the bed naked and did the wild monkey sex thing three times before morning.

He moved in six weeks later when his roommate got busted for drugs and Harley said he'd had enough. So we just fell together like that. He brought over his boxes of things—clothes, some CDs, a few science-fiction novels.

I didn't tell my parents right away. We don't talk about me being gay, not in any explicit terms. So when Mom asked if I would bring Harley when I came home for Christmas, I paused before I said I'd ask him and then see.

He wanted to go, couldn't wait. So I said we'd be there without giving it much more thought, without wondering what kind of signal it sent to them, to Harley, or, for that matter, to me, about what our arrangement might mean.

I think about the Christmas tree back at home. I'm not quite sure now what got me so angry so fast. It wasn't about money and it wasn't about style. I could care less what the tree looks like.

I go into one of the men's stores and look at ties and stuff. I see this great wool sweater, almost too heavy, but somehow I see Harley's chest underneath it, filling it out. So I buy it. It's dressy, not something he would wear any day of the week. I see us sitting in a restaurant and we're eating Caesar salads and Harley's wearing this sweater and there's a candle at the table.

For Pop I get a new Pendleton shirt. For Mom, a sweet perfume. For Ootie, the gifts are the same as always—another beanbag ashtray, a carton of Kools, some lottery tickets, and something I pick up at the music store that makes me chuckle—something I'll give her early.

Harley's already waiting at the Orange Julius when I get there. He's got a big shopping bag. We eat Chicago dogs, then go to the car. If he would just apologize then we could get back to the way it was.

We ride pretty much the whole way in silence.

At home the smell of baking hits us like a warm glove. The kitchen table is covered with wax paper. Chocolate chip, chocolate crinkles, peanut butter, and oatmeal cookies are lined and stacked in neat rows.

For once Ootie's not smoking. She sits at the table and removes cookies from a cookie sheet with a spatula she's holding in both hands.

Ootie shovels a cookie into Harley's big red hand. "Have one," she says.

"Snerkle-derkles," I say.

Harley looks up, his face full of cookie. He fills the kitchen with his body.

"Snickerdoodles," Ootie says. "He couldn't say it right when he was a kid."

"They're delicious," Harley says to Mom.

"I'm going to take a nap," I say. I kiss Mom on the cheek.

"We'll eat dinner at six."

"And then we're going to the Living Nativity," OotieMae says.

"What's that?" Harley asks, sneaking a cookie from underneath Ootie's watchful eye. She gives him a sly grin.

I turn to Harley. "People standing out in the cold pretending to be the Holy Family. They pose in costumes with animals and stuff."

"It's at the Holy Christ Redemptor Church," Ootie tells him. "This year I'm going to get Lester Simms to say 'hey' when I go by."

I go up to the guest room, take off my shoes, and lie on top of the bed. I'm almost asleep when the door opens a bit and Harley comes in.

"You need something?" I ask.

"Presents to wrap," he says, gruff-like, and picks up his packages. "Don't worry your pretty little head about it."

I wake up and it's dark. I've had one of those naps that make you feel like you've been hit by a truck. The feeling lasts just long enough to put a little more edge on my temper.

I can hear muffled sounds from downstairs, Ootie's laugh, Pop's voice deep and cottony. The cookie odor has slipped under the door and draws me downstairs.

"Hey, kiddo," Ootie says from the living room.

The Lennon Sisters are singing on the stereo. That reminds me.

"I got you something today," I tell her as I stop on the stairs. "I think you'll like it." I go back to my room and bring down a small package.

She's wearing her Christmas nails and scratches open the wrapping paper.

"Hot damn!" she exclaims. "Put it on now."

Harley's watching from Mom's recliner; Pop's sitting in his. I put on the disk, wait for it to start up.

The background vocalists, their voices washed out like eunuchs, begin to "aah" as the four opening chords of "Rockin' Around the Christmas Tree" sound.

Ootie smiles. "It ain't Christmas 'til Brenda Lee says it's Christmas."

Harley's puzzled. "It sounds like she's burping," he says. He doesn't make eye contact with me.

"Don't you knock Brenda Lee," Ootie says. She comes over, takes my hand and steps forward, raises my arm as we start a swing step. I give Ootie a careful twirl and pull her toward me the way I learned in junior-high dance class. She's all bones under the sweat suit she's wearing today.

I'm afraid of hurting her, she's so small and her hips bad, but she's smiling big, her hair a bright shock of flame and she's laughing while we dance. When Brenda finishes the song, Ootie collapses back into her chair, her final laugh turning into a cough.

"You all right?" I ask.

"Best ever," she says when she stops. She's breathing hard now, reaches for a cigarette.

Mom comes in from the kitchen, turns down the stereo.

"That's the first record Ootie bought us the year we got our stereo," she says, mostly to Harley.

"Back in the early sixties," Pop says. "One of those fancy console models."

"Danish Modern," Mom says. "With spindly legs and cloth all around the front, real teak veneer on the lid. We played this record until we wore a hole in it."

"It was the only one we had for a while," Pop adds.

"That was the same year you had the aluminum tree," Ootie says.

"Aluminum?" Harley asks.

"A fad," Mom answers, sitting on the couch and chuckling, wiping flour from her hands. "Before Rudy was born. An aluminum tree with a color wheel that sat on the floor and made the tree change from yellow to red to green to blue."

"Psychedelic," Harley says.

"Bad taste," I say.

Harley gives me a look.

After dinner—roast pork Midwest style, cooked dark and crusty, with a milk gravy, crescent rolls, and green beans—we're all bundled up, headed for town. Ootie, small and insulated in a faux fur coat and muffler, looking like a burning can of Sterno, sits between Harley and me in the back seat of Pop's Crown Victoria. She doesn't smoke in the car. She's humming along with Brenda Lee, although the radio isn't on.

"Town looks so different," I say.

A steady line of cars enters and leaves the church parking lot. The grounds are lit up; from here I can see some of the Living Nativity actors.

"They must wear long underwear under those robes," Mom says.

We snake through the parking lot, find a space. I help Ootie out while she tries to put on her gloves. The glued-on nails are causing her some trouble.

"Oh, hell," she says, throwing one glove at me. "I'll just stuff my hands in my pockets." She hooks an arm through mine. "Let's go."

She leads me ahead of the rest, leaving Harley to fend for himself. Pop and Mom bring up the rear.

Cordons guide visitors around the block. Four or five men (and one woman) stand with crooks among several tethered sheep on a small knoll near the outside of the nave of the church. The sheep chew the grass while shepherds look toward a giant gold plywood star lit by flood lamps.

Small children in front of me gasp and goo, pointing with stubby fingers at the animals. A child tries to pet one of the sheep.

"I'm glad you came home," Ootie says to me as we walk past the sheep.

The crowd has backed up at the next scene. I look behind me; Harley is several groups back, standing near Mom and Pop. They're chatting.

"What's wrong with you, anyway?" Ootie asks me.

"I don't understand."

"You're ashamed of who you are. And you don't know what you've got, either." She gives me a look, expects me to chew on what she just said.

I don't want to understand her, but I already have a feeling that I will.

Here are Mary and Joseph. They've got a cow, another sheep, and a piglet in a small stable behind the manger, all flooded in light. Mary is draped in a blue robe, hardly looking as if she's just been through childbirth. The manger itself is raised so you can't see whether there's a baby in it. In the background "What Child Is This?" plays. Joseph is a young man made older with a fiber paste-on beard.

"Isn't Mary beautiful?" Ootie asks. "She's new. They finally got rid of LaiLoris Doody; she'd played Mary for *way* too many years. 'Our Lady of the Menopause,' some of the women called her."

"Ootie," I say, chiding her gently.

"Don't think I've lost my train of thought," she says. "I've been watching you since you got here. The way you are with that boy."

"Harley's twenty-seven."

"You're all boys to me." Harley is still with Mom and Pop behind us. "He's the real thing, Rudy."

We move slowly. OotieMae feels like a bag of sticks; her arm is almost weightless in mine. The flesh I used to jiggle as a child is no longer there, just spongy bones and skin under sweatpants and her gigantic parka.

The Wise Men stand at stiff attention, their gifts in plywood painted chests on the ground, too heavy to hold. The church can't afford camels, so Christ the Redemptor has used llamas instead, draped with elaborate gaudy saddles streaming colored ribbons.

"There's Lester," Ootie says. "Say 'hey,' Lester Simms!"

"Hush," I tell her.

I walk between her and the scene, fearful that she'll take another stab at Lester. But as we walk toward the corner of the church, she looks up at me instead.

"You're my favorite stepgrandson," she says.

I look down. "I bet you say that to Jerold and Keith as well."

"I've been watching you and Harley since you got here."

"There's nothing to see," I tell her.

"That's the point. You act like he's a stranger, not your 'special friend,' or whatever you call him."

"We've been fighting," I say.

"The anger's all coming from you—I can feel it. So can your mother."

"Harley snapped at me this afternoon."

"Why shouldn't he? You've treated him awful since you got here. Ever since the Christmas tree—"

"He told you."

"I wormed a few things out of him while you were having your beauty sleep."

We turn the corner. "Really, Ootie—"

"You've been jumping around like water on a griddle and that boy has just sat and let you do it. That's how much he loves you."

I stammer something, but she nudges me with an elbow.

"You know he's the one, too," she continues, "but I'm thinking you're too stupid to believe it."

My face starts to burn in the cold air.

"There's no shame in love," Ootie says to me, more quietly this time. "No shame at all—only joy, sometimes hurt. Your parents love you, I love you, but you're ashamed of who you are." She pauses. "You can see how he loves you, the way he talks about you. You better watch yourself or he'll be gone and you'll get just what you deserve—a big heap of lonesome. And I'm getting to like him a lot." Ootie turns around, looks behind her. "Harley!" she calls. "Come here."

Harley's beside us now. Ootie grabs one arm; she's between him and me.

"There," she says. "I'm the luckiest gal at the show—except for the Virgin, I guess."

When we get home, Ootie asks Harley if he'll help her upstairs. Mom's in the kitchen making tea, Pop and I sit in the living room watching the tree's lazy blinking lights.

"Sorry you have to go back tomorrow," Pop says.

I'm thinking about what Ootie's said. I'm all knotted up, but something's about to break.

"I am too," I say. "But I've got to get some sleep before I go to work at eleven."

Pop frowns. "Seems wrong, having to work on Christmas Day."

"Where would people eat?" I ask.

Pop thinks about that for a minute. "Harley's a good man," he says. I hear echoes of Mom's words earlier in the day, Ootie's more recent reprimands.

"I know."

At the same time I'm getting some message that whatever I thought about before we got here, whatever fears I hadn't fully considered before I plunged full tilt into this visit, just weren't what I thought they were. It's like I'm tired, like all of the meanness has gone out of me, the anger dribbled out somehow as we walked in the cold.

But my heart is beating fast, a pressure behind it that I have to let out. I'm afraid.

Mom brings in the teapot, four cups. Harley comes back a few minutes later carrying several poorly wrapped packages. He puts them under the tree with the others.

"Ootie says Santa can't make it through the smokestack," he says.

"I hope you're both warm enough upstairs," Mom says as she finishes her tea. "I could get you extra blankets if you need them."

"I'm fine," I say. Harley nods.

"Well, I'm off to bed," she says, rising and moving toward the stairs. "Merry Christmas."

Pop follows, rests his hand first on my shoulder, then on Harley's as he walks away behind her.

Harley sits almost in the dark, just the lights on the tree and the glow of the pellet stove glass door. His face is dark red, the planes of his cheekbones glinting like knives. I can barely see him; I assume he can barely see me. This makes me feel better for what I think is coming.

"You still tired?" he asks.

My heart starts pounding when he opens his mouth.

"Not so much," I say. "The nap helped."

"I'm still full from dinner. Your mom's a great cook."

"It's good to have home-cooked meals again."

Silence.

"The tree's nice," he says, giving a nod toward it. "Good shape."

"Yeah." I take a breath. "But not as nice as the one you got."

He looks over, a silver slice of light across his cheek. I'm seeing that deep calm I saw the night I met him, that peaceful center. It's pulling me out, stretching me until I snap.

"Too bad we didn't get to look at it before we left," he says.

That tree—now I understand. It wasn't anger—it was fear. It was a new thing, like a tradition, starting between us. And I wasn't ready for what that said about what was happening to me, to him—to us. Everything is now clear.

"We can," I tell him. "When we get back home."

We're sitting almost in the dark and there's only a metallic sound every now and then from the pellet stove. I can't stop myself now.

"I love you," I say.

For the first time.

"I've been waiting," he says.

"For what?"

"For that," he says. "I've known I guess since you started working nights."

His voice is low, smooth dark sugar, soothing me out of my panic, but I don't know what he's going to say next.

"You move faster than I ever could—I like that about you," he says. "But you don't know much about yourself. I knew when I moved in that something was clicking for me—what made me more comfortable made you more nervous."

"So?" I ask. I need to hear something more or I'll burst.

"So I decided to wait it out. But I don't know that I could've waited much longer." He laughs, mimics Ootie. "A little shit is what you've been."

"Harley—"

"I love you, Rudy," he says. "I have for months."

We sleep in one twin bed, don't even bother to mess up the other sheets.

Besides Ootie's fishing rod and my Pendleton shirt, Pop gets a new tool box from Mom and some handkerchiefs from Harley. Mom does pretty well, too. She's pleased with her perfume, a new thick cotton robe from Pop, a jar of bath salts from Harley, and from Ootie a gift certificate for a makeover at the Hairport.

Ootie loves her cigarettes and the new ashtray, wins five dollars on one of the lottery tickets. Besides a bottle of Avon Skin-So-Soft, Mom and Pop have gotten her a fancy new cane with four rubber-tipped feet. She looks at it, leaves it by her side, her face a puzzle. Harley gives her a box of chocolates.

Harley brings in a haul—all clothes, a new parka from Mom and Pop (bought while we were out shopping), gloves from Ootie.

"I made him buy them himself," Ootie says behind a veil of smoke. "I told him that he and John had the same-sized hands." She laughs at her cleverness.

From me he gets the sweater—tries it on right over his T-shirt— flexes his lats as he turns—and wears it the rest of the day.

"Don't you look like the stud," Ootie says. Harley blushes.

I get a small haul of my own. Ties—"Dark," Ootie says, "so the food won't show"—a sports jacket from Mom and Pop. Harley gives me a tie bar with a small pink triangle on it.

"What's that?" Ootie asks.

"It means gay pride," Harley says.

Mom and Pop exchange glances.

"Too bad it's not bigger," Ootie says.

Harley's other present to me is a framed enlargement of a picture taken of us at a late summer picnic. We're shirtless—Harley's chest so far superior to mine—arms around each other's shoulders, big shiny faces for the camera. What I see now clearly in Harley's face is that he loved me that day already. And now I know, looking into my own eyes—bright, slightly squinting—that I already loved him, too.

"I'll keep this," Ootie says, taking the picture from me with her gray talon-less fingers. She looks at Harley. "You can get another, right?"

"You bet," he says. He stands up, puts one arm around Ootie, and squeezes. On his way back to his seat on the floor his hand glides across my shoulder.

When it's time to go after dinner suddenly I don't want to—Mom and Pop and Ootie all warm smiles, stuffed from the turkey, dressing, mincemeat pie, and all the rest—Harley offers to drive so I can get some sleep on the way.

Hugs and squeezes at the door. Brenda Lee's singing Christmas.

Mom folds me in her arms, leans in.

"Pray for Ootie," she whispers. "And come visit again—soon." The last word has extra urgency.

I give Ootie a careful hug, feel her frailty, lose myself in the dull light of her hair.

"You take care of yourself," she says, her voice broken. "Take care of each other."

Pop shakes Harley's hand, Mom gives him a hug. Ootie almost disappears in his embrace.

"Welcome to the family," she says to him as I open the door.

THE BOTTOM OF THE CLOUD

James Barr

Robin left the winter coziness of his bedroom and stepped outside into the snow to watch the sun come up behind the distant derricks that fringed the town. Immediately the chill air stiffened the soft leather of his slippers and turned the silk of his pajamas into a wet gale against his skin. He shivered pleasantly, easing himself into the grip of discomfort for the next few minutes, holding confidently to the thought that he could end the unpleasantness at any chosen second by stepping back into his room. It amused him to play with pain when he felt himself safe from it. He breathed deeply of the cold and blew forth a torrent of gray into the frosty air.

There had been an ice storm the day before, and the wheat-stubbled plains, blacktopped roads, and drab buildings were coated with a slick brittle sheen. Every object possessed the lovely unreality of a movie travelogue. The creaking, clinking trees were especially colorful with their chandelier glitter, shifting and blazing blue-white, apricot, and scarlet as they moved clumsily in the wind beneath their unaccustomed weights. The red sun would turn to yellow soon and melt much of the ice, but tonight it would freeze again and the countryside would remain paralyzed for several more days. All but the main roads would be impassable and that meant little work for Robin until the snow plows had finished their monstrous jobs.

With the thought of no work, Robin's exhilaration with the elements mounted and he thrust his arms into the air and his thighs forward for a wonderful moment of stretching. He kicked the snow roughly and laughed as it sprayed over his bare white arch to melt and trickle down into the pad of warmth beneath his foot. With a final snort of steam he hurried inside and dressed.

Inside the kitchen Mrs. Lalo, the Mexican woman who provided him with board and room, looked up with feigned amazement.

"You're in your work clothes," she exclaimed, lifting a wooden spoon from a pan of boiling oatmeal. "I thought you were going to Central City all so fast."

"Got one short load to haul," Robin said. He sat at his usual place and started to eat the ham and eggs already on his plate.

"Is it salt water or oil?" Mrs. Lalo asked, pouring the cereal into a bowl.

"Salt water," Robin answered between bites. "Won't take over an hour or so. Then I'm on my way."

"And oh, the little split-tails look out then." Mrs. Lalo gave a small shriek at her own humor. "Ah, you're blushing, Robin."

Robin grinned and continued to eat in silence.

"They got some nice girls up there in the city, Robin?" asked Mrs. Lalo. She sat down opposite him and poured a cup of coffee for herself.

"Pretty nice," Robin grinned half-heartedly.

This was the part of his present set-up he found it so hard to live with in this damned hick oil town—the lying he had to do. He didn't mind everyone kidding him about his frequent trips to Central City to see the girls. What he did mind was the fact that he couldn't rip out his foulest oath and tell them that he went up there not to see the girls, but the boys! To shock them would be mildly enjoyable, but to tell the truth just once would give his conscience unequaled satisfaction. But the price was too high.

"They got big ones like these, Robin?" Mrs. Lalo tossed her great breasts up and down playfully.

"About like yours," Robin said, stealing a sly glance at her laden hands. Again she shrieked with laughter. Most of his dialogue was carefully planned and delivered for Robin knew that his prosperity in this town lay in the perfection of his role. But it did get monotonous, going through the same routine day after day, and each time he returned from a trip, inventing additional lurid details to let fall in the manner of a stumbling novice to keep the thing going. Oh well, he thought, another year or so and he'd get out of here with enough money to last him quite a while. He had never planned to stay in one place very long anyhow. Then for the West Coast or Hawaii. Gosh! Those sailor towns and the way some of those queens lived! He tensed the muscles of his legs against the chair quickly several times. He'd be ready for Central City tonight all right, all right!

"Better get yourself something closer to home, Robin." The old note of falsity crept into Mrs. Lalo's bantering tone as it always did at this stage.

Robin finished the eggs and pushed back his plate. Immediately Mrs. Lalo was at his side, removing the dish, handing him oatmeal, pouring coffee, touching his hair shyly, hopefully. Robin whacked her on her flabby bottom.

"Careful, Maw, your boyfriends won't like your playing around with this young stuff. It might spoil you."

Again the shriek, as she wriggled away from him. Mexicans must be awfully hot-blooded, he thought, but they were good cooks.

Mrs. Lalo had plenty of boyfriends, both Mexican and American. They came to see her several nights a week from their boxcar barracks down by the freight depot. Sometimes they had drinking parties and he'd hear downtown the next day that she'd taken on all comers. The parties never bothered him in his part of the house. He could sleep through barrages of noise; the army had taught him that. The heavily laden visitors tramped in and out, always at night, but they did not bother him—the Mexicans because they didn't dare, the others because they didn't care. Once in a while, Robin would notice a particularly attractive fellow, but he had never tipped his hand. Too risky. He had a gold mine of a business in this town and he wasn't going to give it up for a little fun. And besides, he often thought, men were all alike anyhow, conveniently located like comfort stations, something you didn't think much about until you wanted one, then you just looked around for a couple of blocks and there one was.

He finished his cereal and coffee. "Well," he said, getting up, "I may see you before I shove off."

"Going to drive through or take the train?"

"Train. I'll leave my car over in Hamlet at the garage." Mrs. Lalo nodded. "Want anything from the big city?" he asked. "Another gut-buster, maybe?" He referred to a girdle he'd purchased for her on one of his trips. She shrieked loudly.

"You're a card, Robin. You're a whole pack of them."

He rolled the doors of the garage all the way back and looked with pride upon the truck and the big new coupé. Both were immaculate despite the business he was in. He climbed into the cab of the truck and turned the starter over slowly a few times, pumped up gas into the carburetor with his foot and then turned on the ignition. The engine took the first time, roared but a second before he caught it with the throttle and nursed it to life gently but persuasively. He let the engine idle for a long while as he tested the heater, windshield wipers, radio, and lights. Then he went around the outside, checking the chains, the doors to the tool compartments, the lengths and connections of the thick high-pressure hose, and last of all the great fifty-barrel tank mounted on the chassis. Everything was shipshape, Robin observed with pleasure.

Five years before, after his discharge, he'd gone in debt to purchase this truck. The prospects had seemed pretty slim then, but today the truck and car were paid for and he had in the bank a balance that would allow him to buy two more trucks if he wanted to expand his business. But then he wasn't at all sure he wanted to expand just yet. It was about time to cut loose and raise hell for a year or two out West. Then too, another war was brewing, and a business would be the last thing he'd want when he was called back to active duty.

Still, he hated to think of giving up anything as lucrative as this. It was lopsided in ways, but it brought in over ten thousand a year. For a young buck and for doing what was considered manual labor, that was all right. He knew of nothing else that would beat it, unless it was wheat farming, but that required a lot of capital and more hard work than he was used to putting out.

His business was tank cleaning, salt water hauling, road oiling, and anything else he could do with his truck. His summers were comparatively light, but in the winter work always piled up and he was able to get up to Central City only for overnight trips. During the big season, more often than not he made fifty dollars a day so he couldn't afford to be away too much in the wintertime.

In this particular field the crude petroleum was of a very poor grade and carried a high percentage of impurities that settled out in the storage tanks before the refineries ran off the best in their own pipelines. When the residue grew deep enough, it was drawn off into a truck such as Robin's and spread over the dirt roads to make a surface impervious to rain and snow. Salt water, which was settled out in special riser-equipped tanks, had to be hauled away also to disposal plants rather than be allowed to soak back into the earth to contaminate the farmland, streams, and pastures. This was a state law, and because of it men in Robin's business did well.

For drawing off bad oil from a tank, a job that usually took an hour or so, Robin got a flat rate of fifteen to twenty-five dollars, according to the size of the tank. For road oiling, five dollars an hour; for salt water hauling, four. The work was not hard. Unlike most of his competitors, he worked with the fast high-pressure hose which some tankies believed to be dangerous because the nozzle often struck sparks inside the metal tanks. Oftentimes the work was dirty and this caused him a good deal more anxiety than the possibilities of being blown up. Mrs. Lalo always complained about his laundry, but good-humoredly because he paid her well.

In the beginning, he had been a little ashamed of doing what was considered manual labor. After all, he had a college degree and during the war he had carried braid. However, his feeling of shame disappeared quickly when he learned the social setup of the oil fields. There was no leisure class in the small towns. The very rich always moved away from their source of wealth. The educated of the town, the book-keepers and the schoolteachers, were poorly paid and hardly ever held in esteem. Tradesmen comprised the highest social order, but the laborers and bosses of the oil companies were the envied. They were independent, proud, and very well paid. They married the best-looking women, who prized their maleness highly. All in all, in their easygoing manner, these men shaped the characteristics of their communities. It was with this group Robin chose to identify himself, which was natural since he got all of his work from them, plus invitations to supper and card parties, and too often for comfort, the glad eye from not only the unmarried sisters but also the wives. Life was pleasant enough for Robin, so close to Central City and its secret joys.

Robin climbed into the truck again and raced the engine a few times before easing it backward into the alley. As he was about to release the clutch, he glanced into the rearview mirror which was attached to an arm outside the window to see that the way was clear. As he did so two boys on a bicycle rode slowly into the range of the mirror. Robin had seen them often in the neighborhood. Impatiently he waited for them to clear the way. The older one, a nine- or ten-year-old, was pedaling leisurely. The other, who was perhaps a year younger, sat sideways on the frame in the curve of the older boy's arms. The basket on the handlebars was full of milk bottles. Robin could hardly believe his eyes when suddenly the older leaned forward and kissed his young passenger on the cheek. Almost immediately they were out of sight, but the picture remained sharp in Robin's mind—the gentle, protective insistence of the older, the casual acceptance of the younger who had carried a toy pistol in his gloved hand. How naturally it had been done. Robin grinned broadly.

"I'll be damned," he muttered. "I'll just be damned!"

So those two babies were on to it already, he thought, and for a moment he wondered how much of that sort of thing went on in this slow predictable town. He hoped there was a lot of it. He hoped it was well submerged, well guarded, for it could be a frolicsome thing and give zest to the mediocrity of day-to-day living.

"Those little devils!" He laughed and eased the truck backward out of the garage.

The roustabout who awaited Robin at the tank battery wanted two loads hauled instead of one. The disposal plant was nearby and the road had been scraped free of ice the entire distance. He took his time, enjoying the unusual sparkling day, and spent most of the morning hauling salt water and emptying it into concrete pits. At eleven o'clock he drained the big tank completely and drove back through town to his garage. When he had parked the truck inside and backed the coupé out, he locked the doors and turned to look at the tracks of bicycle wheels in the snow. He remembered himself at the age of ten on a summer day in the caves along a creek. He had swum with a red-haired boy much older than himself and afterwards they had slept in the cool dry caves. His eyes grew unseeing to the present and his smile became tender upon his lips.

The house was deserted as he expected it to be. In order to escape Mrs. Lalo before he left he hurried through his bath, splashed himself with alcohol, and admired himself briefly in the steamy mirror. He put on new shorts and socks and dived upward into a freshly ironed shirt, which was stiff as cardboard. He selected a blue wool tie and took out a light gray suit of English flannel, cut expertly along the lines he favored, and a Cashmere topcoat. His shoes had been polished and his hat brushed. Mrs. Lalo was an accommodating old whore, he thought happily.

Half an hour later his car was moving majestically through town. The air was never crisper, the prospects before him never more alluring. The car gathered speed slowly, picking its way over the frozen gravel of the streets daintily as if it hated to jar itself while it was still cold. Robin smiled and looked down fondly at the steering wheel in his hands. He loved engines, powerful engines. Such lovely things they were, so quiet and well bred, and yet so—so powerful. He was in a great mood, he thought, much too fine a mood to be broken, as it was in the next instant.

As he turned the car to the highway out of town, a roaring, deafening blast from somewhere to the north rocked the car momentarily and shattered ice from the trees and telephone wires in showers along the road. Robin scanned the horizon fearfully, knowing too well the sickening, paralyzed quiet that had fallen over the town like a great invisible tent. Almost directly ahead of him he saw the first results of the explosion, a thunderhead of black smoke that billowed upward into the crystalline air, staining the ice-blue sky. It spread quickly on the wind like ink through cloth. Near the horizon orange tongues of fire proclaimed the disaster was well out of hand.

Robin drove off the highway into a service station, his heart beating rapidly, and pulled up to await the news. If it was bad, he might be needed for rescue work. All plans for Central City were temporarily abandoned.

A group of men had poured out of the station and stood watching the growing smudge in the sky with silent apprehension. At last from the babble of voices that arose timidly, the station attendant emerged and asked Robin automatically, "Fill 'er up?"

"Yeah. Wonder what happened out there?" Robin's own voice had grown infinitesimal to him in the face of that rolling, spreading cloud.

"Don't know. Probably thawin' out a leadline. Looks like the whole battery's goin' up, don't it?"

"Yeah."

A heavy Diesel truck with a bulldozer chained to the trailer lumbered by with a dozen men clinging to it. The watchers' eyes devoured it hungrily as it appeared, broadened, and disappeared down the road.

"Looks like the Byington lease," Robin said.

"Byington or the Stringer. Both of 'em's pretty big."

"Yeah."

Mechanically the attendant wiped off his windshield and then, as if aware of Robin's identity for the first time, asked, "You goin' som'mers?"

"Central City on business."

"Goin' try ta drive through?"

"Nope. Train from Hamlet."

"Guess it would be safer today."

"Yeah."

"That'll be two sixty-three. Want it on your bill?"

Robin nodded. He had hardly taken his eyes from the spreading blaze as he talked, glancing avidly at each truckload of workers or carload of sightseers that hurried by, but without comment. A well-known dread had possessed him tenaciously since the explosion. But for a rigid discipline, he knew he might now babble like a fool, leap into his car, and speed to the scene for the most electrifying view of the horror that rested somewhere out there on the snowy plains. As a youngster reared in the oil patch, he had once done such a thing and the hideous details of burned and bloody remains, the cries of dying terror had never left him. With each new disaster he had witnessed—and in the oil fields they were frequent—the weight of terror and fascination had accumulated. In college he had learned something of the significance of these experiences and he came to know that the great fear of his life was to be burned alive. And he had learned, too, that perversely enough he had devoured the hideous spectacles with shuddering eagerness because for some insane reason he wanted them for himself. Because of this, during his later years he had learned to clamp a shut-off valve over his brain, as it were, forcing himself to remain calm, forcing himself to keep away.

Robin left his car and went inside the station where some of the observers had gathered to escape the cold. He lighted a cigarette and dropped a nickel into the Coca-Cola machine. There was a sound of falling metal. Digestive organs whirred, purred, gurgled, and thrust forth an icy bottle from its rubber slit. The thing was almost obscene.

"Oil's dangerous stuff," one of the loiterers said. "Don't take much to blow up a whole township."

"You talk like a man with a paper A-hole!" said another scornfully. "There ain't enough oil in this field to blow up anything. Now down in the natural gas fields of Texas—"

"Aw, take Texas and go to hell!"

Robin went to the phone and picked up the receiver easily. A familiar voice at the switchboard requested his number.

"Mabel," he said softly. "Me, Robin. What's the explosion?"

"Oh, hi, Robin," the operator replied. He was on good terms with the operators who sometimes helped him get work. "It was the Stringer lease. Bunch of men laying a new line near where Jim Heath was cleaning a tank. They said his hose struck a spark inside the tank. Must have been an awful lot of gas accumulated. Gosh, I'm glad it wasn't you!"

"Thanks, keed," Robin said. "Anyone killed?"

"They haven't been able to get close enough to find Jim yet. Mrs. Beedly turned in the alarm. She said some of the men were pretty bad burned."

"Jesus! What a way to die!" Robin shuddered.

"What did you say?"

"Oh. Nothing. Well, thanks, Mabel. Give me Mrs. Lalo's number, will you?"

"Sure thing, Robie."

Briefly Robin told his landlady what had happened, knowing she would worry about him until she heard.

"You still going on to Central City?" Mrs. Lalo asked.

"Yeah. Everything seems to be under control. No need of delaying my trip."

"Well, be good, and if you can't be good, be careful," the voice simpered in his ear.

"Okay. Take a good hitch on the gut-buster before you throw that whingding tonight." He hung up before the shriek could reach his ear.

As he was leaving the station, one of the men said, "Somethin' like that's going to happen to you one of these days, young fella." He pointed to the fire and then to Robin.

"Not if I can help it," Robin said, starting out the door.

"Where you goin' all dressed up like that?"

"Business trip," Robin winked.

"Yeah? Sure wish I had some of that kind of business tonight."

Robin, as he closed the door behind him, muttered, "I doubt it, you old fart!"

He left his car in a garage in Hamlet with instructions for the attendant to wash and grease it, went next door to a beer joint and ordered a bottle of beer and a ham on white. He glanced at the expensive watch he always wore on these occasions and told the girl to hurry. It was ten before two and the train might be on time. He drank the beer, wolfed the sandwich, and hurried to the station a block away. He had time to purchase a ticket before the whistle sounded at the five-mile crossing and the station master closed the window. Robin continued to refuse to think of the disaster that had claimed Jim Heath or to let it invade his anticipation of happiness. Thank God the people with whom he lived and worked were not demonstrative.

He stood on the icy platform, his topcoat flung about his shoulders, conscious of the unusually elegant spectacle he made against the dull background. He slapped his gloves lightly against his leg. Life was, after all, tremendously good sport.

The train ground down upon him, hoary and black, thrillingly huge, hissing, clanking, pounding, turning, grinding, snapping—a thousand sounds combined into one unbelievable nightmare of leashed fury. Blood sang in his ears. Instinctively he stepped back beside his traveling bag and picked it up. Though he loved the spectacle of approaching locomotives and was always fascinated by their powerful mechanisms, he was always frightened. Suppose one of them leaped free of its confining rails and tore toward him. No power on earth could save him if such a thing happened. Again he found it necessary to turn off these dangerous thoughts. The train stopped and he gave his bag to the porter and climbed aboard.

Inside the coach he tossed his coat over his arm, stamped the snow from his shoes and walked unseeing through the double row of faces to the club car at the rear. As the train started to move again, he ordered another beer and gave his hat, coat, and gloves to the attendant to hang up for him. From now on he was anything but a man who worked for a living. Briefly he glanced down the car at the other passengers who stared at him with the frank curiosity that is born of travel's boredom, and settled himself with a copy of an oil journal he had brought along to pass the journey as quickly and uneventfully as possible.

For three-quarters of an hour Robin read, glancing at the wintry landscape from time to time to rest his eyes. Next to him sat a young marine who looked somehow as if he had just returned from active duty abroad. He had eyed Robin quietly since he had entered and Robin was pleased but not expectant. Probably the man would start a conversation before long. Robin didn't really care if he did or not. He looked at his magazine a while longer and fell to meditating about himself as he always did on his way to Central City.

He began wondering, as usual, where this present course of his life was taking him. No student of psychiatry, he was not morbid or pessimistic about the fact that he was homosexual, whether congenital or nurtured or whatever else experts cared to call him. But once he had done a lot of thinking on perversion. He suspected the conclusions he had reached at that time were quite elementary so far as authorities were concerned, but then authorities were apt to be very dull people with rather unpleasant academic aspects, so he didn't mind being considered elementary by them at all.

Everything boiled down to a few basic facts for Robin, the most important of them being that essentially he was like every other young man he knew—unmarried, free, in comfortable circumstances, living a fairly interesting life, hunting the same jungles for his sport as others, but preferring the male to the female of the species for his entertainment. But he was not trapped; at least he did not feel that he was, which was as important, and his difference in preference was not obvious. He supposed he was just plain lucky. He knew that he could stop what he was doing at any time he wanted. Of course, he did not want to slop, and if he ever did, it would involve a lot of self-chastisement that would be damned unhandy for a while, but Robin was reasonably sure that if circumstances arose that required him to live the life of a respectable normal man, he could do so without too much sacrifice. But, he thought with a smile, living as he was was so pleasant. He thought of the hunt, the thrills and the pleasures of the hunt.

He had his likes and dislikes in partners. He preferred redheads in the youthful, more effeminate types; blonds in the older, heavier, more masculine types; but there was a type of brunette that approached that standard of his perfection which, he had to admit, was for him a menace. Usually the few of this particular type were not big men, but extremely compact ones with short, easy, graceful movements and a quiet air of virility that was discernible almost as far as they could be seen. They were usually fairly normal in their habits but so hopelessly oversexed that they were driven to roam from their firesides to compensate for the wifely rationing. They were happy family men for the most part so they hunted the safer pastures where Robin's kind, in both sexes, was to be found to receive their left-over passions.

But this highly desirable type was quite rare, Robin had discovered early in his career. Once they were found, however, they could be had as frequently as one wanted. More often than not these men turned to women for their extramarital relations, as the newspapers put it, but occasionally they sought those of their own sex for extreme safety. In this small group lay the gravest danger to Robin. Whereas their meetings could mean little to them since their primary desires remained in the homes they had been forced to leave for sufficient satisfaction, to the partners of their rendezvous the opposite was true. The homosexual without Robin's intelligence and instinct might think that these relations were the beginning of his happiness, but he would be wrong, for these men had nothing more than a few casual meetings a month to give anyone. They arrived, anxious to be relieved and to be on their way, and at the first possessive sign they thought of their own safety and moved away from any danger. In these few men, Robin knew, lay the power that could pull him from his safe conveyance on the surface of this world and literally drown him in the depths where there was no volition. Because he knew this, he steered a wide course about them; and when he did meet them, he treated them with sarcastic flippancy, giving no quarter, demanding outrageously and consequently holding the whip throughout the brief but always shattering relationship. His knowledge of coquetry was not meager and he saw to it that he did not become too involved with any of this group. He would not let a suggestion of permanency enter his mind or any admission other than general impersonal admiration and satisfaction. With wisdom he was cautious and with caution he was safe.

The others he had observed in the homosexual world were really a pretty stupid lot when one got right down to it. They dolled themselves up in outlandish finery that could be spotted by an idiot, they sat in the same notorious bars too frequently, they mooned over affairs when they had them, and worked themselves into states over partings. They had mad passions for the ballet, or classical music, or feminine fashions, or crystal, or decorating, or old china. They picked up effeminate idiosyncrasies of speech and manner and gushed at each other, hoping they were showing the world how clever and important they were—and all the while they were willing to play to any audience they could shock into watching them.

Robin enjoyed attention as much as any exhibitionist and he liked fine clothes, so long as they were quiet. He saw to it that his speech remained a little crude, his choice of subjects and attitudes masculine, and he tried to care very little what the rest of the world thought of him so long as it accepted him as an equal. That was most important. He suspected the same was true for the others in this world too, but they were not so wise as he in going about achieving this respect. As a result, Robin succeeded where they usually failed, for he knew that the only possible understandable element to the rest of the world who sat in on them as judges was this intense appreciation of that which is male. He also knew that departure from maleness led to personal disaster quicker than any other infringement.

Of course, there were many exceptions to any rule he used as a measure, but these exceptions in his world were hard to meet for they lived and hunted in his manner, not in parks like the others. It was in this group of individualists like himself that a possible future for him lay, he supposed, if he didn't break with all this before it was too late. Yet he hated the thought of settling in one place and putting down roots and being enveloped by the tendrils of a comrade. The other escape he saw was in marriage when this present penchant was exhausted or outgrown, but marriage was not too alluring. He was fond of a few girls and supposed that any of them would do nicely, but they were for the most part older than he. It was difficult to escape the possibility that he found in women only an answer to a need for a substitute mother. Oh, well, better that than nothing so far as society was concerned with him, he supposed. When he decided to turn his talents to preserving society in a more genuine manner, women wouldn't question his motives too closely so long as he married one of them. But in the meantime, there was pleasure to be had and—

"Excuse me. Do you have a light?"

"What? Oh, yes, just a moment."

It was the marine. Robin handed over his lighter and studied the serviceman. Not bad. The man lighted his cigarette and examined the golden gadget.

"That's nice. Got your name on it too. Robin S." He handed it back. "I'm Bruce A." Robin laughed and took the proffered hand.

"The lighter was a present from a fair admirer."

"Some admiration, I'd say."

Robin nodded. "I paid for it and more before I got out."

"Married her, huh?"

"Not that bad."

There was a pause indicative of polite disinterest on both sides, and then Robin asked, "On leave?"

"Yeah. Going home for ten days."

"That's good."

"I suppose," the serviceman replied, leaving the opening for Robin to enter, but Robin remained uninquisitive. "Live out here?"

"Yes, I do," Robin answered.

"I noticed some oil wells near the stop where you got on."

"That's right. Quite a field they've brought in there. Know anything about the industry?"

"A little. I'm from Pennsylvania."

Robin raised his eyebrows appreciatively and gave a short nod. "Ever work in the field?"

"Nope. That's one thing I haven't done yet."

"Quite an experience."

"I guess so. Where are you going?"

"Central City. I come up often on business."

"Your home office there?"

Robin laughed. "I own my own business. I label my trips business, but I guess they're really for relaxation."

"How is Central City? Quite a town?"

"Yes, quite a town." Here Robin found the pattern growing more familiar. He looked the man over carefully, noticing every feature separately—head, body, hands, legs, eyes, teeth—weighing them against his private standards before deciding.... There was nothing wrong with the man. He just didn't quite meet the requirements. Then too, servicemen could be the dullest of the lot, or even troublesome on occasion, especially if they were as interested in being friendly as this fellow seemed.

"I might stop over there for the night." The man uttered the expected. "Getting tired of riding. Been on since 'Frisco."

"Traveling can wear you down, all right," Robin agreed.

"What's a good hotel?"

Robin considered a moment. "The Luckendam is fairly good and right downtown. Not far from the station and reasonable. They can usually find a room for a serviceman."

"Is that where you're staying?"

"No. I'm putting up at the Town House. It's out a ways and rather expensive."

"Oh."

Robin glanced at his watch. "Care for a drink?" he asked.

"Don't mind if I do," the marine agreed warmly.

Robin raised his hand to the barkeep who came on the double.

"What'll you have?"

"Double Bourbon and a coke," the marine answered promptly. Robin's stomach turned at the thought of the concoction. He was quite sure of his decision now.

"Bring me a Martini," he said, "and take this away." He indicated the beer. "I guess it won't hurt me to start my imbibing an hour early for once."

"It shouldn't," the serviceman smiled, turning his chair a little more to him. "You must do all right in your business."

"So-so," Robin replied, thinking the man duller than he had originally supposed. He calculated the number of minutes he'd have to get through before the train got in and he could decently escape.

The drinks arrived and as the serviceman grew more acutely aware of Robin's lack of interest, he tried to become more entertaining by reciting his stock of well-exercised observations gathered from his run-of-the-mill experiences in the Philippines.

Robin felt sorry for the fellow, so he tried to listen with interest, but the man was hopelessly boring. Robin recognized the type; he was looking for a good time on someone's expense account, which probably meant a steak dinner, a nightclub or the fights afterward, a good bed where he would square up his end of the bargain, and a spot of cash to speed him on his way in the morning. He might be manna from heaven for some queen, but from Robin's viewpoint, he had little to offer. The Martini was abominable, so he left it unfinished.

When Central City was announced, Robin called the waiter, ordered his companion another drink, and paid the bill. As the sheds came into view, he stood up and took down his hat and coat.

"Lots of luck," he said and held out his hand.

The marine lurched to his feet and squeezed Robin's hand with un-due warmth. "You're a damned good joe."

Robin cupped his hand to withstand the pressure and smiled indifferently into the probing eyes. The porter appeared with his bag.

"Right this way, sir."

"Goodbye." Robin released his hand, promptly wiping the man and the past hour out of his mind forever. He followed the porter down the long moving aisle.

In the station he paused long enough to make one call. Though it was heartless of him to do so, he always rang up Freddie, a clerk from some man's shop who had picked him up one night when he had been very drunk. He reported that he was in town, "but pretty busy this trip, seeing some new equipment and meeting some business acquaintances for the evening." With this explanation he left himself free of Freddie for his stay. In return he got a quick summary of the local gossip that might interest him and valuable tips on where not to be seen at the moment. Freddie was a cloying, nauseous little fellow, but he had a certain usefulness.

Robin stepped out of the booth and walked through the high glass-covered, bubble-like station to the taxi ramp. He got into a cab, told the driver his hotel, and settled back to watch the town roll by the windows in the press of after-five traffic. The War Memorial atop Hillside Park came into view, a tall slender shaft of concrete set among promenades, parapets, and long sweeping lines of fountains, and flanked by broad stairways. At the top of the shaft, commanding the entire city, floated a diaphanous flame of orange. The city's lights were still dead and the crepuscular stillness far above the dinning traffic about him helped to fill his mind with memories of those long, shadowy night walks one might take up there in the park, the faces one saw or did not want to see, the whole forbidden atmosphere of expectancy. He drew his breath in sharply and looked up again at the flame, floating like a scarf of bright silk against the deepening blue-black sky, and quite without warning he shivered with cold—and, yes, it might have been fear—not for an instant but for several minutes. The cab moved on until the monument was no longer visible, and the paroxysm left him as unexpectedly as it had arrived. He huddled into the warmth of his top coat. Perhaps he was coming down with a cold. He'd try to remember to drink only whisky tonight.

His arrival at the hotel was without incident. He went immediately to his room which was nice enough but without the view of the city he had been anticipating. He was too exhausted to call the desk and demand another room, and since the lobby had had that convention look, they were probably crowded.

He fought a sudden desire to fall on the bed and sleep, telling himself he hadn't come all this way only to sleep. He went into the bathroom and started filling the tub with hot water and came back to the phone. He noticed his voice was weak and he said, "Give me the masseur, please." He waited for a few seconds and replied to the voice that answered him, "I'm in 622. Can you come up in a quarter of an hour?" The voice said it could and Robin dropped the telephone into its cradle.

Refusing to look at the bed, he made the tub with effort and climbed in hardly caring that the water felt scalding to his skin. He submerged and closed his eyes. Slowly, very slowly, he relaxed and let his arms and legs float to the surface. Strange, strange, this sudden lethargy. He was not ill. He was chilled from the drafty train. That was it. Or had the shaft and the flame had something to do with it? It was as if someone had walked over his grave. His laughter was a weak snort of contempt. Still it was such a funny old idea, shivering when someone stepped on your grave. But then he'd never have a grave, he was going to be cremated, they'd have to step on his ashes.

A knock awoke him and he called to come in for he had left the door unlocked. The door opened and a high, table-like bed rolled in before a man wearing the whites of a hospital attendant. Several towels and a flat pillow lay on the fresh sheet, and bottles clinked lightly from the shelf below. The attendant came to the bath door. "Good evening, sir."

"Hello." Robin sat up with some effort. He hoped he felt better. "I think I'm coming down with something. Chilled and a sudden fatigue. Don't know what it is," he finished thickly.

Instantly the masseur was on his own jovially familiar ground. "We'll have you fixed up in a jiffy, sir." He gave Robin a hand to help him rise and brought a great white towel and wrapped him in it before opening the drain. "If you'll just lie on your stomach on the table here, sir."

Robin decided he was hungry. "Order me a couple of Gibsons," he told the masseur, "and get yourself a drink if you want it."

He stretched out on the sheet completely relaxed, almost asleep while the masseur ordered the drinks. Then the man toweled him dry and started kneading the muscles in the small of his back, rubbing in unguents that smelled faintly of Vick's ointment and lavender water. Robin dozed feverishly.

"Here you are, sir." The masseur awakened him. "Your drink."

Robin raised himself on his elbows and looked at the handsome young bellhop who stared at his nakedness with unconcealed interest.

"My wallet's there on the bureau." He smiled, lifting himself up more and turning on his side. The boy appraised him further. "Hand it to me, will you?"

The bellhop offered him the tray of cocktails and then brought him his wallet. He managed to touch Robin's hand as he handed over the wallet.

"Be interested in a little lovin' tonight, sir?" He grinned impishly, his eyes leaving Robin's face slyly.

"Have you any suggestions?" Robin asked, immensely amused.

"I can fix you up with anything you want, sir. Blonde, brunette, redhead—anything you might want."

Robin gave the boy a wink of understanding and a bill. "We'll see later. Keep the change."

"Thank you, sir. I'm on duty until one o'clock. If you want me, call for Number Seventeen." He touched the brass tab on his dark green chest and backed out the door with an answering wink.

Robin drank his first cocktail, took the second, and lay on his back for the remainder of the massage. The masseur's joviality seemed to have frozen. So he had caught on. "What the hell," Robin thought, closing his eyes and exhaling the pleasant fumes of gin through his nostrils. What the hell. He was beginning to feel wonderful. He was glad when the doddering old dodo was finished and left with his wet towels and clinking bottles. He drank his second drink and thought of Number Seventeen. It might be nice to have him up for a few minutes. Sort of a preliminary to the evening to come. He could order another drink. He toyed with the idea for a moment and decided against it. Tonight, he felt, was going to be something special. He would save himself for it. With a sudden excess of good spirits he picked up a rather heavy chair and held it straight out before him, admiring his modest corded muscles in the mirror above the bureau. Then he dressed and went down to the hotel bar.

There is nothing like an expensive cocktail lounge to bring out the very best in an exhibitionist, Robin thought happily as he walked down the few deeply carpeted steps to the hostess in her too smart black dress. He paused a moment, aware of the eyes on him, and looked over the dim crowded room with a subtle show of indifference. It was a gorgeous setting for gorgeous people, tall mirrors flanked by tall slabs of onyx marble and small white plaster chandeliers of pink lights. He smiled at the hostess and said, "A table, please." From the bar, appreciative eyes watched him across the room.

But from the moment he was seated, he knew his adventure would not begin here tonight. The place was too civilized. Its possible passions were too well-known to him, too burned out. Two tables away, an unbelievably good-looking man smiled tentatively but Robin looked away, hating him for attempting to intrude on such a promising night as this might be. Without waiting for his drink, he put money on the table and walked out. He went to the dining room, ordered drinks and dinner and sat morosely listening to the unctuous strains of chamber music.

What was this business of homosexuality anyhow, unless another narcotic for the jaded, the used-up of the world? He was not thinking of those who could not escape from the trap of their natures. They didn't count. They were faceless before humanity in any light you examined them. He was considering those like himself who conceivably might get out but who always chose not to. Tonight why didn't he pick up a girl, take her to his room, and make a night of it? And in the next instant he knew why he would not. It was the possibility of that fantastically satisfying experience he would have one night, perhaps this night, an experience that would set the mark for all others to follow. It was the fact—and this jarred him soundly—that already he was in too deep to get out with a whole skin. He knew now that he'd been in too deep the second time he had willfully sought out this type of satisfaction, so many years ago. The first might have been excused for several reasons: curiosity, lack of control from drunkenness, inexperience, or a number of others. For the second attempt there was no excuse. It was too bald a fact to allow qualification.

Robin sighed. It had taken him years to admit this point. For a moment he was worried, but he turned his attention to his dinner thinking, "Oh well, that's life," and began to eat.

He walked through the city for an hour. Fog threatened and for a while it seemed to grow warmer. That was good for he did not want to be out too late if it started growing colder. He might be having influenza and there was no use inviting a long illness. He walked along with a cigarette, looking into the shop windows, admiring or discarding the treasures they offered. He found a few things he liked, but nothing he coveted. He seldom did in shop windows. The things he bought were usually kept exclusively out of sight.

His feeling of adventure had grown rather dim during dinner but the longer he walked the streets, the more it revived. He still did not know exactly what he wanted to do. He stopped in a cafe for coffee and sat at the counter beside a heavily muscled man with a great head and dirty nails. Immediately the feeling of anticipation spread through him like a warm glow of liquor. Big and brutal. Power. Power to conquer, power to control, a machine, an engine, power to own, to make work for you at your whims. His pulse grew sluggish in his throat.

"So that's what you want," he said to himself. "A bit of roughing up, is it? Well, okay, but excuse this one, please. He's much too filthy. At least get one that looks as if he bathes regularly."

When he left the cafe it was snowing so he entered the next bar he saw and had a double rye. He lingered a few minutes studying the habitués and went out. He had seen nothing that interested him.

Like a beacon between the walls of the tall buildings, he saw the War Memorial atop the hill with its elusively contoured flame almost obscured by the light falling snow. His pace quickened. At last he had a destination. He knew that it was there he had wanted to go from the beginning. There on the promenades about the flame-bearing shaft might await the shadowy personage he would know this night.

As he walked briskly along the quieter streets, the reasonable part of his brain argued that the place would be deserted on such a bad night, thus conditioning him for possible disappointment. But a second part of his mind told him that there would be no disappointment. And still a third thought neutrally, "You can always call Number Seventeen."

He crossed the last street and stood before the first long flight of steps up the hill. A policeman strolling nearby looked at him a while before deciding to nod and speak. Probably this minion of law and order had decided he had come from the nearby railway station for a walk between trains. Robin nodded in return and looked up at the great shallow urn atop the shaft that held the flame. How high it was, how great was the bowl, how tremendous the fire. Once more he shivered and, fearing another paroxysm, he looked down and started the ascent.

Halfway up he started encountering people, either seated on the benches or standing fairly near the lamps. A vagrant, little more than a heap of hopelessness, grief, and rags, sat half frozen in the meager protection of a stone bench. Robin's heart ached with sudden pity and he took a couple of pieces of silver from his pocket.

"Get yourself a drink," he said hoarsely, dropping the heavy coins into the rags. He hurried on, not wanting to hear the servile whine of thanks. Why did such people deliberately torture themselves in such a way? Didn't they know about the institutions that would feed and clothe them? Or bridges where one could jump?

On the next bench a soldier and a girl were embracing in the darkest shadow. As he approached, their rhythmical movements stopped and they stared at him until he passed. The girl, her leg over her companion's flank, looked cold. Robin hoped she was prompted by love.

Nearer the top Robin came across the first game, two figures sitting near a lamp. Like fowls from underbrush, they watched him tramp past them. At last one got up and followed at a timid distance. He could hear their soft girlish voices and indistinct words that probably invoked the gods of love and luck. He did not look back.

There were others, standing or moving stiffly in attitudes of embarrassed bravado at their lack of respectable motives for their presence, and some that looked more likely than others, but none that proclaimed at the first glance, "*This* is the one you seek."

Robin climbed the last flight of stairs and stood looking down the long shining pavilion before the monument. Along the parapet that overlooked the city to his right were the sitting ducks. With a heart beating an old exotic tempo, he lighted a cigarette, and started the walk peering intently but briefly into each face that turned as he walked by.

Long yellow hair...a furred flying jacket...a hungry face there...a man blowing on his gray hands to warm them...a camera case suspended from the neck...a bright muffler, gloves, and a beret...one who spoke softly...one who did not speak, but smiled....

Robin walked along, aware of the sickening thrust of his heart as each prospect was examined and discarded. Which would it be? There were not many left....

A knot of three chattering like birds, hungry snow birds...an old one in a homburg...a suave profile held for its dazzling effect against the city's light....

That was all of them. For a moment Robin was stunned. He considered going back to see if he had missed one. But bitterly he knew he had not. Slowly he walked to the opposite stairway and put out his hand to the stone balustrade to descend. He poised his cigarette on his fingertip to flip it away when he heard, "A light, if you please."

"What?" Robin turned to the voice at his shoulder.

"I said, a light if you please."

Two bare hands reached for his cigarette and as he would have surrendered it, the hands enfolded his own and carried it to a narrow lean face. The cigarette tips touched and glowed, revealing dark eyes and heavy brows under black curling hair, hollow cheeks beneath high bones, and wide soft lips that were nearly purple with cold. The hands were like two husks about his own, but husks that were tough and green, not ready to be shucked off. He was not a tall man, nor a heavy one. But he was aware of his endowments for obviously he did not feel it necessary to parry in the accepted manner. He continued to hold Robin's hand while he looked at him. Robin cast about for some excuse to shatter the pose they held.

"I didn't see you. Where did you come from?"

The shining wet head jerked toward the shadow of the tall stone shaft. In the sudden flash of light on the face, Robin thought he must be an Italian or perhaps one of the other Mediterranean peoples.

"You want some fun?" The accent was thick and labored. Robin realized the man had not spoken more because he was unsure of the language.

Robin nodded. "I want some fun."

The hands released his. "We go."

They walked rapidly down the darkened stairway and down the curving paths of the hill. Once as they rounded a corner into pitch blackness, Robin felt himself jerked to a stop and the lean face was thrust down animal-like into his. The man was like a steel spring bent to its utmost tensility. At the street Robin signaled a taxi. The drive was completed in silence and Robin stopped the cab half a block from the hotel, paid, and watched it move away.

For the first time Robin noticed the man's disreputable state. His clothes were cheap, frayed, sodden. The threadbare coat collar was turned up against the falling chill. Impossible to take him inside in this condition and too risky to ask him to use the service elevator. Better bluff it out, he decided. Quickly he moved into the doorway of an un-lighted store and took off his topcoat, hat, and gloves. Luckily they were near the side entrance of the hotel. He helped the man into his coat and saw him stroke its wet silkiness with wonder. He gave him the hat and gloves.

"I stay there," he said distinctly, pointing to the hotel. "You follow me in. Up to my room. Understand?"

"I understand," the man said, putting on the hat that sat grotesquely on the top of his head.

Robin laughed. Better carry it," he said. Then he laughed again as a thought struck him. "What a hell of a lark if this poor, hungry son-of-a-bitch ran away with his clothes. Three hundred bucks worth of hat and coat disappearing up an alley. What an experience. He almost wished it would happen.

Robin lighted a cigarette and stepped casually out of the store front. To anyone who noticed him, he must seem to be a hotel guest out for a breath of air. He looked behind him at the man in his coat. Already he was moving to follow him, so Robin strolled toward the hotel entrance. Pretty fair deception so long as no one noticed the dilapidated shoes. He took out his key and played with it idly as he approached the marquee. He nodded to the doorman, passed him and then, calculating the time the man behind would reach him, turned abruptly and asked, "Oh, by the way, can you tell me where I can find a Chicago paper?"

The doorman replied, "You might try the newsstand just off the lobby, sir."

Robin saw his coat enter the revolving door, "Thank you. Quite a crowd at the hotel tonight."

"Yes, sir. Another convention."

"Well, good night."

"Good night, sir."

Inside Robin picked up his shadow once more and felt the man follow him to the elevators. Robin entered the first car, turned, and saw it enter too. Robin was somewhat surprised at the man's manner. He seemed to be fairly at ease.

"Six, please." Robin looked at his companion. The man moved a step nearer and smiled down on him showing dazzling white teeth. How theatrical he looked, like a prewar troubadour from a very schmaltzy movie. He even wore a neat mustache and he was immaculately shaven. "Maybe he works in a barber shop," Robin thought with amusement. The elevator stopped and they went down the hall to his room.

"Nice place," the man said. "In Poland, once, I work in place like this."

"Indeed?" Robin concealed his grin and unlocked the door. "Go ahead."

"Thank you." The man bobbed him a little bow and walked in.

Robin closed the door and shot the bolt into the jamb.

"You'd better get out of those clothes. They look wet to me."

The man took off the topcoat and laid it tenderly on the bed. Then to Robin's amazement he went to the closet, brought out a hanger, and hung it up.

"Hey, fellow, you're all right. A gentleman's gentleman, no less."

The man beamed and Robin went to the bathroom for towels. Coming back, Robin saw that the man's suit was really nothing more than a dripping rag.

"Better give me your clothes and I'll have them pressed for you." Obediently the coat and trousers were handed over after being flushed of a dime and a few pennies, a fresh handkerchief, a penknife, a small roll of copper wire, and a tube of preparation that could have but one purpose. Robin's mounting mirth burst forth in unapologetic laughter.

"You're always prepared, I see," he said as the man deposited the articles on the bureau. "What's this," Robin asked, touching the wire.

"I use in my work."

"Oh, well, you'd better hop into a hot bath. You're probably chilled."

As he called room service, Robin watched the man remove his shoes and socks and put them on the radiator. Then with rising tension he watched him strip the rest of his clothes.

"You might have been a homeless war refugee once," Robin said to himself, "but there's no evidence now that you were ever starved." The man was splendid and proud of it. He walked away from his clothes and posed consciously for Robin, at last coming nearer and holding out his hands.

"Not now, Pedro." Robin waved him away. "Go take a bath while I get this stuff taken care of." He indicated the clothing near the door. The man went off to the bathroom taking the towels with him. When Room Service answered, Robin said, "I've got some clothes to be pressed and mended. Can you have them ready in the morning?" He was assured they could. "Fine. And bring up a bottle of good rye whisky when you come."

Robin took off his coat and hung it up, smoked a cigarette while he waited for the bellhop, and listened to the sounds of running water and a deep rich voice that hummed what might have been a lullaby.

When the bellhop knocked, Robin closed the bathroom door. He went to the door and saw with relief that it was not Number Seventeen. He took the tray, gave up the suit, and told the boy to do whatever was needed but to be sure to return it in a presentable state. He locked the door again and half filled two glasses with whisky and added ice. Holding them both in one hand, he opened the bathroom door and looked in.

"Hello. You sound happy." He handed the man a glass. "For your bugs."

"Bugs?"

Robin gave a mock cough by way of explanation and said, "Germs."

The man looked bewildered but smiled, lifted the glass to his nose, rolled his eyes with appreciation, and drained the glass in one attempt. "Good," he said.

"Like another?" Robin asked, concealing his astonished amusement behind a habitually sarcastic countenance.

"Please."

Robin gave him his own glass and the man drained it as he had the first drink. He turned and escaped to the other room to shake with silent laughter. This guy was a clown. He belonged in a circus. Robin stood by the window until he was possessed of sobriety again. The night ahead would certainly compare with nothing he'd ever experienced, he was sure of that. He fixed another pair of drinks and went back to sit on the stool and regard the man splashing in the tub. If this guy drank two more like the first, he'd be flat on his damned face in another half hour. He held out a glass to him. But the man shook his head and laughed.

"I get drunk," he protested.

"No." Robin exclaimed with condescending irony. "How old are you anyway, Pedro?" he asked, looking him over admiringly.

"Thirty-four," the man said. He seemed never to miss an opportunity to display those teeth. They were marvelously even, but on him they looked like a wolf's. "How old are you?"

"Twenty-nine," Robin replied,

"You are a nice boy," the man said solemnly and went back to scrubbing his foot. "You live here all the time?"

"No."

"Where you live?"

"Out west a hundred miles in the oil fields."

"You come here often?"

"Not often."

"You take me to the oil fields to work with you?"

"Don't tempt me, Pedro," Robin said. "I'd probably never get any work done myself."

The smile appeared again, as if in understanding. "You come in with me?" He patted the water in front of him.

"No, thanks. I don't think I could swim for my life in such a small place." Robin laughed at the man's puzzled look. "Hurry up, Pedro."

Immediately the man stood up and started drying himself. Robin went into the other room and finished his drink. The man appeared and drew himself up at the edge of the rug like an acrobat about to go into a tumbling routine. Robin felt his mouth curve with mirth again.

"Have you ever worked for a circus?"

"I was farmer over there," the man said with a trace of sadness in his tone. Robin shrugged and nodded.

"Are you cold?"

"Some cold."

Robin took his dressing gown out of his bag and tossed it to him. The man took it and caressed its silk against his chest with his big hands before putting it on. "Fery soft," he said.

"Glad you like it. Pedro."

The man came to him and sat down on the arm of Robin's chair. He took Robin's hand in both of his. "Why you think me funny?" he asked quietly. There was a frown between the heavy brows and hurt in the dark eyes.

Robin shrugged his shoulders restlessly. How in the hell could he explain anything to a poor dope that didn't even understand the language well enough not to appear comic. How could he explain that it didn't matter what either of them thought so long as they got satisfaction from each other. How could he say to this pot of flesh, "Forget you have a brain. Forget you can talk or laugh or think or cry. Forget everything but that you are an animal and give me and yourself what we both want so I can give you a couple of bucks in the morning and throw you out."

Robin knew there was no way he could say these things to this man. As human beings they were alike, yet tragically separated. Only as forces, blind mute forces, could they meet. So Robin made his voice light as he replied, "I think everyone is funny. Don't you?"

The man shook his head. "You must not play with this—" He groped for the word but Robin understood what he meant. He bobbed his head up and down encouragingly but Robin gave him no help. "You want to be happy," the man faltered on like a child learning to walk, "then you must not play. Suffer, be killed, die, but not laugh and be funny."

Robin freed his hand and stood up hurriedly. Damn it all! This was exactly what he had fought to escape all this time. Keep it frivolous and keep it safe. That was his motto. The best cure for a heavy passion is a sense of humor. And now this goddam peasant was trying to shove the whole damned mistake down his throat. And what else was he trying to do? Ingratiate himself to the point of receiving a comfortable handout for a while?

Robin's eyes fell on the objects on the bureau, the pitifully few coins, the tube, the wire he had said he used in his work. Robin seized the opportunity to get the conversation back to the rollicking tempo it had had a few minutes earlier.

"What kind of work do you do, Pedro?" he asked, turning to him with a smile. The man looked at him with eloquent sadness.

"My name is not Pedro," he said heavily. His dark eyes dropped and he said softly, "It is Karl Tadeuz Horejscai." He offered it humbly, the only gift he had to bestow, and he added, "I work at the bone yard."

Robin frowned for a moment and asked, "Do you mean the cemetery? The graveyard?" For no good reason he felt himself shiver.

The man nodded and looked up uncertainly at Robin's tone. Something was falling into place in Robin's mind. He tried to smile as he asked his next question but he knew the expression he wanted had not appeared. "You mean you—dig graves?" His voice was actually unsteady. The man studied him closely, the sadness leaving his face. Slowly he shook his head. A look that might have been craftiness crept into his eyes.

"I," he said softly, "am the cremator!"

A thousand impressions packed precariously into the dark spaces of Robin's mind came loose and hurtled down the long dangerous limbs. Among the confusion he recognized a smudge against a thin blue sky, an explosion that shattered ice-like broken glass about the streets. "Name of God! What a way to die!" A train thundering down on an ice-bound station, a floating flame at the top of a tall shaft, a floating flame and from its shadow coming to him as if it were the whim of a hilarious god. A cremator!

He shook his head helplessly, and his hands sought vainly for something to grip. He saw recognition of his fear dawn in the man's beautiful eyes. He saw him stand and move toward him, the silk falling apart to reveal the long thrust of bronze flesh.

"Don't," Robin tried to say with authority. "Don't." But his voice escaped its control. "You've got to get out of here. I'll send for your clothes. I'll give you money, but you've got to get out!"

He spoke rapidly with pleading incoherence but the man did not pause. He came closer. He smiled. The teeth, so white. Robin aimed a swift blow at them but his arm was sluggish and easily deflected by the man's hands that reached for his throat. As the hands touched his neck, Robin desperately remembered a fragment of his Army training. He lifted his knee hard for an attack to the groin and felt it hit. The face before him blanched sharply but the hands did not loosen their firm pressure. The thumbs bit down so easily, so very easily. He struggled until he was unconscious.

The overhead lights were out and his head ached. The only light in the room seemed to be coming from the bath. He could not breathe freely. Something was stuffed loosely into his mouth. He tried to move his head and a biting pain seized his wrist and held. He moved the other hand and a similar pain attacked him there. He yelled and the sound was muffled but for its ringing echo inside his head. He tried to move his legs and again pain struck him in his ankles. Gradually he realized what had happened to him. He was bound, spread-eagled on his stomach to the four posts of the bed by thin strong wires. He was loosely gagged and a towel was tied about his face. He knew he was undressed. He knew his captor was a cremator named Karl something unpronounceable.

Out of the darkness gentle hands touched him, stroked his back and legs lovingly, tenderly. A voice in a language as strong and harsh as stale tobacco half sang to him. For a moment he almost relaxed when the voice grew suddenly silent and something burned briefly into the flesh of his back. He screamed his surprise as pain ricocheted up and down his spine but again no sound came forth. The song began again and a cooling, soothing unguent was massaged into the fresh wound, and the gentle hands went exploring, coaxing him to a passion he could not restrain. The voice stopped again and a sharp object was driven into his flank and quickly extracted. This time he did not scream but bit down hard on his gag and felt tears slip from his tightly closed eyes. To his horror he found that the manifestation of passion had not fled but remained waiting for release. Again the voice began to sing.

Near daybreak the wires were taken from his chafed wrists and ankles. The man named Karl took away the towel and wiped Robin's face with a cold cloth and gave him water to drink. Robin was spent, not from actual pain but from the anticipation of it. And yet he was no longer terrified. Strangely, in a way he could not yet comprehend, he was certain of something important, if still somewhat elusive. He lay relaxed in the arms that held him and looked up into the anxious face that studied his own intently. "Why?" he asked at last. "Why did you do it?"

"To show you must not laugh," the man replied softly. "Suffer, be killed, but not laugh. I had to show you it was not funny. I will never do it again. You know? You understand? I never hurt you again."

Robin nodded weakly. He understood that the man was not a sadist. What he had done had been but a token of what he might have inflicted upon him. Robin knew from his own past that some cures can be effected only by extremes. So it was all over at last. The light threads and fabric of his existence had at last been burned and cut away. He lay where he had fallen, at the bottom of the cloud with the rest of those like himself. He lifted his hand and touched the man's chest. It was rough and compact and warm with life like an animal's. Instantly he was crushed closer and words he could not understand poured passionately over his head.

"My back," he gasped with pain.

"It will grow well fery soon," the man assured him. "I stay with you and see it grow well."

"No, I must go back this morning," Robin said slowly. Realization of what lay before him was becoming more apparent every second. No longer did he think of fighting the irrefutable. He could only make adjustments now. That was all that was left him.

"I go too, with you."

"No." Robin shook his head. "Not this time. I'll come back for you in a week or so."

"You will go away," the man said sadly, "because I have hurt you."

"No," Robin smiled. "I'll not run away. Not now. I understand. And I won't laugh anymore."

The man searched his face carefully and at last his smile appeared. "What is your name," he asked.

"Robin."

"Robin," the man repeated it slowly, "Robin."

"You like it?"

"I like it, Robin."

When the sun was high, they rose and bathed and Karl dressed his woundswith the medicines sent up from the drug store, touching them carefully and repeating that soon they would heal. They dressed when the pressed and mended suit arrived, Robin giving his new friend one of his shirts, a tie, and his extra shoes. He took all the money from his wallet and gave it to the man.

"Take this and find yourself a decent room in town somewhere. Get yourself some clothes. Don't spend it foolishly — and for God's sake, get yourself another job."

He smiled affectionately as the man nodded in heavy seriousness. He was like a great, gentle animal, Robin thought, but an animal that is miraculously wise.

"Then we go to the oil fields perhaps," Karl asked.

"Yes, perhaps," Robin agreed. "You'd better go now. I've a train to catch."

"I will help."

Karl moved about the room collecting his possessions and packing them expertly into the suitcase. As Robin watched him he felt a silly desire to weep, thinking all the while what a hell of a setup he'd been saddled with.

At last they said goodbye reluctantly and Karl went down the hall. At the elevators he turned and lifted his hand. "Robin," he called. "Robin." The door slid open and with a last wave the man stepped out of sight.

On the train, Robin settled back against pillows to alleviate as much pain as possible and reviewed the experience of the previous night. He was not happy with the present state of affairs, but he was resigned, perhaps even content.

He felt no hatred for the man who had tortured him, nor a desire for revenge against him. There was no bitterness in his heart, he knew, for what he had endured had been but a device to free him of what the man had recognized as an artificially superior attitude. And now that he was free of it he was glad, for in freedom, he recognized at last, he could love without fear. And most important of all, he did love at last. True, by some standards he had been treated abominably. But he knew also he had been treated in such a manner because he was wanted in a genuine way for perhaps the first time in his life.

Robin looked out of the window at the snow-packed landscape racing silently by. He realized he had gotten too close to the rim and his footing had crumbled away. He was in for good at last. And being in, he looked again at his new responsibilities and sighed.

He'd speak to Mrs. Lalo (My God! Who was Mrs. Lalo!) about another room. He'd look around town for a job for the man. Better still, he'd take him out on the truck for a while. He'd arrange to buy another truck immediately and thus expand his business.

And Robin looked inward upon himself with new eyes. How docile he had become, how quiet and unbelievably at peace. How willing he was to make adjustments. Yet there was fear within him still, fear that he did not identify. If only he could get through the next week safely in this unaccustomed role until he saw Karl again, he knew he would be safe. He was walking in a dream and in dreams there is only that which is new, present, and unpredictable. Before his present breath could be exhaled, he knew he could find himself facing, yes, even death. He knew it was possible to face it and be claimed by it because he was no longer his own master. He was alone in a strange land with no one to guide him. He was at the mercy of anything that might decide to attack him until he learned to protect himself again. He was a Grimm hero, turned into a mouse by a force of magic; and a cat, in eating the mouse, would digest the man. Instantly his fear became the dull terror of the dying. It had been a mistake not bringing his new friend with him, for the man knew the way out. The man was protection and he had blindly left him behind. Robin closed his eyes. What to do? What to do? Better not think of himself. Bluff it out as always. Think of Karl. Think of him and find comfort there in his plans for their future. But his new friend was alone, too, poverty-stricken in a country that had evidently not treated him too generously as yet.

After a few moments' thought, Robin took up his address book and wrote on a fresh page:

"In the Name of God, Amen: The Last Will and Testament of the Undersigned. I, Robin, being of sound mind and memory, but knowing the uncertainty of human life, do now make and publish this, my last will and testament. That is today, I give, devise and bequeath unto Karl Tadeuz Horejscai, a recent immigrant into this country and lately residing at 7703 Cokely Street in Central City, all my real and personal property.

"I do hereby appoint Karl Tadeuz Horejscai executor of this my last will and testament, and he is to serve without bond or inventory."

He signed his name and wrote again:

"Signed, sealed, and declared by the said aforesigned, the testator, as and for his last will and testament; and we, at his request and presence, and in the presence of each other have hereto subscribed our names as witnesses thereto, this 27th day of January A.D. 1949."

He drew three lines on which his bankers would witness the paper and closed the book. He stared at the wide, monotonous landscape with a sense of finality. At last he felt that in a small way he had matched Fate to his last farthing. He massaged his bandaged wrist.

In Hamlet he got his car and drove slowly along the roads toward his town as if he were seeing them for the first time. A pall of doom, white and everlasting, hung over the quiet countryside, and high in the pale sky faint flat ice clouds lay in a pattern of a spreading mottled pheasant's wing. Oil wells pounded and pumped and trucks ground along the dangerous roads. Robin wished he were out of the oil game, for here he felt alone, and for him aloneness now spelled only destruction. He looked at a farmhouse set far back from the road in a belt of snowy cedars and smiled wistfully.

In town he stopped by the bank, saw the will typewritten and witnessed, and took a carbon copy with him. To the banker's puzzled inquiry, "This fellow a friend of yours, Robin?" He replied, "My best."

"Know him long?"

"Not long."

"Then, why —"

"He tried to help me once," Robin said. "There is no one else I owe that much to if I should die tomorrow."

"I wouldn't be too hasty."

"I'm not hasty, sir. He risked himself to save me. I think he's a deserving man. I'm sure you'll agree when you meet him."

He drove his car into the garage and sat in it for a while. He'd better sell it soon and buy something less pretentious. He looked around the darkened garage at the truck, the various spare parts and equipment hanging on the walls, calculating their value.

Outside the door the sun on the snow was dazzling. Yesterday at this time two children had ridden by on a bicycle. He wished they would ride past again and enact their scene once more. But he knew that such tableaux are not enacted twice. One sees them the first time or not at all. Stiffly he climbed out of the car.

Inside the house he remembered he had not brought Mrs. Lalo a present. She expected one so he took five dollars from his replenished wallet and gave it to her, explaining, "The train was late and the stores were closed. Get yourself something useless."

"A gut-buster, eh, Robin," Mrs. Lalo shrieked.

"Yeah. A gut-buster," Robin replied, knowing that he would never bring Karl here. He'd have to find another place. "Any calls?"

"Dozens of them." Mrs. Lalo lifted her beringed hands. Funny, he'd never noticed the cheap rings before. She handed him a list of seven or eight names. "The one at the top is a rush job. He says you've got to transfer some oil right away. He say his tank's full." Suddenly Mrs. Lalo shrieked and Robin jumped. "I told him to take a leak!"

Robin tried to smile but started for his room.

"Something wrong, Robin?" Mrs. Lalo asked.

"I—had an accident. My back's a little stiff."

"You'll be all right?"

"Yeah. Fine."

Slowly he changed clothes and went out to start the truck so it would warm up. His head ached and his shirt was a bed of cactus against his back. He went back to his room and sat wearily at his desk. On a sheet of paper he wrote, "I'm awaiting your arrival, hurry." He folded the copy of his will into an envelope, sealed, addressed it, and put it out for Mrs. Lalo to mail. In a daze he went back to the garage and got into the truck.

Though the roads were glassy with ice, his boot was heavy on the accelerator. Several times he was forced to lift his foot off completely and let the heavily laden truck roll down to a safe speed. Brakes were useless on this kind of surface, he told himself again. Yet his mind would not stay with what he was doing. It roved back through his years with a desperateness that aroused his objective pity for it. He tried to discipline it into remaining aware of the job he was doing, but it was impossible to do so. He listened to the icy crust on the road break beneath the chains on his rear wheels, faster and faster as he picked up speed. His mind filled with thoughts of the explosion of the day before. Jim Heath had been burned to a crisp. They'd had difficulty finding enough of him to bury, the bankers had said. He had left a wife and baby. Some insurance. The town was taking up a donation for the widow. Robin's lips parted and curled with horror. He looked down at his speedometer. He was going much too fast and a rather steep grade was coming up with a narrow bridge at the bottom of it. He tensed himself over the wheel and kept his eyes on the bridge below. He recognized his danger, and from force of habit when he was in a tight place, he slowly started to count.

Barely a quarter of the way down he felt the rear end of the truck give and slip sideways. "Three, four, five, six...." He gave the wheel a little compensating turn. His speed was still mounting. Silently he prayed that the rear end would hold and yet he knew before it started to give again that it would not. "Twelve, thirteen, fourteen, fifteen...." When he felt the slip coming, he turned the wheel carefully, knowing that it was going to be of little use. The slip was going to be a slide. The truck would approach the bridge broadside and there wasn't a chance in a million that it would remain upright. Laden with live oil and traveling at its present speed, if it turned over now, it would be a rolling ball of fire. "Twenty-one, twenty-two, twenty-three...." Before his eyes flashed the explosion that would come, and he saw the great dark smudge of suddenly wasted energy that would spread again over the sky and the orange flames the townspeople would see, floating, floating, floating above the one who had to be taught he could not laugh at Fate. The truck was almost crossways in the road. The steering wheel was bent as far as it would go. He had done everything he could inside the cab to save himself.

Terrified into effort, he broke the hypnosis of the atmosphere about him, threw open the door, and leaped as the truck hit a rut and started rolling. The ice-hard ground struck him like a hundred quivering spears inside his flesh, muffling the exploding roar a short distance away. He lay unmoving as he saw the sheet of flame cover the bridge and the truck, tear through the concrete buttress and disappear into the stream below. Robin rolled over and let his head fall back on the icy road. Only half conscious he watched the smoke roll up past the trees into the pale sky.

Thus it was that a man named Karl left Central City and came to live on a wheat farm near Hamlet.

"He's the best darned worker this county's seen around here for many a year," the natives are fond of saying. "Why, his employer just deeded him an interest in his farm the other day. *That* should give you an idea how good he is, I'd think! A good-natured devil too, always laughing. Drinks, but not too much, and courts the farm gals like a fool! Never seems to find one to settle down with though, and nobody's ever seen him mad. Robin's mighty lucky to have a hired hand like Karl, I'll tell you! Yes, sir, mighty lucky indeed. Best hand with a sick milch cow I believe I ever seen!"

PASSING NOTES IN CLASS: SOME THOUGHTS ON WRITING AND CULTURE IN THE GA(Y)TED COMMUNITY

Wendell Ricketts

I.

"We're here! We're queer! We're not going shopping!"
(Chant at an early Queer Nation demonstration at a California mall.)

I have a confession to make. As much as I reject the notion of collective identities, as much as I despise the Stepford Fag mass hallucinations of gay "community" rhetoric, and as much as I long to be the fierce and independent warrior of spirit that the label "queer" conjures, the genesis of this book was a much more fragile concept. *We.*

As in: Where are we? How do we imagine our lives and reconstruct our histories? Given the chance, what kinds of stories would we tell?

That last question intrigues me particularly. I am more and more convinced that imaginative literature—creative writing—possesses the ability to embrace ruction and rupture, union and invention, slippage and paradox in ways that are simply, inevitably absent from pride marches, consciousness-raising groups, "lifestyle" magazines, tavern guilds, gay churches, waves of same-sex couples lining up to get married at city hall, press releases, election campaigns, award-winning documentaries, civil-rights-litigation teams, queer-theory classes, gay-dad potlucks, town-hall meetings, square-dance clubs, and cadres of activists, no matter how pure of heart.

Short stories and novels capture the extemporary, plastic, kaleidoscopic, everything-at-once nature of being alive. They stand in marked contrast to those other mannerisms of culture and community whose goal is the reduction of reality to a proposition on which a majority can agree. It's not for nothing that works of fiction are never written by committees.

And that's why this anthology. Men who are working-class—who cannot or will not compromise that piece of their complicated selves—and who also love/fuck/pine for/build lives around/lust after/experience themselves in common cause with other men, well, we don't see ourselves much in American gay fiction. Though perhaps that only begs another question: why bother to look there in the first place?

For someone coming out in 1976, as I did, what was remarkable about being gay was that you simultaneously knew so much about it and almost nothing about it. Before I came out, I had never read a book with a gay character in it; I had never seen a gay character on a TV show or in a movie. Even in the entire first year after I did come out, the number of gay or lesbian people I knew personally remained a single digit. Of course, I intimately understood every loathsome, despicable thing about queers that everyone else did, because in America you imbibe that much with your colostrum.

So what was a boy to do? Fortunately, I also came out at a time when it was still possible to give a friend fifty dollars, send him on his annual pilgrimage to San Francisco, and have him return with a copy of every new gay book of fiction that had been published during the previous year. Today, fifty dollars wouldn't cover the sales tax on a year's worth of queer stories.

The point is, my coming out, because it was essentially a small-town one, took place against the backdrop of the lives of the gay people (gay men, specifically) I found in books. I knew someone in those days who lived in Laguna Beach, and we read *Tales of the City* together long-distance, inspired by our reading to write each other long, gossipy letters in which we referred to Armistead Maupin's characters by their first names and pretended they were our buddies, boyfriends, neighbors.

Well, but wasn't that precisely the point?

Cliché as it sounds, I read in those days to discover myself and my "people," and the characters in novels and short stories *were* more real to me than the few flesh-and-blood queers I knew. Books offered alternative possibilities; they promised a world in which secrets were optional, in which longing was quite often requited, in which figuring out where "gay" was and going there was The Quest, was the answer to—well, to *everything*.

I don't know if that goes on anymore—whether seventeen-year-old American gay boys still look for their first glimpse of "community" between the pages of books or, indeed, if they even come to believe that such a thing as community exists, as I did, mainly *because* the gay men they read about appear to live in one.

I can report that something similar happened in Italy in 2003, where I happened to be when the publication of the translation of the first volume of *Tales of the City* (ironically enough) was greeted with both genuine delight and a certain samizdat zeal. If you were too embar-rassed to walk into a bookstore to buy your own copy, a friend would slip you his. Everyone was talking about it—and fantasizing trips to the other edge of the world. I can't recall the last time a gay novel in America got that kind of reception.

The Italians, of course, were reading against invisibility and as counterpropaganda, just as I had done in 1976. (Anita Bryant mounted her "Save Our Children" campaign two months after I came out.) In a country where gay community—even in the restricted sense of gay-friendly physical spaces—barely exists, *I Racconti di San Francisco* described Oz.

But perhaps we have no need for that anymore in America. You can scarcely watch an hour of prime-time television these days without seeing a gay or lesbian character who's doing all right, and the producers of reality television are positively obsessed with gay men (though lesbians remain an unfathomable mystery), so we're not exactly invisible, right?[1]

Or are we?

The "boom" in lesbian and gay writing, which began as a trickle in the mid-seventies and was already a flood by the mid-eighties, was related in major ways to the enormous social and political changes that were taking place then—the Anita Bryant campaign; the defeat of the Briggs initiative in 1978 (which attempted to outlaw gay and lesbian school teachers in California); the election (and later assassination) of San Francisco supervisor, Harvey Milk, the first openly gay elected official in the United States; waves of movies with queer themes and more-or-less sympathetic characters (*The Rocky Horror Picture Show* and *The Naked Civil Servant* in 1975; *The Ritz*, *The War Widow*, and *Norman...Is That You?* in 1976; *La Cage aux Folles* and Peter Adair and Rob Epstein's outstanding documentary, *Word Is Out*, in 1978; *Making Love* and *Come Back to the Five and Dime, Jimmy Dean, Jimmy Dean* in 1982); and prime-time television shows like *That Certain Summer* (1972), *Soap* (1977), and *A Question of Love* (1978). By the early seventies, in fact, talk-show hosts like David Susskind and Dick Cavett had interviewed so many homosexuals on the air that they had become the butt of newspaper cartoons and stand-up routines.

There was unquestionably a new national momentum in those years to organize, to lobby, to protest, but there was just as strong an impetus to publish, to produce movies and plays, to bring gay and les-

[1] Lance Loud, of course, was television's first "real" gay man. He came out on national television in 1973 during the broadcast of *An American Family*. When sections of the series were shown again in 2002, on the occasion of a documentary about Lance's death, what struck me was how deeply the Louds' story is rooted in class. Lance himself characterized his childhood as "drowning in the luxury of late-'60s suburbia," and Shana Alexander, reviewing *An American Family* in *Newsweek* in 1973, described the Louds as "nice-looking people [who] act like affluent zombies. The shopping carts overflow, but their minds are empty." Lance's decision to "run away from home" at age twenty, meanwhile, in order to exist in faux poverty in New York City's Chelsea Hotel, strikes me as way glam and *très boulevardier*, but not especially daring, in precisely the way that Thoreau is not daring when he goes to live "deliberately" in the woods—fully cushioned by his family's money and the comfort of the knowledge he could return at any time to the mansion in Concord. Still, one understands Lance's desire to escape the WASP-y, relentless, and slightly creepy impassivity of his natal home, though the adult gay life he constructed for himself in Manhattan proved to be no less superficial, consumer-driven, lonely, and spiritually empty. Gay, in other words, couldn't save him.

bian literature and studies into the university. The two impulses, of course, were not separate. Literature is the propaganda of a culture, and a lot of people thought we needed better propaganda.

And that—if you can stand my mushing together more than a decade of complicated sociopolitical and sub- and mass-cultural phenomena—is how gay and lesbian literature up and married identity politics.

Now, for someone reading as I read in those early years of my initiation, it hardly mattered. Like so many readers then and even now, I firmly believed in role models and evaluated fiction on the basis of whether it provided "positive" images of gay and lesbian people. All I wanted in my reading was some reflection of myself and of my group. But if you had asked me who I thought that was, I'd have said "gay people" and cut my eyes at you for asking such a silly question. "We are here!" Horton hears the Whos chanting. For a long time, I wasn't much concerned with figuring out what I meant by "we."

II.

Hey, faggot. The Castro is that way!
-------------------->
Hey, redneck. The trailer park is that way!
<-------------------

(Bathroom graffito, El Trebol Restaurant, San Francisco)

But how long could that go on? As my sense of self grew more complex over the years—a process that comes to anyone who doesn't struggle too hard against it—I abandoned the naïve belief that all my contradictions and pluralities could be crammed into a single identity, and, when I went looking in fiction for my li(fe)(ves) to be reflected back to me, I did so with an increasing sense of disorientation.

Blue came about, then, because I understand something I once didn't: literature instructs us. We must be vigilant, then, as we take our pleasure in reading, because one of the main ways that literature instructs is by what it refuses to name, by what it omits, elides, or just plain fumbles. Literature is never neutral and it is never still.

In one of the first post-Stonewall gay novels that came into my hands, Andrew Holleran's Dancer from the Dance—a book that still haunts me—Holleran creates a mid-seventies world of Manhattan circuit queens who are rich, stylish, rapacious, desperate for sexual attention (which, paradoxically, they often reject), terrified of aging, and defiantly superficial. The main character, Sutherland, actually comes from a poor Southern family, but he affects such Ur-Blanche DuBois entitlement and regal scorn that he seems more like the heir of a de-

posed czar. These, Holleran suggests, are the people participating mean-
ingfully in gay life.

The one identifiable working-class character in the book is Frankie
Oliveiri, an Italian American transit worker from Bayonne, New Jersey,
who has left his wife and child to be with Malone, one of Holleran's
gilded young men. Here is Holleran's description of him:

> Frankie had never gone to a bar, had never wanted to, had
> heard of Fire Island but considered it "a bunch of queens" and
> lived a life that, save for the fact that he slept with Malone, was
> hardly homosexual. (82)

> ....

> Frankie read the papers, asking Malone to pronounce for him
> the words he had never come across before, and tell him what
> they meant.... He came home with ideas and schemes. "Maybe
> I should be an electrician," he said, "we could move to Jersey
> and have a house. Just you and me and all those honkies...."
> [Frankie] wanted to improve his lot; he wanted to learn a skill,
> fix TVs, and move to New Jersey with Malone to a house in the
> pine barrens. He was a true American. (87-88)

In addition to being "hardly homosexual," Frankie is also patholog-
ically jealous and becomes physically violent when he learns that
Malone has cheated on him. Part of his macho charm is his lack of formal
education (Malone tutors him in newspaper English); and his ethnic
masculinity, while highly attractive, is ultimately incompatible with
"real" gay life. Moreover, Frankie's "truly American" desire to escape
Manhattan's gay scene for the suburbs is depicted as incomprehensible
and when, toward the end of the book, he finds a more accommodating
partner and does exactly that, Sutherland and Malone have this to say:

> "He's bought a house in Freehold, New Jersey," said Malone,
> as they sat down for a moment and Sutherland slipped off his
> satin pumps.... "He's making twenty thousand a year now and he'll
> have a pension, too. Never say America isn't a worker's paradise."

> ....

> "Oh, well, we lived for other things," [Sutherland] smiled....
> "At least," he murmured in [Malone's] ear, "we learned to
> dance. You have to grant us that. We are good dancers," he
> said. "And what," said Sutherland, "is more important in this
> life than that?" (230-231)

Well, probably a lot of things, but the point of *Dancer from the Dance* is that there's something fishy about a homosexual who wants the things that Frankie wants—Frankie, in fact, is in danger of forfeiting his gay identity.

It would be an exaggeration to hold *Dancer from the Dance* responsible for the single-handed creation of a genre, but it is accurate to say that Holleran put his finger on the crack-that-would-become-a-chasm in gay male self-representation and -imagination during the 1980s. "Truly" gay men lived in cities (or fled to them) where they lived not lives but lifestyles. All other aspects of their identities fell into place beneath the capstone of gayness—a process, as any number of commentators have noted, that has only intensified in the years since.

III.

"It is a truth universally acknowledged that a man in possession of a gay lifestyle must be in want of a fortune."
(With apologies to Jane Austen)

That's the way it happens in John Caffey's *The Coming Out Party*, originally published in 1982.

Sid and Calvin, bored and besotted with luxury and possessions in their West Hollywood mansion, decide that the solution to their malaise lies in finding a boy in need of gay metamorphosis and modeling, from his unlikely clay, "The Ultimate Homo." The more dubious the prospect, the more enviable the "rescue" effort. Thus, when they come upon nineteen-year-old Hal, broken down by the side of the road in Santa Monica, a pale, overweight "Hee-Haw reject" (20) from Xenia, Ohio, they've found their (im)perfect man.

The transformation begins (of course) with the physical: the gym, the personal trainer, Keratin masks, the starvation diet, contact lenses, the hair stylist, the fashion consultant. Hal is next made to read Gore Vidal and is instructed in the appreciation of classical music; he is taught how to engage "properly" in casual sex and drug-taking; and he is quizzed on his ability to identify the source of such quotations as "Jungle red, Sylvia!" and "I have always depended upon the kindness of strangers."

Up to this point, *The Coming Out Party* is a rather broad farce on gay male "community" mores at the time of its writing. What makes the plot timely more than twenty years later, however, is that the imperialist, colonizing energy of the bourgeois class and, in particular, of its avatar, the gay-male coming-out process, has not changed. Indeed, the comedy would fail if the serious truth behind it were not still fully legible.

The cultural imperatives evident in Sid and Calvin's "project" were, in fact, the running joke behind the four-part "Fagmalion" episode of the NBC sitcom *Will & Grace*, as recently as 2003. Barry, the dowdy cousin of Karen Walker, has come out at the age of thirty-five, but his "debut" as a gay man (at a black-tie Human Rights Campaign fundraising dinner) is unthinkable until he undergoes a complete makeover. Jack and Will, guardians of the well of gay knowledge, serve as Barry's guides and renovators. (Significantly, it is Karen who arranges for—and funds—Barry's twenty-thousand-dollar crash course in gay, but faithful viewers will recall that the rich (by marriage) and eternally snobby Karen comes from a working-class background; in another episode, her shame regarding her past, and the revelation that her mother works as a bartender, are explored).

What *Coming Out Party* and "Fagmalion" share is the understanding, manifest behind their "light-hearted" superficies, that the possession of a gay "lifestyle" is insufficient unto itself, but is required by its very nature to proselytize. Thus, though no one can take seriously the claim that gay men recruit sexually, the "community's" instinct is demonstrably to hegemonize *culturally*.

Gay-male identity, moreover, is revealed as an almost exclusively *material* site: Barry, like Hal, is marked as "ungay" by the brands of clothes he buys (he shops at Miller's Outpost), by being "twenty pounds overweight," by his unfashionable beard and bad haircut. Will's role in the tutelage of Barry is to "work on his mind"—that is, to teach him "things like gay culture, gay politics, driving up the cost of real estate in affordable areas." The success of Barry's acculturation finally begins to be visible when he buys his first pair of Gucci shoes and when he shows Will and Jack a photo of "fabulous abs" from *Men's Fitness* magazine, stating his wish to resemble the model:

WILL: [TO BARRY] Are those— Is that Gucci on your feet?
BARRY: Oh, yeah. Aren't they great? They kill my toes and cost a fortune, but what the hell? I'll take out another credit card.
WILL: [VOICE BREAKING] I think I'm gonna cry.
JACK: Will, do you know what this means? Unrealistic body expectations.
WILL: Choosing fashion over comfort.
JACK: Living beyond your means.
WILL: Boy George, I think he's got it!

Without the gay-male diktat, of course, another show in which gay identity is synonymized with bourgeois consumption, *Queer Eye for the Straight Guy*, would be unintelligible. The humor of *Queer Eye* frequently hinges upon the ridiculing of working-class men for their grooming, clothing, living spaces, and eating habits,[2] while suggesting that the creation of "metrosexuality" (that is, homosexuality without the sex) depends upon the literal stripping of the classed body and its subsequent reconstruction. In every episode, then, the object of the makeover is shown all-but-naked at the moment of his transformation, just as he prepares to resignify his remodeled self with new cosmetics and new clothing.

In these precise terms, Hal is trained in *The Coming Out Party* that successful participation in male homosexual culture requires that he remove all traces—from his body, from his speech, and from his psyche—of his previous heterosexual (read: lower-class) life. That he has a home and a natal culture and may yet desire to remain fluent in their idioms is considered not only irrelevant but actively antagonistic to his homosexual rehabilitation.

Thus, the gay existence is one without a past-a life that begins *de novo* at coming out, the instant of queer conception.[3] There can be no dispute that great potential exists for the release of creative and psychic energy in processes that result in self-acceptance, but the insistence that the newly inscribed "gay" or "queer" body must pass through the portals of the gay village *by means of* renunciation of previous moral, ethical, and cultural training and *through* abandonment of prior allegiances to geography and to clan is essentially to rob the individual of civilization. The indigenous baby, that is, is tossed out with the gay bathwater.

What emerges to "queer" Sid and Calvin's increasingly cruel regimen for Hal, however, is that most savage of all forces, desire. To the men's horror, their incipient creation falls head over heels in love with the decidedly déclassé Pool Man ("Not a penny to his name." [63]), and Calvin is particularly incensed by their liaison ("The Pool Man was a hunk, but Cal'd be damned if he'd have any daughter of his sleeping with the Hired Help." [65]).

---

[2] Food frequently emerges as a potent marker of class. The four-part 2001 PBS documentary, *People Like Us: Social Class in America*, devoted a segment ("The Trouble with Tofu") to a controversy over the building of a new grocery store in Burlington, Vermont. Low-income and middle-class residents clashed viciously over whether the new store would stock "regular" food or only more expensive "health" and "gourmet" lines. *Queer Eye* episodes frequently depict refrigerator and cupboard raids in which unacceptable food is discarded with evident disgust. In *The Coming Out Party*, Sid and Calvin are able to convince Hal to participate in their scheme because they first seduce him with a meal made entirely of frozen Stouffer's TV dinners and Sarah Lee desserts. Later, Calvin tells Hal that it's Perrier for him from then on, no longer "Cragmont soda."

[3] "Families belonged to that inscrutable past west of the Hudson," Holleran writes in *Dancer from the Dance*, "and when a queen walked out a window, and you heard the family had come east to claim the body, it was like hearing that some shroud had come out of the darkness to pick up the dead and return whence the Three Fates sequestered, in the hills of Ohio or Virginia." (235-236)

It is at this point that Caffey inserts the only challenge to Sid and Calvin's project (other than Hal's own weak resistance to it), which comes, significantly, in the voice of Calvin's mother. Arriving for a visit, she accuses Calvin of "[using Hal] to be what you never were," adding, "Better the boy wants true love than what passes for it at the Club Baths"(100). By criticizing Calvin and Sid's treatment of Hal and, by extension, the entirely self-referential gay world the men occupy, Calvin's mother, like a relict of Calvin's "pre-gay" life, attempts to reassert into that world the moral, civilizing principles that were Calvin's birthright. It is to no avail, however, and Calvin's first act upon his mother's departure is to express his rage by deploying his capitalist power to fire the Pool Man.

In the end, Hal's love for the Pool Man triumphs, and they are married in a public ceremony attended by both their gay and natal families. Even Calvin comes to accept the relationship and, in a significant moment near the very end of the book, he finally asks the Pool Man his name (Beau). Just as in E. M. Forster's *Maurice*, which *The Coming Out Party* specifically references, Beau recognizes that his relationship with another man cannot survive in hostile surroundings (the heterosexual middle class in *Maurice*, the homosexual one in *The Coming Out Party*), and he immediately "whisks" Hal away (in his '71 Dodge van). They return, importantly, to the house where Beau was born-a place steeped in Beau's family and class histories—in Hawaiian Gardens, a largely Latino, working-class community in East Los Angeles.

The Coming Out Party is assuredly no manifesto of sustained proletarian resistance—Beau turns out to be the beneficiary of a large trust fund left to him in secret by an "eccentric aunt"—but it pointedly examines, in a way that perhaps only humor can (as Oscar Wilde and Joe Orton taught us), the class-inflected (and class-envious) demands of gay-cultural membership.

The question that *The Coming Out Party* raises humorously is the same one that *Dancer from the Dance* raises in deadly earnest: Does successfully entering the gay male community require the assumption of a market identity? In other words, does not "gay" resemble, more than it resembles anything else, a brand name?

IV.

Marketers worldwide are increasingly recognizing the importance and spending power of the gay community as a dynamic, fast growing economic force in the business world today. As a result of their unique lifestyles, gay men and women are by definition intensely brand loyal, and hyper acquisitive. They for the most part enjoy joint earnings, yielding them high disposable incomes.
(From a letter sent to gay businesses by the Millennium March On Washington's Millennium Festival Street Fair.)

Certainly, no one could blame a guy if he got that impression. But if *Dancer from the Dance*'s answer to the question is probably yes, and *The Coming Out Party*'s is probably no, Kirk Read stakes out a much more ambivalent position in his 2001 memoir, *How I Learned to Snap*. After living for several years in New York and San Francisco, Read received a contract to write a book about his experiences as an openly gay teenager in high school and, in order to focus on his project, moved temporarily to rural Lake County, California, home to "good country people, leftover hippies, and hardcore druggies" whose "prison tattoos and dirty fingernails make me wonder what in the world I'm doing around here" (vii).

Upon his arrival in a town where "Wal-Mart and K-Mart are the cultural epicenters" (vii), Read goes to the "ambitiously named" café at Wal-Mart for a hamburger. There, Read spots a boy he judges to be about fifteen, who is having lunch with his mother:

> His well-conditioned hair hung over the left shoulder of his Calvin Klein tee shirt.... His fingers were covered with silver rings and he ate quickly.... His mother was a round woman dressed in an embroidered Guatemalan shirt I'd seen priced for a dollar at the Hospice Thrift Shop. He was chubby from sharing his mother's snacks. I wondered how long it would take him to reach her size....
>
> I sat at the table behind his mother, catching pieces of their quiet conversation. Names like *Pa* and *Aunt Junebug* floated over to me.... [The boy] looked up from his food to throw glances at me. As he lifted his burger, his pinkies jutted out from the sides of the bun. He was a dainty eater and wiped the sides of his mouth with a small stack of napkins after each bite....
>
> I went through high school dreaming of being rescued by an as-yet-undiscovered older brother who would adopt me and ask me why I looked so sad....

His eyes were full of a need for adoption. I wasn't cruising him, I was gently, carefully letting him know that his tribe was out there, beyond the cinderblocks and hubcaps that filled his front yard.... In that moment, I wished I could have handed him something ... more than a soft-eyed stare that said "hang in there" or "save your money." (viii-ix)

All of this takes place in the space of Read's two-and-a-half-page prologue, which, despite its brevity, nicely compresses the semiotics of class and homosexuality. Read cannot learn, during their silent encounter, the boy's actual sexual preference or class background, of course, so he describes neither literal gayness nor literal working-class status, but their *signs*. In interpreting such signs, moreover, Read assigns a valence to each that is either positive (the escape provided by coming out as gay) or negative (the culture from which the boy needs rescue). Thus, prisoners, dirty fingernails, obesity, thrift-store shopping, the presence of Wal-Mart and Kmart, relatives called "Pa" or "Aunt Junebug," and hubcaps in the yard are "coded" for their working-class (and, thus, *contra*-gay) character, while well-conditioned hair, dismay at prison tattoos and unscrubbed fingernails, Calvin Klein T-shirts, disdain for the absence of non-Wal-Mart- and non-Kmart-based culture, eating "daintily," and the "need for adoption" by an older (presumably gay) brother are coded for their antagonism to or differentiation from working-class milieux and thus, in favor of gayness.

Significantly, Read desires to communicate to the boy that his "tribe" is "out there," the expression of a vision for the boy's life that is entirely hegemonic. Read seems to imagine homosexuality as a physical place (the boy must save his money in order to travel there), a "land," if you will, where the boy's true breed resides. His home culture, meanwhile—the boy's birthplace and blood family—is presumed to be an error and a detriment: the boy, "sharing his mother's snacks" (that is, her literal and metaphoric nourishment), threatens to become like her. This is pointedly *not* his tribe, and it is the discovery of that fact that legitimates escape.

To be fair, there is every reason to consider Read's concern for the boy to be completely genuine, but the question of "tribe" (that is, of community, of belonging, of membership) lies so deeply at the core of the problematics of gay-male cultural (re)presentation—both as a literary theme and in our real-life experiences—that the term cannot be passed over lightly.

To further complicate matters, the body of Read's book, in which he describe his coming out as a high-school student in the small town of Lexington, Virginia, demonstrates an even more profoundly conflicted relationship with the place and people Read left behind:

I never wanted to abandon Lexington altogether.... I loved the people I'd grown up with and even when they scared me, I held out hope that they'd come around on gay issues....

It can be a challenge to go home and explain to them what I'm doing with my life, because their realities are so entirely different from mine. My exposure to sexual adventure, college, and radical politics has created painful cultural differences between us. But they're my people, and I can't give up on them. (111-112)

What is notable about this passage is Read's inclusion of the term *sexual adventure* in his tripartite explanation for the *cultural* differences that have arisen between him and the people in his hometown. Although a university education and exposure to political paradigms diametrically opposed to those of one's natal environment may lead to conflicting, even incompatible understandings of reality, they do not rewrite one's origins, dissolve personal history, or replace preexisting culture with an alternate version.

Read's addition of "sexual adventure" to his list is thus especially intriguing, containing, as it does, the premise that embedded within (homo)sexual practice lies culture or, to put it more specifically, a culture in which Wal-Mart cafés, thrift stores, and unmanicured lawns, acceptable in one's naïveté, are revealed to have been improper all along.

My point is not to criticize what is, in the end, a rather touching memoir, but to call attention to the polarities of class and (homo)sexuality that have become so deeply ingrained that we are virtually helpless to avoid speaking in their language.

V.

"I must constantly assert my difference."
Gloria Anzaldúa, "To(o) Queer the Writer: *Loca, Escritora, y Chicana"*

I refer deliberately in the sections above to gay *men*. Huge differences exist between the ways in which "gay" men were consolidating a national, public (and literary) identity in the post–Stonewall era and what many queer women and lesbians were doing. One of the most striking contrasts between lesbian and gay male community and cultural production in the post–World War II period, in fact, has been the insistence by many lesbian writers, scholars, and organizers on keeping the issue of class (and, more broadly, of economics) in constant intellectual and cultural play. Much of the work of writers like Judy

Grahn, Dorothy Allison, Pat Parker, Audre Lorde, Amber Hollibaugh, Minnie Bruce Pratt, and many others, for example, has been devoted to the working-class-lesbian theme, particularly as class intersects gender, race, and butch/femme dynamics.

In one of the early anthologies dedicated to surveying the state of lesbian fiction (entitled, descriptively enough, *Lesbian Fiction*), editor Elly Bulkin (1981) takes special care to underscore the important contributions of working-class women writers to the expansion of the lesbian short-story form:

> Through much of this century and the end of the last one, lesbian literature has been almost exclusively the province of white lesbians—or of white women of indeterminate or unknown sexual/affectional preference—who are either middle- or upper-class. Only fairly recently has this situation even begun to change: white working-class characters are depicted in some of the fiction in *The Ladder* and of the pulp novels of that period [1956-1972], and a growing number of lesbians of color and poor and working-class lesbians of all races have written much poetry since the late sixties and are, along with other lesbians, producing a growing body of powerful fiction. (xii-xiii)

Bulkin, like many of the women who edited lesbian anthologies in the seventies and eighties, introduced her book with a kind of framing statement in which she expressed the writer's and anthologist's obligation to combat the *silencing* of lesbian voices within the culture, including the ways in which failed considerations of class, race, and disability (to name the categories that Bulkin names) served as exponents of that silence. Literature—what Bulkin called "fictional truth," evoking Audre Lorde's famous formulation, "biomythography"—was thus no mere entertainment, but was a dynamic and vital tool for change. Writing and publishing, in other words, were essential cultural work in the larger project of creating and transforming *political* consciousness, including consciousness about class.

Lesbian Fiction, thus, is no less remarkable for the high quality of the work it contains than for the respect it pays to working-class writers and to the importance of working-class themes in the development of the literature Bulkin saw emerging around her; and working-class-inflected stories like Dorothy Allison's "A River of Names," Audre Lorde's "The Beginning," or Judy Grahn's "Boys at the Rodeo"—each one a classic in its own right—ultimately form something like a fourth of the anthology.

The working-class dyke,[4] meanwhile, was becoming a lesbian literary imago, celebrated in such classic novels as Leslie Feinberg's *Stone*

Butch Blues and Frankie Hucklenbroich's *Crystal Diary*. Both books revolve around blue-collar, "stone butch" lesbian protagonists in the 1950s (Feinberg) or 1960s (Hucklenbroich) and, though often painful, are tales of ultimate survival and perseverance that present working-class experience as both valuable and heroic.

"Underground" writer Red Jordan Arobateau's dozens of largely self-published experimental novels and short-story collections, which date back to the mid-seventies, similarly center the experiences of what Arobateau calls "street dykes." Arobateau's characters live at the margins, moving in and out of homelessness, unemployment, jail, prostitution, and drug use. The lives of Arobateau's protagonist butches are marked by violence, rage, alcoholism, and a restlessness that is only temporarily lulled by rough, marathon sex, which Arobateau describes in eidetic detail. If Arobateau's characters often lack emotional depth, the work remains interesting for its unapologetic focus on a "queered" underclass, for its exploration of gender and racial dynamics, and for its explicit centering of sexual agency as a mechanism by which powerless people experience power (and, thus, engage with the reparative function of sex).

Lesbian fiction writers' work, then, was firmly joined within a tradition of scholarly inquiry that includes such nonfiction studies such as Elizabeth Lapovsky Kennedy and Madeline Davis' *Boots of Leather, Slippers of Gold* (1993), an ethnography of working-class lesbians in Buffalo, New York, and any number of Lillian Faderman's foundational books and articles on lesbian literary and social history. Such work—and what I've mentioned here is merely the tip of a substantial iceberg—is evidence of a sustained, concerted, dedicated effort on the part of lesbian writers, poets, publishers, journalists, and scholars not to allow working-class lesbians simply to be named tokenistically in a litany of oppressions, but to insist that their experiences be brought to the foreground. It is no more than a reflection of that effort, I think, that the important 1997 anthology, *Queerly Classed: Gay Men and Lesbians Write about Class*, was edited by a woman who identifies as queer and that the majority of the contributors were women.

Such an observation in no way mitigates the historical and ongoing struggles of working-class lesbians, and especially of working-class lesbians of color, against what Lynne Uttal (1990) called "inclusion without influence" in lesbian- and feminist-centered scholarship,

---

[4] Anthropologist and social historian Esther Newton (1993) notes the class-inflected use of the term "dyke" in the lesbian summer community of Cherry Grove, New York, during the late 1950s and early 1960s. Though the early lesbian arrivals to the Grove were wealthy and professional women, many of whom bought homes, working-class Irish and Italian women began arriving in the 1960s. "The remaining 'ladies' [as they called themselves] intended an ethnic and class slur by calling the new women 'dykes,'" Newton writes. "The working-class women identified with the word." (529)

literature, and community life, but it is meant to hold the lesbian-feminist "example" up for purposes of contrast—and by so doing to make the point that the counterpart in American gay-male cultural commentary barely exists.

VI.

The workman started pulling tools from his belt and making adjustments here and there. At last Billy had a man, a sweaty he-man day laborer and not those polite and gentlemanly teenagers at school. This was, he was sure, what they called "rough trade." He knew it was for him.
Boarding House Chicken, 1978

Except perhaps in pornography. Boy, are we present in pornography. (As we are in "erotica," the name given to the genre that now constitutes approximately one-third of all fiction published for gay men each year in America.)

I hardly need to recite the names of internet porn sites and listservs or the plots of "adult" novels to make the point that there's no gay sexual iconography quite so tried and true as the sex object who is a truck driver/prison guard/construction worker/ranch hand/Army grunt/auto mechanic/street hustler/beat cop/jailhouse rapist/squaddy/skateboard punk. In each case, of course, the "consumer's" gaze is assumed not only *not* to be working-class but to be inexorably drawn to the fetish quality of sex with a (class) difference.

In the pornographer's imagination, moreover, working-classness in men means masculinity and lots of it, such that, in queer porn, the fetish category "laborer" is indistinguishable from the fetish category "he-man." And masculinity, of course, means insertion. The exec in the three-piece suit *could* screw the scruffy bike messenger, but he virtually never does.

There's a good deal more to be said about gay male pornography's obsession with race and class as markers of iconic masculinity and, indeed, about gay-male pornographers' profound ambivalence regarding masculinity in the first place, but I want to focus here on two *non*-pornographic examples of the ways in which working-classness is fetishized in a gay-male cultural context.

In November 1999, that stop-calling-me-gay magazine, *Men's Health*, published a two-page spread entitled "Blue-Collar Brawn," which described, complete with color photos, a "blue-collar workout for men." The exercises, which include the "Sandbag Lift," the "Shovel Lift," and the "Car Push," purport to duplicate the "real life" activity of guys who "spend [their] days moving big stuff around for a living"

(118). The magazine's call to reproduce a (fantasized) working-class male body invites the reader to envision the musculature (and masculine attractiveness) that may result from physical labor, but simultaneously requires the reader to annul all knowledge of the actual blue-collar man who "moves big stuff around for a living." That man—whose "blue-collar brawn" is a mechanism of survival and not a form of recreation; whose literal body ages prematurely, is often scarred and burned, and is plagued by early arthritis, bone degeneration, and tendonitis; and whose pain and injuries not infrequently go unattended for lack of health insurance—is rendered invisible by the need to re-imagine "blue collar" as a commodity category.

J. G. Hayes' fine short-story collection, *This Thing Called Courage: South Boston Stories*, suffered a similar "re-invention" when it was published in 2002. Michael Lowenthal, whose "prepublication review" is included in the book's front matter, lauds Hayes' work:

> Though they're only blocks apart, there's a world of difference between Southie, Boston's blue collar Irish stronghold, and the South End, its gentrified gay ghetto. Likewise, there couldn't be a greater gap between Hayes' authentically muscular storytelling and the steroidal puffery that passes as some gay fiction. Unlike so many gay characters whose heroism depends upon fleeing their origins, Hayes' heroes prove their courage by staying put. From the tectonic violence of his hometown's class conflict, Hayes' voice thrusts to craggy heights.

Lowenthal could certainly not have known, when he wrote his comments, that his words would occasion a strange irony, because "steroidal puffery" describes precisely the image Hayes' publisher chose for the cover: the nude torso in profile of a young, muscular white man, his right deltoid decorated with an obviously fake tattoo in which the words "South Boston" (and not "Southie") surround a Celtic cross.

That such a body is chosen to represent—indeed to embody and exemplify—the blue-collar or working-class "condition" of Hayes' writing exemplifies the ways in which mainstream gay-male cultural representation actively refuses to acknowledge working-class men, even when they are gay, beyond the fetishized, sexualized category.

The flawless, evenly tanned skin in the cover image—entirely free of hair and entirely free of scars—marks the body in question as the opposite of a working-class body and, indeed, inscribes its owner unequivocally as a denizen not of Southie but of the "gentrified South End." It is a body created not through the physical demands of working-class labor but through the decidedly middle-class exploitation of the leisure time and disposable income necessary to belong to and attend a gym, to eat well, to spend time in the sun.

Like *Men's Health*, Hayes' publisher sought to evoke the real working class by "quoting" an imaginary working-class body—one, in this case, onto which fantasies of young, sexually attractive, tough (meaning masculine) Irish kids in South Boston were meant to be projected. That the photo is cropped at the neck seems significant as well: robbed of the individuality of a face, the body becomes more generic and, thus, more pornographically available.

It is essential, however, to underscore the fact that none of Hayes' stories has anything to do with the cover image; his work is by no stretch of the imagination "erotica," and Hayes is not particularly concerned in his seven stories with his characters' sex lives. But his publisher could not release itself from the rapture of the commodified, pornographized fetish-consciousness to which contemporary gay urban middle-class sexual culture is in thrall, literally could not read the nonerotic experiences that Hayes' book sought to illuminate.

This, I would argue, is a peculiarly gay-male alexia. A few years before *This Thing Called Courage* appeared, Beacon Press published Michael Patrick MacDonald's heartbreaking memoir, *All Souls: A Family Story from Southie*. Though *All Souls* is nonfiction and though MacDonald is heterosexual, he and Hayes traverse corresponding territory. There is not the remotest possibility, however, that Beacon Press would have considered a cover similar to the one that appeared on *This Thing Called Courage*; indeed, in a nongay context such imagery would have been viewed (correctly) as vulgar in light of the book's serious content. For a gay men's publisher, however, the appeal to the (perceived) interests of gay-male consumers trumped concern about whether the sexualized cover art neutralized the working-class gay voice within.

That transaction, too, recapitulates the familiar power dynamic in which the products of the labor of working-class people (creative writing, in this case) comes to be "owned" by the holder of capital. (Many people don't realize that writers do not control the cover and design of their books and are, in fact, typically required to sign contracts to that effect.)

Once writing is transformed into a physical object destined for the marketplace, to be sure, it necessarily becomes subject to the laws (or, rather, the superstitions) of advertising: that is true of any book. What is instructive about the example of *This Thing Called Courage* is the publisher's assumption that a sexualized, idealized male image was required both to invoke working-class men as the subjects of fiction (that is, was tied to the content of the book) and to render that content attractive to the consumer (that is, was tied to the gay-male buyer's inability to "read" without the mediation of beefcake).

The omnipresence of such subcultural cryptography may serve to illuminate another phenomenon. If there was one kind of story I rejected more than any other for this collection, it was the one with the implausible soft-porn plot featuring (and I am not making this up) construction workers. The fact is amusing, but also telling. Writers find it no simple matter to project working-class men into the imagination, especially if they are sexually and emotionally tied to other men. When we look there, we see clichés and advertisements, Stanley Kowalski and the Marlboro Man, the inflated (and inflatable) cops and cowboys of Tom of Finland, the generic white boy with gym muscles who is transformed into a "he-man laborer" by the strategic application of a tattoo or a smear of axle grease. So successfully have our own minds been colonized that what we do not much see are full-fleshed characters with complex lives.

Because most people who write are readers first, and because reading so often leads directly to writing, there's little mystery here. Fiction writers, particularly when they're starting out, tend to copy what they see being published, and queer fiction that is commercially rewarded with publication (which is, to be fair, very little of it), often follows formulae in which, as Larry Kramer famously argued, "the goals of gay fiction (are) so small" (1997, p. 60). The one current growth industry in gay fiction, in fact, is the surprisingly successful subgenre—but I'm probably the only one who's surprised—that unashamedly characterizes itself as "beach reading" and whose entire point is to publicize the fabulous lives and fabulous romances of fabulously young, assimilated, and consumer-very-friendly gay men.[5] Literature is, after all, the propaganda of a culture, and working-class queer men have been propagandized right out of the picture.

VII.

I have been breaking silence these twenty-three years and have hardly made a rent in it.
Henry David Thoreau, from *Journals*, February 9, 1841

You don't do much better with nonfiction. Visit the HQ section at your local library (or the 305-306s, if they're on the Dewey system) and glance

---

[5] My own unscientific survey of new (i.e., not reprinted or reissued) fiction published for gay men between 1998 and 2004 breaks down this way: literary fiction—45.2%; erotica—30.1%; romance and "beach" reading—14.6%; genre (mystery/sci-fi/horror)—10.1%. Since the figures are averaged, they don't show some interesting trends: the number of new gay romances and "beach" titles (*Wearing Black to the White Party, Trust Fund Boys, Man of My Dreams*), e.g., which came in at only 5% during the 1998-2000 period, nearly tripled between 2001 and 2004. These figures are based on information available from the Library of Congress catalog and Amazon.com and exclude self-published and print-on-demand books.

at the tables of contents and indices of the scores of books on LGBT "culture," "politics," and "studies"—books with titles like *Historical Sourcebook of Gay and Lesbian Politics, Ethnic and Cultural Diversity among Gay Men and Lesbians, The Gay and Lesbian Encyclopedia, The Culture of Queers,* and *Inside the Academy & Out: Lesbian-Gay-Queer Studies & Social Action.*

You will not find in these five books any discussion of class, nor are you likely to find much analysis of the subject in the billions of words published over the last decade on the dissection of male homosexual "culture." David Bergman, in his otherwise excellent study, *Gaiety Transfigured: Gay Self-Representation in American Literature* (1991), includes chapters on camp, race, AIDS, family formation, and gender, but cannot manage to wrap an analysis around the way that gay-male self-representation in literature is *classed.* Suzanna Danuta Walters, in her *All the Rage: The Story of Gay Visibility in America* (2001), devotes two chapters ("Consuming Queers" and "If It's Pink We'll Sell It") to a consideration of gay wealth and entrepreneurship—and brings herself to use the word "class" once, on the last page of the last chapter, without a word of comment.

When Michael Bronski, writing in *The Pleasure Principle: Sex, Backlash, and the Struggle for Gay Freedom* (1998), congratulates popular culture for creating the space in which gay and lesbian liberation could finally succeed, he sidesteps the *classed* nature of pop culture's idioms. "The politics of popular culture," Bronski writes, "is the politics of pleasure and personal freedom" (36).

On the contrary. American commodity culture—a more accurate name for it—is diametrically opposed to personal freedom (except as that freedom is expressed in consumption), discourages the unfettered expression of pleasure by valorizing heterosexual coupling above all other forms, and actively corrodes human(e) interaction by insisting that only those able to meet unreasonable standards of beauty, youth, and wealth are eligible to participate. Pop culture does not—cannot—exist outside of economics, nor does gay (male) participation in it. Here again, however, scholarly discourse on the nature of queer life cannot admit of class.

Bronski is absolutely correct that pop culture and the gay "community" can barely keep their hands off each other, but to confuse liberation from oppression with "open, celebratory displays of gay sexuality and the gay body" (108) is simply sinister (not to mention misogynist and racist, since that "celebratory" body is invariably male and white). To assert, finally, that "because gay and lesbian identity is defined by sexual attraction to members of the same gender, sexuality is, necessarily, at the heart of gay culture" (54) is to iterate the middle-class insistence that gay cultural membership is open only to those who are willing and able to place sex-object choice at the center of their lives. If class (or race or gender or any one of a number of other subjectivities, or perhaps all of them together) lies closer to *my* heart, am I admissible then only to the queer auxiliary?

And then it sometimes happens that we disappear even when we appear. In 2001, Alyson published Dan Woog's *Gay Men, Straight Jobs*, a collection of interviews with gay men who work in what Woog identified as "'heterosexual jobs,' as most people—gay as well as straight—would call them" (vii). Leaving aside the curious process by which Woog operationally defined occupations like judge, public-relations executive, investment banker, and doctor as "heterosexual jobs," I turn to more vexing questions.

First, more than half of the men Woog interviewed are employed in *working-class* occupations (prison guard, oil rig mechanic, trucker, forklift driver, mason, lumberyard man), though he never engages with that fact. Second, the sole job-related issue that interested Woog in his interviews was whether or not the man was "out" at work:

> [A]ll out gay men—no matter what profession or job—share certain experiences that straight men never can. These experiences revolve around overcoming homophobia, be it subtle or overt, in the workplace.... Some of the men I talked with...are not out, or are semi-out at work and way out at home; for them, every day is a demanding, energy-draining balancing act. (viii)

A "demanding, energy-draining balancing act" because of "homophobia," but presumably not, for the working-class men, because of the nature of their jobs, their lack of control over their time and their work, or the stress of financial insecurity. I scarcely need to add that the cover of the book is decorated with a handsome, hunky guy wearing a sweaty undershirt and a hard hat. One wonders whether he is the straight man emblematic of the "heterosexual job" or the gay man who holds one; he is, in any case, visually marked as working-class, a juxtaposition that conflates the categories of "working class" and "heterosexual" in a way that Andrew Holleran's Sutherland and Malone would have grasped instantly.

VIII.

*"Excuse me for saying so but isn't gay and working-class kind of a
contradiction in terms?"*
Posted to the Working Class Academics listserv in response to
the *Everything I Have Is Blue* call for submissions, November 22,
2002

"There's no such thing as a working-class gay man."
The best-selling Manhattan-based gay author of some seven
novels and numerous books on theater, in an April 28, 2003
telephone conversation

"The great thing about gay is that it erases class."
Ditto

Perhaps that helps explain why it is so hard to find legitimate contemporary American queer fiction—meaning the kind that appears in those
semiannual "best" anthologies or which is recognized with publication
by mainstream houses (including mainstream gay houses)—in which
the boys in question aren't spending the fall at a villa in Tuscany (or
summering in Provincetown, or taking a three-month excursion through
the "ruins" of Mexico); aren't decorating their lofts in SoHo (or their get-
away home in Vermont or their Victorian in Pacific Heights); aren't
pulling out credit cards to pay for first-class flights to Bangkok (or a new
set of Baccarat bibelots or dinner at Elaine's); don't have cleaning ladies
(or real-estate agents or personal trainers). They are white-collar professionals—or, if they aren't, they either don't need to work or are merely
working their way *up*. They have taste and culture and subscriptions to
Architectural Digest, but they have no politics (or would have no politics
were it not for AIDS). They are products of the queer Diaspora, and they
have come to the urban centers where "we" are presumed to thrive and
(significantly) to prosper.

I'm exaggerating, but not as much as you might think. The publishers' descriptions of recent gay men's fiction tell the story (the last two
quotes are actually from *Publishers Weekly*):

• ...a funny, playful, endearing slice of life from the late-20-
something Chelsea crowd in Manhattan's fast lane...
• ...four young, image-conscious New York gay
men...attempt to recalibrate their out-of-whack love lives while
looking their best in the latest designer fashions...
• The boys are looking forward to Rex Gifford's Red Party,
which promises to be even bigger than the White Party on the

gay party circuit...
* ...a young posse of preppy Upper East Siders with a taste for high fashion, top-shelf liquor and other men...
* Nigel Adams and cynical, aristocratic Nicky Borja...are accidentally thrown together in a Tuscany villa...
* ...filled with bright and sympathetic 20-somethings trying to make their way in the world...
* ...a blissful bachelorhood of drugs, circuit parties and dance floor groping in Boston...
* ...bittersweet romance in Provincetown with Eduardo, twenty-two and a vision of gorgeous, wide-eyed youth...
* ...a younger, prettier set who spend their time at resorts with names like Babylon and clubs with names like Universe...
* Powered by the same type of giddy, clichéd fluff that is common to so much contemporary gay fiction...
* ...adheres to the flourishing genre of gay pulp fiction, simple stories churned out to affirm gay souls and pass the time on beaches and couches.

To my mind, it is no coincidence that the invisibility of nonurban, non-middle-class, unfabulous, and unwaxed queers in the agendas of our national political organizations and in gay journalistic coverage of "our" community exactly parallels the absence of such images in "our" fiction.

And so. A working-class queer man comes out and enters a/the gay "community" (almost always a physical place, a neighborhood, a social milieu). Apprehending the pressure to leave behind/disguise/transliterate his life as he knows it, he is presented with a choice: if his kind is not there—well, he'll need to change his kind. The magazines he leafs through, the television he watches won't tell him much different. Neither will the books he reads.

The part of the title of this anthology that lies east of the colon—the "more-or-less gay" part—is no accident. It's an attempt to represent linguistically a failure of thought. It's an accusation. I don't pretend to speak for the other writers in *Everything I Have Is Blue*, and I don't presume to know how they have, over the course of their lives, managed their relationship to that vexed and freighted notion, "gay." But I'll bet there's not one of them who hasn't at one time or another in his adult life been in serious conflict over the label, hasn't worn it sometimes not because it fit or was flattering but because it was the only shirt in the closet.

I can say this: I have experienced my most profound moments of bonding with other men when I have worked in prisons and jails in Texas, New Mexico, and San Francisco, places where poor and working-class men are not the majority, they are quite simply the whole. As a teacher, I have entered without fear rooms full of murderers and gang members with the fanciful intention of interesting them in poetry, but I no longer have the guts to walk unescorted into a party full of gay men I do not know. In theory, the one group might injure my body, but the distinctly nontheoretical wounds inflicted by the second group threaten, like Philoctetes' snake bite, never to heal.

And I will say this: the point of an anthology like *Everything I Have Is Blue* is not to elevate working-class "identity" to a place in the catechism of oppressions recited by good liberals and by smug moderates, eager to do the least they can to disguise their Darwinian politics. It isn't to ask for a place at the table or a slice of the pie, for what would be the point? The queer bookshelf already groans beneath the weight of books by, for, and about people raising their voices to be heard: gay, lesbian, and bisexual Jews, Chicanos, African Americans, Italians, Native Americans, and Cubans; lesbians with disabilities; transgendered couples; lesbians and gay men who are deaf; queer youth; gay, lesbian, bisexual, and transgendered people with developmental disabilities; lesbians who are fat; gay men who are elderly.

Almost all of this writing speaks in some measure, just as I have done, about invisibility, about silences; almost all of it attempts to stake out a plot of land on the landscape of queer public consciousness. I have not even considered the dozens of books (like Mark Simpson's *Anti-Gay* [1997]), the scores of magazine and scholarly articles (like Ian Barnard's "Fuck Community, or Why I Support Gay-Bashing" [1996]), or the uncountable numbers of websites (like www.gayshamesf.org) that critique, with varying degrees of bitterness, the institutions, agendas, and cultural products of the mainstream gay community.

Increasingly, the response to such expressions is to view them as churlish, exaggerated, and naïve; to dismiss them as what majority-group members like to call "political correctness" (on the theory, I suppose, that to be *incorrect* in matters of human interaction is the more principled position); or to characterize them, the way *Village Voice* Executive Editor Richard Goldstein did in *The Advocate* in 2000, as disloyal "backbiting."

"For every three gays there are four acronyms," Goldstein quips. "At this rate there will soon be more divisions in the lesbian community than there are lesbians." Such "constant carping," he continues, "threatens to turn our movement into an activist equivalent of the Balkans" (39).

I want to suggest an alternative reading of those divisions. I want to ask how it is possible that such a shining place as the "gay community"—that redoubt, as Michael Bronski would have it, of unrestricted personal expression and uninhibited sexual freedom; that "tribe" as

Richard Goldstein also calls it; that rainbow culmination of decades of struggle—has become the site of so much resistance from within, the locus of so great a sense of being disregarded, constricted, *altered*. I want to ask, in short, how many points determine a line.

IX.

> *I do not know which to prefer,*
> *The beauty of inflections*
> *Or the beauty of innuendoes…*
> Wallace Stevens, from "Thirteen Ways of Looking at a Blackbird"

In the end, *Everything I Have Is Blue* came about because I'm still trying to figure out who and where "we" are, because I wonder whether there is ever any way to stop, during the great bullet-train ride of our lives, to say, *There! That's what I am!*—or whether the slippage of successive moments past the window is the whole story: the constant lap dissolve, never the freeze-frame. Reading is like that as well: the skein of words plays itself forward, and no single page tells you everything.

And yet, to freight the metaphor a little further, we are also whatever we carry with us on the train.

This project, this collection of stories I find so powerful, answers in part my need for a response—not so much to the silence, but to the noise. A reminder (again) of the qualities of experience, of the subjectivities that are elided, obscured, overlooked, manipulated, misunderstood, or simply out-shouted. It was a way, simply, to feel less alone.

There was always plenty of occasion for that—something I found out the moment I began to circulate the idea for this book. The language I used in the call for submissions, I was immediately informed, would "turn working-class people off." My insistence on short fiction (as opposed to essays or "life writing") was bourgeois. I sounded like an academic (or, worse, an "intellectual") and so couldn't really be working class. The project was impossible because, by definition, literature "excludes working-class subjectivities." The very idea of a book was anti-working class because everyone knows that working-class people don't read. I was perpetuating historical exploitation by making money off the backs of the working class (anyone who thinks the editor makes money off a project like this has never done it).

If I rejected someone's work, I was an imposter who knew nothing about the "real" working classes; if I asked for revisions, I was elitist because I was trying to "control the language of" working-class people.

Of course, comments like these hurt (and all of them are real), but they were also familiar. In these criticisms I heard the echoes of my own family's cautionary mantras and ever-ready willingness to find fault:

You'll never be able to make that work. You're getting above your raising. Who are you to even try?

That, of course, is the essence of capitalist injury: if the ruling class can get you to participate in holding yourself back, they are free to deploy their resources elsewhere.

My fear, if we don't root out such tendencies, is that we will never get out of the business of shrinking the world. I don't want to be told that I'm not queer enough, and I don't want to be told that I'm not working-class enough. I'd never say that my experience of either one should be anyone else's, but I do say that the issue of "realness" ought to be left to drag contests, where it still makes some sense.

And I do want to read literature about a world that's as complex as what I know in my bones. In *Brown*, the third and final installment of his memoirs, Richard Rodriguez writes that:

> American bookshelves of the twenty-first century describe fractiousness, reduction, hurt. Books are isolated from one another, like gardenias or peaches, lest they bruise or become bruised, or, worse, consort, confuse. If a man in a wheelchair writes his life, his book will be parked in a blue-crossed zone: "Self-Help" or "Health." There is no shelf for bitterness. No shelf for redemption. The professor of Romance languages at Dresden, a convert to Protestantism, was tortured by the Nazis as a Jew—only that—a Jew. His book, published sixty years after the events it recounts, is shelved in my neighborhood bookstore as "Judaica." There is no shelf for irony. (11-12)

Everything I Have Is Blue strikes me as a good argument for building a brand-new bookshelf. And what better project—one that involves both interior decorating and power tools—for a collaboration between the myth of the modern homosexual and the archetype of the working class. Not matter and antimatter, but iron and carbon. I can't think of anything queerer than that.

REFERENCES

Alexander, Shana. (1973, 22 January) "The Silence of the Louds." *Newsweek*, pp. 28+.

Barnard, Ian. (1996) "Fuck Community, or Why I Support Gay-Bashing." In Renée R. Curry & Terry L. Allison, Eds., *States of Rage: Emotional Eruption, Violence, and Social Change*. New York: New York University Press, pp. 74-88.

Blue-Collar Brawn. (1999, November) *Men's Health*, 14(9), 118-119.

Bronski, Michael. (1998) *The Pleasure Principle: Sex, Backlash, and the Struggle for Gay Freedom*. New York: St. Martin's.

Bulkin, Elly. (1981) "Introduction: A Look at Lesbian Short Fiction." In Elly Bulkin, Ed., *Lesbian Fiction: An Anthology*. Watertown, MA: Persephone Press, pp. xi -xxxviii.

Caffey, John. (1982) *The Coming Out Party*. New York: Pinnacle Books.

Feinberg, Leslie. (1993) *Stone Butch Blues*. Ithaca, NY: Firebrand Press.

Goldstein, Richard. (2000, 15 February) "Cease fire!" *The Advocate, 805*, pp. 36-40.

Hayes, J. G. (2002) *This Thing Called Courage: South Boston Stories*. New York: Southern Tier Editions/Harrington Park Press.

Holleran, Andrew. (1978) *Dancer from the Dance*. New York: William Morrow and Company.

Hucklenbroich, Frankie. (1997) *Crystal Diary*. Ithaca, NY: Firebrand Press.

Kennedy, Elizabeth Lapovsky & Davis, Madeline D. (1993). *Boots of Leather, Slippers of Gold: The History of a Lesbian Community*. New York: Routledge.

Kramer, Larry. (1997, 27 May) "Sex and Sensibility." *The Advocate, 734*, pp. 59+.

Newton, Esther. (1993) "Just One of the Boys: Lesbians in Cherry Grove, 1960-1988." In Henry Abelove, Michèle Aina Barale, and David M.

Halperin, Eds., *The Lesbian and Gay Studies Reader*. New York: Routledge, pp. 528-541.

Raffo, Susan (Ed.). (1997) *Queerly Classed: Gay Men and Lesbians Write about Class*. Boston: South End Press.

Read, Kirk. (2001) *How I Learned to Snap: A Small-Town Coming-Out and Coming-of-Age Story*. Athens, GA: Hill Street Press.

Rodriguez, Richard. (2002) *Brown: The Last Discovery of America*. New York: Viking.

Simpson, Mark (Ed.). (1997) *Anti-Gay*. New York & London: Freedom Editions/Cassell.

Uttal, Lynne. (1990) "Inclusion without Influence: The Continued Tokenism of Women of Color." In Gloria Anzaldúa, Ed., *Making Face/Making Soul: Creative and Critical Perspectives by Feminists of Color*. San Francisco: Aunt Lute Books, pp. 42-45.

Woog, Dan. (2001) *Gay Men, Straight Jobs*. Los Angeles: Alyson Books.

CONTRIBUTORS

Timothy J. Anderson is a writer, horseman, and truck driver with sixteen years of over-the-road trucking experience throughout North America. He is a graduate of Lutheran Bible Institute of Seattle (now Trinity College) and Seattle Pacific University. He is co-author of the study, "Chicken Haulers and the High Liners: CB Talk Among Interstate Truckers," published in *Communicating Ethnic and Cultural Identity* (Rowman & Littlefield, 2004). He is president of the Gay Truckers' Association and has served as a consultant on the NIH/Emory University Community and Truckers' Health Project. Anderson's writing has appeared in *Guide, Frontiers, Second Essence,* and the anthology *Bend, Don't Shatter: Poets on the Beginning of Desire* (Soft Skull Press, 2004). His website (www.highmountainranch.com) was chosen as Website of the Month by www.roadstaronline.com and won Cross Trucking's award for excellence. An excerpt from his essay "Bodacious" was nominated for a "PREN-D" (Public Radio News Directors' Award), and his piece "Drive Through This" was commissioned for inclusion in the award-winning 2003 season of Public Radio International's *Outright Radio.* He resides in Pend Oreille County, Washington.

Rane Arroyo is a Puerto Rican poet who was born in Chicago. He is the author of four collections of poetry, including the Carl Sandburg Prize-winner, *The Singing Shark* (Bilingual Press, 1996) and, more recently, *Home Movies of Narcissus* (University of Arizona Press, 2002). His first collection of short stories, *How to Name a Hurricane,* a gathering of his experimental fiction about gay and Latino identities, is forthcoming in 2005 from the University of Arizona Press. He started work in a factory at the age of thirteen. Since then, he has held temp jobs and has been a banker, an arts administrator, and a dancing ape at a Mormon disco. He lives and teaches in Toledo, Ohio, and is currently wrestling with the ghosts in his memoirs manuscript. He can be reached at RRArroyo@aol.com.

Keith Banner's novel, *The Life I Lead,* came out from Knopf in 1999, and his stories have appeared in *Kenyon Review, Washington Square, Third Coast,* and *Witness,* among others, and have been anthologized in *O. Henry Prize Stories 2000* (Anchor, 2000), *Full Frontal Fiction: The Best of Nerve* (Three Rivers Press, 2000), and *Best American Gay Fiction 3* (Back Bay Books, 1998). His book of short fiction, *The Smallest People Alive,* was published in 2004 by Carnegie Mellon University Press. Currently, he lives and works in Cincinnati, Ohio. He started his work life at thirteen as a carhop, running burgers out on little trays to cars parked in a gravel lot. After that, he moved on to Kentucky Fried Chicken and Ponderosa Steakhouse, just to name a few. He has also been a part-time telemarketer, library-book-shelver, group-home worker, janitor, and convenience-store cashier.

James Barr was born in 1922 "in an oilfield boomtown in either Texas or Oklahoma," according to a biographical sketch he wrote in 1990. He never knew his father, and his mother died shortly after his birth. Barr served in the U.S. Navy from 1942 to 1946, later moving to New York to begin work on his first novel, *Quatrefoil*. When it appeared in 1950, Barr became an instant gay celebrity. (*Quatrefoil* was reprinted in 1991 by Alyson.) Barr reenlisted in the Navy during the Korean War, but the Office of Naval Intelligence learned he was the author of *Quatrefoil* and ordered him discharged. His collection of short stories, *Derricks* (from which "Bottom of the Cloud" is taken) appeared in 1951. Both books were eventually pulled off the market when the U.S. Post Office threatened to prosecute Barr's publisher for "peddling pornography." When Barr's foster father was diagnosed with leukemia, Barr returned to Kansas where he worked as an oilfield roustabout and continued to write, including stories, articles, and reviews for *One Magazine* and *The Mattachine Review*. He later moved back to New York for a time, where he struggled with alcoholism and drug addiction, only to make another return to Kansas and a new career as a newspaperman in the mid-sixties when his foster mother fell ill. A second novel, *The Occasional Man*, appeared in 1966. Barr died of liver cancer at the Oklahoma Veterans Center in 1995. (Excerpted with kind permission from Hubert Kennedy's excellent article, "A Touch of Royalty: Gay Author James Barr," available for download at: http://home.pacbell.net/dendy/Barr.pdf.)

CAConrad is the author of three forthcoming books: *FRANK* (Jargon Society: PO Box 10, Highlands, NC 28741), *advancedELVIScourse* (Buck Downs Books: PO Box 50376, Washington, DC 20091), and *DEVIANT PROPULSION* (Soft Skull Press). He co-edits *FREQUENCY Audio Journal* with Magdalena Zurawski and edits *BANJO: Poets Talking* (http://banjopoets.blogspot.com) and *The 9for9 Project* (http://poets9for9.blogspot.com/). He is working on a collaborative series of poems with poet Frank Sherlock. He can be reached at CAConrad13@aol.com.

C. Bard Cole is a cartoonist and writer. The author of *Tattooed Love Boys*, six other illustrated chapbooks, and a collection of short stories, *Briefly Told Lives* (St. Martin's, 2000), he is also the co-creator of the 'zine

Riotboy. Originally from Baltimore County, Maryland, and a longtime resident of New York's Lower East Side, he currently teaches English in Tuscaloosa, Alabama.

Marcel Devon is a twenty-eight-year-old bisexual writer and artist who has been incarcerated in Texas since the age of fifteen. After eight years in solitary confinement, he has developed his artistic and writing skills as well as a grasp of four other languages. Recently out of solitary, he is hoping for a release this decade into free society where he can contribute to causes of social benevolence. His current works include the comic strip "Ambiguous Ambrosia" and contributions to *Fanorama*, an LGBT punk rock 'zine (http://www.freewebs.com/fanorama/). "There Are No Pretty Girls at the Tabernacle" is his first published story.

Dean Durber is a PhD candidate in the Department of Communication and Cultural Studies at Curtin University in Perth, Western Australia (and can be reached there at D.Durber@curtin.edu.au). His thesis considers the silencing of nonhomosexual male-male sex within the gay liberation movement. He holds a master of arts in theatre studies and a bachelor of arts in Chinese and Japanese studies. He lectures in queer theory, media studies, cultural studies, and drug culture. This academic world is a far cry from the government housing estate where he (mis)spent his youth. His publications include a novel, *Johnny, Come Home* (Marginal Eyes Press, 2002) and short stories in such anthologies as *The Best Gay Erotica 2003* (Cleis Press, 2002), *Straight? Volume 2* (Alyson, 2003), and *Boy Meets Boy* (Griffin Trade, 1999). His research may be serious, professional, and deep, but the sex he does is downright dirty. He has studied, worked, traveled, and bummed his way extensively around the world. He speaks Japanese, Chinese, and German. His biggest fear is sitting still. When you're still, they can find you. When you're still, they can get you.

Rick Laurent Feely grew up with a single mother in the mountains of southern California, where he became a runaway at the age of twelve. He spent his youth escaping from psychiatric institutions, hitchhiking around the country, and defending himself with straight razors. He is now twenty-four and lives in Philly, where he organizes around queer, youth, and class issues; engages in a variety of part-time work; goes to school; writes; makes art; and obsesses about the human condition. "Skins" won the Spring 2003 Judith Stark Fiction Award at the Community College of Philadelphia and is his first published story. He can be reached at warrantsoutstanding@yahoo.com.

John Gilgun says: "I had shit jobs until the fall of 1960. I define shit jobs as jobs a person cares nothing about except for the money—always minimum wage and sometimes with tips in my case—and from which you are always fired. I was always fired. In 1960, a miracle happened. I was offered a job as a college teacher. Teaching was so wonderful that I did it for thirty-nine years until I had to retire because I was going deaf and couldn't hear my students. From busboy to college professor: that's my bio. I taught at working-class colleges (except for my four years at Drake University in the sixties), and I taught working-class kids like myself who were in college because they hoped that with a degree they could escape the shit jobs from which they were also always fired. In those thirty-nine years I published six books, including *Music I Never Dreamed of* (Amethyst, 1989) and *Your Buddy Misses You* (Three Phase, 1995) and hundreds of stories, poems, and essays in little magazines."

Rigoberto González is the son of migrant farm workers from Mexico. His childhood is the subject of his forthcoming memoir, *Butterfly Boy* (University of Wisconsin). He has also authored two books of poetry, including *So Often the Pitcher Goes to Water Until It Breaks*, a 1998 National Poetry Series selection (University of Illinois Press, 1999); two books for children; a biography of the late Chicano writer, Tomás Rivera; and an award-winning novel about California grape pickers, *Crossing Vines* (University of Oklahoma, 2003). He is the recipient of a Guggenheim Fellowship and is a member of PEN and of the National Book Critics Circle. His reviews of books by Latina/o authors appear twice monthly in the *El Paso (Texas) Times*. Since 1998, he has lived mostly in New York City. Visit his website: www.rigoberto gonzalez.com.

Jim Grimsley grew up in a working-class family in rural North Carolina. His novel, *Winter Birds*, published by Algonquin Books in 1994, was a finalist for the PEN/Hemingway prize and winner of a Sue Kaufman Prize from the American Academy of Arts and Letters. *Dream Boy* (Algonquin Books, 1995) won the American Library Association GLBT Award for Literature and was a Lambda Literary Award finalist. Other novels include *My Drowning* (Algonquin Books, 1997), *Boulevard* (Algonquin Books, 2002), and *Kirith Kirin* (Meisha Merlin, 2000). Jim is playwright in residence at 7Stages Theater in Atlanta and at About Face Theatre of Chicago. In 1987, he received the George Oppenheimer/ Newsday Award for Best New American Playwright for *Mr. Universe*. His collection of plays, *Mr. Universe and Other Plays*, was published by Algonquin Books in 1998 and was a Lambda Literary Award finalist for drama. He received the Lila Wallace/Reader's Digest Writers Award in 1997. He teaches writing at Emory University in Atlanta, Georgia. He recently won the Asimov's Readers Award for his short story "Into

Greenwood." His second novel in the science fiction/fantasy arena, *The Ordinary*, was published by Tor Books in May 2004 and won the Lambda Literary Award.

Ryan Kamstra (sCRATCH) is a Canadian bi poet, songwriter, and sometimes fiction writer originating from small-town Thunder Bay, Ontario, and currently residing in the big bad smoke of Toronto. His songwriting has drawn comparisons to Bob Dylan, Ani di Franco, and Tom Waits, and his poetry has been compared to Canadian poets of dissent Milton Acorn and Dorothy Livesay. He currently performs in odd clubs as a gender-challenged sparkly militant mime for the Most Beautiful on Earth, his one-creature band & declaration of war with the hidden agenda of creatively breeding an army of pacifist pretty mimes to upstage & outmode more traditional modes of war. He has released one album, *aLL fALL dOWN* (independent, 2001: 1244 College West Toronto, ON, Canada M6J 1X5) and one book of poetry, *lATE cAPITALIST sUBLIME* (Insomniac Press, 2002: Suite 403, 192 Spadina Avenue, Toronto, ON, Canada M5T 2C2). His second collection of poems, *iNTO tHE dROWNED wORLD*, is due out in 2006 & a second album, *aT tHE eDGE oF lIGHT*, in 2005. In his spare time he works as a temp, a grocery clerk, a paralegal, a busker, a data-entry clerk, an art gallery prop & so much more!

Christopher Lord was born in Astoria, Oregon, in 1955. His stories have appeared in *Men on Men 7: Best New Gay Fiction* (Plume, 1997), *His 3: Brilliant New Fiction by Gay Writers* (Faber & Faber, 1999), *Harrington Gay Men's Fiction Quarterly*, *Confrontation*, *The James White Review*, and online at *Blithe House Quarterly* (www.blithe.com) and *Lodestar Quarterly* (www.lodestarquarterly.com). He has completed three novels and is actively searching for interested agents and editors. Lord is the recipient of a Fellowship to Writers from Literary Arts, Inc., a nonprofit organization that supports writers and sponsors the Oregon Book Awards. He lives in Portland with his long-term partner, Evan.

Wendell Ricketts was born on Wake Island, an atoll in the middle of the Pacific Ocean, and raised in small towns on O'ahu, Hawai'i. For nearly twenty years he has written about politics, education, literature, the performing and visual arts, lesbian and gay family and legal issues, and responses to AIDS in the arts and media for such publications as *Contact Quarterly*, *The Advocate*, *Out*, *Dance Ink*, *Spin*, *Gay and Lesbian Literary Heritage*, and *Silent No More: Voices of Courage in American Schools*. His fiction and poetry have appeared in such publications as *Blithe House Quarterly*, *James White Review*, *Mississippi Review*, *modern words*, *Harrington Gay Men's Fiction Quarterly*, and the anthologies *Rough Stuff:*

Tales of Gay Men, Sex, and Power and *Bum Rush the Page: A Def Poetry Jam*. For his translation of the plays of Natalia Ginzburg from Italian, he received the PEN American Center Renato Poggioli Prize in 2000. He holds a master's degree in creative writing from the University of New Mexico, where he received the highly specialized training that has enabled him to pursue a career as an office temp. He can be reached via his website, www.mondowendell.com.

Alfredo Ronci was born in Rome in 1958, and he still lives in the community of Colle Mattia, just south of the city. In 1992, he founded the literary magazine, *Il Paradiso degli Orchi*, for which he served as editorial director until 2000. His first novel, *Moana e l'Atletica del Dilettante* was published by Moby Dick (Faenza, 1999) and his second, *L'Insonnia delle Rondini*, by Addiction (Milan, 2000). His short stories have appeared in the Italian collections, *Men on Men* (Mondadori, 2002) and *Men on Men 2* (Mondadori, 2003). His father worked for many years as a marble quarryman and his mother was a farm woman. Today, Ronci works as a librarian in the archive of the Italian State Railroad.

Jan-Mitchell Sherrill was nominated for the American Book Award for his first volume of poetry, *Blind Leading the Blind* (New Poets Series, 1978), and for the National Book Award for his most recent work, *Friend of the Groom* (Brick House Books, 1994). His poetry has appeared in *The James White Review*, *Art and Understanding*, and *The Carolina Quarterly*; he was a contributor to *Hometowns: Gay Men Write About Where They Belong* (EP Dutton, 1991) and is the author of New York University Press' *The Gay, Lesbian, and Bisexual Student Guide to Colleges and Universities* (1994). His new book of poetry, *Gunfire in Oz*, is due out from NPS/Stonewall in 2005. He is Associate Dean of Students at George Washington University in Washington, DC.

Royston Tester grew up in Birmingham, the English Midlands. Before emigrating to Canada in 1978, he spent time in London, Barcelona, and Melbourne. He has been a fellow of the Hawthornden writers' retreat in Scotland and the Valparaiso Foundation in Spain, and he is a frequent Leighton Studio artist-resident at The Banff Centre. He has published short fiction in numerous Canadian literary journals, including *Descant*, *The New Quarterly*, *The Antigonish Review*, and *The Malahat Review*; his work has been anthologized in *Rip-Rap* (1999) and *Intersections* (2000), both from the Banff Centre Press, and in the *Quickies* series (Arsenal Pulp Press). In 2003, he was short-listed for Pagitica's International Literary Competition. In the U.S., his stories have appeared in online publications such as *Blithe House Quarterly* and *Lodestar Quarterly*; in 2002, he was a finalist in the U.S. New Century Writer Awards. His first collection of linked stories, *Summat Else* (2004), was followed by a second, *You Turn Your Back* (2005), both published by Porcupine's Quill. Currently working on a novel, *For the English to See*, he lives in the Little Italy area of Toronto.